PENGUIN BOOKS

LIFE BEGINS

Praise for Amanda Brookfield

'Few contemporary British novelists writing today explore the messy tangles of close human relationships with quite such warm perceptiveness as Brookfield' Henry Sutton, *Daily Mirror*

'Amanda Brookfield could lead the woman's novel a few steps further out of its cultural ghetto' *Sunday Telegraph*

'The novel walks a line between comedy and wrenching sadness. It is fluently written and its depiction of domestic chaos . . . is all too recognizable' *Sunday Times*

'What is refreshing here is the author's conspicuous sanity and her sharp line in defence of reason . . . It could be sentimental, but it isn't' *Guardian*

'Intelligent and perceptive' *Sainsbury's Magazine*

'This book, about deep and complex family love from this accomplished author, is told with true passion' *Family Circle*

'Through her characters, Brookfield skilfully illuminates the relationships, dilemmas and compromises that define so many lives' *Sunday Express*

Life Begins

AMANDA BROOKFIELD

PENGUIN BOOKS

PENGUIN BOOKS

Published by the Penguin Group
Penguin Books Ltd, 80 Strand, London WC2R ORL, England
Penguin Group (USA) Inc., 375 Hudson Street, New York, New York 10014, USA
Penguin Group (Canada), 90 Eglinton Avenue East, Suite 700, Toronto, Ontario, Canada M4P 2Y3
(a division of Pearson Penguin Canada Inc.)
Penguin Ireland, 25 St Stephen's Green, Dublin 2, Ireland (a division of Penguin Books Ltd)
Penguin Group (Australia), 250 Camberwell Road, Camberwell, Victoria 3124, Australia
(a division of Pearson Australia Group Pty Ltd)
Penguin Books India Pvt Ltd, 11 Community Centre, Panchsheel Park, New Delhi – 110 017, India
Penguin Group (NZ), 67 Apollo Drive, Rosedale, North Shore 0632, New Zealand
(a division of Pearson New Zealand Ltd)
Penguin Books (South Africa) (Pty) Ltd, 24 Sturdee Avenue, Rosebank, Johannesburg 2196, South Africa

Penguin Books Ltd, Registered Offices: 80 Strand, London WC2R ORL, England

www.penguin.com

First published by Michael Joseph 2008
Published in Penguin Books 2008

3

Set in Monotype Garamond
Typeset by Rowland Phototypesetting Ltd, Bury St Edmunds, Suffolk
Printed in England by Clays Ltd, St Ives plc

ISBN: 978-0-141-02183-6

www.greenpenguin.co.uk

Penguin Books is committed to a sustainable future
for our business, our readers and our planet.
The book in your hands is made from paper
certified by the Forest Stewardship Council.

For Rod and Gyll

Truth is rarely pure and never simple.
Oscar Wilde

Chapter One

I sit where only the tips of the waves can reach, slapping my palms at the foamy water. The sand is gritty between my toes, the ties of my sun bonnet tight under my chin. Big hands scoop me high. My father's face is close, leathered and smiling, his blue eyes sharp against his tan. When he throws me I laugh, safe in the knowledge that I shall be caught. My mother sits reading in a deckchair, her slender white freckled limbs neatly circled by the protective shadow of a large wooden parasol. She wears a blue sarong and matching headscarf, from which one wild curl of auburn hair has broken free to bounce across her forehead. As I shriek she peers over the black ridge of her sunglasses and smiles, her lacquered eyelashes blinking in the glare.

Charlotte unlocked the door and pushed, with some difficulty, against the pile of morning post lodged on the mat. As she did so her neighbour emerged from his own front door wearing his faded tartan dressing-gown and the backless leather slippers that exposed the yellow crusts of his heels. 'Happy Valentine's, my dear,' he barked, bending down to swap the empty milk bottle in his hands for the full one parked next to his recycling box. He straightened and clutched his back with a grimace.

'Thanks, Mr Beasley, same to you.'

'Young Sam well, is he?'

'Oh, yes, thanks . . . I've just taken him to school.' Charlotte, now riffling through the mail, cast a doubtful glance at the Volkswagen, which sat like a large frosted tea-cake next to the for-sale sign stapled to her gate-post. Late as usual for her twelve-year-old's school run, she had hurled the contents of the kettle at the front and rear windscreens, only to have to chisel most of the ice off with her fingernails as the water instantly froze. Sam had watched her stony-eyed from the front seat, resting his chin on the top of his rucksack. The car had refused to start on the first three attempts, then performed its new clunking noise, the one that hadn't yet lasted quite long enough to warrant further investigation, as they approached the roundabout.

'I expect you'll have a few cards in there.' Mr Beasley nodded towards her hands, showing off his yellowing teeth as he grinned.

'I doubt it.' Charlotte smiled. Her neighbour meant well, she knew. In the ten months since Martin's departure, each week had been peppered with similar efforts at communication. But it was a raw morning to be lingering on the doorstep and, of course, there weren't any cards. There hadn't been a home-made offering of gluey glittered hearts from Sam that year either, which was entirely understandable and healthy, given her son's advanced age, but it had caused her a moment's lament all the same.

'Sold the house yet?' Mr Beasley rasped, just as she was edging inside.

'No – but there's someone coming to look this morning. Any minute now, in fact . . .' Charlotte glanced pointedly at her watch.

'Been a while, hasn't it?'

'A few months, yes.'

'And you've not found anywhere to go yet, have you?'

'No, Mr Beasley, I haven't.'

'I've forgotten, what was it you were looking for?'

'I –' Charlotte broke off, distracted by the envelope uppermost in her hand, brown, with a court stamp. 'Something smaller, a little cheaper, a lot nearer the park,' she muttered, delivering a summary of the brief she had given Tim Croft the estate agent eight months before. Under her anorak her heart was pumping fast – relief, joy, a million things. It was the decree nisi – it had to be. She felt as if she had been pushing at a huge heavy door that had at last given way – no more hideous haggling over numbers, what she spent at the hairdresser or in department stores; no more miserable sessions with her pocket calculator and a pile of bills. It was all over at last. She was free.

Mr Beasley was sucking in his cheeks and shaking his lugubrious unshaven old face at the dank February sky. 'The park . . . Oh, they're pricy, those are, even the poky ones.'

'Really? Well, I'm hopeful, *very* hopeful.' Rejoicing now, because of the brown envelope, Charlotte clasped the pile of post to her chest and escaped inside.

There was still a palpable quietness about the place without Martin, almost as if her refusal to mourn the demise of their unhappy union meant some spirit of the house was doing it for her. In her wilder moments Charlotte even wondered if this was why it was proving so hard to sell. At other, saner, times it seemed grossly unfair that while Martin and his adulterous love, Cindy, could spread their wings in their new spacious riverside house in Rotherhithe, she was left trying to sell a property that seemed, no matter how many vases of fresh flowers she arranged around it, to exude something akin to an atmosphere of bereavement.

She took her time with the brown envelope – made herself a cup of coffee, found a biscuit, relished the moment. And once the document was in her hand she made herself read it, every word, skimming none of the jargon or small-print, forcing herself to recall the sourness of the final months and the sly anonymous note that had finally provided the nudge – the courage – to put an end to the misery for good. *Your husband is seeing someone else, from a well-wisher.* Even at the time Charlotte had felt a sort of sick triumph – all the years of disintegrating affection, the needling suspicion, Martin's denials – and there at last, in ten words, was the verification, permission to give up, as official as the stamped document cradled in her hands.

And now a house viewing – the first in five weeks. It was going to be a lucky day, Charlotte decided, flying with something like exultation round the ground-floor rooms, shuffling papers into tidy piles and scooping up the random items that had found their way into inappropriate places: a wet towel, a phone charger, two odd clean socks. Arms full, she set off up the stairs, musing on the curious business of inviting strangers into one's home, the compulsion it induced to present an image of perfection where none existed.

Arriving on the threshold of Sam's bedroom on the top floor, she forgot all such notions and swore out loud. Drawers and cupboards spewed their contents like escaping entrails. Scattered across the floor, transforming the carpet into some sort of imploding mosaic, were the entire contents of the crate of Lego that had for months – or was it years? – been gathering dust under the bed. Strewn among this were his once treasured miniature Subbuteo figures, unsheathed CDs, sweet wrappers, a bowl encrusted with flakes of cereal, a plastic boomerang and a range of torn comics and magazines.

Charlotte gripped her bundle, fighting a host of familiar emotions – irritation, resentment, resignation, despair – and beneath that a guilty sense of responsibility. What sort of man would this boy of hers make, she feared suddenly, what sort of partner, husband? She was still standing in the doorway, frozen with doubt and foreboding, when the doorbell rang.

'Sorry, I'm early.' The man, who had thick dark hair, peppered with grey at the sideboards, and a large nose, visibly red with cold, extended a hand that gripped hers too firmly to suggest genuine penitence.

'That's fine . . . don't worry . . . Come in.' Charlotte managed a handshake through the tangled flex of the phone charger. 'Though you've caught me slightly on the hop, I'm afraid, no baking bread or fresh coffee to win you over. You'll have to take things as you find them.' She deposited her bundle on the hall chair, inwardly scolding herself for managing to sound – a mere two seconds into the process – so apologetic, so *desperate*. 'Shall we start with the kitchen?'

'Fine. Whatever suits.' He hadn't even smiled when she said the thing about the bread and the coffee and now he was peering at the hall ceiling, right at the spot where Martin's overflowing bath had yellowed the paintwork two years before. They should have had it replastered, repainted, of course, like the damp above the back door and the delta of hairline cracks that had appeared round the ceiling rose in the sitting room after Sam and six friends had performed gymnastics at a birthday sleepover. The house, Charlotte saw, with sudden, horrible clarity, was a testimony to the failure of her marriage, and not just for its subtle emptiness. It was like the proverbial millstone: ugly, heavy, holding her down. The sooner she was shot of it the better. She glanced again at her prospective viewer – visibly nervy, arms pinned stiffly behind his back – wondering if he would soften up at a hint that she would be prepared to accept something below the asking price. Tim Croft had been implying she should do as much for weeks.

In the kitchen she talked fast – too fast – about the

waste-disposal unit and how the sun lit the back of the house. Her visitor cast a doubtful glance at the garden, then at his watch. 'You could nose around on your own if you'd prefer,' Charlotte offered casually, leaning against the kitchen table, which wobbled because the bit of paper keeping it steady had, as usual, worked its way free. 'It requires a bit of attention, I know, a lick of paint and so on.' Stop trying so hard, she scolded herself, cocking her head, crossing her arms and then, for good measure, her ankles.

'Thank you, but . . . well, to be perfectly frank, I can see already that this isn't quite what I'm looking for.'

Charlotte clung to her elbows. 'Oh dear. Never mind . . .'

'I'm on my own, you see – that is, I have a daughter and don't really have time for a house that needs anything doing to it, even a lick of paint. Also, from what the agent said, I'd thought it would be near enough to her school for her to walk. She's just started at St Leonard's and I have to get to work and the traffic round here is so bad . . .'

Charlotte pushed herself off the table and held up her hands to forestall the embarrassment of any further apologies or explanations. 'Please, I know *exactly* where you're coming from. My son is at St Leonard's too, and I can tell you the school run is a pig from here – not as the crow flies, of course, which is where the *A–Z* can be so deceiving but with three main roads to get across . . .' She shook her head in a show of ruefulness. 'If that's a priority then you would, in all honesty, be mad to buy this house. In fact, leave now,' she joked, pointing towards the door. 'I command it.'

'Er . . . right.' He offered her a doubtful smile and backed into the hall.

'I'm on my own too,' Charlotte found herself saying, as she trotted after him. 'Wasn't the plan . . . but life has a knack of not turning out quite as one expects, doesn't it?

6

You sort of look back at where you started, then at where you've arrived and think, *Yikes*, how did *that* happen? Like examining the lives of two quite unrelated people or –' She stopped at last, halted by the pained expression on his face and the speed with which he was doing up the buttons of his smart charcoal grey overcoat.

'Well, thank you, Mrs Turner. I'm most sorry to have put you to the inconvenience – you might tell your agents to be a little clearer about the details next time.'

'Yes. Absolutely. Of course. Goodbye then, Mr . . . er . . .' Charlotte could feel her cheeks burning. She had forgotten how to *be*, she reflected helplessly. These days, words and responses seemed to ricochet out of her of their own accord. She didn't miss Martin – how could she miss the source of so much unhappiness? – but was increasingly aware that having a husband, no matter how unsatisfactory, had provided some sort of essential *ballast* to her personality. Without it she was freer but also, still, until she got properly used to it, somewhat unbalanced, rootless.

'Porter. Like the beer.'

'Pardon?' Charlotte reached across him to release the catch on the front door.

'My name is Porter,' he repeated frostily, leaning out of her way. 'It's an old word for beer.'

'Is it? Right . . . Mr Porter, of course, I remember now . . . Oh, I say . . . wow . . .' she exclaimed, momentarily forgetting her embarrassment as he pulled a scarlet woollen pom-pom hat from his overcoat pocket and pulled it low over his forehead and ears. The general impression was not flattering. 'That's quite a hat.'

'Rose – my daughter – gave it to me for Christmas,' he muttered, his sallow face creasing into a flinch of a smile. 'But there's no room for pride when it comes to love, is there?'

'No, indeed,' Charlotte murmured, and fell against the wall with a groan of relief after she had closed the door.

The Asian girl – by far the prettiest of Tim Croft's minions, with a silky curtain of jet black hair and large feline eyes – had a vase of roses parked next to her computer, twelve blood-red beauties with thick green stems and thorns as sharp as knives. Seeing them and the girl's glow of happiness, Charlotte experienced a moment of wonderment that anyone could ever be so naïve as to take any aspect of giving and receiving Valentines seriously. Just you wait, she wanted to say. Just you wait and see where those roses can lead.

Tim Croft, warmly effusive as always, swept her into his office, poured her a cup of coffee and put on a good show of concern at her account of the viewing with Mr Porter. 'Not the easiest customer,' he said, rubbing the neat semi-circle of a beard that ran along his jaw-line. 'The wife died apparently. Ovarian cancer – caught very late. Diagnosis to death in three weeks.' He clicked his fingers.

'*Died.*' Charlotte clapped both hands to her mouth. 'I assumed, when he said he was on his own . . .'

'Tragic, of course, but there we are.' Tim cleared his throat twice in succession. 'The good news is I've had a call this morning from a Mrs Burgess who's keen for an appointment to view your property next week.'

'Oh good,' Charlotte muttered, her mind still locked on to an image of the hapless widowed Mr Porter cringing under the force of her over-familiar chatter about the burdens of life and single parenthood.

Tim Croft's big-knuckled fingers were flying over the keys of his computer. 'Shall I offer her Thursday afternoon, say three p.m.? You don't give Ravens Books your services on a Thursday afternoon, do you?' he added, his voice softer and more *knowing*, as if he rather relished the fact that months of failing to sell her house meant he had an intimate knowledge of her weekly routines. 'Don't despair, Charlotte,' he went on jovially. 'Everybody gets there in the end.'

Where? Charlotte wondered, nodding and smiling as she pushed away her coffee cup. Where did everybody get to? And how did they know when they had got there? 'Thursday, three p.m., Mrs Burgess. Thanks, Tim. And I've been thinking about the asking price – perhaps I could take a bit off, but not too much or I won't be able to afford to move. Things are *so* expensive by the park.' She blinked at him, feeling suddenly in the mood for one of his boosting monologues about the market and things going up and down and possibly even repeating the stuff about getting there in the end.

'Aha.' Tim, never one to disappoint, patted the side of his nose. 'I've had word, unofficially, that there's something within your range on Chalkdown Road. A stone's throw from the park, not in the toast-rack – it could be just what you're looking for. The vendors have been advertising privately but I'm going to see what I can do.'

'Wonderful, that sounds really promising. Thanks, Tim. Do keep me posted, won't you?' On her feet, ready to leave, Charlotte held out her hand, which Tim shook, but then, to her puzzlement, did not immediately release.

'Charlotte, I was wondering . . . forgive me if . . .'

He had lowered his voice so much that she had to lean across the desk to hear.

'Only I just thought . . .' he glanced warily in the direction of his colleagues '. . . it might be nice to . . . meet up . . . for a drink or something. Not tonight, obviously – I'm sure you're busy tonight, of all nights – but perhaps next week some time, or the one after that?'

'A drink?' Charlotte whispered, casting a wary glance over her own shoulder as she eased her hand free. 'A *drink*?'

Tim laughed, tugging nervously at the point of his chin where the hairs were longest. 'Yes, you know, traditionally presented in a glass . . . sometimes with the accompaniment of food.'

'Oh, my goodness . . .'

'Not tonight, obviously,' he repeated, patting the springy top of his wiry brown hair and gazing out of his office window, as if considering the logistical possibilities of diving over the filing cabinet and hurling himself through the pane.

The answer had to be no, of course. The man was her estate agent. While having vowed to girlfriends that, when ready, she would play the field with gusto – have some fun after all the years of discontent – it had never occurred to Charlotte to imagine the solidly built, square-faced Tim Croft as a target. He had a beard. She didn't like beards.

But it had been a Valentine's Day with no cards, she reminded herself, and she had her decree nisi safely stowed in the bulging beige file labelled *Divorce*, and maybe the still elusive urge to launch herself into the alien business of having a good time required a bit of a kick-start. And then there was the inescapable fact of feeling sorry for Tim – desperately sorry, with all the twitchy looks out of the window, the terror of rejection flashing like a red light. So, while still thinking, *No*, Charlotte muttered instead that she was out of practice with baby-sitters and that this might prove a problem since Sam, at twelve, still needed consider-able supervision through the travails of homework, supper and being persuaded into bed.

'My neighbour's sixteen-year-old is always up for baby-sitting jobs,' Tim gushed, forgetting to keep his voice down and eliciting a raised eyebrow from the Asian girl. 'She's called Jessica,' he continued, with a little less exuberance, 'mad about children. I could give her a call. How about eight o'clock next Wednesday? Just to talk houses, if you like, over a drink instead of this filthy coffee.' He grinned, tugging his chin again, his eyes pleading.

Charlotte agreed, then spent the rest of the afternoon regretting it. By the time the tall black gates of St Leonard's came into view, pointing like a line of gleaming black weaponry towards the washed-out February sky, she had hatched and abandoned several elaborate pretexts to cancel. It was almost a relief to have the usual hunt for a parking space – scouring for gaps between driveways and double yellow lines – to distract her. By the time she found one the sun was already a sinking silver disc – more of a moon than a star. Watching it from the warm cocoon of the Volkswagen, aware of a subtle slide in her spirits, Charlotte hurriedly switched off the engine and stepped out into the raw chill of the afternoon.

'You can't park there. Your bumper's right over the end of my drive.'

'Is it?' Charlotte looked over the shoulder of her accuser, a jowly-faced man in a beret, seeing nothing but the unwashed hump of the Volkswagen. 'But I thought I –'

'There's a white line,' snarled the man, flecks of spittle gathering in the corners of his mouth. 'There's a white line and you've crossed it.'

Down the street a crowd of parents had now gathered in front of the gates. Charlotte could see Theresa in her funny hat with the ear-flaps talking animatedly to Naomi, whose twin three-year-old boys were tugging at her arms. 'I'm only collecting my son, I won't be a moment.' She cast the man an imploring look, hoping that his obviously advanced age might make him more likely to succumb to the dubious faded charms of a pallid thirty-nine-year-old with violet smudges under her eyes and messy auburn hair, which had begun the day as a bun but was now bursting out as a makeshift ponytail.

'If you don't move, I'm phoning the police. We're fed up with it, I tell you, *fed up*. Every bloody day it's the same. Useless bloody women parking your huge bloody vehicles across our driveways . . .' He paused, perhaps at the realization that the Volkswagen did not match this insult, or perhaps because tears were pouring down Charlotte's face.

Appalled by herself, swiping furiously at her cheeks, Charlotte ducked away and stabbed blindly at the door with the car key.

'Five minutes, then,' the man snapped, backing off and shaking his head. 'And I'd better not find you here tomorrow.'

Sam was easy to spot – face masked behind his flopping shock of white-blond hair, shoelaces and shirt tail trailing, his rucksack bumping along the Tarmac like a recalcitrant pet on a lead. Several classmates were horsing round alongside, towering above him as they all seemed to now, their pubescent bodies ripe and thick for manhood. Sam, with his waif-like smallness and stick-thin arms and legs, cruelly in evidence thanks to a wayward decision that morning to wear shorts, seemed more closely related to the skinniest of the girls.

'Sam!' Charlotte hurried towards the gates, blinking away the ridiculous tears. He hung back, inspecting something on the sole of his shoe while George, unmistakably Theresa's son with his thick dark curls and round ruddy-cheeked face, bowled out of the group for brief but enthusiastic entrapment in his mother's arms.

'Mah-jong, my place, a week next Friday,' yelled Theresa,

dodging the lollipop lady as they set off towards the mud-spattered Volvo on the opposite side of the road, where the bobbing, pig-tailed head of her youngest was visible through the passenger window.

'I don't know how she does it,' said Naomi, strolling over with the twins, who were now hanging from their sister Pattie – she had been in the same class as Sam since nursery school but these days turned up her nose at play dates with boys in favour of closed-door consultations with girl-friends. 'Four children, four schools. The woman's mad.' Charlotte nodded and smiled at this well-worn line of commentary. They all admired Theresa – organized, cheerful, self-deprecating, with a high-powered medical consultant of a husband who was often away presenting papers at important conferences. She would claim she wasn't coping but managed to cope superbly all the same. With the friendships between their children wavering, it had been Theresa's idea that the mums should keep seeing each other anyway over games of mah-jong (she had no time to read a book a month, she said, and abhorred bridge). Sporadic, enjoyable, the sessions had started at about the same time as Charlotte's marriage had entered its death throes, and proved nothing short of a lifeline. The warmth of her friends' support had been like oxygen, giving her the strength to plunge back into the awful disintegration going on at home.

'I thought Theresa had decorators in,' remarked Naomi, making a desultory attempt to pull the twins off their sister.

'She does, but they'll be gone by then.'

'Leave Pattie *alone*,' Naomi shouted, in a gunfire explosion of impatience that had the desired effect, before turning back to Charlotte and saying, in the mildest voice, 'Jo's asked me to pick up Ellie because the au pair's sick. Have you seen her?'

Charlotte scanned the thinning group of children. Josephine Burrows, a marketing executive with three off-spring and a history of problematic home-help, made up the fourth of their close-knit group. Ellie was her youngest; two elder brothers got themselves to and from a school in Wimbledon by bus. 'Hey, that's her there, isn't it? On that wall, reading.'

'*Reading*. Do you hear that, Pattie, she's *reading*, without being asked.' Naomi glared at her daughter, before switching her attention back to Charlotte. 'Hey, are you all right?'

'Yes, fine, absolutely fine.'

Naomi cast her a quizzical look. 'Martin hasn't been renegotiating Sam's weekends again, has he?'

'No . . . in fact, this morning the decree nisi came through. At last.' She punched the air.

'So why the long face?'

'Oh, I don't know – hormones possibly, and not selling the house . . . and, just maybe, accepting a *date* with my *estate agent*. I tried to refuse,' Charlotte wailed, 'but it came out wrong.'

Naomi was guffawing in a manner endearingly at odds with her petite frame and delicate features. 'Well, I think that's great. So long as it's not the fat old one, but the nice youngish one with short hair and he's not married.'

'Of course he's not married,' Charlotte put in a little sharply. 'I'm hardly likely to play that game, am I?'

'Nope, I guess you're not,' agreed Naomi, still laughing. 'And don't worry about the house – they always sell in the end. Remember it took Graham and me eighteen months to get shot of our first place in Milton Keynes? The market had nose-dived and refused to come up again, but here we are, safe and sound, in sunny Wandsworth. Now, I'd better retrieve Ellie and get this lot home.' She gestured with sudden weariness at her twins, who were playing a vicious game of tug-of-war with a pencil case. 'You said you were going to have a good time, remember?' she added, perhaps still not convinced by the expression on Charlotte's face. 'That you were just going to go with the flow, *enjoy* yourself. It's been months now and you were so unhappy . . . Do you remember that, Charlotte? How unhappily married you were?'

There was a trace of impatience in her voice; enough for Charlotte to roll her eyes, say, 'Of course,' and signal to Sam that it was time to head for the car. She felt impatient with herself too. The turning point she had longed for had arrived that morning and here she was already finding reasons to be blue.

She walked fast but Sam skipped on ahead. There were red patches on the backs of his knees – a flare-up of his babyhood eczema – and a bruise on his calf. Charlotte hurried to catch him up, the self-pity displaced by the much more understandable and familiar sensation of guilt – for what she and Martin had put him through, for knowing only too well what it felt like to be the child of a cheating dad. 'You okay, love?'

'Yep.'

'I thought maybe a Coke and a slice of chocolate cake at that nice café.'

It was a cheap ploy, Charlotte knew, but like many of the simplest stratagems it worked. The past could not be controlled – what was done was done – but the future, she reminded herself, was now more within her power than ever.

Sam's face lit up as she had guessed it would – a treat in recent weeks and beautiful to behold, like curtains parting on daylight. 'Let's dump your bag in the car and walk. Or maybe run,' Charlotte cried, taking off down the street the moment the car door was closed, knowing he would overtake her in seconds, loving it that she could still astonish him.

Chapter Two

There is a workshop — always — wherever we live; a dusky, woody-smelling room lined with shelves of small, sagging boxes, each containing different-sized nails, bolts and screws. Hanging along the wall above the workbench are hammers, screwdrivers and spanners, arranged in graduated order of size, the smallest so appealing that I long — as with the smallest of my beloved babushka dolls — to fold it tightly in my palm. Sometimes — the scenes merge — my father lets me sit on his lap to help tighten a piece of wood in the vice. I use both hands to work the heavy handle, then watch the tightening clench of the metal jaws as he finishes the job. Like teeth, he says, a monster's teeth; and he presses his mouth to my neck and I squirm and squeal with that afraid-pleasure that comes so easily to a child.

The following Wednesday afternoon Sam ate tea with more than his usual methodical reluctance, cradling the side of his head on one hand and using his fork to spear too-large pieces of chicken and solitary slices of carrot and potato into a barely open mouth. Charlotte sat next to him with a mug of tea, resisting the urge to reprimand. They had already had a scuffle about not being able to eat in front of the television, which she had managed — within a hair's breadth of caving in — to win.

'I won't be out for long. A nice girl called Jessica is coming to baby-sit. Are you okay with that?'

Sam placed a shred of carrot in his mouth and chewed slowly. 'Whatever.'

'Dad phoned. I'm dropping you there straight after school

on Friday as Cindy has the afternoon off. He said they might take you to the cinema. That will be nice, won't it?'

'I guess.'

'School all right?'

He raised his head to look at her, his pale blue eyes flashing with scorn behind the straggle of his hair. 'School sucks.'

'Miss Hornby said you're doing much better this term, that you –'

'Miss Hornby is a spastic.'

'That's a horrible word, Sam. You're not to use it about anyone.'

He dropped his fork on to his empty plate and pushed back his chair. 'Can I watch telly now?'

'Don't you want a pudding – yoghurt or maybe a biscuit?'

He shook his head, sticking out his chin, reminding her momentarily – vividly – of Martin.

'How about a yoghurt *and* a biscuit *while* watching telly?'

Sam knitted his eyebrows together, fighting her kindness, the softness of her voice, holding out. 'Can I play on the computer?'

Charlotte drummed her fingers on the table, pretending to think. 'Yes, but only *after* eating and . . . let me see . . . I think that will require a hug too. A massive, gigantic one that no one else need ever know about.'

Sam shuffled towards her and allowed himself to be held, while Charlotte felt a swell of emotion as strong as the one she had experienced when the doctor first tugged him free of her womb and placed him, tiny and slimy, in her arms. She put her nose into his hair, treating herself to an inhalation of the little-boy mustiness of his skin, feeding the animal need that had begun that day in the hospital, so instantaneous, so all-consuming that she had looked at Martin hovering by

18

the bed with a sort of wonderment that she could ever, until that moment, have had the remotest knowledge of what it meant to love.

An instant later Sam had wriggled free and was delving into the biscuit jar.

'Did you have games today?'

'Nah. Can I take two?'

'Yes – hey, let's see that bruise a minute.'

'What bruise?'

'There, on your leg, and there's another by your elbow. Two bruises.' Charlotte tried to grab his arm, but he snatched it away and skipped out of the kitchen.

An hour later she was welcoming a pimply-faced teenager and Tim Croft into the hall, noting with mixed feelings the effort the estate agent had made on her behalf – his wiry light brown hair, lustrous from washing, his beard freshly trimmed, his large teeth gleaming. In place of the usual work suit there was a tan leather jacket, a black polo-neck jumper and faded blue jeans, tight enough to reveal either a natural athleticism or hard work at the gym.

In fact, he was quite attractive, Charlotte realized, tensing rather than relaxing at the observation as she ushered them into the dining room to meet Sam. Her own ablutions had been limited to a hasty bath, followed by a torturous scanning of her overcrowded wardrobe for an outfit that would appear presentable without communicating any suggestion of a conscious desire to please. Pulling faces at her reflection, feeling, with some disgust, like a teenager who had gone nowhere, learnt nothing, she had settled at last on a staid (too staid) pair of chocolate corduroy trousers and a cream top with mother-of-pearl buttons.

'We – I – keep the computer in the dining room so I can see if Sam's eyes are going square, don't I, darling?' Charlotte chattered, trying to strike a tone that would make up for her son's rude growl of a hello. 'I bet you're good with computers, aren't you, Jessica?' she prompted, peering over Sam's shoulder, pleased to see it was dancing dots that were transfixing him, which meant a harmless football game as opposed to something sinister, like a chat room, whatever they looked like. Martin had been in charge of all that – child locks, spam blocks, firewalls and other ungraspable concepts that constituted technological health and safety. The extent of her own abilities, as Sam knew only too well, reached no further than websites and emails.

'I'm not bad,' Jessica replied slowly, exposing heavy rail-track braces that Charlotte suspected might account for the poor girl's evident reluctance to speak.

'Shall I show you round, then?' she offered, fighting fresh doubts about the evening and her selection of the cream top, which she had forgotten had an infuriating habit of riding up to her ribcage.

'Thank you, Mrs Turner.'

'Excellent.' Tim, clearly the happiest by far of their unlikely gathering, slapped his hands together and strode across the room to ask Sam who was playing who and where they stood in the league. Charlotte warmed to him, especially when – getting glimpses during the course of her guided tour with Jessica – she saw the hard time Sam gave him in return, his eyes not leaving the screen, his answers monochrome and monosyllabic. 'The estate agent,' he had snorted, when she confessed the identity of her escort. 'What for?' Charlotte had hesitated, stumped by the multitude of possible answers, all inappropriate (because I felt flattered and sorry for him, because since your father left the only male I have spent time with is you, because with the closure I so craved within reach I seem to have been pitched into a baffling, maddening state of immobility, of back-sliding, of retrospection . . .). '*Hah!*' Sam had spat the word into her silence, making his special gagging face as he bounded up the stairs.

'Are you ready to go?' Tim met her and Jessica as they returned to the hall.

'I think so, unless there's anything you want to ask me, Jessica?' Charlotte murmured, smiling encouragingly at the girl, who had chatted very sweetly between having the fridge pointed out to her and receiving instructions about bathtime and bed. 'He'll argue about going upstairs, of course. So don't give in, will you? He can leave his light on if he wants . . . He likes to sleep with it on. Not that I'll be late –' Charlotte broke off, flustered, with Tim cracking his knuckles and Jessica staring at her feet, both clearly dying to get on with things.

'I thought we'd get out of town a bit.'

'Did you?' Charlotte gripped the buckle on her handbag and looked out of the window, straining to focus beyond the blur of her reflection to the neon lights of bars and shops streaking behind. Tim had escorted her down the street to a sleek two-seater she had never seen parked outside the estate agent's. It was more like being in a cockpit than a car. Outside, what she could see of the world seemed equally compressed: huddled figures scurrying under the dark March sky, phones pressed to their ears, each absorbed in the tight, complicated package of their own life. *Relax*, she scolded herself. *Go with the flow*. After further doubts and several postponements, her expectations for the date were almost too low for disappointment. Fun, not love – how hard could that be? And if it went wrong she could relay it as a hilarious anecdote to her friends; prove to them, and herself, that she hadn't lost her sense of humour, that the long stint of playing the complaining wronged wife was well and truly past. Charlotte inhaled and exhaled deeply, releasing her grip on her handbag and noticing that the hard edge of the buckle had left a red ridge across her palm. Like a lifeline, she mused, determined not to let the nerves back in, a new, vivid lifeline, pointing who knew where?

Beside her, the padded leather steering-wheel made small swishing sounds as Tim slid it between his palms.

'Don't worry, not too far. We're heading for Kingston. Are you too warm?'

'No . . . I – Well, maybe just a little.' Charlotte shifted her legs away from the island of controls while he pressed various buttons. She could smell his aftershave, a faint but penetrating scent of something citrus. Beneath his earlobe were three long hairs that he had missed with the razor. Every time he changed gear his elbow brushed against hers. The outline of his thigh muscles was surfacing visibly through his trousers as he worked the pedals. 'Look, Tim,' she blurted, 'I think I might have given you the wrong idea – I mean, accepting to come out tonight. I never meant –'

'I know.' He shot her a grin. 'Seriously, it's fine. I made it difficult for you, didn't I? Bulldozed you into accepting. I can be like that, I'm afraid, when I get an idea into my head.'

'The thing is, I only recently . . .'

'Separated? I'd worked that one out a while ago. I'm not long out of a relationship myself,' he added smoothly, swinging off the main road. 'Ten years, you think you've found your soul-mate and then *pfff*,' he clicked his fingers, 'you're on your own, watering dead pot plants and watching crap on the telly and wondering what the hell happened to your life. You have to do something about it or you go mad.'

'Yes, you do,' Charlotte agreed, liking him so much that

it was all she could do not to confide the going-backwards feeling, haunting her still, every time she had least reason for it.

'So, I thought, why not have a drink?' Tim continued. 'Even with a girl who doesn't fancy you. Even,' he pressed on, unperturbed by Charlotte's failure to interrupt, 'if that girl is a client and every rule in the book warns against mixing business and pleasure. Ah, here we are.' He braked sharply and turned past a wooden pointing arm carved with the words 'El Ranchero'. A few moments later they had pulled up in front of two large wooden ostriches guarding a walkway to an empty stretch of decking and a large door. 'A friend recommended it. One of those Spanish tapas places – nothing heavy, snacks and drinks. Just a bit of fun, eh?' He leapt out of the car and gallantly opened her door, then jogged ahead to be able to offer the same compliment at the restaurant entrance.

The ostriches were hideous close to, crudely carved and so poorly attached to their moorings that their spindly legs juddered visibly as a gust of wind whipped across the car park. But Tim beckoned her towards the warm, bright interior with the confidence of a hotel doorman, and soon they were settled most comfortably on bar stools in front of chilled white wine and dishes of prawns, ratatouille and fluffy miniature tortillas. They talked easily and at length about houses; prices, streets, deposits, surveys. Tim had several funny stories about difficult clients and collapsing transactions, one in particular involving a milkman and a pet cockerel that made Charlotte laugh so hard she almost fell off the stool. And then, quite suddenly, when she was truly relaxed and off her guard, Tim announced that he had liked her from the start, that from the instant she had walked into his office it had been like a light going on. 'It's okay,' he assured her hastily, patting her hand as she flushed and squirmed, 'you've made it clear how you feel and I understand – I *respect* – that, but . . .' he lowered his voice '. . . even as your friend I would like to know all about you, Charlotte Turner, or at least a *little* more?' he pleaded, turning the confession into a joke by holding up his thumb and index finger as if indicating a tiny portion of something edible.

Flattered, her instincts softened by wine, at a loss as to what to make of this man with his twists and turns of tone, so *unknown* (so unknowable, as it seemed, after twenty years of no one but Martin), Charlotte countered feebly that there was nothing to tell and what about him? She found herself deciding in the same instant that the beard wasn't so bad. At least there were no specks of oil or food in it; he had been careful about that, dabbing with a napkin between mouthfuls. He ate daintily, too, for a man, which she liked. Martin had gone into a sort of trance when it came to food, shovelling in forkfuls, incapable of sensible conversation until his hunger was appeased.

'I asked first.' He topped up her glass.

'Okay, let me see.' She took a sip, and then another. 'A potted history would be roughly . . . born in Sri Lanka – or Ceylon, as it then was – because my father was into tea, then we moved to Constantia in South Africa –'

'*Tea* in South Africa?'

'No, wine by then.' Charlotte laughed. 'Okay, I'll leave it there.'

'No, no,' he protested. 'Don't leave it there. Go on. I want to hear more.' He ran his fingers across his lips in a charade of zipping them shut.

'I was despatched to boarding-school at the tender age of nine. A few years later my parents came back to England for good, to Tunbridge Wells. My mother still lives there.

We don't get on too well. Er . . . what else? Oh, yes, my father died when I was eighteen. I had just started at Durham University. That's where I met my husband. We had Sam, moved to London, separated last year, divorced this – I hope.' Charlotte picked up her glass and put it down again, twiddling the stem and smiling shyly. 'I think that's about it. A simple thing, a life, isn't it? The bare essentials, I mean.'

'Oh, yes, so simple,' Tim agreed, although his attention had long since drifted from the substance of the conversation. He liked the way she had left the top three buttons on her cardigan undone, drawing the eye – deliberatcly, he was sure – to the modest swell of her breasts. They looked in pretty good shape, too, given that she had had a kid and had to be pretty close to forty. Through the thin cream wool of the top he could just make out the edging of her bra. Or maybe it was a camisole, a piece of pretty silk with a lacy trim. And her mouth was enticing, having the natural cherry redness that so often went with auburn colouring. In his view it was even more irresistible now that the lipstick had worn off.

It was wrong, Tim knew, to let such thoughts in. He had said he understood how she felt, so he should stick to that, play out the charade of wanting friendship. Talking was so important to women, sharing feelings and so on. Phoebe had rammed that home often enough, ticking him off for not listening to her, for having feelings that were either insufficient or never about the right things.

'What about you?'

'Pardon?'

'Your potted history.'

She was leaning on the bar and turned towards him to await the answer, resting her left cheek in the palm of her left hand, her sharp green eyes properly alive at last. A moment before, she had run her fingers through her hair, raking it off her face and letting it fall in two silky sweeps across her ears. Tim suddenly remembered reading somewhere – in one of his men's magazines probably, brought out of hiding since Phoebe's departure – that such preening by a female denoted genuine physical interest. Body language was everything, the article had said. Undisguisable, it proved that behind the elegant structures of our sentences – the so-called *communication* that Phoebe had been so keen on and eventually abandoned – humans were no more advanced than the rest of the animal kingdom. Love, hate, hope, fear, desire – none of it needed any words. It was all there in eyes, hands, elbows and legs. You just needed to know how to look for it. Inspired, Tim mirrored her position – elbow on the bar, head resting on his hand. Making eye contact, holding it as he moved closer, he delivered the less than inspiring pronouncement that his father had been an electrician and then, with great speed and, he hoped, gentleness, lowered his mouth on to hers.

After rain the grass sings. I listen, standing in the shade of the jackfruit tree, its great emerald leaves dripping. Above me one of the fat knobbly green fruits dangles, heavy with moisture, big enough to kill, my father says, should it land on my head. I look up, studying its gnarled features – like an old man's face – wondering what it would feel like to die, or whether it would be like sleep, which you couldn't feel. I am supposed to be asleep now. It is after-lunch time when the heat sits like a pillow on your face and the strays lounge in scraps of shade, snapping at flies. My mother thinks I'm lying on my bed under the whirl of the ceiling fan, the amah *nodding in the wicker chair, my lunch settling. She is meeting someone, a someone with a girl my age whom I was supposed to meet, too, but who is unwell.*

I cross the grass, my bare feet sinking into its new softness, leaving prints that do not last. I look through the hole in the fence and see the gardener curled in a Z-shape next to his tools, the white-pink soles of his feet towards me, his thin black legs like dusty sticks. Around him, half over him, the bougainvillaea and frangipani explode like the fireworks on the Queen of England's birthday. I am bored, the thrill of disobedience quite gone. I think of my mother's friend's sick child and wonder if she is nice. I wonder whether she has lovely dolls with elaborate clothes like my playmate Freya, who has gone back to England. I want to be in England too, near the Queen who has such grand birthdays, near Freya and her toys and her mother's home-made scones.

My skin prickles in the heat. My hair is wet on my neck. Through the hole the gardener stretches, raises his head and looks towards me as if he can see through the wood. I scamper back across the grass. The door of the workshop is ajar and I slip through the opening, one leg first, then my head and shoulders. It is almost as good as diving into the sea from the jetty – the plunge of my hotness into the wet cold. But then something snags. I pull but I am caught. I can hear the gardener approaching the fence. I can feel his eyeball boring through the hole, rolling in its socket, looking for trouble. He will find my amah *and tell on me. He likes her. They sit on the back step sometimes sharing the juice of a king coconut, sucking at two straws, their lips close. I pull harder and hear the rip of cotton. Looking down I see that a rusty nail has gashed my shorts – my favourite gingham shorts. The front panel hangs open; the torn edges are frayed and brown, like a wound.*

I want to cry but I don't want to be found. Inside the darkness of the workshop it is like being stroked by cool fingertips. It is soothing to be stroked. My amah *does it sometimes when I cannot sleep, running the backs of her roughened nails up and down my legs and arms, humming one of her funny songs that have no tune.*

I step towards the worktop where the vice gleams in the dim light. I am taller now and can reach the tools pinned along the back. Knowing they are within my grasp makes the urge to touch them less strong.

Even the tiniest screwdriver, with its neat tip and little wooden handle, looks ordinary. I sigh, sensing something lost as I turn back towards the room.

It is only then that I see them. I see the whites of her eyes first, huge in her black face. She makes no sound as she presses her lips to my father's ear. I see the back of his head, the hair curling up from his shirt collar. He is on top of her, on the rush matting next to the dolls' house whose roof came loose and which he has promised to fix. He is on top of her and moving. His trousers are round his ankles, his shirt tails trail over his backside and thighs. The moment holds, endless. I know what they are doing. I know because Freya has told me, giggling, as she points up under the skirts of her dolls.

The eyes are wider, whiter. As her lips leave his ear he stops moving and turns his head towards me. But I am already running, out of the shed, my gashed shorts flapping. I race back across the grass, past the butterfly petals of the flowers, past the hole in the fence. The whip of the sun stings my head. The ground, dry now, is silent and hard, yet I feel as if I am running through air, upside-down, weightless, lost.

Jessica had been surprisingly nice. She had let him stay up late and told him about trying to eat only fruit for ten days straight and a boy named Darren who never called. It had reminded Sam that once upon a time, before the new silliness at school about who liked whom and how much, he had got along pretty well with girls. Once upon a time, even longer ago, he had actually quite fancied having a kid sister. George had one called Matilda with puce cheeks and knotty hair who would fetch and carry for him like a slave. On one occasion she had eaten Airfix glue because George asked her to, and then not told on him, not even when George's mum – a terrifying spectacle, eyes popping, her face livid – had screeched about dying and stomach pumps.

It had occurred back in the days when George still invited

him to tea. Sam had witnessed the episode in awe, both on account of the display of sibling loyalty (to have such an *ally*!) and the shouting – not just by George's mum but by George himself and his little sister and the brothers, joining in for good measure. And then, suddenly, like a storm passing, or a language everyone but him understood, there had been rounds of hugging and quietness and toasted muffins. Returning to his own household, Sam had felt more acutely than ever the *not* talking going on between his parents – his father shaking the newspaper like a shield, his mother laying knives and forks with fierce, terrifying precision; it was like white noise, constant, invisible, deafening.

Hearing an echo of it now, in the dark of his bedroom, Sam switched on his light. He had a favourite Astérix book that lived under the bed for emergencies, but for some reason he wasn't in the mood. He stretched instead, to his very fullest, pointing his toes and fingertips in the hope that it might have some permanent effect on his length. His body was invisibly diseased, he was sure of it. Each night for weeks now he had been measuring himself against the babyish wall-hanging of a tape-measure that lived behind his bed-room door (a giraffe with a grinning mouth and a lolling tongue; it had occupied that spot ever since he could remember) and each night there was no change. After his nice time with Jessica Sam had felt especially hopeful, especially *tall*. He hadn't even tried to cheat as he usually did, but had pressed his palm lightly on the flat of his head and kept it steady while he performed the contortion necessary to get a reading. And yet it had been the measly five feet two it always was, just by the tip of the giraffe's big black nose.

Staring at the stupid creature now, feeling it was staring at *him*, Sam experienced such a wave of loathing that he scrabbled in his bedside drawer, among penknives, flints and other treasures, for his darts. Balancing on the mattress, he hurled all three across the room in turn, pinning the giraffe's silly cartoon face to the wall. His mother would tell him off, of course – *holes* in the *wall* when they were *selling* the *house*. Sam mimicked her under his breath as he bounced back under his duvet. He didn't want to move house anyway, and she was the one who had got his hopes up about growing – *any minute now*, she always promised, *any minute now*, saying what was nice, as per usual, instead of what was actually true, so you couldn't trust any of it, not really.

Sam was almost asleep when he heard a car pull up in the street outside. Ducking up under the curtains, he couldn't help thinking how cool the estate agent's long red sports car looked next to their silly old Volkswagen. To console himself he thought of his dad's BMW and Cindy's Saab, both black, both convertible. The cars sat on the hard standing outside their new home, gleaming, sleek, like two members of the same family. They had matching bikes as well, and all the gear to go with them – helmets, pumps, Lycra T-shirts and shorts. Recently they had given Sam a bike too, as an early birthday present, his dad had said, so they could go on expeditions together. They hadn't done that yet, but he had been out with Cindy a couple of times, along the walkway next to the river, which had been sort of fun but also weird, like they were playing at having a good time instead of really having one.

Half on the window-sill now, his knees aching with cold, Sam waited, wondering why his mother wasn't getting out. He opened the curtain wider, craning his neck to get a better look, wishing he had Superman's laser eyes so he could bore through the roof. Then, suddenly, the passenger door swung open and there she was, looking as she always did in her old black overcoat.

Sam slid back under the bedcovers, pulling them up to his chin. She would come up, surely. She would because she always did. She always had, even during the worst times, after shouting and door-slamming when not even the dark could hide the puffiness in her eyes and he knew that the slightly salty taste of her kiss was from crying.

And yet now those same lips might have touched the hair-framed mouth of the estate agent . . . during that time in the car, those long minutes. Sam exhaled slowly, closing his teeth round the cotton fringe of the duvet cover. When the landing creaked, he rolled on to his side, burying his face in the pillow. He couldn't control anything, he realized, good or bad. The mattress tipped as she sat down. Sam didn't move, not even when he felt her mouth brush the crown of his head, soothing the exact spot that had failed to outgrow the giraffe.

Chapter Three

Theresa hummed quietly as she always did when she was busy. The curry was taking shape now, the rich aromas of frying beef and spices conveniently masking the smell of fresh paint seeping in from the sitting room. Next to the oven top, splattered with brown drops of meat juice, was the final invoice from the decorator. Through the wall she could hear the muffled clatter as the man folded away his ladders and shifted the furniture back.

With both hands full – cardamom, a fresh chilli, the dripping wooden spoon – Theresa tugged up the sleeve of her sweatshirt with her teeth to get a glimpse of her wrist-watch, performing in the same instant a rapid complex mental calculation encompassing all the things that had to be achieved in the half-hour remaining before her school run. And after that – Theresa hummed louder as her mind whirred – George would require cajoling through some trumpet practice for his exam the following Friday, Matilda, her youngest, needed a nit-check, while the middle two, Alfie and Jack, would, as usual these days, need supervising through absolutely everything, from homework to the insertion of toothbrushes between their jaws. Fifteen months apart, her two younger sons had reached a stage of such competitiveness – for her attention, for the number of spaghetti hoops that made it on to their plates, for who could get to the top stair first – that it required the tactical skills of a wily diplomat, not to mention exhaustive vigilance, to keep the peace.

Theresa placed the lid on the casserole dish with a contented sigh. She could, she knew, have done many things with her life. She had always got high grades at school and been bright and popular. Her parents, both teachers, had been stunned into silent disappointment when she shunned university and opted for nursing. She had excelled at that, too, just as she now excelled at the management of her large family. It was like running a ward, or a small company – supervision of projects, seeing to practical details, rewarding good behaviour, trying to bring out the best in everyone, thinking and planning ahead. How anyone ever thought motherhood unchallenging or dull was beyond her. Though people did it badly, of course, everywhere, all the time, just as lots of people made a hash of running businesses. It was wrong to judge, Theresa knew, but really, when one looked at the mess some people made of their lives – dear Charlotte, for example – it was impossible not to count a few blessings at least.

The curry, mild enough to suit the children, was also sufficiently large to serve as dinner for the mah-jong group, and for Henry, who would make himself scarce as he always did on what he called her 'hen nights'. He would put his head round the sitting-room door, his thinning hair askew after his walk from the station, his deep-set blue eyes crinkling with mild amusement at the assembly of females gathered round the card table, plates and wine glasses slotted between the little walls of tiles, then retreat via the kitchen to the den. Later, after clearing up, Theresa would find him asleep, glasses on the end of his nose, his chin on his chest, the TV murmuring, a half-read journal still open on his lap. He would wake instantly, as all doctors learnt to do, marvel at the lateness of the hour, then shoo her upstairs so he could lock up and set the alarm.

Theresa, hurriedly writing a cheque for the decorator, scraping the worst of the meat blobs off the invoice with her thumbnail, paused in her humming to smile as the scene formed in her mind's eye. They had their fall-outs, of course, but even those, during the course of fourteen years, had acquired an element of predictability that was almost comforting. The hardest time for them by far had been early on, when Henry worked long hospital shifts as a houseman and she was still climbing the career ladder as a nurse. Tired, lonely, disillusioned, she had had an affair with one of his colleagues – or, rather, a one-night stand – to which she had confessed almost immediately, flinging clothes into a suitcase between sobs. Instead of being angry, or offering to help her pack, Henry had taken her to Paris that very evening, frogmarching her to Gatwick and then to a hotel so expensive they had spent the next few months paying off the overdraft. Looking back, Theresa often thought that the incident, though in many ways terrible and unforgivable, had been the making of them; like a horse knocking a first fence that wobbled but did not fall, and keeping its hoofs higher in consequence, they had bounded on all the stronger for the crisis.

Decorator paid, sitting room dusted, curry simmered, rice washed, ironing folded, washing-machine loaded, dish-washer unloaded, alarm set, door double-locked, Volvo launched into the afternoon traffic, Theresa found her thoughts returning to the demise of Charlotte-and-Martin. There was no going back for either of them now, which was sad, of course, but also – if she was totally honest – a tad inconvenient. Martin was extremely nice. Henry, in particular, got on very well with him – computer talk, rugby-watching, dad-only sessions in the park. With the marriage beyond repair, he was in danger of losing quite a friend.

Now it was Rotherhithe and a woman called Cindy. A couple of days before, they had received an invitation to a house-warming, a large, ostentatious card, studded with pictures of champagne corks and glitter. Flicking the duster round it on the mantelpiece that afternoon, Theresa had wondered suddenly whether it wouldn't be better off hidden in a drawer, at least until the mah-jong was done with. Her first loyalty lay with Charlotte after all. They had become friends eight years before – via George and Sam's Montessori and an incident with a flat tyre on the South Circular when they'd left the hazards flashing and bolted into a wine bar.

Martin and Henry hadn't stepped into the frame until many months later and then only because she and Charlotte had orchestrated it, promoting the relationship to an official adult level with invitations to dinner and the theatre. Now such occasions would have to involve either a fund manager called Cindy, who was ten years younger and childless (not the most likely-sounding soul-mate for either her or Henry) or, apparently, an employee from one of Wandsworth's leading estate agencies.

Theresa, accelerating and slowing with practised ease between the road humps lining the final approach to her daughter's primary school, shook her head in disbelief. To go out with one's estate agent smacked of desperation. And where would it get Charlotte in the end, she mused, other than into another relationship that would eventually require effort, a willingness to launder male socks and the need, sometimes, to feign an interest in sex when all one really wanted was a cup of tea? Love, Theresa had learnt, lay on the other side of such trials, the extraordinary waiting in the shadows of the ordinary. It could take time to find, not to mention trust, commitment . . . She gripped the steering-wheel harder. *Staying power.* That was what all marriages needed, and her friend had simply never had enough of it.

As we wait on the station platform I observe how fresh-faced the other parents look, how energized, wielding bags and younger siblings, how young. Mine hang back, different, uncertain, old. Compared to the other women's smart hairstyles, my mother's looks limp and long, the red salted with white, while my father's once full head has shrunk to a ring of brown that circles his baldness like a too-small nest holding a large egg. Their clothes are wrong too – her loud yellow shawl, his red-spotted neckerchief. I blush to belong to them.

The garters of my new school socks cut into the ridge under my kneecaps. The material of my skirt feels rough against my thighs. My plaited hair tugs at my skull. I long for the train to arrive, for the farewells to be something to look back on instead of dreaded. I wish my parents weren't different, but I ache already from missing them, especially him, with his big, bear-hugging love, his games and jokes, and that special smile, which even after two years still says, 'I know that you know but we shall not speak of it.'

We have a woodshed in Constantia but I never enter it. The dolls' house, mended, pristine, lives on a table at the foot of my bed. Through its white-framed windows I can still see the figures I used to cherish, the man sitting in an armchair, his spindly legs – wool woven round wire – bent awkwardly, the woman in the kitchen propped up against the miniature mangle I bought with saved pocket money from a magazine. Her hair is coming unglued and she leans unrealistically, like the doll she is. Nearby, in a pink wooden cot, the tiny china face of a baby – their baby – peeps over its gauze blanket, its pencil-dot eyes blank. I see them but I no longer want to touch. They must manage alone, as I do.

On the train I hold my hat on my lap. It is made of straw and has a blue ribbon round it. In the middle at the front is a badge with a crest on it and the words 'In Omnibus Veritas'. At the station café my mother, scowling at the watery grey tea (the dust off the factory floor, my father complains loudly, proud of his knowledge), has explained that this means 'Truth in all things'. She said it twice, glancing from me to him, as if she knew . . . but, of course, she couldn't because she had been lunching with her friend that day, and if she knew she wouldn't have agreed to go to Africa, to swap tea-leaves for grapes and a damp, sapping heat for one so dry it burns through to your bones.

'Are you new?'

'Yes.' *I pluck at the blue ribbon and try to smile, as if being new is normal and bearable. The girl who has put the question has dark blue eyes and hair the colour of honey, curling in silky tips across her shoulders. She is sitting opposite, with a magazine on her lap. She chews gum, pushing it out between her teeth and sucking it back again. On her fingernails are jagged traces of red varnish. She wears her school boater pushed back on her head, like a halo. She tells me that she is thirteen and that a blue ribbon means we are in the same house. I am overjoyed to have a friend already, an older, beautiful friend, in the same house. She says she is called Letitia and then asks me my name.*

'Charlotte Boot.'

She pauses, the blue eyes widening. 'Boot?'

I sense danger and turn to look out of the window. The English countryside is like a washed-out picture compared to the landscapes I know: greys spilling into greens and browns, like something created by a painter with too much water on his brushes.

'Boot, as in Bootface?'

I stare hard at the smeary palette of Surrey, seeking something lovely or certain, something to hang on to. I do not look at her but I hear the change in her voice, the edge, as sharp as the blade our old cook had used in the hill country, slicing new cuts into the criss-crossed map of her chopping board. For a moment — a blissful moment — the tunnel of the memory closes over me and I am standing at the cook's elbow, watching the dark hairs on her arm glisten as she slides the knife

37

across a pineapple, decapitating its prickly head and then the stubbly armour of its body. One, two, three, four strokes and the juicy yellow innards are there — mine for eating. 'No, just Boot.'

'Yeah, Bootface, like I said. And Carrot-top. Carrot-top, Bootface.' She swings her foot as she talks, banging my shin with the hard toe of her shoe.

A woman in a brown suit and thick tights slides open the door of our carriage and checks off our names on a clipboard. She teaches a subject called Divinity, she says, and is a deputy housemistress. She smiles at me and says it is nice to have me on board and that I will soon get the hang of things. I stretch my lips back at her, willing her never to leave. But a minute later the door whooshes shut and she is gone. Letitia tucks her feet under her seat and returns her attention to her magazine. I breathe quietly, slowly, absorbing the knowledge that an English boarding-school will offer no haven from the complications of living, that pretending not to care remains the only sure way to survive.

Fresh from the most unsatisfactory of meetings with Miss Hornby (no, Sam wasn't himself, yes, they were keeping an eye on him), it was in a somewhat distracted frame of mind that Charlotte map-read her way via the *A–Z* towards Chalkdown Road. Yet at first glimpse the virtues of the location were so obvious, even in the dim light of a March afternoon, that she delivered a thump of delight to the steering-wheel, accidentally sounding the horn and prompting a dark look from a sprightly jogger for whom she had slowed to allow safe passage across the road.

The park was a minute's walk away, quite a nice walk, too, by the look of it, along a winding avenue of large grey and white Victorian houses sporting pruned shrubs on their doorsteps and gravelled off-street parking slots for small, expensive cars. In Chalkdown Road itself, there was a more motley assemblage of buildings, including a disused and dirty red-brick church and a section of ugly square flats studded with graffiti, satellite dishes and concrete balconies full of rusting white goods and chipped flowerpots. But it was a long street and number forty-two was one of a cluster of semi-detached cottages set away from such unsightliness. It had a neat front garden of well-tended grass, bordered by flowering thickets of winter jasmine – a dazzling and welcome splash of colour on a day that had begun with such heavy downpours that Charlotte had been reminded of the grey monsoon lashings of her early childhood when the rain streamed so thickly it hosed gullies in the soil as it fell.

A charming cottage in Wandsworth, near the park and only just out of her price range . . . Charlotte peered through the windscreen of her car in happy disbelief, her imagination leaping forwards to visions of Sam skipping merrily to school and her waving him off from the doorstep. She might even give in to the years of pleading for a dog, she decided dreamily, not a squat silly dachshund like her mother's, but a *real* dog that bounded and licked and fetched and gave affection on demand. Sam's delight alone would make it worthwhile. And with Sam back on an even keel she was sure she, too, would be able to embark at last on the new beginning she had promised herself, to start relishing her freedom instead of being frozen by it.

The interior did not disappoint. While Tim (having arrived very much the estate agent rather than as a would-be suitor) consulted some notes and punched in a set of numbers to decode the alarm, Charlotte skipped round the hall, exclaiming at every detail – the stained glass in the front door, the low beams, the polished pine floorboards. Thus inspired, it was easy to forgive the somewhat worn kitchen units and note instead the original tiles on the floor, the handy hooks and shelves housing scrubbed pans, strings of garlic, family photos, teacups and jars of dried herbs.

There were darker beams in the sitting room, and a limestone fireplace, offset by a handsome décor of lemon and faded blue. In the darkening light a crescent-shaped patio was visible through the double doors overlooking the garden. Fringed with beds of lavender and an ebullient japonica, bursting with scarlet berries, it lit up the back of the house just as the jasmine had the front. Beyond stretched a long wide lawn which, like everything else, exuded a sense of something nurtured, something *loved*. And it was this she was falling for, Charlotte realized, scanning it greedily, just as much as the house's cosy rooms and proximity to the park.

Absorbed, enchanted, the arrival of Tim's hands on her shoulders, his smart polished shoes silenced by the carpet, caught her by surprise.

'I think I might want this place,' she murmured, letting her weight shift against him, thinking in the same instant that, even with the lowest of expectations, there was a simple, profound pleasure in having someone to lean on, to share food with, and thoughts on houses.

'And I want you,' Tim replied, slipping his arms round her waist. 'I've been dying for you to call. You said you would. Why didn't you?'

Charlotte hesitated. She hadn't called because she wasn't sure she wanted to go on another date. And yet, receiving his formal handshake in the street, a small part of her had felt faintly rebuffed, and even wondered, dimly, whether her kissing the previous week – rusty, a little shy of the geography of a new face – might not have been up to scratch. 'Because it's wrong, Tim, that's why.'

'Wrong?'

'Inappropriate.'

'Nonsense. We're grown-ups.' He slid his hands over her hips and pulled her more firmly against him. 'I was thinking . . . we could finish here and then go back to my place. I'm not a bad cook. I'll rustle something up and then . . .'

'I'm afraid I can't tonight. I'm already busy.' She wriggled free and turned round.

'Oh.' He looked crestfallen.

'My girlfriends,' she explained, more kindly. 'Every few weeks we meet at each other's houses and play mah-jong together.'

'Mah-jong? Very fancy.'

'It's to talk, too, of course – a bit of a girls' night, you know the sort of thing. It's a small group but they're good friends and, frankly, I don't know how I'd have got through the last few years without them . . . I say, do you mind if we get on with looking round?' she ventured, impatient suddenly, both to see the rest of the house and at having to pitch the question – to him of all people – as if it were some kind of favour.

'No, of course not.' Tim clicked his heels and saluted. 'At your service, madam. All inappropriateness to cease forthwith.'

Charlotte laughed, flinging up her arms in despair at the awkwardness. 'Look, Tim, I'm sorry. This whole business – you and me – I'm just not sure if it's wise, or what I want from it or . . . but I do like you,' she continued hurriedly, seeing his dismay deepen, remembering how good it had felt to be held, 'and maybe – if we agree there's no pressure and so on – we could perhaps meet again soon. Okay?'

'*Okay.*' He rolled his eyes and made a face, like a child being told something he knew already. 'I just think you're great, that's all. I think you're great and I'm not very good at hiding it. But that's fine,' he added, jaunty once more, tossing the house keys from palm to palm. 'It's my problem, not yours. I will, as they say, take what I can get.' He clenched the keys in one fist. 'And now would madam like a tour of the bedrooms or is she too worried I'll rugby-tackle her on to a mattress?'

Charlotte giggled, taking his hand for the walk up the stairs, which were steep, with spindly wooden banisters and a T-junction of a landing at the top. There were three bedrooms and a bathroom, all pleasantly decorated and of a good size. The back one had its own balcony, decked with window-boxes of miniature cyclamen and winter pansies, and a little wrought-iron chair. It was on seeing this – on seeing herself, in fact, sitting in the little chair with a book and a cup of tea and peace in her heart – that Charlotte spun round and declared that she had to have the place at all costs, that she would accept anything Mrs Burgess offered and beg a loan from the bank, from Martin if necessary, to make up the difference. She *had* to have it, she gabbled, the colour rising in her cheeks. Did he understand?

Tim, busy grappling with an unfolding ladder from a hatch in the bedroom ceiling, said he would do his best and did she want to go up first or should he?

'Tim,' Charlotte pleaded, 'can you get me this house?' She tugged at his jacket. She didn't care about the attic. They were pointless places, used for storing things probably better off in a skip. She didn't like their dusty cool either, the sense of the unknown crouched inside. Sam would love it, though, she reflected, glancing upwards with a trace more interest. Sam, who didn't want to move, who was too young to see the sense – the importance – of a clean slate for the pair of them, would *love* it. As a little boy one of his favourite places had been the tank cupboard behind the eaves on the top landing of her mother's house. Discovered during a game of hide-and-seek, he had taken to retreating there when no need for concealment was required, staying sometimes for alarmingly long periods, but emerging always with dirty knees and the dazed, triumphant expression of an explorer returning from a distant land.

'Hey, I'll do my best, okay?' Tim promised, clearly somewhat surprised by the urgency in her tone. He patted the ladder. 'Now, are you going to take a look or not?'

Charlotte shook her head. 'Not now, thanks. I'll save it for Sam. Talking of whom,' she glanced at her watch, 'I ought to be going. I've got to pick him up from after-school club, drive him to his father's and get back in time to go out. I'm a bit worried about him, actually,' she confessed, stepping out of the way of the ladder.

'Who?' puffed Tim, still trying to seal the hatch.

'Sam,' Charlotte murmured, momentarily transported back to her unsatisfactory consultation with the very young, very smiling, faintly condescending form teacher earlier that afternoon. Charlotte had left the meeting feeling humoured rather than reassured, angrily contemplating the empathetic deficiencies of a creature whose talents extended only to the dates of Henry VIII's wives and how to inscribe those dates across a whiteboard in straight lines, a creature whose sole knowledge of childhood was her very recent own.

'You're worried about Sam?' Tim prompted, brushing patches of dust off his suit.

'Oh, it's nothing,' Charlotte protested, heartened nonetheless at this display of interest. 'I saw his teacher today . . . Something unpleasant is going on at school, I'm sure of it. But Sam, like all children, I suppose, would endure anything rather than the hassle – the *embarrassment* – of complaint.'

'Bullying, you mean?'

Charlotte shrugged. 'Maybe. A bit . . .'

Any temptation to elaborate was cut short by the slam of the front door. Starting a little guiltily, they hurried downstairs to exchange hasty pleasantries with the owner of the house, a Mrs Stowe, in her late fifties with pale blue eyes and long grey hair kept in girlish fashion off her face with a wide blue hairband.

'We were just going, but it's *lovely*, thank you *so* much. In fact, I might . . .' Charlotte glanced at Tim, who had shrunk back into composed, estate-agent mode, clutching his sheaf of papers and staring hard at the briars of tight green rosebuds springing round the front door '. . . that is to say – and I know this is probably premature and unprofessional – but I might be interested in putting in an offer.'

Mrs Stowe smiled uncertainly. 'Well, that's very nice, dear, but as I hope Mr Croft explained, this was very much an unofficial visit. My husband, in particular, is still keen to sell privately. In fact –'

Before she could reach the end of the sentence Tim had abandoned his flower-study and was bringing the encounter to a smooth close with farewells and thanks and promises to call.

'I can't believe it,' Charlotte wailed, once they were out of earshot. 'Either it's on the market or it isn't.'

'Well, no, actually, since people are entitled to change their minds. And as Mrs Stowe said, that was something of a *premature* viewing, agreed to by her thanks to my powers of persuasion. Getting a foot in the door, Charlotte, that's so often the key. I shall talk to her first thing tomorrow, see what I can do to move things forward, maybe drop in the idea of sealed bids . . .'

'*Sealed bids?*'

'If Mrs Burgess comes back with an offer on your place

and you can, as you say, raise a bit more money, you could be in a very strong position.' Tim couldn't keep the heartiness from his voice. One of Charlotte's reservations about him, he suspected, was that he was *only* an estate agent. Well, here he was, showing her how important that could be, how he could guide her and help her; that he could be depended upon. She looked lovely, too, standing all flustered by her car, with the wind knotting her extraordinary hair and her green eyes a bit wild. He even liked it that she was complicated, blowing hot and cold, keeping him guessing, keeping him on his toes. 'You enjoy your mah-jong and don't worry about it, okay? I'll phone as soon as I have any news.' He touched her cheek with the back of his fingers. 'Okay? This is my job,' he added, aware that he was pushing his luck, but riding high now, unable to resist. 'It's what I *do*. I'm good at it. You go off and have a nice evening. We'll talk soon. And, Charlotte?'

She paused, one foot in her car. 'Yes?'

'The other business . . . us . . . No pressure, I promise. Scout's honour.' Her face collapsed into a warm, relieved smile that made his heart surge. He'd quite forgotten the thrill of a chase, the sweetness of a prize that required patience.

Chapter Four

I am three people: the daughter who writes home each Sunday with talk of the occasional tasty meal, the results of maths tests and hopes of selection for the swimming team; the quiet, carrot-headed girl called Bootface, who keeps her eyes down and feigns sleep when the teasing starts, holding the sheets tight against her clammy skin; and I am Charlotte, friend of a day-girl called Bella, who sits next to me in class and invites me to her house for leave-weekends and half-terms, where we play with her mother's makeup and try to handle cigarettes like film stars, letting the smoke stream between our teeth, pressing the pink prints of our lips round the cork tips.

Bella has an elder brother called Adrian, who is short and thick-set, with whiskery hairs on his chin, and ears that stick out like brackets. I like him because he rides horses and because he doesn't care that he is ugly. His eyes are a sharp blue and full of teasing. He smells of saddle soap and the mulch of the stableyard. He calls me Charlie and orders me around. I fetch and carry tack, buckets, brooms, brushes with a singing heart. Between the clammy sheets I seek consolation in dreams of his piercing gaze and big hands. Calloused, the nails stubby and full of dirt, I want them on me, stroking the nape of my neck and pushing up through the long orange burden of my hair. And in such dreaming I start to believe that maybe there is another me – a fourth – sitting like the miniature Russian doll inside the others, waiting to be found.

The Rotherhithe house was everything Charlotte had always assumed Martin would despise: part of a modern development within a gated compound, one in a row of identical homes overlooking a mini roundabout filled – at this time of year – with regimental lines of daffodils and tulips. Entering the place always made Charlotte feel as if she was in some sort of adult Toytown, where grown-ups could play safely at the normally hazardous business of living.

Sam, however, claimed to like it a lot. It was 'cool', he said, to be able to see the river Thames from his bedroom and not to need a helmet for riding his bike round the compound's network of plump, humped Tarmac pathways. And when Charlotte pressed (gently, oh-so-gently, resisting the urge to howl that the only mothering worth anything was her own), he claimed to like Cindy, too. She cooked home-made pizza and let him choose the topping. She allowed him to get out three DVDs at a time in Blockbuster and on Sundays he could stay in his pyjamas till lunchtime if he wanted. Charlotte received such pieces of information (randomly and infrequently delivered) with as much stoicism as she could muster, fighting urges to scour cookbooks for pizza recipes and sweep shelves of DVDs into her shopping basket.

Of course, Sam's happiness was all that mattered; Charlotte knew that, had always known that. Far better an indulgent, saccharine Cindy than a cruel one, though she did marvel that Martin clearly colluded in such cosseting – Martin, who had spent so much of their son's brief life reprimanding her for being too soft, who, on one particularly horrible night, had locked Sam's bedroom door to discourage his nocturnal wandering into their bedroom. When the whimpering started, he had locked theirs too, pinning her to the bed, ranting about some childcare tactics he'd seen on the telly, telling her that this was it, that she had to choose – to act with him or against him. As if he was the one being hurt rather than their six-year-old, sobbing in voluble confusion across the landing.

Charlotte had chosen. It had been easy. She had crawled into Sam's bed and stayed there all night, telling herself he needed her, even though he had fallen asleep in seconds and she had lain awake, listening to the pumping of her own heart till the birds sang.

'Okay, here we are,' Charlotte trilled, doing her best to sound cheerful as they pulled up on to the slab of spare Tarmac next to Cindy's Saab. 'Did you remember your toothbrush?'

'*Mum.*'

'Well, don't forget to use it, then.'

'*Mum.*'

'You haven't had George round for a while, have you?' she offered next, in a fresh bid to lift the gloom that seemed to linger after each school day now, even the ones that hadn't involved the ordeal of after-school club. 'I'm seeing Theresa tonight – shall I fix something up?'

Sam made a noise suggesting rather than actually articulating the word 'No.'

'No – thank – you – Mum,' Charlotte corrected sternly, hoicking his bag out of the boot, then kissing his head to sweeten the reprimand. In the same instant a light came on in the kitchen, which overlooked the drive, bringing the room to life like a flickering TV screen. Cindy, in pink velour jogging bottoms and a white T-shirt, her blonde hair gathered in a fashionable spiky knot, strolled across the centre, her back to them as she reached for a cupboard. Charlotte couldn't help staring, at the slim honey-coloured arm, at the ample curve of the bustline, the trim indent of the waist. Freya, she recalled suddenly, had had a doll called Cindy, with wavy yellow-blonde hair, pearl studs in her ears, red-painted fingernails and a chest so pointy and hard that when they gave up on playing and fought each other instead she was often the top choice of weapon.

48

When they were greeted on the doorstep, however, Charlotte couldn't help noticing that her husband's new partner looked rather below her usual dolly-perfect self. Though she smiled as she always did and said '*darling*' to Sam, who surprisingly – annoyingly – didn't cringe and make his gagging face, but merely offered a shy smile back, there were blue-black smudges under her eyes and evidence of thick concealer to hide several large blemishes on her face. Charlotte, poised as always to scuttle back to the refuge of the car, couldn't resist asking if she was all right.

'Oh, absolutely fine, thanks – a bit of a hard week at the office. Crazy markets – nobody can read them at the moment. Thank God it's Friday. Hey, sweetheart, nice to see you.' She patted Sam's head, offering Charlotte the torchbeam of a smile with which she had managed every one of their encounters: fierce, sharp, bright, there was never any way round it other than retreat.

''Bye, Sam, be good.' Charlotte ruffled his hair and called, 'See you Sunday night,' as he ran off. Then she confided to Cindy, in a much quieter voice, that she needed a word with Martin some time over the weekend.

'You can call any time you want, you know that, Charlotte.'

'Yes . . . I . . . of course. Thanks.'

'But I'll tell him if you like.'

Charlotte blinked in the glare of the smile as a dizzying, violent sense of usurpation took hold. This woman had had an affair with her husband and now was sharing his bed permanently and playing mother to *her* child. She had trampled upon the fragile, threadbare remains of her and Martin's happiness by making herself available to him. And now here they were with their Toytown house and matching cars, playing at happy families, while she grappled with the vile realities of money, houses, parenting ... It was intolerable. Martin always said to consult him about everything to do with Sam but he certainly didn't make it easy. Drop-offs and pick-ups were never a good time to talk and on the phone he either sounded rushed and distant or old enmity crept into the conversation, steering them off course.

But having managed a civil farewell, the feeling passed, like a bout of nausea, leaving only pity; Cindy was welcome to Martin, and he to her. Their marriage had been a limping, draining thing. She was well out of it, *well* out.

She had reached the bottom of the drive when Martin's black BMW swung into sight. 'Hey.' He got out quickly, pulling his briefcase after him and running one hand through his hair as he always did when agitated.

'Hello.'

'You've dropped him off, then?'

'Yes, just now. I'm in a hurry I – I'm going to Theresa's.'

'Fine. See you Sunday, then.'

They were standing several feet apart, Martin at one end of his car and Charlotte taking small steps backwards towards hers. His hair, youthfully fair still, was visibly thinning and in retreat from his forehead, yet physically he looked in better shape than he had for years, his suit trousers hanging loosely off his hips, his upper body exuding poise and strength that seemed new.

'It might be a bit earlier than usual – I hope that's okay. Say, four o'clock?' he added.

Charlotte bit her lip, weighing up the easy option of agreeing against a small inner shout of protest at being taken for granted. She was visiting her mother on Sunday. The early drop-back would mean rushing home from Kent, having to make sure there was something sensible for Sam's tea. 'May I ask why?'

She saw him tense, a visible bracing of his entire body, as if he was preparing to maintain his balance against the approach of a large wave or a violent gust of wind. 'Cindy and I have joined a choir. The rehearsal time is five o'clock on Sunday. I need to drop Sam and get back here so as not to be late.'

Charlotte couldn't stifle a snort of disbelief. '*You* – a *choir*?'

'Just tell me if that's okay,' Martin muttered, hugging his briefcase, almost bashful, as if he, too, somewhere deep inside, recognized the incongruity of the old Martin whom she had known so well – obstinate lover of punk rock and Led Zeppelin – offering the services of his scratchy bass to the classical formality of a choir. 'Can I deliver Sam back at four o'clock on Sunday or not?' He clenched his jaw, casting a wistful glance at the illuminated window from where Cindy had offered a stagy wave to acknowledge his arrival, then disappeared.

'Yes, yes, I suppose so,' Charlotte conceded, incredulity giving way to weariness. 'Four o'clock. I'll be there. I'm having lunch with Mum that day – probably be glad of an excuse to get away,' she admitted ruefully.

'I see . . . Well, thanks.'

'But I do need to talk to you,' she called, as he turned for the house, the worries about Sam rushing back at her, together with a dim terror at the prospect of daring to ask to borrow money.

Martin set down his briefcase on the doorstep and folded his arms. 'I thought you were in a hurry.' Cindy, studiously not looking out of the window, had stepped back into the frame of the kitchen. Next to her Charlotte could just make out the dishevelled top of Sam's head and then one of her son's stubby chewed-nail hands, stained with some felt-pen doodle, pointing at something.

'I am. I meant tomorrow – on the phone. It's to do with Sam.'

'Well, I assumed that. Why can't you tell me now, for heaven's sake?' A fine rain had started, more like a floating mist, its droplets glittering as they caught the sheets of light streaming from the house. Martin stepped back under the protection of his porch.

Charlotte put her handbag over her head and ducked towards her car. 'Not now, there isn't time.'

'Charlotte.' The syllables flew through the wet air like missiles, sharp and angry. 'If it's important tell me now, for fuck's sake.'

Charlotte flinched, remembering all the bad stuff – suspicion, hostility, the desire to be free. 'Tomorrow, Martin. I'll call you.'

A moment later Martin appeared on the illuminated stage of the kitchen, an arm round Cindy's smooth white shoulders, a hand ruffling the soft straw tangle of Sam's head. Man, woman and child: the perfect human triangle. But not perfect, Charlotte hastily reminded herself, turning the ignition once and then a second time to get the engine going, because Sam wasn't their child, Cindy looked drained and Martin would tire of her one day – if he hadn't already.

En route to Theresa's, she stopped at the off-licence in the high street. Emerging with a bottle of rioja, she caught sight of a familiar figure in a bright red bobble hat on the pavement opposite. A tall skinny girl with frizzy orange hair walked at his heels, shoulders hunched inside a school blazer that was several sizes too large. Edging back into the traffic a few minutes later, Charlotte spotted the pair again, getting into a silver Mercedes. They were laughing about something this time, with such gusto that she found herself pondering what it would have been like if Martin had died instead of being unfaithful, whether the end of a marriage was easier to accept with death as its instigator instead of human failing.

There was a full moon that night, large and melon-yellow, hanging so low over the skyline that George, studying it through the upper pane of the bathroom window, imagined it cartwheeling across the treetops like a giant Frisbee. He had been commanded to wash by his mother, who had an uncanny knack of keeping track of such things even when she appeared to be paying no attention. Not a shower, a *bath*, she had said, as if she knew about his secret trick of running taps and splashing water on his hair when time was short or he wasn't in the mood. He hadn't been in the mood that night, but she had bustled into the bathroom before he had had time to lock the door, set the taps running and tipped in so much of her special bubble bath that when he got in a great shelf of foam spilled over the end on to the floor.

It was nice now, though, George had to admit, lying among the suds, safe from the annoyance of his younger siblings and the awful hubbub of his mother's dinner-party preparations. Pattie's mum, Naomi, had already arrived and was sitting on the sofa with a glass of wine, which George had been instructed to pour for her while his mother frisked his little brothers for mah-jong tiles. They were in bed now upstairs, on pain of death not to wake Matty, who had bawled so loudly during her nit-check that she had actually puked up some of her tea. Alfie had squatted down in fascination to point out the undigested baked beans to his brothers (Matty hadn't liked the curry), which had been gross but also sort of interesting until their mother had said if they liked peering at it so much they could jolly well clear it up.

George had sought refuge in trumpet practice, working at it far longer than he really wanted to out of fear that his mother might carry out the threat. When she had slipped into the room he pretended not to notice and restarted his piece even though it had gone really well the first time. But instead of talking about the puke, or his wrong notes, she had said, in her softest, nicest voice, that she was sorry if she had been on his case about the music exam and would he like her to organize a sleepover for the following Friday to celebrate it being over and what about Sam?

It had gone a bit wrong after that because George had said no – not to the idea of having a friend over but to Sam. At which point the motherly niceness had turned into a lecture on what Sam was going through and supporting friends in times of need, to the point at which George had wanted to say that if she was so keen on Sam Turner why didn't she invite him over herself? He hadn't, of course – answering back was never a good idea with his mother – and then he had been let off the hook by the doorbell and the business of helping with the wine.

It wasn't fair, though, George mused now, sucking the sodden flannel noisily through his braced teeth, that his mum should try to make him feel bad about whom he chose as a friend. Sam had been okay once – way back – during the days when anybody played with anybody. But nobody liked him much any more. He had become a sad show-off, all the more annoying because he had nothing to show off about: how much his dad earned, what phone he was going to get, scores in computer games – who cared? And it was probably lies anyway. So what if his parents were getting divorced? It wasn't like he was the first kid it had happened to. Rose, the new girl in their class, had had a mother who *died*. Now that, in George's opinion, was far more dramatic and impressive. If Theresa had said to be nice to Rose Porter he would probably have done his best, because the thought of losing his own mother, for all her bossiness and cunning, was so impossible to contemplate that he actually felt a little sick just trying.

As it happened, the motherless Rose didn't seem to need much looking after. She was one of those scary girls, who sat in the front row and shot her hand up to answer everything and buried her nose in a book at breaktime. She was as tall as several of the boys in their class, with carrot-coloured bird's-nest hair, skin as white as sunblock and blue eyes that stared so hard you felt she was seeing through you to something on the other side. Instructed to partner Sam for an exercise in Drama that morning (a stupid exercise where one person had to be a tree and the other the wind), she had looked so fierce and towering, so scornful of Sam's puffing efforts round her stick-like outstretched arms, that George had felt almost sorry for his erstwhile friend.

But not sorry enough, George vowed, slopping more water on to the floor as he scrambled out of the bath, to invite the irritating loser over for the precious treat of a Friday-night tea.

Downstairs in the sitting room Naomi had been joined by Josephine, whose stylishly cropped blonde hair was dark and damp from having been caught in the rain, but who looked immaculate nonetheless in a navy trouser suit and high heels. Theresa bustled between them, setting out bowls of vegetable crisps, offering top-ups of wine and checking the card table, which had been unfolded from its usual storage behind the piano and set up in preparation for the evening game. Safely retrieved from her sons' pockets, all the mah-jong tiles were now neatly arranged in the two-tiered square required to start the proceedings. Sitting in the middle, like two loose teeth, were the faded misshapen dice that had come with the mah-jong set (acquired on a whim at a car-boot sale a few years before), with a small booklet of instructions, held together by Sellotape so old it had dulled to a dirty brown and lost most of its stick. Naomi, left alone with her glass of wine for long enough to be driven to picking up the little booklet and studying it, warned her friends now that she fully intended going for one of the more high-scoring difficult hands.

Josephine groaned. 'I can never remember them. I get my winds and my dragons muddled and some of those bamboos are just like flowers.'

'It's like cards, Jo – different suits, extra points for winds and dragons – and we *must* do the North Wind thing this time, Theresa.'

'What thing is that?' asked Theresa, absently, more concerned for the curry, which was showing severe signs of dehydration, while the rice, being kept warm in the top oven, was starting to look clumped and sticky.

'I don't get the North Wind thing,' complained Josephine, stretching out her long legs and settling back with obvious relish into the deep folds of the sofa, hands and wine glass resting on her stomach. With a reputation among her management-consultant employers for being keenly intelligent, ruthless, inexhaustible, she found such evenings particularly relaxing. As her friends well knew, she didn't really care a jot about the North Wind or whether she muddled bamboos and flowers. Before mah-jong she had been a member of a book club but had found it too much like hard work: fierce, often intellectually frustrated women holding forth, fighting to have nonsense opinions heard and respected – as if it *mattered*. She read Dick Francis, these days, or fluffy stories about women who shopped and had a lot of sex. 'I've always thought the South Wind should be more important than the North, anyway. Because it's nicer, more *clement* . . . Oh, I could so do with some now.' She sighed, pulling a face. 'March is so long and hateful, with Christmas a distant memory and still months and months until the summer hols. I'm pushing hard for an Easter trip somewhere but Paul says he can't get the time off.'

'Paul always says that and then you persuade him,' said Theresa, smoothly, glancing at the clock and wondering what could have happened to Charlotte.

'Graham's got a conference in Dubai this summer,' said Naomi, crossing to the mantelpiece to study Martin and Cindy's invitation, which, thanks to the distraction of her various domestic dramas, Theresa had forgotten to hide. 'He's going to try and fix it so I can go too.'

'With Pattie and the twins?'

'I haven't got that far.'

'You never get to spend time with husbands at conferences, though,' Theresa pointed out. 'I know Graham's banking, not medicine, but it's all the same. You end up seeing more of the room-service boy than you do of your partner.'

'Not always a bad thing,' quipped Josephine, her brown eyes glinting.

They laughed, united in a gentle, effortless companionship that offered no real threats to husbands or room-service boys, but was instead a simple acknowledgement of the fact of being female and young enough still to lament some of the constraints of the marital state.

No longer an issue for Charlotte, however, Theresa mused, crossing to the window to peer out into the street, wondering if this was a fact over which, after a few more swigs of wine, she might even be able to muster a frisson or two of jealousy. Bell-boys, estate agents – Charlotte, in her newly single state, could have her pick. Glancing down at her chest – a little too slack and ample since the children, but attractively displayed in a favourite blue lace-trimmed top – Theresa spent a moment trying to imagine the face of a nubile young man, as opposed to Henry, owl-eyed without his glasses, nuzzling at her cleavage. Then she thought of her stretchmarks, the large mole on her thigh that needed checking, the sag of flesh masking her hips, and the dear face of her husband came more clearly into focus. A stone overweight, aged thirty-eight, she was well past her physical best and any new lover would see that. Henry, on the other hand, she reflected happily, had known her at her best, just as she had known him before the glasses, the clicky knee and the tummy that swelled or shrank according to his level of self-discipline. For her there would always be that first enriching memory to fall back on – of the handsome, twinkly-eyed, newly qualified surgeon who had asked her to a rugby match and kissed her dry, freezing lips afterwards, saying now that he had found her he would never let her go.

'We'll have to start without Charlotte,' she declared, dropping the curtain and turning back to the room.

'Maybe she's with her *new* man,' suggested Josephine, casting a sideways glance at Naomi, normally her closest ally in the group.

'Oh, but I think we should offer Charlotte nothing but encouragement,' Naomi cried, releasing a snow-shower of glitter on to the carpet as she flapped the invitation. 'It must be so hard, don't you think, to feel any sort of confidence about *dating* when you're nearly forty and you've been on the receiving end of such deception?'

Josephine rolled her eyes. 'You mean Martin and *Cindy*?'

'Of course.' Naomi carefully put the invitation back in its place. 'And the others. Remember, Charlotte thought there were others.'

For a few moments the three women fell silent, recalling the woeful tales of the Turner marriage, recounted with increasing bitterness and frequency as the years of their acquaintance with Charlotte had ticked by. Difficult, unloving, unfaithful – Josephine had quickly dubbed him Martin the Monster, and pioneered early efforts to get Charlotte to leave. But then Martin had finally pitched up for a school parents' evening and she had found herself talking to a mild-mannered, good-looking man with anxious eyes and a ready smile. She had dropped the nickname overnight and, while remaining supportive, stopped trying to tell Charlotte what to do.

'But Charlotte's got her estate agent to look after her now, so she's fine, isn't she?' pressed Josephine, as she took her place at the table, determined to get a rise on the subject from at least one of her companions. 'And she's beautiful,' she exclaimed, with some exasperation when neither responded. 'It wouldn't be fair to look like that *and* be happy, would it, now?'

'Jo, you're horrible,' said Naomi, amicably, sitting down next to her.

'Let's throw to settle who's the North Wind,' commanded Theresa, shooting both of them dark looks. 'I'll be me as well as Charlotte.'

With a precision that would have been impossible to orchestrate, Charlotte arrived on the step just as Henry was slotting his key into the front door. Thus unheralded, she had time, while easing off her coat, to hear her name being mentioned through the half-open door of the sitting room. Henry, hearing it too, looked momentarily panic-stricken and barked an unnecessarily loud reprimand as George's dark curly head bobbed through the banisters. 'You should be in bed.'

George rolled his eyes, announcing, with some pride, 'Look, Dad,' and proceeding to push his tongue up over his upper lip until the tip made contact with his nose.

'Does young Sam have such social graces, I wonder?' asked Henry, grinning once his son had been ordered back to bed.

'Not that particular one. But he used to be able to put both legs behind his head and do somersaults round the room.'

'Blimey – how alarming.' Henry chuckled, pushing open the sitting-room door. 'Here we are, ladies, your missing member.'

There was a half-beat before the three women responded, like the pause before applause at an inconclusive conclusion of a performance. It was enough to confirm for Charlotte that she had indeed been the subject of conversation and to leave her with a dim, irrational sense of exclusion, which persisted in spite of the warm greetings that followed.

They had been talking about Tim, probably – understandably – and she was being over-sensitive, she reasoned, trying her best to enjoy the usual chaos of the game with collapsing walls and Josephine shrieking 'pung' every time she meant 'cong' and one of Theresa's delicious curries to oil the wheels. And, of course, not having a husband did make her different, Charlotte reminded herself, wondering that it had taken so long for this feeling to dawn. Holding back on her own news, she tried to lose herself and the niggling sense of separation in the merry stream of anecdotes that bounced around the table. Only to find the feeling getting worse:

family life, family holidays, family tiffs, husbands this, husbands that. It was as if all three friends were speaking a different language.

She was rescued eventually by Theresa, who caught her gaze and held it, generously insisting that their Suffolk cottage (inherited a few years before from Henry's parents) was at her and Sam's disposal for an Easter as well as a summer break if they wanted it. Whereupon Naomi, having suggested they abandon the game and retreat to comfortable chairs, asked with touching concern how things were going with Tim.

'We've only had the one date and it was a bit of a blur, to be honest,' Charlotte admitted, basking in the warmth of the kindness, ashamed that she could ever have doubted it. 'We went to this weird Spanish place and ate salted almonds and lots of little dishes of oily snacks. It was okay, I suppose, but then I let him kiss me in the car when we got home, which has made him think we've got a proper *thing* going and I tried today to tell him that we haven't but now he's gone and found me this totally perfect house in Chalkdown Road so I really don't feel I can ditch him altogether.'

'A house!' exclaimed Theresa, over the laughter of the other two. 'But that's fantastic news. So long, I suppose, as you have a buyer for yours . . .' She tailed off, glancing round the freshly painted walls and carefully selected furnishings of her sitting room, thinking how loath she would feel to part with it.

'That's the point. It looks as if I might have. She's called Mrs Burgess and Tim's sure she's keen.' Charlotte chattered on, loving the feeling of relaxing properly, of being part of the old circle at last. 'It's more a cottage than a house – there's all this lovely jasmine in the front garden and a bedroom balcony and two dear little stained-glass windows in the hall. The owner said they might not go with Tim's agency, which would be bad for him but not the end of the world for me, now I know where it is and how much I like it. And it would be *so* good for Sam to have a fresh start. He'd be able to walk to school, of course, and we'd be so near the park I've been thinking we might even get a dog . . .'

'Whoa there – a dog?' cried Theresa, raising both arms to stop the flow. 'But what about your job in the bookshop and keeping it entertained? Anyway, you hate dogs.'

'Correction: I hate my mother's dog for being dull and overfed and spoilt. And my job at Ravens is only part-time. And Sam has always wanted a dog. And at the moment Sam is –' Charlotte stopped abruptly. She had drunk far too much, she realized, with some surprise, carefully setting down her wine glass. She had been on the verge, stupid goat that she was, of mentioning the very subject she had privately vowed to avoid. Miss Hornby had said they were on top of the situation. Martin would almost certainly agree with that view. The last thing she wanted was for these dear friends to think that, with clear water ahead of her, she was still finding cause to be unhappy; that with one major worry solved she was immediately on the track of another. And how would it sound, anyway, to tell the mothers of Pattie and George, Sam's two oldest friends, that she suspected some sort of foul play? 'Sam is still so . . . unsettled,' she finished lamely, looking round for her handbag.

'Sam will be all right,' coaxed Theresa, gently. 'He's still . . . adjusting, that's all.'

'And children are *so* adaptable,' put in Josephine, brightly, slipping her feet back into her shoes and nodding at Naomi, who had promised to give her a ride home.

'Of course they are,' echoed Naomi, unhooking her handbag from the back of her chair and standing up.

After their farewells, and having double-checked the state

of the downstairs loo before she allowed Charlotte to enter it, Theresa sought out her husband in the den.

'I'm not asleep,' he croaked, waggling the two feet she could see sticking up over the end of the sofa. 'Is it safe to come out?' He peered over the back in the manner of a soldier checking the edge of a trench.

'Ssh,' Theresa scolded fondly, pressing her fingers to her lips. 'The others have gone but Charlotte is in the loo. I want to invite her to a Sunday lunch – her and Sam.'

'Of course.' Henry pushed his fingers up under his glasses and rubbed his eyes.

'Because George and Sam appear to have fallen out and getting them over here might help sort it. And though Charlotte did her best tonight I think she's pretty blue.'

'You are the wise one, my love.'

'Yes, I am, and if you're coming out of here before Charlotte leaves you might want to consider doing up your flies first. I relish any opportunity to ogle your Y-fronts, of course, but I'm not sure Charlotte would share my enthusiasm.'

A few yards away, sitting in the ill-lit cramped confines of the downstairs loo, her knees almost touching the door, Charlotte had to steady herself against the basin. The walls on both sides were crowded with framed collages of family snaps, cleverly spread like scattered playing cards to reveal toothless baby faces, tottering toddlers, Henry with a fatter face and thick sweeps of hair, Theresa laughing and pregnant in a Laura Ashley smock, pushing a buggy. The images shifted and blurred, pressing in on her. Struggling upright, she studied her reflection in the small mirror above the wash-basin, pinching her cheeks and tugging at her lips in quiet despair at her pallor. 'Like a ghoul,' she hissed, grabbing the basin again as she swayed. 'An ugly *ghoul*.'

Venturing back into the hall, she found Theresa and Henry standing with their arms loosely round each other's waists, laughing about something. Speaking in a steady, careful voice, fighting a fresh, even worse bout of dizziness, she announced that she would like to pick up her car the next day and phone for a cab, if that was all right by them, if they had a number, though, of course, she could use her own phone. She plunged her hand into her bag, groping, finding only keys, the mirror, her purse, an unravelling tampon. Then the hall floor heaved and she had to reach out to steady herself again, knocking a print of bluebells that hung next to the stairs. 'Sorry . . . I seem to be a little . . .'

'Oh, poor you,' cried Theresa, rushing over and pulling her into her arms.

Enfolded in the motherly softness of her friend's embrace, Charlotte closed her eyes, for a moment so intensely at ease that she could have gone to sleep. When she opened them again the hall floor was rushing past, like a fast, dark river.

'Poor thing,' Theresa crooned, stroking Charlotte's shoulder-blades with the same tenderness that had soothed away Matilda's crying fit a few hours before. 'You look worn out. But don't bother with a taxi. Henry will drive you home, won't you, Henry?' She exchanged a glance with her husband over the top of Charlotte's head, meeting his rolling eyes with a beseeching glare.

'Of course.' Henry adjusted the bluebells and reached for his coat.

A few minutes later Charlotte was hunched in the passenger seat of the Volvo, her feet wedged between a plastic bag bulging with library books and a pair of football boots shedding brittle clods of mud. 'Sorry about this.'

'No need.'

Charlotte hugged herself, rolling her neck from side to side in a bid to ease the throbbing in her head. 'Are you going to it?'

'I'm sorry?'

'The party. Martin and Cindy's party. Are you going? I saw the invite.'

'Ah ... that.' Henry, as if in hope of escaping the unmistakable, incomprehensible danger of female emotion, accelerated through a red light.

'Not that I mind,' said Charlotte, stiffening as the pressure of the car's sudden speed pushed her back into her seat. 'I don't mind in the least,' she added, bursting into tears.

'Oh dear, oh dear, oh dear ... Charlotte.' They were at another red light, impossible to jump this time.

'Ignore me,' Charlotte gasped, batting furiously at her streaming eyes. 'I've been doing this sort of thing lately – not just when I'm drunk. It's unspeakable. I have nothing to cry about – *nothing*. I'm almost forty, I'm a free woman, I should be able to control myself.' She rocked backwards as Henry accelerated again, from a standstill this time. 'Are you ever unhappy when you shouldn't be, Henry?' she sobbed, groping through the blur of her tears for a tissue and finding nothing but the tampon.

'Of course. Everybody is. Here.' He took a hand off the wheel and pulled a crumpled but clean handkerchief out of his coat pocket.

'Thank you ... You're so kind ... Everybody's so ... kind.' She dabbed at her eyes and blew her nose loudly. 'I'll keep it and wash it ... Thank you, Henry.'

'Here we are,' said Henry, with some relief, pulling up outside the wrong house and then having to edge along the pavement to a much darker patch of the street. He double-parked with the intention of making a quick getaway, but then, moved by the stillness of the undrawn curtains, the front gate creaking on its half-broken hinge, he pulled into a space instead. 'I'll see you to the door,' he declared gruffly, feeling a twinge of something like anger on Charlotte's behalf. He hadn't taken sides – one did one's best not to with divorcing friends – but Martin had a lot to answer for, he mused grimly, taking Charlotte's elbow as she got out of the car and keeping hold of it for the walk down the disintegrating tiled front path to the doorstep. 'Got your keys?'

'Yep . . . somewhere.' She shook her bag, which jangled. 'Thank you again, Henry.' She put up her face for a kiss, which was duly delivered. And then, because of the stony silence of the narrow black-windowed house – the sudden nose-pressed-up-against-it glimpse of what she was going through – Henry put his arms round her and hugged her hard. Which was fine and brotherly and generous, except that Charlotte emitted a little sigh and pressed against him so fiercely that he could not but feel the litheness of her slim frame and the quick bird-pulse of her heart. Oh dear, he thought, not for the reasons he had used the phrase in the car, but because she was attractive and needy and he had never thought of her like that before. Oh dear. Copper hair, the scent of lemon on her neck – what man wouldn't have felt the same?

Floppy, tipsy, oblivious, Charlotte clung on until Henry had wrested the keys from her hand and steered her towards the open door. He reached inside and put the light on, keeping his feet and as much of his body as he could on the doorstep, resisting the urge to help as she battled with the sleeves of her coat.

'Good night, then.'

'Good night, Henry, and *thank* you.' The coat came free at last, exposing in the process a portion of bare shoulder and accompanying bra strap of over-laundered pale grey. Henry was sure he would have found a man-eating strap of lacy satin infinitely less affecting. As it was, the flash of underwear, like the dark, unblinking windows of the house, opened his eyes to an entirely new version of his wife's friend – wronged, attractive, alone.

But not alone, Henry reminded himself, shaking his head in some bemusement as he walked back down the path to his car. She had Sam, after all, and a bunch of close friends that included his wife and himself. The knee-jerk of attraction was just that – an involuntary twitch, typically male, probably – or so Theresa would say if he were ever to confess to it.

Which would be an act of madness, obviously, Henry mused, kissing the back of his wife's dark curly head some twenty minutes later as he snuggled into bed next to her, remarking, when she said he had been a long time, that there had been a conspiracy of red traffic-lights to slow him down.

Chapter Five

Gradually my hair thickens and darkens to an auburn flame. I grow tall. I grow breasts. I turn heads. I have become acceptable. I learn how to shave my armpits and the finer pale hairs on my legs. I pluck my darkened eyebrows to thin arches and show off my calves in short skirts, tights and suede pixie boots. Adrian becomes a bore, hanging around on my weekend breaks with Bella, his wide face heavy with hope and disappointment. Bella and I lose interest in the stableyard, trading pleadings to be allowed to ride horses, with negotiations on night-time curfews for excursions into town. We listen to the Boomtown Rats and Genesis, swap lipsticks, and test each other on valency tables and French vocab.

During the autumn term that I turn fifteen, Letitia becomes bug-eyed and skeletal and leaves the school. I am Charlie to everyone. I am free.

My parents are to return to England at Christmas. My father has been told he has a weak heart and should replace office work and overseeing vineyards with rest. Bella comes to stay for two weeks of my last holiday in Constantia. The warm wind blows hard across the valley, flicking our hair across our hot faces as we lie by the pool. We wait until my mother goes shopping and mix cocktails of vodka, Martini and lime juice, which we suck from long glasses through straws. We each put an animal sticker on our tummies and watch as our skin goes pink round them. Bella's is a cat, mine a snail. We smoke and gossip about our friends, our teachers and our families. Bella confides that she cheats in maths exams by writing formulae on the inside of her elbows. She says that once, towards the end of a long day's hunting, she felt small spasms of pleasure deep in the pit of her pelvis. She says that she likes our English teacher, not Mr Coots, who does grammar, but Miss Garth, with whom we have been studying Jane Eyre. She slurps her cocktail, not looking at me. I say Miss Garth is pretty and that her secret is safe with me, that I am good with secrets. But something is called for in return, I know that. One confidence requires another. I have only one secret that I care about, that burns still, fuelled by the velvet brown eyes of the girl who comes each day to clean and cook. She is called Charity and she watches my father intently, swinging her wide hips in her brightly coloured dresses, her pink heels slapping against her flip-flops as she works the mop across the floors.

I have this secret but I find I cannot release it, not even with Bella, open like a soft blowsy flower on the sunbed beside me, not even with the floating sense of well-being from our vodka limes.

So I tell Bella instead that I hate my mother. And as I speak the words I feel their truth. I hate her for the distant look in her green eyes, for the limpness of her arms when I need to be held; for the dog-eared novels that shield her face as she takes her rests on the sofa or in the middle of her wide, canopied bed. I hate her for sending me, so ill-equipped, to the grey skies and grey slate roofs and soggy hockey pitches of England. But above all I hate her for her ignorance, for the state of not knowing in which she coexists with my father. Even in the thickest African heat, her fingers, her face are icy cool, detached, ungiving. If she feels so to me, how must she feel to him? Where is the striving to love and be loved? Where is her heart?

On the last day of the holiday we peel off our stickers and squeal with delight at the white silhouettes on our bellies. Bella's, less well tended against the hazards of bathing and washing, is a little blurred, especially round the tail, but mine is a perfect snowy cartoon of a snail, the hump of its shell-house firm and round, the feelers on its head pointing like arrows that know their mark.

The upheaval of the move to England seems to last for ever. The house in Tunbridge Wells is small, apparently, so we have to sell many things. The lines on my father's sun-weathered face deepen. Perhaps wanting to make the most of his weakening heart, he works harder –

or, at least, for longer hours — than I can ever recall, leaving as the sun is only just beginning to burn the horizon and returning when the darkness is as thick as tar and the winds cold. My mother's naps grow longer, while Charity kneels at open boxes, folding tissue paper round the points and curves of our worldly goods.

As the jaws of the removal-van doors bang shut, I feel the closing of something else, deeper and irretrievable. During the farewells to the servants it is my father who weeps. Their future is unsure, he explains. They have no savings like him, no pension plans and investments, no certainty of a roof over their heads. Charity, I notice, stands a little apart from the others, her yellow-turbaned head high, her black-eyed gaze fixed somewhere between the still green slopes of the hills and the scrubby tops of the higher skyline beyond.

There is a last-minute glitch on the house, forcing us to spend several nights in a small hotel. The walls between our bedrooms are thin. I listen to the rise and fall of their arguments, starting softly, then louder, then soft again, like a song. The snail fades, shrinking to invisibility, shrinking into my skin.

By Saturday evening Charlotte was still feeling so under par that, phoning Theresa to reiterate thanks for Henry's gallantry, she dared to speculate that a virus, rather than her over-indulgence, might be responsible. But Theresa cackled so loudly in response that she hurriedly withdrew the suggestion, inwardly squirming at what Henry must have reported when he finally got home. Charlotte herself could recall only snapshots of what had followed Henry's kindness – holding the banisters to get upstairs, spilling her first effort at a glass of water, waking several times with her temples pulsing and her nightie wringing with sweat.

Jason, who took it in turns with his partner Dean to man the bookshop on a Saturday morning and who was the softer-hearted of the two, had taken one look at her and pointed at the storeroom, where there was a comfy chair to sit on and a pot of fresh coffee. Even so, it was only with the aid of mouthfuls of analgesics that Charlotte had got through the shift, resenting the swarms of customers brought out by the spring sunshine instead of enjoying them as she usually did. Most were *en route* to cafés or the park and had buggies and small children in tow. Normally Charlotte relished the challenge of eliciting delight from despairing parents by plucking hidden or unlikely winners out of their small section for younger readers. That morning however, she had clung to the till, leaving her boss to charm customers, and concentrated hard on making no mistakes with the chip-and-pin machine, which was new and likely to flash commands she did not understand.

The highlight of this endurance test had been a phone call from Tim, announcing that Mrs Stowe was dithering still – but promisingly – and that Mrs Burgess had offered the asking price on her house and wanted to organize a survey. 'And what about dinner?' he had added cheekily. 'Do I deserve that yet?' Charlotte, aware of Jason listening intently from the far corner of the shop, curious and critical, since her contributions that day had been so visibly flawed, had whispered, yes, of course, and promised to call him back.

Instead, she had retreated to bed with a mug of soup and slept for fourteen hours. She awoke groggily the following morning to the double-blow of a realization that she still hadn't called Martin and had her mother's company to look forward to over lunch.

'Are you on your own?'

'You mean *sans* Sam?' quipped Martin.

Charlotte hesitated. She felt nauseous still and there was music in the background, reminding her unhelpfully of how her husband had often liked to conduct conversations with the volume up, insisting he was listening if she spoke, but tapping a foot or a finger so that she knew his first allegiance was to the rhythms of the soundtrack rather than her voice. 'I'm worried he's getting picked on at school.'

'Really? He hasn't said anything to me.'

'Well, he wouldn't, would he? I mean, you don't, do you?'

'Don't you?'

'Martin, are you really listening?'

'Of course I am. Have you said anything to the school?'

'Yes, I saw Miss Hornby on Friday. She said he was a bit quieter than usual, that they were keeping an eye on things.'

'Well, there you are, then.'

'Right. Fine. Stupid of me to mention it.'

He sighed heavily. 'Charlotte, don't start, okay? Look, I know kids bullying each other is a subject close to your heart –'

'No, Martin, you don't know anything,' she snapped, wishing suddenly that she could erase his knowledge of her, the little things gleaned, inevitably, during the course of twenty years. 'Sam is not himself. I *know* him and he is not himself.'

'That's hardly surprising, is it now?' Martin said slowly. The music had stopped, leaving a stark backdrop of silence. 'We're all feeling our way along here, Sam included. And he's almost thirteen – it's a difficult age. And he's got a thing about being small, he told Cindy. I've had a word with him, explained that I didn't get my growth spurt until at least fourteen, that some boys start really early and with others it can take much longer.'

'Yes, well, that's good,' Charlotte conceded, trying not to mind the Cindy aspect of the story, the thought of Sam curling up next to her on his bed, or maybe the sofa, opening his heart.

'Was there anything else?'

'I may need to borrow some money,' she blurted, unable to think of any clever or subtle approach to the subject. 'I've found a house – it's just a semi-detached cottage, but it's more expensive because it's next to the park. I've at long last found a buyer for our place, but there might be a shortfall.'

A moment of unmistakably stunned silence was followed by an incredulous laugh. 'I'm sorry, Charlotte, but *no*. We've just settled everything, remember?'

'I meant as a *loan*.'

He laughed again, more kindly. 'Look, I can't. Cindy and I have got a big new mortgage on top of what I'm already shelling out for you and Sam. Financially I'm right up against the wire – I thought you knew that. In fact, I cannot *believe*,' he continued, the sneering incredulity back, 'that you could actually think I might be in a position to help.'

'Neither can I,' Charlotte replied quietly, reminding herself that there was still the bank manager and ways of getting anything in life if one wanted them enough.

A heavy downpour had brought a small army of snails out from the flowerbeds on to the zigzag of crazy paving leading up to her mother's front door. Charlotte trod carefully between them in her high heels, musing upon the appealing notion of carrying one's home on one's back instead of having to wrench free of one place and crawl in search of another that suited better.

Halfway down the path she paused to look at the familiar black and white mock-Tudor front of the house, recalling how physically crushed her father had seemed from the moment he had been forced to occupy it. It was the heart, of course, the weakening heart, but Charlotte, thinking of him as she always did on any trip home, remained certain that some deeper spirit had died as a result of the enforced transfer from Africa to England. He had taken up gardening, but only in the most desultory fashion and because it allowed him to chain-smoke his untipped Player's cigarettes out of earshot of the muttered reprimands of her mother. His only other occupations had been sleeping and watching television, often at the same time, with a half-drunk mug of tea, or an ice-packed gin and tonic balanced on the arm of his chair.

Her mother, in contrast, as if it was merely the African heat that had sapped her energies, had found something akin to a new lease on life. She joined the Women's Institute and a bridge club and went regularly to church, taking her turn on the rota of coffee mornings and flower-arranging. During the evenings she prepared dinner on a tray, laying it like a miniature table, complete with napkin, glass of water, pepper and salt and a side-plate of bread and butter, often eating her own meal at the kitchen table with the radio on while he dined alone in front of the television. There had been separate beds too, a pair of narrow singles side by side, and then suddenly, at some invisible moment, separate bedrooms, one at each end of the landing. When he grew too weak even for gardening, Jean had taken these duties upon herself for a while, too, donning green wellingtons and an eccentric floppy-brimmed hat, clipping her secateurs across the rose stems with a businesslike ferocity that matched the expression on her face.

These days, a man called Bert tended the garden and a woman called Prue came on Friday mornings to clean the house. From what Charlotte had seen, her mother treated them with embarrassing imperiousness, playing the role of the colonial boss with far more relish than Charlotte could ever remember her doing when there had been an excuse for it.

Charlotte saw the lace curtain in the front room twitch but knew she would still be expected to ring the bell. She had been careful to dress in a manner that would brook no criticism – a smart brown skirt, heels, a wool jacket. Having pressed the button, she tugged at the hem of the jacket while Jasper, the dachshund, yapped, and her mother, sighing volubly, slid the door bolts from their metal sheaths.

'Hello, Mum – I brought you some daffs. You look well.' Charlotte stepped across the dog and kissed the soft, powdered cheek before handing over the flowers.

Jean shook her head. 'Do I? I can't think why. I'm not well at all. Dr Fairgrove says he's very worried about me, that if it wasn't for *having* to get out and about to look after myself and dear Jas, I'd probably have seized up completely. I'm using my stick more and more,' she added, handing the daffodils back to Charlotte and plucking an aluminium cane from the elephant stand behind the door. 'I get so tired without it.'

'Poor you,' Charlotte murmured, trying not to hear re-crimination in the thwack of the stick on the linoleum as she followed her mother into the kitchen. She focused on the now slightly rounded back of her seventy-eight-year-old parent, the shadow of elegance still evident in the thin legs – so thin that her tights fell into small folds at her ankles. 'Hmm, something smells nice.'

'It's only fish in a bag – cod with a white sauce.' Jean leant the stick against the kitchen table and lifted the saucepan lid, frowning. 'I simply can't be bothered with cooking, these days. Of course I never really learnt *how* to cook until your

75

father and I returned to England. Before that, there was no need.' A forlorn dreamy tone had crept into her voice. 'No need,' she repeated wistfully, bending down – slowly, stiffly – to pluck Jasper off the floor and scratch the silky black fur between the ears.

Charlotte found a vase for the flowers, then pulled open the cutlery drawer to begin setting the table. 'I'm not a great cook myself,' she reminded her mother wryly. 'Maybe it runs in the genes.'

'Nonsense, dear, you could easily *learn*, even now.' Jean's wrist flicked expertly as she whisked a fork round the saucepan of potatoes. 'Men like to be cooked for. The old adage about it being the way to their hearts is *so* true. Take these, for example.' She held up a forkful of the now creamy mash. 'They contain salt, pepper, butter, milk and – most important of all – an *egg*. They are *ingredients*, not the product of divine intervention.'

Charlotte tensed, breathed deeply, then continued laying out the knives and forks and arranging the mats; wintry scenes of villagers skating and gathering firewood which she could remember placing on other tables as a girl, before the colours had faded, when the felt underneath had been spongy and green instead of thin and grey.

Chewing the fish a little later, which was soft but tasty in its too-salty sauce, Charlotte did her best to listen sympathetically to small-talk about the effect of the changeable spring weather on Jean Boot's health and the fact that a fresh spate of malingering by the hapless Prue meant that the house was badly in need of dusting. 'I am sure poor Prue will come when she can,' Charlotte ventured, glancing at the spotless cabinet next to the table, which paraded the best of the crockery treasures to have survived domestic accidents and the hazards of being shipped across the world.

'It's not good enough, though, Charlotte. One needs people one can *rely* on. And my sheets – I hate not having my sheets changed.'

'I can do it, if you like.'

'Would you, dear?' Jean smiled for the first time since her daughter's arrival, revealing the small pearly teeth of which she was still, justifiably, very proud. 'That would be kind.' She dabbed at the tight white curls of her perm, her blue eyes glistening with gratitude.

'No problem.' Charlotte could feel her patience running out, just as she had known it would. It did not help that she was feeling ill again, close to throwing up in fact. She pressed her half-eaten mash and fish to one side of her plate and laid down her knife and fork.

'Aren't you hungry?'

'Not very, I'm afraid. Actually, I've been a little –'

'Jasper! Here, darling. Look what the naughty Charlotte has left for you.'

Charlotte bit her lip and folded her arms while her plate was scooped from in front of her and set on the floor. The dachshund clambered out of his wicker nest and trotted across to the treat, his too-long claws, splayed with age, scraping audibly on the lino.

'I've got cake for pudding. A nice sponge – do you have room for *that*?'

'A small piece, Mum, yes, please,' Charlotte muttered, trying not to watch the dog's pink tongue work its way across the lumps of fish, despairing at how one could feel so trapped by someone one knew so well. 'But I can't stay that long, I'm afraid – Martin is dropping Sam back early today.'

'Charlotte – forgive me – but is there really no hope for you two?' Jean burst out, flinging both arms outwards to emphasize her exasperation.

77

Charlotte stared at her slice of cake, which was sizeable – much larger than her mother's – with a gluey fissure of scarlet jam running through the middle. She thought, with uncharacteristic longing, of the Madeira to which she was usually subjected: plain, at least, not too sweet, though that, too, could stick in the throat.

'Charlotte?' Jean had her cake fork poised. This, Charlotte knew, was her idea of a motherly moment.

'Mum . . .' She folded her napkin and ran her fingers along the fresh crease. 'Our decree nisi has come through. Martin is living with someone else now.'

'I know, dear, but . . .'

'*Someone* with whom he had an affair during our marriage –'

'Aha – but he always denied that, didn't he? He said it was just friendship, didn't he? That ridiculous little note, wasn't it?' She jabbed the air with her fork. 'A child – a boy – needs his father . . .'

Charlotte could feel the dizziness coming back. She pressed the edge of her spoon down through her cake, forcing the jam to dribble from its seam.

'There are ups and downs in any marriage, Charlotte.'

'As you would know, Mum, wouldn't you? Because –'

'I beg your pardon?'

Charlotte tried to swallow. The cake was in clods at the back of her throat. Some deep protective reflex had snagged the rest of the sentence; a reflex connected to the expression on her mother's face, now slack with dismay and something else . . . Fear. 'I just meant . . . ups and downs . . . I . . . Excuse me – I think I might –'

She ran with her hand over her mouth, up the stairs and along the landing to the bathroom. Jasper, excited, scuttled after her, butting her heels with his nose. There was no time to shut the door or to think of anything but gripping the rim of the lavatory to steady herself through the spasms.

'Jasper, *out.*'

From the corner of her eye Charlotte saw the walking-stick nudge the dog into the corridor and the door close. I am alone, she thought, thank God. But a moment later the tap was running and then her hair was being held back for her and a warm flannel pressed gently to her forehead.

'You poor child. There, better now. A sip of water when you're ready. I thought you looked a little peaky. I hope it wasn't the fish.'

Charlotte sat back on her heels, shaking her head as she blew her nose on some loo roll, managing even to smile. 'I've not been right for a couple of days,' she croaked. 'Hope I don't give it to you.'

'I don't get bugs,' Jean retorted. 'My cod-liver oil sees to that.'

'Yuk.' Charlotte reached for the towel rail and levered herself upright. 'I can't bear that stuff, not even in the capsules they say have no taste.' She ran the flannel over her face again, feeling a lot better, dimly aware that she wanted to stretch out the moment. But her mother was already half on the landing, instructing her to have a lie-down if she wanted, not to come down until she was ready.

Charlotte rinsed her mouth, tidied her hair with a dusty tortoiseshell comb from the back of the bathroom cupboard, then walked, treading softly, along the corridor to the linen cupboard, pausing for a quick sentimental peek into the eaves space where Sam had once loved to hide. She saw in the same instant how foolish it was to be talking to anyone about Sam's troubles but Sam himself. She would do it that night, she decided, no matter how much he squirmed. If there was something sinister going on, she would whittle it out of him.

Having made up her mother's bed and folded the dirty sheets carefully into the laundry basket, she went as far as the door of what had, in latter years, been her father's room, then changed her mind and turned back for the stairs. His stuff had long since found its way to charity shops. The bed would be flat and empty, the air scented with furniture polish. The only memento left was the old photo that lived on the window-sill, of him among the tea bushes, hand raised to ward off the sun, two workers standing next to him, their dusty faces grinning, their sacks bulging on their backs, her mother's writing across the bottom: *Reggie at Ratnapura.* Charlotte knew it so well she was past needing to look at it.

Downstairs Jean was in the kitchen, the radio on at a high volume, wiping down the table mats.

'I'm sorry –'

'No need. You're not well. You should get yourself home to bed.'

'I changed your sheets.'

'Thank you, but I would have managed, you know.' She turned off the radio and hung the cloth over the edge of the sink.

'Of course you would.' Charlotte picked up her handbag. 'I'd better go. I might be moving house, by the way.'

'Might you, indeed? I thought you'd given up on that idea.'

'I almost had but . . .' Charlotte left the sentence hanging, warning herself to get out while the air between them was still relatively clear, 'I'll let you know, obviously.'

On the doorstep Jean thrust a carrier-bag at her. 'It's for your birthday.'

'My birthday? But that's months away.' Charlotte laughed. 'I'll see you long before then.'

'Quite possibly, but I should hate to forget and one can't trust the post these days.'

'No . . . right, thanks.' Charlotte peered into the bag.

'And it is your fortieth, after all.'

Charlotte made a face. 'Don't remind me.'

'I suppose you'll have a big party, won't you?'

'I very much doubt it.'

'That one you did for Martin was lovely.'

'Yes, yes, it was, wasn't it,' Charlotte muttered, hastily kissing her cheek and hurrying down the path, so eager to get away that she forgot the snails and crushed two before she could help herself.

'Love to Sam,' Jean called, when she was at the gate. 'Tell him Granny sends her love.'

Sam plugged in the earphones of his portable CD-player for the journey back to Wandsworth. It had come with a case strapped to a belt so that you could walk around listening to whatever you wanted, but every time Sam tried it the music jumped, even when he took tiny steps and tried not to breathe too hard. It was a stupid, gay machine – he couldn't believe how thrilled he had been to get it a year before. What he really wanted now was an iPod like Cindy's, but just when he'd got her on the point of caving in his dad had interrupted and said not until his birthday and only then if he was good and worked hard and got a decent report, blah-blah.

But the CD-player worked fine on his lap in the car. His mum, he knew, would have tapped his head and said, 'Anyone at home?' or one of her funny sayings to try to get him to switch it off and talk to her instead, but his dad was cool about it. That afternoon he had even asked to listen to one of the CDs and clicked his fingers to the beat and said it wasn't bad, which was bordering on pathetic but sort of nice all the same. Except that a couple of minutes later he was suddenly lying next to him on the carpet, eager and earnest and asking if everything was all right at school, which had taken a lot of the niceness away and made Sam see that the finger-clicking had been one of those fake shows that adults put on when they want something from you and need to butter you up to get it.

The world looked different to a soundtrack; more interesting, better. Even tower blocks and spitting grey skies and the stop-start traffic that was blatantly stressing out his dad (fingers drumming the wheel, watch checks, tugging at his hair like he *wanted* more of it to fall out) looked sort of decent with the Gorillaz pumping between his ears. Sam wished he could use a similar filter for the everyday ordeal of school. With music in his head he was sure he wouldn't notice the sniggers at his puny frame when he was down to his pants in the changing rooms, or the sneering gaze of freaky Rose Porter during the horrors of Drama, or George's new way of sitting with his back half turned and his arm spread to cover his work or – almost worst of all – Miss Hornby's mumsy kindness. *Did you enjoy your snack, Sam? Good boy for remembering to use your pencil sharpener! Please join us in Chess Club after school one day – we'd love to have you!*

Like he was a special case. Like he was a special sad little runt who needed protecting. At after-school club on Friday she had even put her arm round him – in front of everyone – leaving it there for so long he had wanted to punch her. *Was he looking forward to the weekend? Was he enjoying the Tudors? Any problems and he was to come straight to her.* It was positively pervy, and Sam had wanted to shout as much to everyone else sitting at the library tables, smirking at his expense. But talking wasn't allowed and by the time his mum arrived they had all gone except Rose, who had kept her head bent over work as usual, writing and writing, like the words just streamed out of her pen along with the ink, no crossings-out or the desire to *die* of boredom that so often afflicted him.

'Sam, sweetheart, I thought we'd go out for tea for a change – have a pizza or something. Would you like that?'

His dad had driven off in a noisy blast of exhaust fumes that Sam knew was connected to the finger-drumming and hair-pulling on the journey. He and Cindy were going to *sing* together and Cindy didn't want to be late. She had said so several times during the last-minute hassle of packing his stuff. He was messy, just like his dad, she had teased; his dad had made a face to show he didn't find the comment funny. Like her clothes always made it into the laundry basket, he had replied, prompting a blatantly unteasing remark from Cindy about wet towels and washing-up, after which she had left the room closing the door really quietly, which Sam had felt was worse than a good slam. The next thing his dad had left the room, too, and the house went totally silent and Sam had put the telly on so he wouldn't have to notice it or think too much about the fact that it was him leaving his socks next to the sofa that had set the whole thing off. A few minutes later they had come back into the sitting room holding hands. But Cindy's eyes were puffy and red, and saying goodbye at the door she had kept a hold of his dad's fingers till the very last second and said again about how important it was not to be late getting back.

Sam shook his head solemnly at his mother, explaining that they had eaten pizza the night before, choosing their own toppings as usual, and he had had pineapple and peppers and ham.

'Peppers?' she exclaimed, like it was something not allowed. 'Since when have you liked peppers?'

'Since whenever.' Sam shrugged. They were sitting in the kitchen. She had poured him an apple juice even though he hadn't asked for it and made herself a cup of tea, which she was holding in both hands and pressing close to her chest, like she needed the heat of it to warm her up.

'How about a burger, then? A burger and chips?'

Sam eyed her suspiciously, shaking his head again. He had only just got home and the thought of trekking off somewhere else, even for the rare treat of junk food, held little appeal. 'We could have pasta,' he said at length, having given the matter some thought, aware that she was trying to be nice. 'With that sauce, I like,' he prompted. 'The one without the lumps.'

'With that sauce – of course we can. In fact, that is *exactly* what we shall have.' She leapt into action, opening cupboards and banging around with packets and saucepans and tins.

'But I'm not really hungry yet,' he admitted. 'Cindy made a chocolate cake.'

'Did she? How *lovely* that she's such a good cook.'

'I like your cooking,' ventured Sam, in a small voice.

'Oh, sweetheart . . .' Charlotte put down the saucepans, crossed the room and kissed the top of his head, then returned to her tea, beaming now and clearing her throat. 'I've got something really exciting to tell you. I wanted to wait until I was sure it was possible – but I've found a lovely house right next to the park and much closer to St Leonard's –'

'Why do we have to move? I don't want to move.'

'Well, of course you feel like that right now, but wait till you see –'

'I don't want to see it.' Sam watched as she put down her mug slowly, returning it exactly into the middle of the wet ring its base had made on the table.

'I would like to show it to you,' she said firmly. 'Maybe after school one day this week. Having a look won't do any harm at all. It has a loft – a really huge one, with its own ladder. And we could . . . that is, I was thinking, with the park so close, we might even get a . . . dog. Would you like that, Sam? Maybe not until Christmas, but – but a puppy of your own?'

Sam twirled his apple juice, not catching her eye. He knew that she wanted him to leap out of his chair and punch the air. A part of him wanted to. A *dog* of his own! At long last! But another part of him felt cross and cornered.

'It's called bribery,' she said, smiling. 'A dog for a house. Not too bad a trade-off, is it?'

'Maybe.'

'Well, you think about it,' she said, brisk and cheerful, like she thought the battle had been won.

Sam pushed back his chair and stood up, but she reached across the table and motioned him back down. 'Hang on, young man, I haven't seen you for two days. I think I deserve another couple of minutes at least.' Sam leant against the chair, not going, but wanting to show that he had no desire to carry on talking either. The lack of desire shrivelled still more when she went on to announce, as if it was some huge cause for celebration, that they were to have lunch with George's family the following weekend. 'And Theresa has said we can use their Suffolk cottage during the Easter holidays,' she continued gaily. 'Won't that be great? I thought you might like to take a friend. It doesn't have to be George – it could be *anyone*.' She made a grand sweep of her arms, as if he had the whole world to choose from.

Sam tried to make a smile come but it wouldn't. He hated how, like all adults these days, she seemed constantly to be *trying* so hard to get stuff out of him, trying to get him to say – to *feel* – the right things.

'Sam . . . darling . . .' She was speaking really softly now and gazing at him with her green, unblinking eyes. 'Are you all right? *Really* all right? I mean, there's nothing going on that I should know about, is there?'

Sam pushed the chair, so roughly that it rocked forwards, slamming against the table before settling back on to all four legs. Needing something else to do, something that wouldn't involve having to look at her, he swiped an apple out of the fruit bowl and took a large bite.

'Sam, darling,' Charlotte urged gently, 'it's a perfectly simple question and I only ask it because I'm a little worried –'

'Yeah, but you – everyone – *always* ask it,' he spluttered, through the apple, which was soft and tasteless. 'And I'm fed up, *fucking* fed up –'

She was on her feet in a second, as if an electric bolt had shot up through the seat of her chair. 'Don't you dare use such language.'

'I *dare*,' he shouted, 'I *fucking dare*,' and then, because he was crying and because he could see no way forward through the dark, terrible sight of her face and the even darker more terrible sound of the words he had uttered, he flung the apple back into the fruit bowl and ran from the kitchen. He tore up the stairs, taking three at a time all the way, using the banisters, his thighs burning. On the top floor he barged at his bedroom door and flung himself on to his bed, pulling his duvet over his head so that there was nothing for company but darkness and the thump of his heart.

Time seemed to stop and then drag. It was hot under the covers and hard to breathe. Sam strained his ears for the sound of footsteps, but none came. He would die of lack of oxygen, he decided, gripping the cotton of the duvet in his fists, thinking with a surge of joy how bad it would make them feel. All of them. For ever and ever. He'd show them. He imagined his mother finding his lifeless body under the covers, wailing and beating her chest like women in long black dresses he had seen in films. He imagined her telling his teachers, telling George and Rose – all that sick guilt they would feel – and how dumb his dad would look for having said no to the iPod. It would be brilliant, except that, of course, Sam realized, sitting up and shaking off the duvet, as a corpse he wouldn't be able to enjoy the show.

Outside, what had begun as a spray of rain had quickly thickened to fat sheets of water. Soon a powerful wind was driving it against the window next to his bed, making splatting noises and causing the glass to shake in its fittings. It was so loud that Sam wasn't aware Charlotte had even come upstairs until she switched on the light. He blinked in the glare, pulling the duvet back across his shoulders. Here we go, he thought, here we bloody well go. 'Sorry.' He tried to spit the word out, but it seemed to trickle from his lips in a whisper, barely audible against the drumming of the rain.

'I took the giraffe down, did you see?' She crossed to the blank space that had once housed the childish tape-measure of a wall hanging and ran her fingers across the wall, very gently, as if she was stroking it. '*Someone* had been firing missiles at it. Look, they've left three holes, here and here and here. Poor giraffe, he needed rescuing,' she murmured, half turning so that he could see the smile on her face. 'I thought we could put that clock you like here instead – the one in the spare room that shows its insides. You've always liked it, haven't you?'

Sam nodded once, very slowly.

'Sometimes it's okay to swear, Sam. Sometimes it isn't. "Fuck" is a powerful word and you should use it sparingly.'

Sam could feel his whole body burning. The word sounded terrible on her lips. He wished she hadn't said it.

'I'm going to start cooking supper now. Come down when you're ready.'

Charlotte folded her arms as she left the room, glad he couldn't see the white of her fingers where they gripped her elbows, glad he could not know how long she had rehearsed what to say, how desperate she was not to foster even an echo of the sense of maternal alienation that she had endured not just as a child but that very lunchtime, aged thirty-nine and three-quarters, seated at her mother's kitchen table.

Leaving the door ajar, she made her way downstairs, wishing she had something – someone – to retreat to other than the empty ground floor of the house. She cooked the pasta and the jar of inoffensively smooth sauce like an automaton, lost in contemplation of life's repeating patterns and the vigilance it took to resist them.

Lying among the mountainous peaks of her most scented, favourite bath foam, with her hair clipped off her neck and the radio humming from its hook above her head, Theresa contemplated the lovely calm of a late – but not too late – Sunday evening. The first half of the day had been fraught, trying to fit church and George's out-of-school rugby round a roast, with Henry on call, the younger boys needing dropping and collecting from two different birthday parties and Matilda throwing up without having coughed herself into it. But then the afternoon had slowed and unfurled into something wondrously peaceful, like a veil lifted on a parallel world, in which children sprawled elbow to elbow doing jigsaw puzzles and reading books while one's spouse insisted on washing up, releasing her to the unlooked-for treat of sipping coffee and browsing through the Sunday papers. Even when George put the television on for the PlayStation he kept the volume so low and was so generous in offering his brothers a turn that none of the usual mayhem broke out. Matilda had dozed on the sofa for a couple of hours and then, instead of waking and grizzling, had set up a hospital for her dolls in the corner of the sitting room, requiring no attention beyond a box of plasters and the occasional cooing exclamation of sympathy for the sickest of her plastic patients.

By eight o'clock she and Henry were alone eating beef and pickle sandwiches and watching a detective solve a spate of grisly murders in a country village. It was what one worked for, Theresa mused, sinking deeper into her bubbles, one of those passages of calm that made the storms worthwhile. But Henry wasn't quite right, she reminded herself, watching him carefully as he came into the bathroom and began to perform his own ablutions at the basin. A little quiet, not quite *there*.

'I've been thinking – maybe we did give poor Charlotte a bug after all, though she seems better now.' She had to raise her voice over the spurt of the taps, which Henry was running too hard as usual, splashing the front of his pyjamas.

'Who? Charlotte?'

'No, Matty. She's seems better, but maybe she gave whatever she's had to Charlotte. Remember I told you Charlotte thought she might have been ill instead of just hung-over? And Matty's not been herself for days.'

'Ah. Yes.' Henry balanced his glasses across the soapdish and laid a flannel across his face, tipping his head back so that it sank round the contours of his nose and eye sockets.

'Henry? Are you all right under there?'

He peeled off the flannel and looked at her. 'Of course. Perfectly. Why?'

'Because you washed up lunch without banging the pans or shouting at the children to help,' said Theresa, drily. '*Most* unusual.'

'Remind me not to do it again.'

'Hey, don't be like that.' Theresa reached for a towel and clambered out of the water. Stepping across the bathmat, she stood behind him and rested her chin on his shoulder. 'I put in too much hot and now I'm puce and sweaty.' She made a face at her reflection, her cheeks scarlet next to her husband's pale skin, strands of damp hair sticking across her forehead. 'Still love me?'

'Of course.' Henry smiled, turned his head and planted a kiss on her nose before reaching for his toothbrush. He worked the bristles thoroughly and hard, covering the corners the hygienist had warned him about. Theresa stepped back on to the bathmat and scissored the towel across her back and down her legs before perching on the lavatory seat to dry between her toes. There were pink blotches on her skin from the heat of her bath. Her arms and legs were shapely still and firm, but her belly, since Matilda, the heaviest of their four at birth, was pitted with silvery stretchmarks and hung in a heavy extra fold under her tummy button. A late-night bath, Henry knew, was a sign that she was very relaxed, very happy, that lovemaking was on the cards should he choose to take her up on it. After so many years such knowledge was like a silent language. He knew she was in the mood for sex, just as she knew he wasn't quite 'right'. And that was something to rejoice in, Henry reminded himself, patting his mouth dry and retreating to the bedroom: communication, understanding, such elements were the cornerstone of long-term love. He propped his book against his knees – a hardback biography of a politician that made his arms ache if he attempted to hold it – and began to read. A couple of minutes later Theresa climbed in next to him and slipped her arms round his waist.

'You don't really want to read, do you?'

'Hmm?'

She put her mouth against his arm and blew till his pyjamas were wet and his skin burnt. 'There,' she said, smacking her lips with satisfaction. 'A hot potato, because I love you.'

'Thank you, darling.' Henry peered affectionately at her over the top of his glasses. 'And would you still love me if I read to the end of the chapter?'

She smiled back at him, too comfortable, too sleepy to take offence. 'Possibly.' She turned on to her other side, bunched her knees up to her chest and closed her eyes. 'By the way, Charlotte and Sam are coming next Sunday. I thought I'd do duck for a change . . . What do you think?'

'Delicious.'

'And I said she could use the cottage.'

Henry turned sharply. 'When?'

'Easter hols . . . a week.' Her voice was slurred now. She was close to sleep.

'Fine.' Henry returned his gaze to the top of the page. He had not taken in a single word. *Sir William presented his findings to the House before returning to his club. Sir William . . . Sir William.* Henry squinted, focused and squinted again, seeing not the portly frame of the protagonist of his book but Charlotte Turner, slim, milky-skinned, auburn hair streaming, green eyes sad and hopeful. If he hadn't *felt* her, he was sure he would have been fine. But he had felt her, for those brief seconds, in his arms. More importantly, he had felt the *need* in her and it had opened a door that he didn't seem able to close: a door that led into a room full of fantastical scenarios. What if he had held her harder, or for longer, or seen her into the house, or helped her off with her coat, or offered to make tea or pour more wine or –

Henry rolled over and put out his bedside light. He was sorely tempted now to put his arms round his wife but she was lost to sleep – deeply, instantly, as was her wont. And it would have been wrong, anyway, he reasoned unhappily, to vent his pitiful, secret lust upon the very person it wronged. And where could such lust lead anyway, other than a catastrophe of multiple hurt? Theresa had betrayed him once and the pain of it, thirteen years on – if he concentrated – could still scythe through his heart. Forgiving her had been instinctive, then hard, but he had managed it. They wouldn't survive something similar now. A drunken fumble, maybe, but not with Charlotte . . . *Charlotte*! Christ, was he losing his mind?

Henry fought the bedclothes in the dark, tugging and twisting until sheer exhaustion got the better of him and he fell asleep spreadeagled between the folds like a wounded combatant.

Chapter Six

Bella takes a gap year, but I feel it would be nothing more than that – a gap, limbo, time to fill. On the advice of a teacher I apply, successfully, to Durham University to study English literature. My mother offers to drive me there. I pack the car the night before we leave, stuffing bedding round the boxes and suitcases, my stereo and a guitar I have bought but cannot play. My father watches from his chair at the sitting-room window where he spends most of the day now, a tartan blanket over his bony knees. His big hands, the fingers on the left stained a dirty yellow, twitch in his lap for the cigarettes he can no longer smoke. His breath is all wheeze; his eyes, dark and heavy-lidded, are withdrawing into their sockets.

Early next morning he is standing by the front door with a small bag at his feet. He is coming too, he says. It is a big thing, he wants to be a part of it. He swivels his gaze between my mother's face and mine, the sunken eyes daring contradiction. I have to rearrange the car, forcing a space for myself on the back seat so that he can sit in the front. It is a long journey and I spend most of it staring at the back of his head, seeing the contours of his skull through the papery scalp and the dear tufts of silvery hair still doing their best to cover it. The space between his collar and his hairline looks so contrastingly soft, so absurdly young and vulnerable, that I long to press my hands there – anything to keep it hidden and safe.

Durham is more beautiful than I had expected, tall dark ancient stones interleaved with the smooth walls and extensive glass of modern buildings, like two time zones existing in parallel. The cathedral dominates the airspace with its vast square towers, a majestic point of reference that makes our cramped car, our lives, seem small. With its aid I study the map and steer us in the right direction. I am nervous but cannot wait to locate my college and for the two of them to be gone. They are staying the night somewhere on the outskirts and planning an early getaway.

Stumped by double yellow lines, I wind down the window to ask for help from a round-faced girl in a duffel coat. She is called Eve, she says, and there's parking round the back and is it my first term and what subject and see you soon. I wind the window back up with a full heart, recalling the hateful send-off on the station platform nine years before — that flimsy little-girl hope. I am so very grateful to be older, armoured, more prepared.

It is bitterly cold. I feel my father's helplessness as he hunches his shoulders against the cut of the wind and watches the unpacking of the car. There are three flights of stairs to my room. My mother, a box of books in her arms, instructs him to take care, to use the banisters. I follow behind, the handles of my bags cutting welts into my palms. I see revenge in her energy and want to make up for it. By the top his breath is all rattle and squeak. My mother marches past, plunging back down the stairwell for a second load.

'I have something for you,' he says. He perches on the edge of the desk and reaches slowly, carefully, into the inner pocket of his jacket. Watching the delicacy of the movement, the fluttering fingers, I have the sudden overwhelming sensation — as sure as knowledge itself — that this will be our last farewell. There is a softness in his eyes that tells me he knows it too. 'Something . . .' He withdraws an envelope, plump and white, and studies it hard. I gawp at it too, my heart galloping. For I know what such envelopes at such moments can mean. I have read George Eliot and Jane Austen and Thomas Hardy: altered wills, deathbed confessionals, setting records straight. I know all the possibilities and feel ready and deserving of my chance to experience a version of them. My throat is tight — because he is dying and because I fear what this letter will say — but I am excited too. Closure. I lick my lips.

94

'Open it later,' he croaks.

I hug him tenderly, hating how tall I am in my heels, how robust my frame feels against his thin chest. I press my lips to his rough cheek, wishing I could transfer some of my youth and strength to make him well. I could not in all my eighteen years have loved him more and would tell him so if I could trust my voice.

As my mother, tight-lipped, flint-eyed, the leads of my stereo trailing round her ankles, re-enters the room, I tug open the top drawer of the Formica desk and drop the envelope inside. My knowledge of his betrayal has been a burden, but I know, too, that it has bound us in a secret, almost pleasurable allegiance. We are the circle that closes, my mother is the one on the outside.

Later, when Eve asks me round for a coffee I almost refuse. Her room is along the corridor from mine, a cosy den of lamps and wall hangings, posters and cushions. She talks about faculties, clubs and tutors, and offers fat fingers of home-made shortbread to accompany the coffee. I nod and smile, nibble and sip, guilty that I cannot focus.

Back in my room at last, I lock the door and light a cigarette before I approach the drawer. I inhale deeply, enjoying the giddy rush, the drama of the moment. The drawer sticks, then releases. I balance the cigarette on the edge of the desk and run my fingers under the flap of the envelope. The edge of the paper cuts my skin, but I ignore it, letting the drops of blood smudge where they will.

Inside there is an A4 sheet, blank apart from one sentence, and folded round four fifty-pound notes. 'For extras', it says, 'love, Dad.'

I stare dumbly, then shake the envelope, as if some explanation, apology, defiance, regret, might yet fall out of it. The notes are crisp, fresh off the minter's press, their edges sharp enough to slice more cuts into my skin if I was careless enough to let them. Down the corridor I can hear the quiet hum of music, footsteps and conversations as other students arrive. My room feels very empty in comparison, very silent, a world within a world. I fold the money into my purse and reach for the nearest box to begin unpacking.

The first object I pull out is my babushka doll, smelling strongly of the fresh coat of varnish that my father – in a pitiful quest for useful occupation – had recently insisted on applying. For a few moments I meet its bemused gaze, pondering that we are not so very different, with our selves layered inside, our carapaces to conceal and survive.

I plug in my stereo and pluck an LP at random from the box on the desk. Give me hope, help me cope, with this heavy load . . . I sing as I work, aware of the silent ebb and swell of my disappointment moving to a different, silent tune inside my head. Two hundred pounds will buy a lot of extras: fur-lined boots, guitar lessons, or a duffel coat like Eve's to keep out the raw northern chill. It is generous and yet I feel let down. I had wanted so much more. Not many words, necessarily, but just enough to convey some acknowledgement of the truth upon which I had stumbled all those years ago under the scorched roof of the garden shed. There might have been allegiance, but there was such loss too, such terror; the tremble in my knees as I raced away across the scratchy grass, I can feel it still. Does he know that? Did he ever know that?

I tear open my purse and look at the notes again, fighting a sudden dark fear – far worse than the disappointment – that they might constitute an attempt to guarantee my silence after he has gone. I turn up the volume, sing louder, letting the fear burn itself out. He would never think in such a way. He would know, surely, that my discretion has never had conditions attached, that even at the age of seven it was as much about protecting the fiction of my own life as his.

Cycling back from the gym, Tim let go of the handlebars for long stretches, steering with a combination of balance, willpower and the strength of his inner thighs. He felt exuberant, masterful, in control, as he always did after a good workout. It was Sunday and spring was in full flow, evinced by the flowers streaking past him, palettes of colour, tumbling over garden walls, from tubs and hanging baskets.

At the garden centre he was forced to resume control of the handlebars to avoid a woman trundling a wheelbarrow of compost bags and bedding plants to the open boot of a double-parked estate car. An empty, dripping jungle just a few weeks ago, the place was now swarming. The woman had a small child who was skipping dangerously round the wheels of the barrow, ignoring commands to stay on the pavement. Tim glared at the pair as he braked. Spoilt middle-class women with kids and cars they couldn't handle, it was enough to make one want to mow them down. Charlotte was middle class, of course, but not in any way that he could see typical of the breed. It was one of the things he liked about her – that while she operated within a certain social milieu she did not seem, quite, to be a part of it. There was something lost about her, something lost and, perhaps on account of that, deeply appealing. In fact, Tim's only real reservation about her was the shrimp of a kid, Sam. He had seen it time and time again: perfectly fun-loving women ruined by their offspring. Although with Phoebe it had been the *idea* of having children that had helped to ruin things. Before they had got married she had been as anti the whole business as he was. Two years in, however, and he was regularly checking the little pack of pills in her bedside drawer to check she wasn't playing games.

But then, Tim reasoned, changing down a couple of gears for the steepish slope up the last section of his road, a woman who already had a child was far less likely to get broody, especially one who was on the verge of turning forty with a crap marriage to her credit and a glint in her eye that suggested she knew how to have a good time. Tim breathed heavily as he pumped the pedals. He had to have her. He simply had to. He was fed up of imagining it. He needed to make it real.

Once inside his house (a three-bedroomed semi, which had put on a thumping fifty grand in the three years since its purchase), Tim sought solace by masturbating quickly and fiercely as he stood under the pummelling jet of his power-shower, then sat down in his favourite armchair to draw up a plan of action. As was his wont when under pressure, he jotted his thoughts in the form of a list. Number-one priority, both from a work and a personal point of view, was Mrs Stowe. Having promised to consult again with her husband, she had failed to return his last few calls. If he could just keep the dialogue going, Tim was sure he could bring the situation round. Mrs Burgess, on the other hand, was coming along nicely. She had found an eager purchaser with no chain for her house and was now waiting for the results of the survey with a view to securing Charlotte's. Hurrah. One tick in the box there.

Tim sucked at the water-bottle he had bought at the gym. A litre after exercise was his aim, though he seldom managed it. He preferred drinks with a bit of fizz and bite, the ones that forced burps between mouthfuls. But then he also liked looking younger than his forty-two years and was determined to do all he could to keep things that way. Water was good for the circulation and the skin and he had worked up a hell of a thirst. His stomach muscles were still pulsing from the push of an extra twenty repeats. He had fixed upon an image of Charlotte to see him through: naked and sitting astride him, the ends of her tremendous hair tickling his face, soft-mouthed and admiring. It had worked a treat.

The next thing for his list was Charlotte herself. She had called him back the previous weekend, but only to say she was ill. Various subsequent communications relating to the house had arrived through the channel of his assistant, Savitri. Where some might have confronted this with a certain lowering of spirits, Tim, his self-esteem riding high on endorphins, viewed it merely as a new aspect of what was proving a hugely enjoyable challenge. He would call her that afternoon, he decided, play up the progress on the house, ask about the boy – yes, that would work – the bullying thing, and about *her*, of course. Tim paused to suck the end of his pen, musing on how best to play his hand. 'Birthday 8 June,' he wrote, after a few minutes, inwardly congratulating himself on having unearthed this gem of a personal detail from his work files. A beautiful divorcée approaching her fortieth, desperate to move house with a sulky son in tow and no distractions beyond board games with girlfriends and a part-time job with two puffs in a bookshop. Christ, if he couldn't use some of that to his advantage he really was losing his touch.

Absorbed in such thoughts, forcing more squirts of water down his throat, Tim almost did the nose trick when his phone rang and Charlotte's voice was on line. 'Tim, I'm sorry, I meant to ring before but what with one thing and another . . . and now it's Sunday which is probably –'

'Fine,' Tim chipped in happily, his ears popping as he swallowed. 'Absolutely fine.' The water-bottle had somehow rolled out of his hands and was dribbling a dark stain on to the Indian silk rug that Phoebe had wanted and he had refused to surrender. 'Fine,' he repeated, aware that the things on the list, his clear thinking, had turned to mush at the sound of Charlotte's voice. 'I still have high hopes of Mrs Stowe, by the way – *very* high. I know how much that house means to you,' he added tenderly.

'Thank you so much . . . and, Tim, about dinner . . .'

Ah. At last. Tim slid from the chair on to the floor, stretching his legs and tipping his head back against the seat cushion. 'I was hoping that was the reason for your call

– that you hadn't forgotten.' Using both feet, he had managed to right the water-bottle. Gently, he told himself. Easy does it.

'Of course not but I was going to suggest that maybe we should wait until the . . . our business transactions have been completed before –'

'And *I* think that's the worst idea I've ever heard,' Tim cut in, sitting up in panic.

'But you must admit it is somewhat –'

'One little dinner, Charlotte, as friends. It's hardly going to threaten world peace, is it?'

Much to his relief, she laughed. 'I suppose it can't do any harm.'

'Might it even be nice?' he teased.

'Hmm, yes, I –'

And then, suddenly, the kid was there – obviously having barged into the room. The laughter had left her voice in an instant. 'Sorry, Tim, but I've got to go now. Sam and I are off for a Sunday roast with friends.'

'Let's say Thursday, then, shall we?' Tim suggested hastily. 'My place, eight o'clock? I'm sure Jessica will be free – I'll give her a call right now. It's Ferndene Drive, by the way, number sixty-three. Turn left by the garden centre – you can't miss it.'

He clicked off the phone, already picturing how it would be. No tacky bar stools and over-garlicky snacks this time. He would consult the French cookbook he had given Phoebe and never once seen her use. He was good at cooking when he put his mind to it; three courses, the best wine, flowers on the table, soft lighting, soft music, he would *woo* the hell out of her. She was beautiful, classy, a little mysterious, down on her luck; a creature more in need – more deserving – of wooing it was hard to imagine. Jessica was bound to be free. Jessica was *always* free. With the pustules and the teeth it was little wonder. He would offer to match whatever Charlotte paid, warn the girl that it might be a late one, promise to make it worth her while.

With the sun streaming through the window it was so warm standing by the till on Thursday morning that Charlotte asked Dean if they could turn the heating off. Her employer, who had arrived with half his face masked by a cashmere scarf and sniffing volubly, responded with a dark look.

'Don't worry. I'll take this off instead,' she offered hurriedly, stepping as far to the edge of the square of sunlight as she could and peeling off her cardigan.

'Nice colour, by the way,' Dean croaked, indicating the garment, which was bobbled from too many excursions through the washing-machine but still a handsome pea-green. '*Exactly* your thing.'

'Thanks,' Charlotte muttered, knowing the compliment was because he felt bad and thinking how much easier Jason was to have around. She returned to unloading a box of recent customer orders, inwardly marvelling that while her two employers complained regularly about the difficulty of keeping afloat against supermarkets they made no obvious efforts to economize. Aside from uncomfortably extravagant attitudes to radiators, the shop front was being painted again, unnecessarily, from lemon yellow to Wedgwood blue, and Dean had recently announced that the perfectly decent worn wooden flooring was to be covered with chintzy mushroom carpet, which Charlotte knew, because she had seen the estimate, would cost several thousand pounds.

But there was only an hour to go, she comforted herself, abandoning the box of books to take payment from a man who had spent ages browsing and bought nothing but a birthday card. Only sixty minutes and she would have a couple of hours to herself before she collected Sam from school. And then there was her dinner with Tim to look forward to. And she *was* looking forward to it, Charlotte realized, with some surprise. And why not? The man was unattached, in the right age bracket, attentive, funny, attractive – a perfect companion for a woman in her position, with no interest in anything heavy or long-term. Phoning on Monday to confirm that Jessica could do the baby-sitting, he had made her laugh several times with self-deprecating quips about overdoing things in the gym and needing a walking-stick to get out of bed. He had asked about the Sunday lunch too, sounding genuinely sympathetic when she tried to explain that she hadn't enjoyed it much and how weird and upsetting this had felt because Theresa and Henry were such good friends. Anyone who had the pleasure of her company should be bloody grateful, he had protested, which was a daft thing to say but endearing all the same.

'Still too warm?' asked Dean, as the door jingled shut behind the man and his birthday card.

'No, I –'

'Not a hot flush, I hope?' he teased, picking up on an earlier conversation that had somehow – without her meaning it to – got round to the subject of age and birthdays.

'Not that I know of,' Charlotte replied, tempted to take offence, but unable to because the gibe had been followed by a bout of vicious coughing. 'Hey, you're not well.'

'I'll be all right. It's not like we're busy.' Dean dabbed his mouth with a tissue and disappeared into the stock room.

Left alone, Charlotte found her thoughts returning to the shortcomings of the lunch on Sunday. The tedious subject of her birthday had come up then, too. Henry and Theresa had even managed to *argue* about it, Henry saying through mouthfuls of plum crumble that such milestones were important and thoroughly in need of celebration, and if she wanted their help in organizing something she had only to ask; to which Theresa had replied that she would, of course, be happy to throw a party for her best friend but what piffle because forty-one was as important as forty and who gave a damn?

Feeling caught in some baffling, invisible crossfire of non-communication, uncomfortably aware of Sam swinging his legs with unnecessary violence back and forth under the table while George did nothing but engage in irritating joshing with his siblings, Charlotte had been tempted to cut her losses and leave. Instead they had set off on a group walk to the park. But even this had proved unsatisfactory, with Theresa too engrossed in zipping her younger ones in and out of anoraks and herding trikes and scooters to talk properly, and the boys managing a half-hearted dart at each other, then charging off in separate directions.

The only cheerful member of the crowd had been Henry, who had remained in step beside her for the entire walk, discussing dates for her borrowing the cottage and saying that he had been planning a work-retreat there himself around the same time. When Charlotte had offered to change her plans, he had protested that, with the granny flat up and running, two sets of tenants wouldn't matter a jot, that each would hardly know the other was there.

'It's just a number, sweetie,' said Dean, returning with a glass of water and observing Charlotte's dazed expression with amused concern.

'What? Oh . . . that.' Charlotte laughed. 'Everyone seems determined to keep reminding me about it, but I couldn't care less, I really couldn't. I was thinking about something quite different.'

'And you're such a looker, darling,' persisted Dean, 'you couldn't possibly be worried, could you? Those cheekbones, that hair. You'll be one of those who go on for *ever*.'

Charlotte raised her arms in protest. 'My God, you'll be offering me a pay rise next.'

They were both still laughing when the phone rang. Dean answered it, then handed the receiver to her, mouthing, 'School,' and looking slightly less amused.

'Mrs Turner? It's Miss Brigstock at St Leonard's. I'm sorry to call you at work.'

'Miss Brigstock?' During the course of the four years in which Sam had moved through the junior to the senior ranks of the school, Charlotte had never received a phone call from the headmistress. A fierce fifty-something with pouchy eyes and an unflatteringly geometric haircut, the head was a somewhat monochrome but dedicated creature, who normally limited communication to wordy introductions at parents' evenings.

'I'm afraid there has been an incident, Mrs Turner. I would be most grateful if you could come into the school.'

'An *incident*?' Charlotte's puzzlement surged into anxiety. 'What's happened? Is Sam all right?'

'Yes, Sam is perfectly well. But we would like you to come in now if you would.'

'Now?' Charlotte glanced at her employer, who was pretending to rearrange the carousel of cards in the far corner of the shop. 'Right now?' she repeated stupidly.

'If you wouldn't mind. Sam, I assure you, is fine,' she added, in a gentler voice, 'but I would prefer to explain everything when you get here.'

Charlotte's hands fumbled as she replaced the receiver. 'Dean, I'm so sorry but –'

Her employer was already rolling his eyes and gesturing

at the door. 'Go. It's fine. Just go. No worries. It's quiet anyway.'

It was only after the doorbell had fallen silent that Dean saw she had forgotten the green cardigan. He picked it up and folded it carefully, wondering what it must be like to experience all that parental angst, to have a creature other than one's partner to cosset and worry about. For a while he had wanted badly to adopt but Jason had said no and weren't they enough for each other and bought two Siamese kittens instead.

Dominic Porter did his best to compose his long limbs into some semblance of relaxation on the slippery leather sofa parked opposite Miss Brigstock's desk. Hateful furniture but a good woman, he mused, recalling their first visit to the school, when she had, quite rightly, given her attention to Rose rather than him, conveying such a gentle genuine interest in his daughter's responses – skilfully letting them control the direction of the conversation – that Rose had opened up in a way Dominic had never seen her manage with an adult before, not even during the days when Maggie had been well and they had had nothing to trouble them but run-of-the-mill things, like bad weather, managing on one salary and what colour to paint the hall.

Rose had closed up again, of course, like some eccentric flower attuned to a private schedule of blooming – seldom, secretly, or when least expected – but it had given Dominic faith in the school and in the difficult decision to take the plunge and leave the Hampshire farmhouse Maggie had so loved and move to London. Setting about it in the middle of a school year had been far from ideal, but having *not* moved earlier for Rose's sake, Dominic had suddenly seen how stuck the two of them were, treading water and nearly drowning as a result: each handmade curtain pleat, the angle of every knick-knack, the *smell* on Maggie's side of the wardrobe (jasmine or whatever the hell it was she had always worn) – all of it such a comfort during the early months, it had simply grown too painful to bear. Without her, commuting made no sense either. Maggie's parents had helped for a while but after that it had been up to a string of sweet, gauche au-pair girls to plug the gaping hole until he got off the train each night. When challenged, Rose always said she liked the girls, that she didn't mind him being late, but since her mother had gone she had become a master at saying the right thing and Dominic had learnt not always to believe her.

Having briefly rented a flat in Trinity Road as a bachelor, and with his brother based just off Garratt Lane, Dominic had alighted on Wandsworth. It was as good a place as any from which to make a fresh start. St Leonard's had come up on a Google search, meeting the criteria for being small, co-ed and near an attractive, affordable residential patch. Not long after he had found it, good reports of the school had ricocheted in from several unexpected quarters, including an old friend of Maggie's, a second cousin and the girl in the Farnham salon who cut Rose's hair, whose uncle had been a teacher there for twenty years.

Connections were so comforting, Dominic reflected, standing up and then sitting down again on the lip of his slippery seat as Miss Brigstock reappeared. A slim fair-haired woman bearing a tray of tea things followed, then Rose herself, her socks bulging round her thin ankles, her sharp blue eyes darting anxiously.

'Are you all right, darling?' She had come to stand next to him, close but not touching. Rose nodded, tugged up her socks, then picked at the chewed strips of skin round her nails.

'We need two more chairs, I think,' commanded the head. 'Gillian, would you see to it?'

The younger woman hurried off, returning a couple of moments later with two plastic chairs which she set down opposite the sofa.

'Rose, dear, would you like some juice?'

Rose shook her head, perched next to her father, then wriggled backwards on to the deep seat, her bare skin squeaking against the leather.

'Thank you so much for coming, Mr Porter. How fortunate that you were at home – house-hunting, I believe? I hope it's going well.'

'Very, thank you.'

She held out a cup of tea, which Dominic accepted gratefully. He was nervous now because Rose was; he could feel it coming off her in waves.

'As I said on the phone,' Miss Brigstock continued, 'Rose is in no trouble – no trouble at all.' She beamed at Rose, who had folded her arms and bowed her head, as if she wanted to sink from view between the sofa's black jaws. 'But there has been an unhappy incident and I'm a great believer in nipping things in the bud so I am going to ask you now, Rose, to tell us in your own words exactly what happened.'

A few doors down the corridor Charlotte, breathless, hot, worried, car keys still in hand, was being shown into a small side room that contained Sam, sitting cross-legged on the floor, and a young man with unkempt dark hair, who was crouching in front of him. The man straightened the moment Charlotte appeared and smiled broadly, offering his hand. 'Mrs Turner? Philip Dawson, school counsellor.'

'Counsellor?' Charlotte looked from the man, about whose arrival on the staff she dimly remembered from a school letter, to Sam who, instead of greeting her, had turned his face to the wall. 'Darling?' She dropped to her knees beside him, the anxiety still rampant but fused now with a certain relief. He was mercifully undamaged. And however horrible the 'incident', as the head, with typical euphemistic PC tact, had described it, at least, with things now out in the open, there was hope of a proper solution. To have the counsellor on board so soon clearly meant the school thought so too. 'Poor darling. Are you all right? Tell me what happened . . . Tell Mum.' She hugged his hunched shoulders.

'Sam?' prompted the counsellor gently. 'It's probably best to explain.'

'I didn't do *anything*,' Sam shouted, spitting the last word with such venom that Charlotte rocked off balance.

'Shall I tell Mum, then?'

Sam shrugged, not looking at either of them.

'Yes, please do,' Charlotte murmured, getting to her feet, dimly aware that the situation was not going to be quite as straightforward as she had assumed.

The counsellor cleared his throat. 'I'm afraid Sam has not been very nice to a girl in his class, a girl called Rose who –'

'That's not possible,' Charlotte interrupted steadily, reaching down to touch the springy top of Sam's head. The hair felt soft and cool, the scalp burning. 'You don't understand. It's been the other way round for weeks. I don't know if it was the Rose girl or . . .'

Philip Dawson shook his head, offering a regretful smile. 'During lunch break today –' He broke off, turning back to Sam. 'Hey, mate, this would really be better coming from you.' When Sam remained motionless, his head still twisted in its uncomfortable effort at invisibility, he sighed and continued, 'During lunch break today Sam pulled Rose Porter's hair and kicked her.'

Charlotte released a breathy laugh of disbelief. 'She must have said something truly horrible.'

'She says she didn't. She also says that there was another occasion, before after-school club last week, when Sam held her arm behind her back and —'

'I do not *believe* this.' Tears were close, but Charlotte knew she had to stay focused and brave. 'Sam is the one who has been having a hard time, needing help, not this girl. I even spoke to his teacher about it because I knew something wasn't right.'

'Absolutely. Something is *not* right and we're going to help Sam to overcome —'

'Where is Miss Brigstock? I wish to see her *now*.'

'I'm about to take you to her, Mrs Turner. At the moment she is with Rose and her father. We're going to sort this out together. Please try to remain calm,' he added, glancing at Sam.

Charlotte, taking a deep breath, felt a huge swell of longing for Martin. She couldn't handle this sort of thing alone, she just couldn't. He would be firm without getting hysterical. He would know what to do, how to handle this scruffy young man with his soft Irish voice, too-long hair and winning smile. Stick to your guns, she told herself. Stick to the truth. 'Sam would *never* deliberately hurt another —'

'There are several children who will vouch for what Rose has told us, Mrs Turner,' he interrupted gently. He paused for Charlotte to take this in, then added, in a tone infused with enough compassion to suggest that, armed as he was with the sword of truth, part of him had no wish to deliver the final blow, 'And we have CCTV footage of the incident last week —'

'*CCTV footage?*'

'All schools have cameras, these days, for security

purposes. We have checked them. I'm sorry, what Rose has told us appears to be true.'

Charlotte turned away to compose herself, pressing her face into her palms. The counsellor dropped to his knees next to Sam. 'We'll sort this out, mate, okay? The first step is you owning up to it. Then, of course, you must say sorry to Rose, promise to be her friend – which you can do right now – and then you can put it behind you. And once a week, or more if you like, you and I are going to meet for a chat about how it's going and how you're feeling. It's tough, I know. All you kids have a lot on your plate, don't you?'

During the course of this speech Sam had slowly swivelled his head to meet the counsellor's gaze. Charlotte, peering over her fingertips, saw both the good, kind body language of the man and the capitulating shame in her son's response to it. So he had done these terrible things. So he wasn't the bullied but the bully. And that was unacceptable and she would make sure Sam knew it. And yet for those few moments all Charlotte wanted to do was barge the counsellor out of the way, grab Sam's hand and run – back down the corridor of brown lino, past the classrooms, the framed pieces of creative excellence and notices about fire drills to a seclusion that would keep them safe from pain, anger, fear and all the other myriad stumbling blocks to the seemingly impossible business of being happy.

Charlotte had certain tricks for getting to sleep, honed over years of battling an inclination towards insomnia. Counting helped, not sheep, but days – until Christmas, Sam's birthday, her birthday, her next period and the one after that, assuming that the cycle was twenty-eight days and not twenty-seven, or -six, as was sometimes the case. If she was lucky, oblivion kicked in before she could work it out. Then there were the little white tablets, secured on a desperate visit to her GP during the final harrowing phase with Martin, when she had wept and gabbled embarrassingly about her husband seeing another woman. The doctor, her least favourite in the practice, with a nasal voice and a habit of tapping his pen against the edge of his desk, had suggested she contact Relate and printed out a prescription for temazepam, which he and his colleagues had renewed during several subsequent visits.

The efficacy of the tablets, the joy of knowing that relief was at hand, had been, for Charlotte, nothing short of a revelation: one swallow and the ghastly nocturnal arguing or, just as bad, the thick silence of *not* arguing, the invisible impenetrable wall of *not* touching, was gone. Except that waking each time to the groggy recollection of reality had been somehow harder, like stepping into precisely the sort of nightmare from which daylight was supposed to offer rescue.

Turning on her side that Thursday night, Charlotte opened her bedside drawer and pulled out the little brown medicine bottle for the first time in ten months. It still wasn't too late to blank out the grim images of the afternoon – more vivid in recollection than they had been in the dazed state through which she had experienced them: Sam meekly, miserably, shaking the girl's limp hand with the adults watching, as awkwardly stage-managed as her own handshake with the father, all carried out against a murmuring backdrop of platitudes and civility. And why these two? Charlotte had despaired then and many times since. The man with the *dead wife* who had hated her house, and the gawky daughter, with her fragile, stick-thin freckled arms and legs. Why couldn't Sam have attacked a creature less pathetic, some gum-chewing fat kid with sticking-out ears and piggy eyes?

Reconciliations done, assurances made – that Sam, too, needed support and would receive it – Charlotte had been unable to shake off the sense that her son's failure to behave decently was her failure too. If unhappiness was the root cause, this too had to be her fault. No one said as much, but she could feel them thinking it. Steering Sam out past the smiles and nodding heads, mustering a show of dignity she could not feel, Charlotte decided she would prefer to face a firing squad than go through anything similar again.

Once home, she had let Sam, ashen, exhausted, beyond talking, eat tea in front of the television before going to bed. 'She didn't like me,' had been his only offering of explanation during the course of these rituals. 'No one likes me.' He had fallen asleep in instants, plucking a grubby white seal from the array of soft toys on the shelf above his bed and tucking it under his chin.

Tiptoeing downstairs, Charlotte had called Martin, only to hear Cindy's singsong voice reporting that neither of them could come to the phone right now, and then Tim, to cancel the date. She gave the reason briefly, baldly, too wrung out herself to care how any of it sounded. After that she had made herself some baked beans on toast and had the first forkful raised to her mouth when Martin returned her call.

'Did you see this *footage*?' he snarled. 'Did you see it?'

'No, I didn't even ask,' Charlotte had stammered. 'I . . . Sam . . . Sam *did* these things, Martin. He's owned up, said sorry. He *did these things*.'

She could hear him drawing breath, faint but distinct, the pull-back before the release.

'Just tell me how,' he exploded, '*how* you could have misread the situation so *catastrophically*? Thinking that someone was mistreating Sam when –' Charlotte had switched off then, in self-defence, stepping away from his voice and the plate of cold baked beans to a tight tiny place inside her head.

How indeed? Charlotte's arm felt heavy as she shook the little plastic bottle and put it down again. They had propped her up during her lowest ebb. To resort to them again would be tantamount to an admission that she had sunk as low again, that even without an icy, hostile, deceiving husband to blame, she was still incapable of finding peace, still ballsing everything up.

The night, without sleep, had its phases. The hum of cars grew more intermittent. Two cats performed a duet of high-pitched yowls. A rowdy group of youths shouted, laughed and kicked cans. The darkness thickened, then thinned to a speckled grey as the moon played cat-and-mouse with clouds. With exhaustion came a sort of manic lucidity. So she had been wrong, thought the best of her child instead of the worst, seen echoes of her own deepest fears rather than his. So what? That just meant she was human. And the school was accountable too – the form teacher with her candy-floss hair and saccharine smile, not to mention Martin . . .

Charlotte sat up and switched on the light. Squinting in its glare, she fumbled for the bedside phone and called Martin's mobile. It was unsociably early but he always switched off his phone overnight anyway and all she wanted to do was unburden herself in a message, to fight back as she had failed to earlier, explain what shouldn't need explaining, that Sam's behaviour meant he was indeed un-happy, as she had suspected, that not feeling loved made people do all sorts of things and it was up to them, as parents, to help him through.

She had said it all, speaking with a clipped lucidity usually beyond her in conversation, when the phone rang back at her and Cindy's voice, soft and wary, was on the line. 'Charlotte?'

'Cindy, I'm sorry, I . . . just left Martin a message. I . . .' Charlotte looked at her clock. It was half past five. In the charcoal dark outside, birdsong had started.

'About Sam?'

'Of course, yes – I'm so sorry to have woken you. I thought his phone would be off.'

'It doesn't matter, I was awake already.'

'Oh?' Charlotte waited, expecting anger.

'Terrible about Sam. Unbelievable. He's such a sweetie.'

'Yes, yes, he is.'

'Shall I ask Martin to call you, then?'

'Well, I've left that message but, yes, thanks.' Charlotte hesitated, suppressing an absurd impulse to ask Cindy if she was okay. She didn't sound okay.

''Bye, then.'

''Bye, Cindy.'

Charlotte switched off the light and pulled the duvet back up to her chin. The bed felt huge suddenly. She skated her foot into some of the icy space on what had been Martin's side, remembering the loveliness of feeling for a warm leg with cold toes. Were Cindy and Martin in trouble? She let the thought float, trying to study it from all sides, testing her emotions. Under pressure Martin could be insufferable. And recently Cindy had been looking drained. Maybe patterns there, too, were repeating. Comforted, Charlotte fell asleep at last, hugging the pillows on the empty side of the bed, warming them with the heat of her chest.

Upstairs, Sam slept soundly until roused by an ache in his bladder. He took his seal to the bathroom, propping it up on the lavatory and keeping half an eye on its whiskery face while he peed. It felt nice, so nice, that he was careful about the drips for once and even bothered to wash his hands afterwards. He was supposed to feel terrible, he knew, because he had done terrible things. To Rose, stupid Rose, who was so good at being a tree, who looked at him like he wasn't there. *Why?* That was all they wanted to know, like there had to be reasons for everything when most stuff wasn't like that, when most stuff just *happened*. He hadn't really hurt her, just a pinch and a twist, to see how she would react more than anything – and, maybe, to sort of show her he was *there*.

Sam turned for the door, then remembered the seal. It was staring with its tiny jet eyes, glittery and knowing. He picked it up and ran his nose along the soft fur. It smelt of his bed, of *him*, probably. It was a nice smell, Sam decided, burrowing his nose deeper and thinking of the weird soapy scent of the sheets at George's house and of Rose for the few seconds that he had held her pinned to his chest, pepperminty, warm. He hadn't meant to hurt her. He hadn't. Sam pressed his face into the soft belly of the seal, letting the grubby fur soak up his tears and the dribble of snot from his nose.

Back in bed, he watched the long metal hands of his new bedroom clock jerk round the dial, wishing there was some way of stopping them, some way of it never being morning and time to go to school. There was, he knew, no question of a reprieve. He had never seen his mother more angry – the chilling silence in the car, her mouth a tight line, her eyes ablaze. But far worse had been the look on her face in the head's study, her eyes glassy and her mouth twitching like his did when he was trying not to cry. Sam had prayed that she wouldn't. All through the talking and the shaking hands and the saying sorry it was the only thing he could think about. And she hadn't. The liquid along her eyelids was visible but it never overflowed and when her lips twitched she bit them.

It seemed only seconds later that the doorbell rang. Sam, alert instantly to the need to curry favour, sprinted down the stairs and scrabbled with the locks, dragging the hall chair across to reach the top bolt.

'For your mum, I should imagine,' said the delivery man, winking as he handed over a large bunch of yellow roses. 'Birthday, is it? Let's hope they're from your dad, eh?'

Sam closed the door slowly. It wasn't his mum's birthday, was it? He ransacked his brain, producing a recollection not of Charlotte's date of birth but that the celebrations tended to coincide with summer half-term. And they hadn't even had Easter yet, so that was okay. He turned for the stairs, carrying the bouquet carefully in both arms, knowing it couldn't be from his father but rather hoping the estate agent with the beard wasn't responsible either.

'Sam, who was it?'

'Hang on.' He took the last few stairs two at a time, spurred on by the realization that flowers, from whatever source, were likely to put her in a good mood.

At first things looked very promising. On seeing the roses, Charlotte propped herself up in bed with a sort of squeal, then tore at the little envelope as if it was indeed a birthday present – the most exciting one she'd ever had. While reading it, she sniffed dreamily at the flowers, then slumped back against the pillows with a goofy smile on her face. They were from Tim Croft, she confessed, goofier still, although Sam, with application that would have given fresh hope to his English teacher, had already worked that out for himself by reading the note upside-down: *With love from Tim. Dinner next Friday? I never give up.*

But the moment Sam laid out the no-school proposal her face went white and hard. She thrust the flowers to one side and said no way, that he was to have a bath and then breakfast, then write two letters, one to his headmistress and one to Rose Porter, and that if he had a problem with that she would think of several others for him to do as well.

'Thank God we ordered,' remarked Henry, the following night, as he, Graham and Paul elbowed their way through the crush to the ledge where the bartender had promised to leave the champagne. The bottle had been opened and parked in an ice-bucket, next to six flutes and two bags of peanuts. His companions, hot and dry-mouthed as they all were from the theatre's over-zealous central-heating system, rubbed their hands in appreciation while Henry poured.

'Should we wait for the ladies, do you think?' ventured Paul, glancing in the direction of the sign for the toilets.

'I take it that's your idea of a joke,' scoffed Graham, who, thanks to a colleague's leaving do, which had almost made him late and earned a death-glare from his wife, was several glasses ahead of the others and a lot thirstier. 'You know women's lavatories, there's *always* a queue. The three of them should have held on, in my view, kept their legs crossed until the end of Act Five. In fact, if they're very much longer we'll have to give serious consideration to downing their share.'

'What do you think of it, then?' asked Henry, making a mental note as he rummaged for peanuts to forgo the bread basket when they got to the restaurant.

'He's good. I'm not sure about her, though. A bit . . .'

Graham frowned, searching for the right word and getting a sudden vivid flash of Naomi the night before, staggering down from a fourth visit to settle the twins. 'Hysterical, I'd say. *Over*acting, like she's been to drama school and wants us to know about it.'

'I think the whole play is being *over*-interpreted,' agreed Paul, with an authority borne of the fact that, in spite of having found his way into accountancy, he had taken an upper second in English at Cambridge. 'The story shines through, it always does with Shakespeare, and they're banging it out like some cheap soap.'

'Ah, here they are.' Henry waved as Theresa, Josephine and Naomi's heads bobbed into view through the doorway on the opposite side of the bar. He watched as his wife led the trio through the throng. She had, he noticed, dressed with particular care that night, a lacy black top designed to show teasing bits of flesh and bra, and a velvet skirt that flared prettily round her knees. And she was in her most serious heels too, the ones she claimed numbed her toes. No doubt she had assembled the entire costume in the space of five minutes, between reading bedtime stories, briefing the baby-sitter and not forgetting the theatre tickets.

In short, he was the luckiest of husbands, Henry reminded himself, handing out glasses as the women arrived, thinking how splendid they were in their finery, how such evenings, with their costumes and chat, were like mini plays in themselves. He remembered in the same instant how Theresa had put her hand on his knee during the second act, just as the ebony-faced actor playing Othello was booming about how 'our loves and comforts should increase, Even as our days do grow'. Henry had responded by placing his hand over hers, dutifully, briefly, wondering at her damnable intuition, calling for reassurance precisely because she could

118

sense he was in no mood to deliver it. Was knowledge of another person love? Henry wondered suddenly. Was it that simple?

'It's so awful, isn't it,' said Josephine, eagerly, 'knowing it's all going to go wrong? Like watching a crash in slow motion.'

'Ah, the fatal flaw.' Graham cast a knowing look round the five faces. 'We've all got them.'

'So what's yours, then, Graham?' teased Josephine, with her customary feistiness. 'Come on, you're among friends, you know.'

Naomi's husband scratched his closely shaven dark hair in a show of deep thought. 'Let me see, working too hard for the good of others ... an inclination towards self-sacrifice ...'

'Yeah, right,' Naomi murmured into her glass.

Theresa was watching her husband's face carefully. There was a fleck of something on his cheek, salt or maybe a peanut crumb. His eyes were crinkled in amusement; his big friendly mouth moved easily between smiles, eating and conversation. He pushed at the bridge of his glasses and twiddled with his ear. He was as he always was. And she was a ninny. A spoilt ninny with so many blessings in her life that she could luxuriate in a sense of wrongdoing at not being made love to for a couple of weeks, and feel jealous of Charlotte – *Charlotte*, of all people – simply because Henry had paid court to her during the course of a Sunday walk, while Theresa had had to play the dutiful mother, attending to runny noses, overturned tricycles and fallings-out between the boys. Henry should have helped and she had told him so, angrily, the moment Charlotte's Volkswagen had made its throaty departure from outside their front door. He had said sorry and she had said fine.

Except that it wasn't fine because there were the other things that Theresa couldn't bring herself to mention: like the flirty teasing at the table about Charlotte's age and the ridiculously generous suggestion that they should throw a party for her fortieth (a *party*!) and later in the week the carefully rehearsed broaching of the subject of whether Charlotte should have been included in the trip to the theatre. They would normally have asked Martin and Charlotte, he had reasoned, looking like George did when he was bargaining for more time on the PlayStation or a second helping of ice-cream, a tightness round the eyes, as if he was fighting shiftiness, so surely it wasn't fair to exclude Charlotte from the treat just because she was on her own? Or Martin and Cindy, Theresa had shot back. Why not ask them instead or as well? That had shut him up. But then she had retreated to the kitchen and seen the pencil arrows in the big diary next to the phone – thin, innocent lines running along the tops of the dates of the Easter holiday. 'Work blitz', he had written, which meant, as it always did, retreating on his own to Suffolk. Except, as they both knew, Charlotte was due to be in Suffolk round the same time – there was a line in the diary for her too. Theresa, flicking her eyes from one pencilled arrow to the other, had seen a sudden, horrible, inevitable collision in their paths – 'work blitz' and 'Charlotte' – destined to meet. Like watching the slow-motion disaster on stage that Josephine had so aptly described, she reflected unhappily, the champagne pulsing in her temples as they made their way back to their seats.

But as the false, fatal evidence of Desdemona's hanky did its dirty work on stage, Theresa began to feel a lot better. What one *saw* and what was *true* were entirely different things. Indeed, the key lesson from the hapless Othello was that too much fear and imagining could make the very disaster one sought to avoid come true. All that mattered was trust. The rest followed. She found Henry's hand for the second time that night, interlacing her fingers with his: fine long fingers, surgeon's fingers, she had always loved them. His palms were a little clammy, but the theatre was warm. 'Farewell the tranquil mind!' groaned Othello, 'farewell content!' But not for me, Theresa vowed, pulling her hand free, sensing that Henry found its presence troubling. 'I'm bloody starving,' she whispered instead, pressing the ninniness away. 'Roll on Act Five.'

Later in the restaurant she volunteered the subject of the dilemma over Charlotte and the theatre tickets herself, easily, confidently. A lively debate ensued, encompassing the difficulty of allocating loyalties between divorcing friends and the burden of balanced couple-groups having to accommodate suddenly single relationship refugees. Then the behaviour of the wretched and disgraced Sam was picked up and punted round the table as well, amid murmurings of horrified pity and disbelief ... The motherless Rose, of all people, being *bullied* by the diminutive *Sam*. The conversation pulsed with the sort of *Schadenfreude* that had no place in the context of close friends.

Theresa, recognizing this ugliness, could not muster the wherewithal to put a stop to it. She would do what she could to help Charlotte, via influencing George (she had already delivered another lecture about standing by friends in times of need) and her own capacity for kindness. She was desperately fond of the woman for all her tangles and foibles; but for that night at least, the security of her own position within this safe circle of friends, at her husband's side, mattered far more. So she let the conversation roll, welcoming the hum of congratulation when the matter of lending the cottage came up and even saying that poor

Henry was going to have to carve one of his prized work sessions round the inconvenience. She glanced at her husband as she spoke, taking fresh heart at his groan of concurrence and the willingness with which he met her gaze.

Chapter Seven

Six weeks into my first term, and the city has become a moonscape of snow. The cathedral, thickly iced, rises from the whiteness like a giant wedding cake. It strikes the hour as I pass, the chimes sounding muffled and uncertain in the blizzard. I am in new fur-lined boots and a duffel coat, late and hurrying for an audition. The snow sticks to my soles in uneven lumps, holding me back and upsetting my balance. It is seven o'clock and I have another half-mile to go.

I am late but I push back my hood and look up at the clock-tower, seeking solace and meaning in its new mysterious wintry beauty. But all I see is a church, covered with snow and bigger than the one in which I stood ten days before, gagging on incense while my mother trembled under her veil, making noises that embarrassed me and would have embarrassed my father, I am sure, had he the power to see through the wooden sides of his coffin. He wouldn't have liked the incense either, or any of the other Catholic touches on which she insisted, but he had left no instruction so she had a free rein. It was a service for her, not him. And yet she wept and wept and wept. Dry-eyed, mute at her side, I wondered if this was hypocrisy or love.

My own tears come in solitude, as now, under the balking shadow of the cathedral, with icy flakes melting on my lips and the muted chimes still echoing in my ears. My closed circle is broken, my point of reference lost. I have only her whom I do not love. I have no answers. I have no home, only a house I do not wish to visit. My course is made up of books that seem pointless, a quest for ideas that I have no desire to hunt down. There is no pattern, no meaning. It is Eve, motherly, clucking, concerned, who has chivvied me out of my room to attend the audition. She is going, too, but arriving from somewhere else. Like me, she has never acted before, but has a crush on the director and is prepared therefore to endure any ignominy in order to breathe the same air. She has said that we can only make fools of ourselves, that if rejected as would-be actors we can offer to find props and paint scenery. She has said that life is about picking yourself up after a fall, about not being afraid to reach for your dreams, from which I have gathered that she is besotted indeed.

Wet-haired, wet-eyed, wet-nosed, skidding on my lumpy soles, I cross the college quad and push open the double doors of the room to which a chalkboard in the porter's lodge has directed me. The door creaks, but no one turns. There are several rows of chairs, half filled, facing away from me towards a makeshift stage lit by two Anglepoise lamps. A girl with blue streaks in her hair and violent red lipstick is on her knees, referring to the script as she shrieks, 'Yes, we all know what you did for me!' Her voice is strained, raucous, compellingly overdone, yet it is not to her that my eye is drawn but to the man standing over her. Loose, messy, sandy blond hair, slim-hipped in tight, faded jeans, wearing a scruffy black jumper with the sleeves pushed up to the elbows. With one of the lamps directly behind him, the light shines through his hair. When he moves I am blinded. I put my hands to my eyes and squint. I had thought he was trying out for Jimmy, but he tells the girl thank you and calls for me to take a seat.

I grope my way along a row to Eve, who hands me a script.

'Isn't he divine?' she whispers. 'Isn't he perfectly divine? I'm on next. We can do any bit we like, he says. I'm going for the ironing scene at the beginning. What do you think?'

Having no view, I nod and start to flick through the play.

'I need a Helena,' he calls, pointing in our direction. Eve stands up. 'Not you, you.' His finger is aimed a little to the left of my chest, at my heart. I stand up, shaking off my coat, raking my fingers through the tangle of my wet hair. I move slowly, aware of many things, including the sheer wonder of how much can be packed into a single human moment. This man and I will sleep together, I know. I know,

too, that Eve knows it, that the connection from the stage to my chair, so instant, so strong, is somehow visible. As I step towards the stage I feel the crunch of her dreams underfoot, but my need is too great to care.

Happiness, I learn that night, comes when the fulfilment of desire not only exceeds expectation but is experienced simultaneously, equally, by another. While we eat pasta and discuss John Osborne and the cheap posters on the bistro walls, being only children and whether mushrooms should be peeled, I know with exalting certainty that the balance of pleasure is absolute. He feels as I do. We will make love, but already there is the delicious sense of a mutual slowing down, the knowledge that we have the rest of our lives, should we choose. At my insistence we divide the bill equally, laughing at our mutual ineptitude with figures, turning mundanity into courtship. Before we leave he swipes a clean paper napkin off a neighbouring table and tears it in two. I write my name and number on one half and he his on the other. I watch his hand work the biro, wondering how I could ever have thought the name Martin ordinary, wondering how his tongue will feel inside my mouth.

There was so much mist that morning, swirling round their scrubby back garden like smoke, that Dominic, nursing his first cup of tea in the draughty chill of their rented kitchen, wondered whether to cancel his planned visit to the Redhill aerodrome and go into work instead. Upstairs he could hear the creak of the floorboards and the gurgle of water as Rose moved between the bathroom and her bedroom, getting herself together in a manner that would have left Maggie reeling in disbelief. Rose setting an alarm clock! Rose, getting out of bed with more than five minutes to spare! Cleaning her teeth without being asked, forcing a comb through the morning thicket of her rebellious hair – unbelievable, fantastic! His wife and daughter had fought hard over such rituals, so hard that sometimes Dominic had been glad to escape out of the door with his briefcase. They clashed because they were so alike – intense, obstinate, wilful – like two tigers in a cage; but so passionate, too, so loving. Dominic swallowed a hot mouthful of tea. It wouldn't do, not today, not any day. Sentimental garbage. He swallowed again, harder.

'Hey, Dad.'

'Hey, sweetheart. I bought a pack of Pop-Tarts yesterday – they're in the breadbin.'

She screwed up the pointy tip of her nose, the only part of her face where the freckles were scattered enough to show the true pearl of her skin.

'I thought you liked them.'

She shook her head. 'Not any more.'

'Right.' Dominic drained his tea. 'Cereal, then.' He began pulling packets out of the cupboard.

'You're not going to work?'

'No.' He laughed. 'How did you guess?'

She shrugged, clearly unmoved by the admiration in his tone. 'You've got jeans on, haven't you? Which means you're either going flying or house-hunting.'

'The former, clever clogs. I don't have to look at houses any more, remember?' he prompted, a little concerned that she could have forgotten such a thing, wondering if it meant she hadn't liked the place after all, whether she had only said she did to please him. 'We've had our offer accepted, haven't we?'

'You did, Dad,' she replied haughtily. 'It's not *my* money, is it?'

Dominic decided to let the matter drop. She was studying the back of the cereal packet, clearly in no mood to continue talking. Maggie hadn't talked much in the mornings either.

Though she was usually the one to venture downstairs to make tea, and would often climb back into bed afterwards, nudging her knee between his legs if she wanted to make love. Dominic turned back to the window as the shadow of longing descended and then passed, like a private silent storm, but easier now, definitely easier.

The mist was lifting, floating in strands across the fence and the branches of the trees like thinning hair. A squirrel was perched on one of the mudflats pitting the scrubby lawn, flicking its tail and glancing over its shoulder as if it knew it was being watched. He missed Maggie, but at times Dominic simply missed sex – a basic enough urge and yet one that was proving maddeningly complicated to satisfy. A blind date organized by well-intentioned Hampshire friends had led to a liaison of sorts; the woman had been a slim, attractive brunette, a divorcée with two children, intelligent, wealthy in her own right, a keen lover – generous, imaginative. Recognizing the potential, Dominic had done his best to nurture it, only to find himself feeling like a spectator to the relationship rather than a participant. Even when making love, he had experienced a distinct, shaming sense of detachment, fighting the urge afterwards to scramble free of her arms and bolt home.

He hadn't, of course. Dominic was too well brought up for that. Instead he had lain still while a head rested on his arm and fingers stroked the shield of dark hairs on his chest and intimate questions were put to him about love and loss. He had realized then that his bereavement held some allure – the romance of tragedy, a man in need of rescuing. He had stonewalled, not wanting rescue, so she had responded to his monosyllables by pouring out confidences of her own, invariably connected to the disappointments of her marriage. All of which had made Dominic cringe in the half-light of the bedroom, shrinking from the sheer *weight* of what she was so desperate to share. Feeling a fraud, after a few such encounters, he had brought the whole thing to an end, citing platitudes – not being ready, needing space – to ease the exit.

What he needed was a clean sheet, Dominic mused, tracking the squirrel as it scampered through a patch of weeds and up a tree; someone fresh and uncluttered as Maggie had been when they'd first met, full of ideals, hope and generosity, holding still to the view that the world would deliver rather than disappoint. Someone, maybe, like the Polish girl whom his sly brother had recently placed at Dominic's end of a dinner table; late twenties, self-assured, saucer-eyed, full of a youthful eagerness to please, to succeed, proud of her unusual career path – au pair, to PA, to fledgling producer in a film company – she had exuded an energy that was impossible to ignore. So some of his clients invested in films, she had exclaimed, in her clipped, school-book English, with the delight of somebody stumbling upon a monumental coincidence, maybe they could talk about it over lunch some time.

'Dad, we're going to be late.'

'No, we're not.'

'But you haven't had your breakfast and it's *eight o'clock* and you feel *sick* if you don't eat before you fly.'

Dominic reached out to stroke his daughter's cheek, missing the harum-scarum creature who had spent the first ten years of her life exercising his patience. She was filling in for Maggie, of course. Even the most amateur shrink could have worked that out. All perfectly understandable, but heartbreaking nonetheless. Something she loved had been taken away so she was damn well going to protect what was left. In his own way Dominic felt it too, had fought it minute by minute during the bad times, letting her be when he wanted to crush her gangly, fragile twelve-year-old body against his chest and howl. It was the new game they played, no sissies allowed, and Rose was still excelling at it. How she had handled the business with the loathsome Sam Turner had been typical: keeping it to herself, not *worrying* him, calmly reporting it to teachers the moment it got out of hand, then putting it behind her as soon the head-mistress's door was closed. Sam Turner was a *saddo* and a *geek*, she had pronounced, during the car ride home, and she would have kicked him back if there hadn't been the danger of getting into as much trouble herself.

Before they left the house Dominic shuffled through the morning post. 'There's a letter, look, for you.'

'For *me*?' Rose snatched it from him, beaming.

'Anyone I know?'

She ignored him, tucking the envelope into her blazer pocket, but adding, because she had her mother's kindness, 'I might show you later, okay?'

As Dominic crossed the M25 the glorious spring day promised by the forecasters – clear skies, light winds, temperatures rising to sixteen – began to push through the mist like some ravishing oil painting emerging through an insipid overlay of watercolour. He felt, as always, a deep reluctance at the thought of the hour or so it would take to shoulder-barge the hangar doors, tug the Cessna out on to the Tarmac and carry out the necessary checks prior to radioing for permission to take off. Enthralled as some members of his flying group were with such technical ritual, Dominic's part-ownership of the little plane had always been about the pure joy of being in the air. In the immediate aftermath of Maggie's death he had, on a couple of occasions, skipped every safety check in the book – ailerons, elevators, lights, oil, avgas, the lot – bumping along the grassy runway with no precaution other than the clearance to do so. No one would know, he had reasoned. No one would care. But the second time he did it, on a loop round the Isle of Wight, a storm had blown up from across the Channel. For half an hour he had had to fly by his instruments alone, which he had managed, sweating with concentration, drawing on the advanced lessons he had taken for just such an emergency. Buffeted in the cramped cockpit, the rain splatting against the screen, he had willed the plane on, his heart swelling with a desire to survive, not just for Rose – of *course* for Rose – but for himself.

That day Dominic's outing did not disappoint. The sky was the densest blue, the sun glaring even through his sunglasses. A thousand feet below, the ordered map of southern England was predominantly rural rather than urban – a green feast of a world, embroidered with the silvery sinews of rivers and motorways and the darker, more geometric lines of its hedges and ploughed fields. Houses clustered round churches like pebbles round a rock, their pedestrian colours studded with the occasional emerald and turquoise jewels of games pitches and swimming-pools.

Dominic turned east, tracking the lower ridge of the North Downs, letting the sides of the control stick float between his palms. In the distance to his right he could make out the thick, ominous shimmer of yellow-grey hovering over London; smog trapped by high air pressure, voluntary human suffocation. Dominic shuddered, nosing the plane south instead, rejoicing in the simple power of being able to turn his back on it. He began to rise higher, until the sheep in the fields were white flecks and the lakes of the chalk pits fingerprint smudges of blue. His heart, his hopes, soared with the plane; such a jewel of a day, so full of beauty and promise; a day, he mused, releasing a sudden involuntary chuckle, when even Maggie might have been prepared to swallow one of her travel-sickness tablets and come along for the ride.

Chapter Eight

Theresa kept within arm's reach of the barrier as she circled the rink, trying her best to glide rather than stagger, as Charlotte was managing a few yards in front of her. Behind them, somewhere among the moving crowd, Sam and George were ricocheting off each other and the edge of the rink as if ineptitude merely added to the thrill of trying to stay upright. Charlotte had only skated on ahead at Theresa's insistence. She was wearing a blue scarf, which flapped among the brilliant auburn tumble of her hair, and had the too-straight back and legs of an amateur but was still graceful, clearly having mastered the knack, which Henry liked to go on about on skiing holidays, of transferring weight to achieve momentum rather than actually moving one's legs. It boiled down to *letting go*, Henry said, allowing instinct to overrule intellect. Which was a fine theory, Theresa mused, steering her aching ankles towards the side for yet another breather, but took no account of the importance of self-preservation; driving, shopping, tackling laundry and marauding children – some silly accident, and the world as she knew it would cease to turn.

She was still catching her breath when Charlotte threaded her way across the ice to join her at the barrier. 'Are you okay? Have you had enough? Shall we sit down? This is brilliant of you, by the way, Theresa, asking us out like this – a mid-week treat, getting the boys together – absolutely *brilliant.*'

'I'd love a cup of tea,' Theresa admitted, wishing her

motives for the impromptu entertainment were as pure as they seemed. Bits were pure, like enjoying Charlotte's company and wanting to do something supportive in the face of the gossip still rippling between the buggies, dogs and bicycles at the school gates, gossip that had made her own tittle-tattle at the theatre the previous week seem positively innocent. One woman who barely knew Charlotte had used the word 'abuse' to a spellbound throng awaiting the end of orchestra practice, adding knowingly that such things always began 'in the home'. When Theresa had said rot and Sam was basically a good boy going through a bad patch – painfully shy, cut up about his parents' separation – they had looked not so much ashamed as disappointed, as if something truly enjoyable had been snatched away.

George's summary of the hiatus – that Rose was stuck-up and Sam an idiot – had struck Theresa as infinitely more likely and honest. Having delivered this verdict, her eldest's attentions had switched, with refreshing speed, to outrage at a spell on the substitutes' bench and a dogged resumption of negotiations to be allowed to give up the trumpet. When Theresa broached the skating plan he had even tried to use that as leverage, saying if she wanted him to befriend an idiot there had to be a pay-back. 'McDonald's,' Theresa had retorted, using a sharp tone to mask her admiration. 'Chips and nuggets afterwards can be the pay-back. And on the subject of music lessons, since we need to give a term's notice, you're committed to the end of the summer anyway.'

The impure aspect of her invitation to Charlotte and Sam was something Theresa had been doing her best not to think about and related to survival instincts of a baser and far more calculated kind than those impeding her prowess on the ice rink. Staying close to the enemy, her mother would have called it. There was no fresh evidence for worry, only the two pencil lines in the diary and a tension that came and went, sometimes feeling real and sometimes not. But if something did happen – some development in the crush or whatever the hell it was, if it even existed – Theresa wanted to be near enough to know it, to *smell* it, as surely as an animal scents its own doom.

'Oh, look, Theresa, look – they're having *such* fun. Quite like the old days,' exclaimed Charlotte, setting down two Styrofoam cups of tea.

'The great thing about boys,' remarked Theresa drily, 'is that generally they don't *talk* they just *do*, and if the doing works . . .' she waved in the direction of Sam and George, who had borrowed Charlotte's scarf and were using it to tow each other round the rink '. . . everything else falls into place.'

Charlotte carefully tore off the corner of a paper sachet of sugar and tipped it into her tea. 'This is so what Sam needs after the ghastliness of last week.' She paused, shaking the sachet, steeling herself to describe what had hitherto been too awful for release, even to Martin, though he had phoned to apologize after her dawn message, admitting coldly but decently that if there was blame for Sam's appalling lapse in behaviour they did indeed share it. 'In Miss Brigstock's office, all of them there – Rose, her father, the *counsellor* – with Sam having done such despicable things and everybody thinking it's my fault . . .'

'Of course it's not your fault.'

'Yeah, right.' Charlotte smiled sadly. 'It's because he's been unhappy, of course.'

'Of course,' cut in Theresa, briskly. 'Everybody knows that's why.'

'And if a child isn't happy, whose fault is it?'

Theresa, catching George's eye as he sailed past their

table in pursuit of Sam and the scarf, waved both arms, secretly glad of the distraction. There might not have been abuse as such, not as the hateful orchestra woman had suggested, but there had been trouble in the Turner household, all right, and Sam had borne the brunt of it. What was more he had always been the centre of his mother's world, which was a dangerous place for any child.

'And yours wouldn't have done it, would they?' persisted Charlotte, with endearing frankness. 'Your kids wouldn't have twisted Rose's arm, would they? And it had to be *her* of all people, didn't it? The girl without a *mother*.' Charlotte groaned. 'You should have seen the way that man looked at me – the father. It was . . . *deathly*, like . . . like I suppose I would have looked at him had it been the other way round,' she conceded glumly, dropping her face into her hands. 'You know he viewed my house, don't you? Or rather *didn't* because he hated it so much on sight.'

'Dominic Porter? No, I didn't . . . Sorry to laugh, oh dear, what a small world . . . Oh dear.' Theresa sat back in her chair, shaking her head. 'But I hope, deathly looks aside, he was reasonable . . . I mean, everybody knows children are capable of all sorts of things.'

'I suppose he was, if silence is reasonable.'

'Apparently he never talks. Naomi says she's tried several times and got nowhere. Poor man, after what he's been through . . . He works for one of those big American banks, yet he's always dropping Rose off, isn't he? And he was at the swimming gala the other day.'

'Well, bravo – I'm sorry,' Charlotte added, in response to Theresa's look of surprise, 'but just because he's widowed and a single dad everybody thinks he's marvellous or heroic or something. Whereas a single mother, even one whose husband had *died* instead of running off with a younger model, would get nothing like the same sort of admiration for doing ten times what he manages. Though I feel sorry for him, of course,' she added quickly, 'what he must have been through and so on.'

'His brother is that actor,' said Theresa, deciding it prudent to change the subject, 'Benedict Porter, the one who was in that thing with the dog and the two doctors. Oh, and George says Rose is very stuck-up,' she offered next, judging from the scornful expression on Charlotte's face that this might be a surer route to consolation.

Charlotte beamed at once. 'I've always liked your son. And I like him even more now,' she murmured, tracking the boys who had given up the scarf game in favour of imitating speed skaters, bending double, left hands pinned behind their backs. 'This will cheer Sam up so much. Although, funnily enough, he does seem quite a lot better already – or at least calmer. I made him write a letter to the wretched Rose, which he hated, but he did it, and after a bit of early resistance he's been going to school like a lamb. This Mr Dawson, he seems a good thing. Sam has seen him a couple of times, though I've no idea what they talk about.' An uncertain laugh escaped her, triggered by the thought of her son opening up to a stranger, pouring out his heart in a way he never would to her.

'The letter thing sounds like a great move,' Theresa assured Charlotte, seeing the darkening expression and puzzling over how she could ever have regarded a creature in such an obvious state of torment as a threat of any kind. 'I've tried to get more out of George about the general situation at school, but as I said, the problem with these males is that they don't *talk*.' She pulled a face. 'Speaking of which, how is it going with that lovely new man of yours?'

'Lovely?' Charlotte, unaware of having said anything so

enthusiastic or unguarded about Tim Croft, glanced up from her tea in surprise.

'The estate agent.'

'I know who you mean, dumbo. I just had the impression that you – everybody – had written Tim off as unsuitable.'

'Nonsense,' Theresa retorted, justifying the lie because she had genuinely changed her mind. 'I can't speak for Naomi or Josephine, but personally I don't think it matters what somebody *is*. It's how a man *behaves* that counts.' She paused, as her thoughts looped back wearily, reluctantly, to the new invisible shadow over her marriage. Of course Henry would behave well. He always had, he always would. Hadn't he been the one to pull *her* back on course all those years before? Hadn't his faith in their union always been stronger than hers? Hadn't he wept tears of joy holding each of their slithery newborns in his arms, gasping that her love and her labour *completed* him? That couldn't change, surely, not with one silly crush, if indeed there even was a silly crush . . . and weren't crushes normal anyway? Hadn't she got a bit starry-eyed for a time over the young music teacher who had insisted George join the jazz band, revelling, just a little, in the man's praise of her son's powerful lungs and quick fingers? Yes, she had been a shade smitten there, all right. But then he had got engaged to a flautist and left the school, oblivious, quite rightly, to any flutterings his dark-eyed sincerity had provoked in the heart of a woman guilty only of being overtired and looking twice where once should have done. Such things were *normal*, blips in a rhythm, nothing to stop a heart.

Charlotte had scrambled off her seat and was crouching at Theresa's feet. 'I think your laces are too loose.' She pushed up the sleeves of her jumper. 'Maybe if I tightened them—'

Theresa let out a small shriek, trying to lift the skates out of reach without causing physical injury to Charlotte's arms. 'Any tighter and I'll get *gangrene*. There's no circulation, I tell you, just heat and pain.'

'Let me see,' Charlotte insisted, settling on to her knees and pulling Theresa's left foot on to them. 'Yes, you see, it's loose at this bit,' she patted the ankle, 'and too tight here. Whereas if . . .' She was soon expertly unhooking, tugging and retying the laces. 'There. Now the other one, please.'

Theresa submitted in silence. The first boot felt considerably better. She leant back in her chair, studying her friend through half-closed eyes, her affection in full flow again. 'You know you're very good-looking, don't you?' she blurted. 'You're very good-looking and that's power. You should use it wisely.'

Charlotte snorted, keeping her head down. 'And you should shut up – shut up and *keep still.*'

For a few moments neither spoke. Charlotte carried on with the task she had assigned herself, inwardly marvelling that a compliment could sound like a warning and at the recent predilection people had developed to remark on her looks. She had never felt less attractive, less sure of herself, in her adult life. Glimpsing her body between the folds of her towel in the bathroom mirror, these days, seeing the sharp points of her elbows and knees, the loud, exuberant topping of her hair, she sometimes felt as if the ugly little girl of her school days was re-emerging, that she had never really left her behind.

'I just meant,' Theresa pressed on, 'now that you're single, you'll probably find yourself fighting men off . . . bees round the proverbial honeypot, et cetera.'

'I haven't moved to another planet,' Charlotte protested, laughing as she tied the last double knot and returned to her seat. 'I'm just getting divorced.'

Theresa sipped her tasteless, now tepid tea, fighting the urge to say that from what she could see divorce *was* another planet – a different game plan, different rules, different priorities; that by separating from Martin, Charlotte had upset the balance not only of her life but of those closest to her, and they should ignore that fact at their peril.

'I wasn't a *honeypot* before, and I'm certainly not one now,' continued Charlotte, merrily. 'My history as regards men is . . .' She hesitated. 'Well, never mind what it is.'

'No, go on,' pressed Theresa, truly curious, since Charlotte had never disclosed much about life before Martin.

Charlotte shrugged. 'A couple of crap boyfriends and then . . .' She had plucked the plastic spoon out of her empty cup and was bending it, as if fascinated by its flexibility. 'Then Martin.' The spoon snapped and Charlotte dropped the two pieces into her empty cup, adding, in a much lighter tone, 'The fact is, Theresa, dear, I don't *want* anybody particularly, and after what I had to put up with who could blame me? What I do want, more than anything, is to be okay on my own and to have some *fun*, which is why I'm having dinner on Friday with the "lovely" Tim Croft who was sweet enough to send me roses after I blew him out because of the hoo-ha with Sam –'

'Roses?' Theresa clapped her hands in delight at evidence of such an advanced state of romance. 'And dinner? But that's fantastic. I do hope you're splashing out on something fabulous to wear.'

'No, I am not,' retorted Charlotte, grinning. 'He can take me as I am, in my standby black trousers and an ironed shirt.'

'Oh, don't be such a spoilsport.' Theresa giggled, truly relaxed now, wagging a finger. 'I thought you said you wanted some *fun*.'

Charlotte pulled a face. 'As everyone keeps reminding me, I *am* almost *forty* –'

'Hah,' Theresa interrupted, on fire now with goodwill and self-confidence. 'On that score I've been meaning to say that I think Henry's idea of us helping you throw a party was inspired.'

'No, no, no!' Charlotte cried, holding up both hands. 'Thank you, that's sweet, but as I said when your dear husband first made the offer, I should hate it. I shall book a table in a restaurant or something, invite a few friends and probably – if I can face it – my mother.'

'Well, if you change your mind,' pressed Theresa, the generosity coming even more easily now that Charlotte had turned her down.

'The only possible change will be deciding to ignore the bloody thing altogether.'

'Now, that I won't allow. What about the new place that's just won an award? Contini's . . . No, Santini's.'

'Theresa, June is months away,' pleaded Charlotte.

'Well, a place like that gets booked up so don't leave it too late. Ah, here come the boys, starving, I expect. Are you starving, darlings?'

George exchanged a scowl with Sam. He hated it when his mother darlinged him, and it was even worse when she did it to his friends. 'Five more minutes,' he yelled, shoving Sam, who shoved him back as they set off towards the ice, galloping precariously on the points of their skates.

By Friday the weather had built to a climax of such unseasonal warmth that pundits were issuing a new spate of warnings about global warming and hosepipe bans. When Tim, in response to the groans of his sweltering colleagues, tried to turn off the heating in the office the control knob came away in his hands. Too busy to deal with it himself, he asked Savitri to get on to the gas company while he rolled up his sleeves to tackle the list of phone calls that needed to be got through before an afternoon of viewings. A spell of spring sunshine, and the housing market went mad; it happened every year yet took him by surprise each time.

Tim moved round his desk as he talked, transferring the phone from ear to ear, pausing to make notes of numbers and appointments and adding to the doodle round his list of things to buy for the dinner he was cooking Charlotte. *Fillet steak, mushrooms, shallots, cream, rice, rocket, cheeses and biscuits, fruit, champagne, wine, FLOWERS, CANDLES –* the latter two items warranting capitals because they were precisely the sort of important details he might forget.

That he wasn't a romantic had been one of Phoebe's favourite accusations; all of his faults – not remembering important dates, not saying the right thing at the right time, not closing the loo door, not noticing new outfits or hair-styles – had served as ammunition for this main theme. Girls cared about that stuff and Tim was determined to show, at this tantalizingly poised stage of his new relationship, that he could more than deliver on it.

The cookbook in which he found the recipe had given him a shock, though. Phoebe *had* used the gift once, he remembered, not as a source of culinary inspiration but as a missile during one of their endless labyrinthine rows, hurling it across the kitchen from over her head with both hands, like a footballer slinging in a throw from the touchline. Tim had ducked successfully, then banged his head on the sharp corner of a cupboard as he straightened. In a reflex of regret, Phoebe had hurtled across the kitchen to croon over the bruise. Minutes later they were tearing at each other's clothes and lumbering between the worktops like first-timers, until Phoebe found anchorage against the kitchen table, clinging to it on her front, like a sunbather on a slab of rock. Christ, what a session. Christ.

Uncomfortably stirred, Tim had briefly considered trying to find another source of practical assistance for the evening. But then the *boeuf Stroganoff* recipe had caught his eye, looking so classy and simple; and not using it because of some ancient sexual memory of his wife had seemed pathetic. He would have new, even better memories soon, he had reminded himself excitedly, if he played his cards right.

After the main course he planned to offer cheese rather than a pudding. He would decorate the board with fruit as Phoebe had always done on the rare occasions they had had guests – sliced kiwi, a small bunch of grapes, maybe a plum or two – something he and Charlotte could pick at and would look pretty. As far as Tim was concerned a more substantial dessert was out of the question, not because of any limitation to his culinary skills but because, while alcohol had never been known to dampen his energies, too much food, particularly when he was nervous, had been known to lead to all sorts of horrors – cramps, indigestion, *wind*, God forbid. Besides which, wine slipped down so easily with a nibble of cheese. And wine, Tim was sure, was going to be key to the delivery of the prospect he so cherished: Charlotte with her defences down, Charlotte unleashed.

All the phone calls went smoothly until Tim got to those that mattered most: Mrs Burgess, thanks to the report of a nit-picking surveyor, wanted to lower her offer on Charlotte's house by a mighty ten thousand pounds, while Mrs Stowe confirmed that they were sticking with the private-sale route and wouldn't require the services of his or any other agency in Wandsworth. They had had a private offer in the pipeline for weeks, she confessed, and her husband was now cross that she had tempted them both to deviate it from it. Tim fought as best he could, marshalling the calm and charm that had seen him through countless tight spots in the past. Some forty minutes later, however, his efforts had secured only the measly compromise that both women would call back if they changed their minds. Short of a miracle, Charlotte's beloved Chalkdown Road was as good as lost.

Tim's spirits were so deflated that he forgot two sets of keys for his afternoon of viewings and managed to leave the supermarket without plums or cheese biscuits. He didn't realize these omissions until he was running seriously late in his preparations for the evening, standing guard over a complicated combination of boiling ingredients, which were supposed to form the basis of the sauce but which refused to *reduce* as the recipe promised. Thanks to the anxiety this caused, with the cooking steam and a hasty, too-hot shower, he was also sweating, so profusely that he could already see a second, cooler shower was going to have to be crammed into his dinner preparations, along with a freshly ironed shirt.

With the sauce obstinately retaining its look of unappetizing soup – copious, thin, lumpy – Tim turned the ring up to maximum and spent a few minutes rummaging in the dusty backs of cupboards for some form of biscuit to serve with the cheese. Clutching an open pack of crumbling Ryvita, he returned his attentions to the hob only to find that his unpromising sauce had 'reduced' at last, to an unusable crust of speckled brown.

Dear Sam,
Thank you for your letter. It was nice of you even if your mum made you write it, which I bet she did. The only letters I get are

from my stamp club, which I don't like much to be honest as I don't
really want to collect them any more but Dad won't let me give it
up. I've got loads and loads and I can't be bothered to put them in
an album. I tell my dad I have and hide them in a drawer. He says
everyone should have hobbies but I don't really apart from writing,
which I REALLY like I don't know why. I can also do crochet
because my mum taught me. My dad's hobby is flying, which is
quite cool, I suppose, except I get travel sickness, like my mum
used to as well.

Anyway, thanks for writing. I am sorry I got you into so much
trouble but you were asking for it.

Your sinscerely,
Rose Porter
P.S. Please don't tell anyone that I wrote.

Inspired, perhaps, by Theresa's gleeful enthusiasm on her
behalf, when Friday evening came Charlotte found herself
jettisoning the safe black trousers and ironed shirt for a
crushed blue velvet skirt and a loose silk top. Streaking green
across her eyelids to accentuate the sharp emerald of her
eyes, slipping her feet into a pair of slingback high heels,
she studied the effects in her full-length mirror warily, half
expecting the ghost of Bootface to skip out from behind
the glass.

So this was being happy again, she marvelled, swivelling
first one way then the other, admiring the umbrella twirl of
the velvet panels and the elegance the fine mesh of her black
tights managed to lend her too-thin calves and bony knees.
This was *living* – relishing life, instead of faltering like a
rambler without a compass. She had direction at last: dear
friends, a suitor who sent roses, a prospective house! Sam
was still quiet, too quiet, but had made no further mention
of being unpopular. Even more encouragingly, three purple

stars for excellence had recently appeared in his homework book and that evening he had asked – *asked!* – if he could go to after-school club an extra afternoon the following Thursday, when Charlotte only worked a morning shift and positively looked forward to breaking the tedium of domestic chores with an excursion to the school gates.

Tucking in a peeping bra strap as she hurried downstairs, Charlotte admitted a rare moment of self-congratulation at her own part in bringing about this small but seismic shift in her son's state of well-being – holding firm about facing the ordeal of school, insisting on the skating outing when he didn't want to go, not quizzing him about the counsellor. She had taken initiatives, taken control, got it right for once *on her own*.

Jessica arrived on a bicycle this time, nosing it into the hall so that Charlotte had to step out of the way as she opened the door. She wore a grey beanie pulled down over her eyebrows, which caused her wispy hair to bunch out round her ears. Strapped to her back was a bulky rucksack that bumped against the wall as she wrestled with the bike.

'Is it okay to park it in here? Only I don't have a lock.'

'It's fine,' Charlotte murmured, lunging for the handlebars to prevent them gouging fresh holes into the already battered paintwork. 'Sam's in the bath. After that he's got some homework to do, if you wouldn't mind making sure . . . ?'

'No problem.' Jessica tugged off the hat. 'I've got a load of stuff to do as well.' She slung the rucksack on to the floor and scratched vigorously at her scalp. 'Bloody coursework. Hey, Mrs Turner, you look really *nice*.'

'Thank you.' Charlotte blushed. 'I won't be too late,' she added, hurrying out of the door and thus being spared the merriment that flashed across the teenager's face.

*

Outside Tim's house Charlotte paused and breathed deeply. She could smell something cooking, something nice. Martin had never been any good in the kitchen — greasy fry-ups, the occasional vast, messy, complicated stir-fry, which she rarely enjoyed and usually resented having to clear up. Suddenly it felt inordinately special that a man should have volunteered this simple compliment of preparing her a meal.

Tim opened the door so quickly that she feared he had been waiting on the other side, maybe even watching her profile through the mottled glass. He was wearing a pink shirt, open at the collar, and black trousers with sharp fresh creases that disappeared at the bulge of his thighs. As he fussed round her, easing off her jacket and warning about a state of total unreadiness, she noticed a pair of polished black leather tasselled loafers parked tidily at the bottom of the stairs. Her host, she observed in the same instant, was wearing neither socks nor shoes. Minor details — microscopic, irrelevant — but they snagged at Charlotte's imagination. She didn't like tassels on shoes. And something about the sight of his bare feet, the toes thickly haired, the second strikingly longer than the big one, was also unsettling, almost too intimate, as if he was divulging information beyond her willingness to process it.

On entering the kitchen, however, her reactions yo-yoed back again. The food smelt so good and everything was laid out beautifully: two saucepans puffing steam on a gleaming stainless-steel hob, a vase of freesias on the table, with napkins, wine glasses, cutlery and a single red candle, already lit. She was still taking it in when a pop sounded behind her and Tim pressed a fizzing flute of champagne into her hand.

'To you,' he murmured, holding her gaze as they chinked glasses, 'and to whatever the future holds. I am entirely yours to command.'

'Well, I'll certainly drink to the future.' Charlotte laughed, pulling a face as the first sip sent bubbles bouncing up her nose.

'It's a rather cobbled-together sort of meal, I'm afraid,' Tim confessed, putting down his glass and flicking switches on a miniature CD-player parked between the toaster and the kettle. 'It wasn't supposed to be. Why is it that recipes always end up being more complicated than they first appear? I had something of a sauce crisis, though I hope I've made up for it with cream.'

'I'm sure it'll be lovely.' A lilting ballad was coming out of the CD-player, a man's voice, a black man, soulful, engaging, familiar. '*Classic Love Songs*,' Charlotte read out, scanning the names of the artists listed on the cover and chuckling at the sudden, obvious absurdity of humankind – masters of microchips and space travel – expending so much creative energy expounding on and trying to understand a single emotion. As if love was a riddle that could be cracked if come at the right way when, as people like her knew only too well, it was a mercurial, whimsical, unsustainable, unreliable *feeling*, dependent on mood and circumstance and certain brain chemicals that one day scientists would probably (she hoped) bottle and sell over chemists' counters.

'What's funny?'

'Nothing.' Charlotte slid the box back towards the CD-player.

'You look fantastic.'

'Thank you.' Seeking escape from his disarming stare of appreciation, she found her gaze inadvertently returning to the bare toes.

Tim, realizing it, performed a little hop of embarrassment, as if he would tuck the offending items out of sight, were it acrobatically possible. 'Sorry – got late showering, couldn't immediately locate socks, the rice was boiling over and then you rang the bell.'

'Oh, but it really doesn't matter,' Charlotte cried, thinking what a cluck she had been to give the informality even a moment's thought, how horribly stiff and prudishly out of practice she was at the business of getting to know someone. She was about to assure him that it was too warm for socks anyway when a thick white froth began to spill over the edge of a saucepan.

Tim leapt into action, emitting expletives, while Charlotte turned her back tactfully and made a big to-do of sniffing the freesias and working her way through her champagne. She wanted, badly, to ask about progress vis-à-vis houses, but feared it might sound callous. She would wait until the food had been safely served, she decided, obeying Tim's command to top up her glass, when his confidence had settled and the mood between them was more mellow.

Instead, sitting knee to knee over full plates at the small table, with the groomed stubble round Tim's mouth glistening in the flicker of the candlelight, Charlotte experienced a fresh, irksome onslaught of nerves. She drank hard to keep them at bay, warning that she had come in a taxi and would need one to get home. Tim, filling her glass, said he would have been disappointed if she hadn't and how important it was to let one's hair down. A pause followed, sufficiently resonant for Charlotte to shy away again from mentioning Mrs Burgess or Chalkdown Road and to embark on a quest for information about his upbringing with the electrician father and a mother who, as it transpired, cleaned people's homes.

Tim relaxed visibly under the attention, recounting a tale of such an obviously deprived childhood compared to her own that it seemed to Charlotte more and more unaccept-

148

able that she should not like him very much indeed for having endured it. By the time the last of the champagne had been despatched, along with a bottle of red and every last morsel of his delicious beef and mushroom stew, she had been stirred almost to tears on several occasions.

'So what happened when your dad's business went bust?'

'We got kicked out for not paying the rent. I had to leave school to get a job. Don't look like that – *sorry* for me – it wasn't so bad. I mean, we were happy enough. I don't see them much these days and my sister still gets on my wick, but that's families for you, isn't it?'

'Absolutely . . . families . . .' Charlotte rolled her eyes, wondering suddenly if he really was going to leave any advancement of the situation in her hands, whether she was up to it. The doubt continued until Tim had cleared the small table to make way for a splendid palette of cheese and fruit. Reaching for a grape, Charlotte found her fingers making contact with his instead.

'Charlotte.' He held just one finger, stroking and tugging it gently.

Here we go, Charlotte thought, staring down on the scene as if from a great height, at her and Tim at the little table, hands linked beneath the flickering candle. Here we go. Go with the flow . . . Go on, move on, go . . .

'Charlotte, you know what you do to me, don't you?' His voice was husky, his eyes hooded. 'I can't stop thinking about you. Not for one moment of one minute. I've tried, but I can't. Please . . .'

He had her whole hand now and was leading her through an archway connecting the kitchen-diner to the sitting room. The journey seemed to take a long time. Charlotte leant back a little, enjoying the feeling of being pulled, persuaded, of abdicating control. They passed a print of a leopard, crouching amid tall grass, the sides of its mouth curled to reveal the white scythes of its teeth; then a photo of a young woman in shorts and a loose T-shirt, long bleached hair blowing across her eyes, dimpled knees, her feet buried in messy mounds of sand. Up ahead, beyond Tim's arm – still stretched in the act of pulling her – was a sofa, dark red, velveteen. It felt soft to lie on, almost too soft, sinking under her spine like a hammock even before he was on top of her.

He moves inside me and suddenly stops, remaining poised on his raised arms. 'You move,' he says, 'when you want. You move.'

I lie still, holding the moment in all its perfection, holding him.

It has taken months to get this far, to get this intimate, this confident. We have argued – about the literary worth of Ulysses, Habeas Corpus, *state education and whether washing-up is best soaked overnight. We have borne each other's moods, his silent tension before a work deadline or a first night, my premenstrual snapping, the glumness before the dutiful necessity of a visit home. We have danced and walked and chased buses; we have sweated and kissed through hangovers, headaches, phlegmy coughs; we have shared secrets and laughed and laughed and laughed, at bad films, at Eve, at Pete, Martin's mate, at ourselves.*

Slowly I tilt my pelvis up, and back. He closes his eyes. His arms are trembling. The moment is moving on, as it must.

He exhales slowly. Keeping his eyes fixed on mine, he lowers himself at last and starts to respond, every so often turning his head, like a swimmer mid-stroke, seeking a gulp of air. 'Never leave me,' he whispers. 'Never leave me. I love you.'

My ear burns in the heat of his breath. 'Never,' I echo, my voice no more than a gasp, but my heart loud and pounding with the lovely certainty that we are at the beginning still, with the best yet to come.

I save my own first milestone declaration for afterwards, pressing the three words into the salty moistness of his chest; I would brand his skin with them if I could, directly over the spot that screens his heart. Entwined, the sweat chilling on our skin, we lie quietly, basking in an aftermath that seems to transcend physical release to a state of communion that feels far holier than anything I have ever come close to in church.

Above all, I feel lucky. No one else could ever love, or be loved, so much; certainly not Eve, with her new crush on a third-year rugby star, or Pete, who changes women more frequently than his underwear, and certainly not our respective parents – Martin's with their petty quarrels and caravan holidays, mine with the now closed sad history of separate beds and separate meals, a shared life shrivelled by betrayal. As to how this history impinged upon my childhood, I have revealed the gist but not the detail. The once sharp outline of the two figures lying on the dusty matting, the hairs on my father's bare thighs dark against the white tail of his shirt, has faded with time and I have no desire to bring it back into focus. And no need now either, with this new system of faith, love making sense of lust, the lost fairytale of my earliest memory retrieved.

Chapter Nine

Martin and Cindy's housewarming took place on a blustery March evening when temperatures suddenly spiralled down into what felt like a last blast of an attempt at a decent winter before the start of British Summer Time the following day. Theresa had already altered the clocks, a somewhat paranoid anticipation of the time change that stemmed from a chaotic transition the year before when she had deposited the younger boys at a birthday party as the entertainer was finishing, and George, having missed almost an entire rugby game, spent the afternoon sobbing inconsolably into his pillow.

'We haven't had any snow,' she complained, as Henry nosed around the Rotherhithe development looking for a parking slot. 'Not one flake, do you realize that?'

'Yes, we did, in January – that week the boiler packed up and the blocked gutter ruined the wall in the sitting room.'

'There was hardly any though, was there? Not enough to build a snowman. I'll never forget poor Alfie trying and the others watching through the window. He was using handfuls of mud in the end and got quite upset, do you remember?'

'Indeed I do,' murmured Henry, although his mind was on Charlotte rather than their son – wishing there was some way she could have been invited to the party too. He hadn't seen her for weeks, which, with Theresa's bloodhound capacity for scenting trouble, was probably just as well. Although, if anything, this paucity of contact seemed to be making his obsession worse – terrible, wonderful, graphic, stealthy thoughts assailed him all the time; and with Suffolk coming up, they had a proper focus now. For while denying the relevance of Charlotte's holiday plans, Henry's imagination had in fact gone into overdrive, nurturing the prospect of long walks and cups of tea, and maybe, if the nights were cold enough, curling up in front of roaring log fires with a glass or two of wine. It would be a chance – possibly his only chance – to get to know her better, to find out if what he felt really had some justification, some reciprocity.

Exact dates for his week of study were still moving around the diary, propelled by clinic commitments and Henry's own terror of showing his hand. With the fantasies, the uncertainty, he was sleeping badly, and yet there was an excitement about the situation that launched him into each new day on an adrenalin high equivalent, he imagined (he had not experimented like most of his fellow medical students), to the ingestion of recreational drugs. It was in the early evenings that he was truly tired, his concentration in tatters; so much so that when Theresa had announced, her tone studiedly light, that Charlotte was no longer seeing her estate agent and wasn't that typical, he had felt such a rush of energy that he half expected it to lift him off the sofa.

Instead he had managed, with a supreme effort of will, to contain himself to a raised eyebrow, a tut and 'Typical', then to enquire in a languid drawl suggestive of deep indifference, if she could think of a word of seven letters ending in *r* that might mean explorer.

'Pioneer,' Theresa had shot back, returning her gaze to the television, an impatient re-crossing of her legs the only remote hint that she had picked up on anything untoward.

Henry had slowly filled in the letters, then let the crossword blur. The estate agent – bouncy walk, bouncy hair. He had spotted the fellow several times, and for Charlotte to dump him certainly showed the triumph of good taste over desperation, loneliness, rebound syndrome or whatever the hell had prompted her to get involved with such a creature in the first place. Of course she was going to make mistakes: she was adrift, alone and with the sort of fragile beauty that provoked a protective impulse the like of which Henry had only ever before experienced towards his children. Theresa had never been the sort of woman to inspire such reactions. Too much gallantry or sentiment from any man, the remotest suggestion that she needed 'looking after', was guaranteed to make sparks fly.

Which was something to admire, Henry mused, watching his wife's pale face in the wing-mirror, hair blasting across her cheeks as she beckoned him into a tight fit of a parking space between a Porsche and a stone wall. And where could anything with Charlotte possibly lead anyway? A platonic bond? An illicit affair? *Leaving* Theresa? It was unthinkable.

Unthinkable, and yet people did it all the time. People like Martin, Henry reminded himself, as his friend opened the door looking ten years younger in loose dark trousers and a charcoal grey T-shirt, grinning like a cat that had had its whiskers dunked in the proverbial cream. Cindy floated up behind him, smiling more shyly, indisputably glorious in a silky blue dress gathered under her ample bustline and falling in watery shimmers to her knees.

'So this is what you meant by "dress smart casual", is it?' Henry accused them, glancing from one to the other and feeling a spurt of pity for Theresa, who had suffered uncharacteristic agonies over what to wear, veering eventually towards the casual end of the spectrum with a pair of trousers that, these days, cut too deeply into her hips (though

Henry had dutifully denied as much when challenged) and which he knew she would now be regretting bitterly.

The gathering was modest but very *slick*, Henry decided, as a passing waiter pressed glasses of Kir Royale into their hands and they were ushered into the carpeted open-plan living space, decorated in minimalist style with towering lithe flower arrangements in its corners and large panels of modern art across the walls. The furniture had been pushed back to the perimeter, apart from a baby grand piano, around which a scattering of other early arrivals hovered. These included Sam, looking refreshingly unslick in a pair of trailing jeans and a crumpled dark green sweatshirt. At the sight of Theresa and Henry he broke away from the group and loped across the room, grinning with evident relief.

'Hey. Horrid, isn't it?'

'Sam!' scolded Theresa, chuckling.

Sam swept his fingers through his hair, pulling out the last bits to create the haywire look to his fringe, which was working really well that afternoon, thanks to some experimentation with aerosols and a tub of wax at Cindy's dressing-table. His mother didn't have a dressing-table. She put her makeup on in the bathroom and kept her hairdryer in a chest of drawers. Cindy's table was an Aladdin's cave in comparison, as was the *en suite*, where every surface was lined with enough foams, scrubs, oils, conditioners, salts and moisturizers to equip a small chemist. Forbidden normally to venture into this sanctuary, even for a pee, Sam had taken advantage of an hour on his own – while Martin and Cindy collected drink and glasses from the off-licence – to have a squirt of almost every bottle.

'How's Mum?' ventured Theresa, judging it the safest line of enquiry among several that sprang to mind, then remembering the estate agent and having second thoughts.

'We just didn't hit it off,' had been Charlotte's only explanation before she had shifted the focus to Sam, explaining how much happier her son seemed and apologizing – needlessly – for a somewhat puzzling insistence that his thirteenth birthday the previous week pass without fuss. And he had rejected the idea of taking a friend to Suffolk too, she had explained, unwittingly scuppering Theresa's hopes of sending George.

Sam was frowning and fiddling with his hair, as if the enquiry about his mother presented quite a challenge.

Seeing the hesitation, Henry thought wildly, Charlotte is unhappy. She feels as I do and is suffering.

'Mum's fine,' Sam declared at last, 'except her bookshop man was ill again today so she had to bring me here early. She was cross because she's only supposed to work every other Saturday and only in the morning, not the whole day.'

'Poor Mum. And I gather you've had a birthday, haven't you?' continued Theresa, brightly.

'Yup. We went to see the latest James Bond and Dad gave me an iPod.'

'Fantastic. A teenager, at long last, eh?'

A waiter arrived, bearing a tray of canapés, each one a Lilliputian version of a food traditionally designed to take up an entire dinner plate. Sam put up his hand and then, remembering his manners, snatched it away again so the adults could choose first. He slipped his fingers inside the back pocket of his jeans instead, feeling for the corner of the latest letter from Rose:

We are moving house soon. I like this one quite a lot but it will be cool not to have to catch the bus to school. I hate the bus. Felix always wants to sit next to me and he STINKS.

Beside the last word she had drawn a little cartoon face with the mouth turned down and the nose screwed up. Sam, who couldn't draw for toffee, thought it very clever and planned to tell her so in his reply. Defeated by the logistical challenge of stamps, postboxes and avoiding parental detection, they had taken to swapping notes during school. It was weird because in spite of doing this they didn't actually *talk* to each other, at least not about anything except pointless stuff like borrowing pencil-sharpeners and how long till the bell. But then Rose *was* weird and had been from the start. Once part of the reason Sam had felt compelled to twist her arm, it was now what he liked most about her.

When it was his turn Sam took two miniature pizzas and three baby hamburgers off the plate and shoved them into his mouth in one go. The adults were bored now, he could tell, looking over his head and twiddling their glasses. When George's dad remarked, licking his fingers, 'You've grown, mate, haven't you?' he responded with as polite a nod as he could manage, then shot off in search of his father and permission to retreat to their big double bed and the telly.

Theresa groaned. 'You shouldn't have said that. You know he's got a thing about being small.'

'Has he? How was I supposed to know that?'

'Everybody knows.'

'Do they? Well, poor little bugger, it's no wonder he's got a *thing* then, is it? Anyway, I said he'd *grown*, didn't I? Which he has . . . dramatically, I'd say.'

They were rescued from this unsatisfactory but, Theresa decided, pleasingly *normal* husband–wife exchange by Martin and Cindy, working their way round the clusters of guests like a pair of conjoined twins. When it got to their turn the four of them discussed, with vigour, the windy weather and the virtues of silk flowers versus dried. Henry could feel his wife's gentle contempt for both the trivial conversation and the juvenile inseparability of their hosts. It was like a radar signal, but visible only to him. Outwardly, she was warm, smiling and delighted, as was he. Pondering this and his own, rather more serious, state of emotional hypocrisy, Henry remembered suddenly a quote from Auden from his school days, about 'the sane, who know they are acting, and the insane, who think they are not'. At least I'm sane, he consoled himself, at least I know that.

As the pair moved away, duty done, and Theresa began to voice contempt – were they *barnacles?* Not to be able to *stand up* alone? What did Martin think he was proving with that skimpy T-shirt? – Henry found his own similarly critical reflexes softening towards understanding. A new woman, a new life, a clean slate, a second chance, reinvention . . . yes, he could understand the appeal of that, all right. Appearing to need to keep each other upright or not, the pair looked happy enough to him. And often, he reflected sadly, it was those most ready to knock happiness who were the least contented themselves.

Every so often the wind actually rocked the car. Charlotte found her hands leaping to the anchorage of the steering-wheel, as if she was trying to control her little vehicle in full flight instead of it being parked tight up against the kerbstone, with the engine off and the street empty. She felt secure under its domed roof, with the thump of the wind outside, and not too cold, even though the heating was off and there was a small hissing noise where air was pumping through the tiny crack at the top of the back window that didn't close properly. And it was quite nice to watch the way the trees writhed, to witness but not suffer the violence of tossing branches, cartwheeling dustbin lids and the two cones, which had been marking some hazard in the pavement but were now on their sides, rolling against the fence of the derelict church.

The last of the light was fading fast. The bloody remains of the sun streaked the sky above the slate tops of the houses and the flailing trees.

I am in a bubble, Charlotte thought, in my bubble car. Nothing can touch me. I am alone, but safe. Up ahead the yellow jasmine tumbling along the wall fronting the cottage had been joined by other dots of colour: candy pink roses and something blue – irises, or were they stocks? Could one stalk a house? Charlotte wondered. Was that what she was doing – trying to stay close to something loved but unattainable? She had taken her own house off the market now, left a message with the pretty Indian girl to pass on to Tim. It was a defeat, of course, the dreadful quibbling Mrs Burgess with her shopping list of faults, the limitations on her budget, the pain of falling for things one could not have, Sam's crushing lack of enthusiasm. She had surrendered at last, held up her hands, given in.

Tim had left her a message in return. *I am so sorry. Please call at once – any time – if you change your mind.* About the house business, of course, but Charlotte knew that he meant the other thing too, the thing that had ended on the night of the dinner, when the ghost of Martin . . . no – she corrected her thoughts – when the ghost of her *love* for Martin, known, remembered, but not *felt* for two decades, had risen out of the soft red cushions and smothered her to the point of screaming. She had screamed, hadn't she? There had been a noise certainly, sudden, shrill, nerve-jangling, like a screech of brakes. And Tim, sheeny-faced, heavy, grunting, pushing, lost in the final thrall of his climax, had pulled out in the same instant, spilling his cum half on her belly and half among the crumpled folds of her skirt.

Some deep, reflexive female part of her had felt violated. But it wasn't rape, of course. Charlotte knew that. In her newly discovered exuberant state she had led him that far, taken him, poor man, to the point of no return, never imagining that her own point of no return lay coiled inside, behind the new hope and the trying and the wine.

'Christ, Charlotte, what did I . . . ? Did I hurt . . . did I . . . ?' In different circumstances – in the absence, for instance, of the image of her twenty-year-old self, with her soon-to-be fiancé poised over her, inside her, ready to explode with love as well as physical desire – she might have pitied Tim enough to pat his beefy knee and murmur platitudes, allow some salvaging of his devastated dignity and pride. But Charlotte had been too devastated herself, too mown down by the onrush of the past, the living memory of what it had been to love – *really* to love – to be able to muster anything beyond a whimper. Tim had clutched at his belt buckle and scrabbled for a box of tissues, pulling out three at once, then dabbing at her stomach like someone attending in panic to a wound.

After that they had sat, like the strangers they were, waiting for her cab, lost in different mute incomprehension. When the cab was late, requiring a second phone call, drawing out the agony, Tim, stammering, had released the bad news about the Stowes' decision, saying it looked like they had had someone lined up for a private sale all along. He had meant to tell her before but hadn't wanted to ruin the evening, but now the evening was ruined anyway. He had done his best, he was sorry, there would be other houses, of course . . . other vendors, purchasers. He had gathered a bit of steam then, spurred on, perhaps, by the familiar solidity of the jargon of his trade, something to cling to amid the wreckage.

At home she had found Jessica asleep on the sofa, her laptop open, her books strewn across the carpet. Embarrassed to be woken, the girl scrambled for her possessions and shot off into the night on her bicycle, the rear light bouncing as she rode the bumps. Charlotte, her head icily – terrifyingly – clear, had gone straight from the doorstep to Sam's bedroom. He, too, was asleep, mouth open, showing the strong, even line of teeth that looked curiously manly against the still childish lips and the little-boy peachiness of his skin. She knelt by the bed and moved a single hair off his forehead, lifting it between her forefinger and thumb and placing it on his head, his lovely head with the new, ridiculously long, messy fringe and the geometrical precision of the crown, so many thousands of strands, such a miraculously perfect interlocking circle.

Charlotte wanted, more than anything, to crawl in next to him, under the duvet of swarming superheroes. But she could smell the wine on her breath and skin, and Tim, she could smell him – his citrus aftershave, his sweat, his seed. In her shock-induced state of heightened sobriety, she fully recognized the dubiousness of any instinct to reach for Sam. The abyss that had opened up under her that night was hers and hers alone. It had been waiting for her, she realized, yawning and invisible, behind the years of complaint, the wifely railing, the recent superficial efforts to pick up the pieces, the claims of desire for independence. She had loved Martin *so much*. She had forgotten. She had wanted to forget. The trigger for such feelings could never be packaged in bottles. He had been her belief system, her *world*. She didn't want Martin back but that lost faith was something to mourn indeed. Did he feel the same thing now with Cindy? Charlotte wondered. Did feeling it twice make it any less real? Was love only an act of imagination anyway, a willingness to believe? Without that what was there?

Charlotte stared hard at the sweet sleeping face of her son – the product of honest passion and yet from the first so much simpler than that, so unbreakable, as easy to respond to as a smile and a thousand times deeper. When had the trouble started? The distance, the distrust, the resentment – had it been after Sam or before? And who *had* written that note? Who had wanted so badly to bring their miserable struggle to an end?

The little car rocked again, backwards and forwards this time, as if some giant malevolent hand was gripping the back bumper and trying to tip it on to its nose. Charlotte tried not to think of everyone at the party – Sam, Theresa and Henry, Naomi, Jo, Paul, Graham, all of them – except her. She tried not to think of Martin, *moving on* with Cindy, going through the ritual of opening up their home, inviting people in, heralding, sealing their public partnership, even though, she recalled, there might already be problems there too, cracks behind the scenes. Hah! Cracks – hah! But even her vitriol felt half-hearted. Vitriol took energy and she had none.

Sickened, a little hungry, Charlotte decided it was time to end her pathetic vigil and head home. She would dig out the treacherous note, she decided fiercely, some resolve returning, have another proper look, burn it, even. But as she reached for the ignition a fresh patch of colour rose above the clumps of flowers outside the cottage. Brilliant red . . . the pom-pom hat – again. The horrible hat, and a matching scarf, too, this time, blowing round his neck like a noose. Charlotte gawped: Dominic Porter was on the doorstep, shaking Mrs Stowe's hand – *shaking Mrs Stowe's hand.*

Her next thought was flight. He mustn't see her. This horrible, hateful, gaunt-faced man, with his equally hateful daughter, criss-crossing her and Sam's path like a pair of bullying incubi. He *mustn't*. Indifference, defiance, friendliness – whatever might be called for during the course of an encounter, she couldn't manage it, not now, she just couldn't.

She turned the key. The engine made its grating sound, its special dreadful sound, reserved for late mornings, late afternoons, as if the only cue required was a sense of urgency in her fluttering fingers. Charlotte tried again, twisting the key viciously, only to produce a grinding sound even worse than the first, like metal striking metal.

Dominic's mind was on fixtures and fittings, on the persistent serendipity of connections (the Stowes knowing Benedict, who had mentioned his need for a house), and whether it was too late in the day to call his solicitor to discuss exchanging and completing on the same date. It was the stalling scrape of the Volkswagen engine that caught his attention. Even then, when he turned in search of its source, it was not Charlotte Turner he first saw behind the wheel of the little black car but the blurred image of his fiery-haired wife: Maggie in her old black Mini, crooning at it, coaxing it to start, as she did with anything uncooperative, regardless of whether it happened to be a person or a machine.

Except it wasn't Maggie, of course: the hair was longer, smoother, closer to chestnut than red, and the eyes were green instead of blue and there were no freckles to speak of and this woman was much slimmer too, with the hips of a boy and long, agile fingers that looked designed to curl round flutes or whip up and down piano keys. Dominic had no need to approach the car to contemplate these details.

He had studied Charlotte Turner closely, not just in the grim circumstance of Miss Brigstock's office but before that, in the narrow confines of her front hall and the kitchen with the south-facing garden and the waste-disposal unit built into the sink, warning himself even then against the private pitiful indulgence of being drawn to a woman with red hair.

'Having trouble?' He lowered his head, mildly put out that she did not immediately wind down the window, this woman whose son had briefly traumatized his daughter (though Rose seemed far from traumatized now) and whose plight he could easily have chosen to ignore, given the number of important phone calls he had to make and that he had promised Rose spaghetti Bolognese and had yet to purchase the ingredients.

'It does this.'

She had lowered the window, but only halfway, as if fearful of contamination, from the violent weather, Dominic assumed, rather than him. 'I'm parked back there. I've got jump leads.'

'No need.' She tried the engine again, visibly gritting her teeth as it delivered another cacophonic response. 'It does this,' she repeated, with evident mounting desperation. 'Sometimes, if I wait, give it a moment . . . please, don't concern yourself. If the worst comes to the worst, I'm a member of the AA.'

'Ah. Right-ho. The fourth emergency service. Excellent.' Dominic straightened, baffled more than hurt that she should give his Good Samaritan act such short shrift. Sam had been horrible to Rose, hadn't he? The woman should be on her *knees*. And she didn't look anything like Maggie, he decided in the same instant, not a trace, *nil*. And Maggie would never in a million years have been so hostile to an offer of help. Never. 'See you, then,' he muttered, backing

164

away from the car, a small part of him reluctant still to admit defeat. Was he that ghastly?

'Excuse me . . . I hope you don't mind my asking . . .' She had wound the window right down now and was projecting her mouth out of it. Her face, Dominic noticed, was not pale so much as white – white as the startling teeth – and her eyes, though electric green, were pink-rimmed, like Rose's when she was on the verge of tears. Her voice was firm enough, though, shooting at him across the whirr of the wind. 'But I couldn't help noticing that you came out of number forty-two and it made me wonder . . . Do you know Mrs Stowe? I mean, obviously you do, only . . .'

Dominic stepped back towards the car, tucking his hands into his pockets. 'Yes – at least, my brother does. Mrs Stowe's daughter is an actor and so is he. They were in something together last year. It's thanks to that that I'm buying the place – been on the cards for weeks now but we're finally there.' He took his hands out of his pockets and rubbed them together. 'They've just kindly agreed to move out before Easter so I don't have to renew my lease. It's a private sale,' he added, driven to add the clarification by the expression on Charlotte's face, as she ducked her head back into the car. Like a tortoise withdrawing, Dominic decided, studying her.

'I know – I knew it was for sale. I wanted to buy it.' She stared at the windscreen.

Dominic hesitated, absorbing the implications of this. One finger, seeking warmth in the corner of his coat pocket, had found a hole, a bad hole, big enough to lose keys through as well as pound coins. Maggie would have seen to it in an instant – anything to do with thread and needles, wool and homecrafts, she had been a wizard. And cooking, she had loved that too, to the point sometimes where he had had to insist on taking a turn, reminding her that food preparation was as much of a passion of his as aeroplanes and that getting the short straw on doing the dishes every night simply wasn't fair. Arguments – who would have thought one could miss them? 'How unfortunate . . . I . . . It's a delightful house.'

'Yes, yes, it's *lovely*. I wanted it very much. Except it was out of my price range and only shown to me unofficially, and almost certainly shouldn't have been by the sound of things . . . I mean, I knew about the possibility of a private sale but had no idea they already had someone in mind.' Charlotte twisted the key again and the Volkswagen chortled smoothly into action, as it tended to when she was drained of hope.

Dominic bent closer to the window, raising his voice against the engine, resenting the certain impression that he was being told off. 'Look, I'm sorry, okay?'

'No, I am,' she shouted back. 'I shouldn't have said anything. It doesn't matter.' She offered him a broad, rueful grin, displaying the extraordinary teeth. 'Good luck with it all.'

'There are always other houses . . .' he began.

Charlotte shook her head, shoving the gearstick into first and glancing in her wing-mirror. 'I've decided to stay where I am, make the best of what I've got.' The grin was still there, but hanging on now, the lips tightening.

'Great. Good luck with *that*,' Dominic offered, feeling a little helpless now. 'Good luck indeed,' he murmured, as she raced off down the road.

For the walk back to his car the wind was directly against him, squeezing tears from his eyes and batting at the flaps of his coat. Divorced, with a difficult little boy and *quite* an attitude, he told himself, as the helplessness threatened to bulge into sympathy. His thoughts shifted to the needy, embittered woman with whom he had briefly – unsatisfactorily – shared a bed: all that history, all that *baggage* when he had quite enough of his own to contend with; he wasn't going to make that mistake again. Making the best of what one had wasn't a bad adage, though, he decided, recalling Charlotte's parting words as he slid behind the wheel of his own car. And he was certainly managing that now, with Rose so much more settled and the pair of them on the verge of making a new start in a house that had fallen into his lap like a gift – thanks to Benedict, dear Benedict, with his own complicated private life but a relentless ability to shine light into other people's. It was also thanks to his wonderful, scheming brother that on top of this huge blessing he now had the clever, striking Polish girl more within his sights. She was called Petra and had recently left him a message about lunch, suggesting somewhere local as she was working out of studios in Battersea – if that wasn't too inconvenient, if he had the time, if he would like to, some time in the next few weeks, or months, if he was busy. It had been a long message, suggesting, behind the too-long clauses, the stilted English, both an appealing uncertainty and real eagerness.

The prospect of following up on it was exciting, Dominic acknowledged happily, blowing on his frozen hands while the car heating got into its stride. He'd ask Benedict to recommend somewhere good locally. He'd look ahead in his office diary and find a quiet day, maybe arrange to work from home, pick Rose up from school, pin down the paperwork for the move . . . Yes, a good plan, something to get his teeth into. Dominic took a deep breath. Sometimes he was sure he forgot to breathe. He summoned an image of Petra's fresh intelligent face, the silky bobbed hair, the long legs; he *loved* long legs. 'And it's time to move on, my darling,' he murmured, pausing for a last admiring look at his future home. 'It really is.'

> *Dear Rose,*
> *We aren't moving house any more. I am pleased because it means*
> *Mum is less stressy and I won't have to keep my room tidy all the*
> *time. The only bad thing is that she said if we moved we could get a*
> *dog, so I suppose we can't now. The other bad thing is she says*
> *we've got to have lots of painting and stuff done here and clear out*
> *junk, etc. Right this moment I am supposed to be sorting out things*
> *I want to give away like old toys and stuff. BORING. And also*
> *to pack for going away. BORING. It is only to Suffolk, to*
> *George's dad's house. We went there once before for a weekend and*
> *it rained all the time. Sorry this letter is so BORING.*
> *Sam*
> *PS For my birthday I got an iPod, an upgrade on my mobile and*
> *loads of new PlayStation games.*
> *PPS You are really good at drawing.*

Sam folded the letter into a tight, fat square, pondering whether he was the only boy in the world to be spending the Easter holidays *missing* school. It would be impossible ever to admit to such a thing; almost as impossible as admitting that the person he had once been famous for hating had somehow – *how?* – morphed into a friendly pen-pal. Exchanging notes with the class weirdo – not only unpopular but a *girl* – he would be a laughing-stock.

Except the funny thing was, Sam had never felt less in danger of being a laughing-stock in all his life. With the Rose business – the *new* Rose business – and having to be on his best behaviour work-wise, he had stopped trying to hang out with George's gang and detected, to his astonishment, a new keenness on their part to hang out with him. It was insane, like getting something after – or *because* – you'd stopped wanting it. During the last week of term George had even hinted that, if there had been the remotest chance of wriggling out of a new plan of his mother's to visit his granny in Cornwall, he would have welcomed an invitation to Suffolk. He had a kite in the attic there that he'd never flown, he said, and there was a place he wanted to show Sam among the dunes, perfect for a hideout. He had scribbled a map of it, with arrows and crosses, like directions to buried treasure.

Sam missed Rose's notes and little pictures. But more than that he missed the thrill of their secret handovers, the looks over the top of books and behind people's backs, the lovely warm feeling of having something going on that no one else knew about, not even Mr Dawson, to whom he had told all sorts of stuff but whom he didn't have to see now, unless he wanted to.

Sam hovered on the landing, scared suddenly as to how his latest effort at written communication might be received. Rose's last missive, slipped into his hands two weeks before, during the enforced tedium of a lost-property session on the last day of school, had ended, 'see you next term'. Like she meant it to be just a *school* thing. And there had been no hint of exchanging mobile numbers either, which had been a bitter blow.

And now there was just the afternoon left and they were going to Suffolk, where his mum said mobiles didn't work and posting a letter required a car journey. Sam leant over the banisters, craning his neck in a bid to establish Charlotte's exact location. He had last seen her entering the spare bedroom on the first floor clutching a pagoda of empty cardboard boxes, but now the door was closed, and she was kneeling on the wrong side of it, one hand rummaging in a dusty, battered suitcase, the other tucking strands of hair behind her ears, from where it immediately fell forwards again, dangling against her nose.

'Hey, you,' she said, not even looking up.

'Hey.'

'Have you done what I asked?'

'Nearly,' Sam lied, folding his fist tightly round the note. 'Can I go to the shop to get some sweets?'

'If you've sorted out your cupboard and packed, yes.'

Sam made a noise designed to sound like a yes, while not actually being one, so that, when accused later, he could deny having lied. Rather to his surprise it seemed to have worked because as he ventured down the stairs towards her she carried on talking, not about sorting his gear but about other tedious things she had already mentioned at least five times since breakfast.

'We've got to leave early or we'll get stuck in traffic. I'm sorry it's only for four days, but I've got to get back to help out in the shop because of Dean still being so ill. And then not long after we get back your godmother's coming to stay – did I tell you that?'

'Yeah, *Eve*, who started sending you emails out of the blue and who I've never *met* because she lives in *Boston*,' Sam chirruped, leaping on to the banister, bracing himself for the usual telling-off as he let go, but too keen for the thrill of the slide, not to mention the chance to whip an envelope out of the sideboard drawer while she was still upstairs.

'And George's dad has promised to drop by with the keys before we leave tomorrow,' she continued, as if he hadn't said anything and wasn't riding the banisters, 'which is so kind of him.' She glanced at her watch. 'And, *Sam . . .*'

Here it comes, he thought, in full flight now, a split

second from the tricky final leap on to the hall floor, skidding on the rug if he was clever. Here it comes.

'While you're at the corner shop could you buy some bread – sliced, brown, white, whatever you fancy having under your scrambled egg.'

'Yeah, sure,' Sam puffed, glancing back up the stairs in surprise. He had missed the pad of the hall carpet but landed safely on all fours. She was still on her knees bending over the suitcase, singing something softly as she took out clothes and papers and arranged them in piles. She had been at it for days now, like someone who *was* about to move house instead of one who had decided not to.

A few miles away Theresa was moving with rather more purpose between cupboards and a large suitcase that was filling fast. Dressing-gowns and slippers – the Cornwall house was draughty – toys and games in case it rained (it was *bound* to rain), wellingtons and macs, and at least one each of the various home-knit jumpers that had arrived in jiffy-bags during the course of the last year. Alfie and Jack would wear theirs, no problem, but George, at thirteen, was growing understandably resistant to sporting loopy-stitched, brightly coloured knitwear – even to please a grandparent whom he loved very dearly – while Matilda . . . Theresa sighed in fond despair at the thought of her six-year-old's new, obstinate fashion-consciousness: since her release from the constraints of school uniform, she had taken to flinging clothes out of her chest of drawers each morning with the despairing petulance of a teenager. Only items that were pink or *glittered* were currently in favour; and since this basically limited her to her ballet outfit, and a couple of too-large garments from the dressing-up box, few mornings that holiday had passed without ructions.

Naomi, who had invited herself for tea, bringing the twins but not Pattie and staying well into the time Theresa had allocated for packing (she was leaving that night), had said it was mid-April, mostly sunny and so what if a child wore a tutu to the supermarket? Theresa had laughed and said so what indeed, apart from paedophiles and pneumonia and the fact that the tutu in question had a 'handwash only' label that added considerably to the already sizeable chore of family laundry.

And control, Theresa thought now, standing on the suitcase, which was too full. Not allowing tutus in the supermarket was part of keeping everything manageable, within the boundaries of a chaos she knew would swamp her if she let it, and, from the manner in which the twins had run riot during the course of the afternoon, appeared to be slightly in danger of overwhelming Naomi. Control. She would take it where she could, these days, she reflected grimly, kneeling on the lid and hissing curses as the contents bulged between the two sides of the zipper.

'Need a hand by any chance?'

'Henry . . . no, I mean yes – yes, please.' She moved off the case and watched as her husband hoisted it on to their bed, using brute force to close the zip.

'There we are. All set.'

'All set. And you?' Seven weeks and two days, she thought, seven weeks and two days since he has laid a hand on me. Lips, yes, in scattered pecks, before and after work, before and after sleep, avuncular, inadequate. And there had been no protestations about her going solo to Cornwall either, not one hint of a lament about considering or wishing he could abandon the wretched work blitz and come too. 'Was Charlotte okay about you dropping the keys?'

'Oh, yes, fine – absolutely fine. She thought it was hilarious that we'd all forgotten.'

Privately Theresa considered it ridiculously inept rather than funny on all their parts. Over a hasty sandwich lunch the week before, she had remembered to offer Charlotte advice on the final tricky leg of the journey, to apologize in advance for the idiosyncrasies of the boiler, but not once considered how her friend was supposed to get through the front door. Charlotte, busily cursing Dominic Porter for hijacking her perfect house and the increased demands imposed by her employer's continuing ill health, hadn't thought of it either. She had been full of a new, almost manic energy, babbling about moving on properly at last, about pieces falling into place, about her determination to make a go of staying where she was. She had been bullish, too, on the subject of the next mah-jong session, insisting she host it in spite of extensive redecorating plans and a possible clash with a visit from Sam's long-lost godmother. She and Eve would play together, she said, so as not to muck up the numbers.

Theresa, who did not fancy the intrusion of an outsider into their comfortable little circle, unbalancing things, requiring politeness and effort, had momentarily caught herself missing the more familiar version of her friend: the one who needed constant support, counselling . . . pity. For years she had felt superior to Charlotte, she realized with some surprise – superior, smug, *happily married*, and she rather missed it.

It had been Henry who had first picked up on the omission of the keys, jangling his set in her face after Naomi had finally left, when Theresa was straining broccoli and wondering why she had committed herself to four hours of night driving when six, even in foul traffic the following day, would probably be infinitely less stressful. 'Doh . . .' Henry had exclaimed, doing an imitation of George doing an imitation of Homer Simpson, his eyes twinkling with satisfaction at having been the one to spot the oversight. He had then speedily – *ebulliently*, or so it seemed to Theresa – volunteered to phone Charlotte to sort out a handover of the offending items the following morning. His own plans involved travelling up by train the day after that and staying on for a few days after the pair had returned to London. The entire family had been talked through it so often, with such conscientious attention to detail, that Theresa could have repeated most of her husband's phrases on the subject verbatim . . . He was going to *hole up* in the granny conversion in order to *break the back* of his latest paper, finding energy and *inspiration*, as he *always* did, in the holiday landscape of his childhood.

'Hilarious?' repeated Theresa, dully, pushing the word out through her reverie and damning the generosity that had prompted her to offer Charlotte the cottage in the first place, allowing the whole ridiculous situation to arise.

'In fact,' continued Henry, lightly, keeping his back to her as he lifted the suitcase on to the floor, 'Charlotte suggested that instead of waiting a day and taking the train, I drive down with her in the morning when I deliver the keys, which makes sense if you think about it.'

Theresa, without having to think, could see that it made perfect sense; perfect, hateful sense. 'Great. How nice of Charlotte.' She followed Henry down the stairs, wrestling with the warring voices inside her head: one screeching the old instinctive wifely terrors, the other scolding the pointlessness of probing for phantom problems, making them exist in the process. There had been barren patches in their sex life before. It was no big deal. A marriage was a journey, a long journey through a constantly changing terrain, moods, phases, colours. It was in a permanent state of flux. *Trust* was the constant. And love, of course. 'I just hope . . . I mean, I'm a bit worried that . . .' she faltered.

'Yes?' Henry stopped in the door of the sitting room and peered at her over the rims of his glasses – not their usual smeary mess, Theresa noticed, but polished, showing off his deep ultramarine eyes. 'What?'

'. . . worried about whether you'll be able to work . . . with them there distracting you. Wouldn't it be better to stay here after all, with the house to yourself? You could take the phone off the hook and –'

'It wouldn't work,' he cut in, then added more gently, 'You know how hopeless I am at knuckling down to anything up here.'

'And can you just leave a day early like that anyway? I mean, you're so busy, aren't you?' she pressed lamely.

'It won't be a problem. I've already cleared the decks. Look, Tessy, if for some *unfathomable* reason you'd prefer me to stick to the original plan of taking the train, then for heaven's sake just say so.'

'No, you're right, it wouldn't make sense.'

'Tessy?' Henry took his glasses off, as he tended to during moments of high domestic drama, and squinted at her. 'Are you okay?'

Theresa shuffled up against him, resting the side of her face against his chest, feeling the buttons of his shirt pressing her skin through his jumper, which was an old favourite and very thin. 'I'm sorry. I'm het up about driving to Cornwall tonight, that's all. I'm too tired – I should never have agreed to it.'

'Well, go tomorrow morning, then,' he suggested, sounding faintly exasperated.

Theresa pulled away, shaking her head ruefully. 'No, you know what Mum's like. She hates a change of plan. She'll be sitting up with a torch, one of her home-made soups and the biscuit tin. If I leave now we'll be there by eleven,' she added firmly, her brisk self once more as she yelled up the stairs for the children to gather any last-minute things and get down to the hall.

. . . And what on earth would Charlotte – especially in this new assertive grab-life-by-the-balls phase – want with her Henry anyway? Theresa mused, feeling much brighter as they sped along the A404, the travails of Harry Potter keeping two of her children spellbound while the other two slept. An absent-minded doctor with bad eyesight, a thickening waistline and an ever-so-slightly hairy back. She laughed out loud, prompting a look of baffled annoyance from George who was hanging on to every syllable about swooping death-eaters.

And what, for that matter, would Henry want with Charlotte? A woman who could muddle house-hunting and love affairs to a point of farcical implosion, one of his wife's closest friends, for God's sake? And if he *was* remotely interested, surely he wouldn't be so obvious as to coincide with her in Suffolk? Of course he wouldn't. The clashing lines in the diary had been proof of *that*, not evidence of scheming. Theresa slapped the steering-wheel. She was a fool, a bloody fool.

Ignoring the hoo-ha it caused from her two non-sleeping companions, she stopped Stephen Fry mid-flow and dropped her phone into George's lap instructing him to dial home. 'Safe journey tomorrow and I love you,' she murmured, the moment Henry's rumbling voice answered.

'You too, Tessy,' he replied. 'You too.'

*

Charlotte was having a good dream, a brilliant dream, of searching – not for the snide well-wisher note that had got her rummaging in boxes and transmogrified, much more usefully, into a general clear-out – but something infinitely better, much more important; something her dreaming self understood but she couldn't. She awoke as the search seemed on the point of finding its object. In the pitch dark outside a lone bird had started a jaunty dawn sing-song, repeating the same pattern of sound, as if hoping to cajole some of its sleepier mates into joining in. Lying there, feeling thwarted, with the lovely dream quite lost, Charlotte found that she knew where the note was anyway, so surely that there was no instant need to leap out of bed and check. She laced her palms under the back of her head instead and spent a couple of minutes contemplating the quiet, unexpected upturn in her spirits during the two weeks since the nightmare that had begun on Tim's spongy crimson sofa and ended with the humiliating vigil outside number forty-two Chalkdown Road.

The self-drama of it made her blush even now. But there was no doubt that through the awfulness something had been dislodged. Driving home, Dominic Porter's expression of hopeless pity etched on her brain, what had begun as a feeble resolve had strengthened into something close to inspiration. Before she knew it there were ten black sacks waiting for a trip to the dump and a list of recommended decorators next to the phone. On top of which, her responsibilities at work had mushroomed to the point where, manning her shifts alone and with her Suffolk trip imminent, Jason had hired an assistant for *her*. The girl was called Shona and had so far proved keener to gossip about Dean's illness ('pleurisy, my arse') than learn how to take credit cards or find book listings on the computer. She sometimes added to pressure rather than alleviating it, but Charlotte was aware nonetheless that the presence of this hapless aide made her feel contrastingly capable. Putting in orders, doing stock checks, changing the window, liaising with two local authors about book launches, she had begun to question how she had ever filled her time before. She was connecting with something properly at last, something other than Sam and worries about what other people thought of her and why the defining relationship of her life had lost its footing.

When the lone bird fell silent Charlotte slipped out of bed and padded into the spare room. In the bedside table there was a battered copy of Wordsworth's *Prelude* from her college days, several paperclips, an empty ink cartridge and a biro engraved with the name of the first company Martin had worked for, when he had finally traded theatre directing for computers and a nine-to-five. The note was sticking out of the book, just as she had expected, between two pages smothered with messy underlinings and faded pencil notes. *Bliss was it in that dawn to be alive, But to be young was very heaven.*

'Mum, what are you doing?'

'I might ask the same of you, young man,' Charlotte retorted, with a smile, hastily popping the note back into its hiding-place and closing the drawer. Being young had been heavenly. It was supposed to be. Wordsworth had nailed that, just as he had nailed the sadness of losing such sensations – she had known that once, written essays on it, yet never imagined *living* it. 'Are you hungry?'

Sam rubbed his eyes with his knuckles, like a child literally unable to believe what he was seeing. 'Mum, it's, like, four o'clock.'

'I know, I know.' Charlotte reached for the dressing-gown, an old one of Martin's, that lived on the back of the bedroom door, spared the black sack only because she hadn't seen it. 'But I'm starving. That scrambled egg didn't really hit the spot, did it? I was thinking . . .' she stroked her chin, frowning '. . . maybe, given that we've got a long drive ahead, we could have *two* breakfasts, beginning now with some toast and honey – or jam – and I'll have tea, but you might prefer hot chocolate. Fetch your dressing- gown first,' she shouted, as Sam bolted through the door.

Charlotte switched off the light and left the room. She had needed to see the note again, if only to remind her of the tiny part it had played in her and Martin's downfall. However deeply in love they had once been, there had been *years* of trouble, she reminded herself grimly, years of arguing, about Sam, about her suspicions, about Martin's denials. The nasty message had merely been the proverbial straw alighting upon the camel's back, collapsing something that was in a state of near-collapse anyway. The only unanswered question was the identity of the person who had 'wished her well' enough to write it. Martin had always denied all knowledge. For a brief while she had secretly suspected Jo, who had been very anti Martin at one stage and, working in the City, might well have spotted him wining and dining Cindy. But even that hardly seemed to matter now. None of it mattered. It was done with.

Charlotte took the stairs slowly, aware that happiness was a mercurial thing, that if studied too hard it had a tendency to slither out of reach. She focused instead on the lovely sound of clattering from the kitchen and of Sam whistling. It was a disjointed, tuneless twittering – Martin had kept his musical genes to himself – but, like the birdsong in the dark, it lifted her heart beyond whatever words even the mighty Lake Poets might have managed.

Chapter Ten

By the time Henry arrived Sam and Charlotte were parked in the hall with their bags, looking at their watches and trying to think of things they had forgotten. As the doorbell rang Sam remembered George's map of the hideout, still sitting in the side pocket of his satchel, and raced upstairs.

Henry set down a heavy leather holdall and leant forward to plant a kiss on Charlotte's cheek, pressing his lips so firmly that Charlotte, imagining the greeting over with, suffered momentary embarrassment when it became clear that he was expecting to offer the other side of her face the same compliment.

'This is *so* kind of you,' she murmured, wondering about the holdall and thinking it a little early in the morning for such social niceties. 'To forget *keys* – and you've had to come by taxi,' she cried, as his cab roared away. 'How horribly inconvenient.'

Henry did not look remotely inconvenienced. He had his hands on his hips under the flaps of his brown corduroy jacket and was grinning. 'Theresa has the car. She left for Penrith with the children last night. A tour of *mothering* duty,' he added, pulling a face.

'Yes, she told me.' Charlotte was rummaging in her handbag for her purse. 'I should contribute or something, and we'll drop you back, of course, or at the station, wherever you need to go.' She glanced again at the holdall. 'I really should have insisted on coming via you to pick the stupid keys up myself, you having one car – I never thought it through.'

'Except that would have meant you beginning a long journey by going in the wrong direction and anyway . . .' Henry hesitated '. . . I have a hatched a slight change of plan.'

'Have you?' Behind her Sam flew off the banister post and skidded towards the front door on the obligingly slippery hall rug. 'Hey, Dr Curtis.'

'Hello, Sam. How are you?'

'Good, thanks.'

'Great.'

'A plan?' Charlotte repeated.

'Only if you don't mind, of course, but I thought maybe . . .' It was Henry's turn to look at the bag, privately hoping as he did so that his small lie to Theresa wasn't going to turn out to have been for nothing.

'That you come down with us now – of course!' Charlotte cried, clapping her hands together, genuinely thrilled at the prospect of adult company for the journey, not to mention an adult who would preclude the necessity of having to remember Theresa's instructions about humpback bridges, pub signs and keeping to the left to avoid hazardous cattle grids. 'I don't know why I didn't think of it myself. It's like forgetting the keys,' she chatted, ushering Sam out of the front door and offering a string of thank-yous as Henry swooped inside gallantly to take charge of their bags. 'I don't know if Theresa told you but I've been *so* busy lately, with the shop and so on. My mind's all over the place.'

'Yes, she did mention it. She also said you'd taken your house off the market,' remarked Henry, tugging a little more sharply than was necessary on his seatbelt at the unwelcome reminder of the estate agent.

'Yes, I'd got it all wrong,' Charlotte confessed gaily, returning a wave to Mr Beasley as they pulled away, 'thinking that trying for a fresh start meant having to change the scenery when in fact it's not about that. People say the same sort of thing when someone dies, don't they?'

'Do they?' murmured Henry, his attention fixed on the long curve of Charlotte's thigh through her jeans and the luxurious prospect of hours – days – with such sights readily at hand.

'That after these traumas it's always best to wait, let the dust settle and see how you feel.'

'Dad hasn't *died*,' Sam snorted, untangling the wires of his iPod. Down the street he could see the postman, the bald skinny one with the earring who winked at him sometimes. It made him think of Rose, of his letter, on its way now, he hoped, to 13 Trinity Hill. Unless they'd moved already. Sam's heart pounded. Could they have moved already? To that house his mum had raved about. All the houses in London and they had to pick the same one. She had been furious, but Sam had thought it incredible – and sort of nice, like a sign that he and Rose were meant to be special friends.

'Hey, I thought you were safely plugged into that new machine of yours,' Charlotte countered, knowing from the snort that there was no suggestion of Sam being upset. 'Your father, as far as I am aware, is in perfect health.'

'If he *did* die,' pressed Sam, diverted from the possibility of wrong addresses, 'would we be really rich?'

Charlotte laughed and rolled her eyes at Henry, who grinned back in admiration at her humour, at how well she seemed to deal with everything. He liked the way she drove too, he decided – steady, safe, unlike Theresa, who harried slowcoaches, exceeded the speed limit between cameras and generally made the curtailment of back-seat-driver assistance impossible.

'No, Sam, we would not. You might get a little something, though – his watch or maybe even his precious record collection,' Charlotte teased, glancing at her son in the rear-view mirror, loving the new ease between them, evinced most recently by the feasting on wedges of toast, dripping butter and honey on to their dressing-gowns as they kept their feet warm under the sofa cushions. They had watched two cricket teams in bright tracksuits on the other side of the world until Sam had fallen asleep and she had tucked his duvet round him, then retreated back to bed to await the shriek of her alarm. 'Most of what there is would almost certainly go to Cindy. If you want to know more you'll have to ask him, won't you? Oh, my word, yes, Dad would love that,' she concluded merrily, delighting in the fact of no longer needing Martin for money or anything else, of having left the intensity, good and bad, behind. He could leave his worldly goods to Cindy and good luck to him – if they lasted that long and Cindy didn't end up scouring his credit-card receipts as Charlotte once had, scrabbling for evidence like a blind cuckold in the dark.

Getting out of London seemed a breeze with Henry directing. In little over an hour they were on the A12, doing a steady seventy with nothing to negotiate but the occasional lumbering lorry and sunshine so bright that she asked Henry to fish out her scratched old sunglasses that lived in the glove compartment. When the Volkswagen started to emit the ominous clunks it reserved for long journeys – one after they had left the A12 and another as she slowed for the infamous humpback bridge – Henry laughed at her groans of panic and promised to give her the number of a brilliant mechanic when they were back in London.

'Oh, Henry, what a *saviour* you are – thank you!' Charlotte exclaimed, on a little rush of missing – not Martin but some of the manly fearlessness that he had brought to their partnership. She experienced something similar when Henry leapt out to open the heavy five-bar gate at the end of the cottage's little drive, and then again when he swung the luggage out of the boot on to the doorstep.

'Your keys.' He dropped them into her hand.

'Thank you, Henry, so much –'

'I'll take these upstairs, shall I?'

'Really, Sam and I can manage now.' Charlotte watched, touched and helpless, as he ignored the refusal and started up the short, narrow staircase with their two bags. 'I'll press the override button in the airing cupboard so you've hot water right away,' he called. 'What about heating? Do you want it on? Or maybe just tonight? Or do you think you'll be okay with an open fire? There should be more kindling in the shed, but I'll check. The firelighters are under the papers in the basket next to the hearth.'

'Henry, please, you've done enough,' Charlotte begged, when he came back downstairs. 'We'll be fine. I know you've got work to do and we really don't – we really *won't* get in your way. I promised Theresa – the barn is your zone and this is ours. Letting Sam and me camp here is so unbelievably generous of you, it would make me miserable if I thought we were interrupting.'

'Don't be silly.' Henry had taken off his glasses and was rubbing the lenses vigorously with the hem of his jumper.

'I thought we'd unpack,' Charlotte continued, 'then walk to that famously well-stocked village post office for some supplies. Tell me what I can get for you – it's the least I can do, given that you won't take any rent.'

Henry slipped his glasses back on and shoved his hands into his pockets, glancing as he did so through the hall window at his holdall, which was still sitting on the gravel beside the car. 'I might come too, if that's okay . . . Good to stretch one's legs after the drive. Bang on the door when you're ready. Tell you what,' he added, turning to Sam, 'if the wind gets up George has a racing kite stowed somewhere about the place. We could have a go with that, if you like?'

Sam sneaked a look at his mother before he replied. He wanted to say yes, of course, but feared that might be the wrong answer, given her little speech about them not getting in the way. 'Yeah, George told me I could use it,' he began carefully, adding in a rush, 'I probably won't need too much help, though.'

Henry let out a hearty laugh. 'Oh, trust me, you will. That kind are a pig to get up. See you in a minute, then.' He was still chuckling as he walked away.

I open my eyes and the Moses basket is there. It rests on the makeshift stand that worries me because it wobbles so. Over it hangs the lopsided canopy I have stitched and hung myself, in a bid to make the basket look less of an object designed for laundry and more like one of the exquisite receptacles for newborns photographed in my maternity magazines.

Drugged still with tiredness, I let my eyes close. Sleep is the new obsession in both our lives now, rare, treasured, fought over. It is Saturday afternoon, an hour since the last feed, after a night without rest. Eve is coming to tea so we can ask her to be godmother. Behind me, curled away, one arm bent over the side of his head, fist pressed against his ear, as if ready to muffle the next cry, Martin, too, is sleeping. Later, dimly, I become aware of Eve in the room, bent over the basket, clutching tulips. Martin is next to her, arms folded across his chest, smiling and proud.

'We want you to be godmother,' he whispers.

Eve gasps and flaps her flowers. 'Ohmygod,' she whispers back,

185

'I'll be useless – oh, thank you.' *She puts her arm round him as they tiptoe away.*

A moment later, it seems, Sam is braying his dry newborn hee-haw, the one that makes my milk flow. The basket creaks as I lift him out. As he sucks, I cup his soft, downy head, breathless with joy, needing nothing else, nothing.

'When can I see your films?'

'Well . . . I suppose when you're fifteen, unless I get the call-up for the next Narnia blockbuster. That would be nice.' Benedict plucked a blade of grass and chewed it, squinting at his niece. They were lying fully stretched out on their sides in the park, heads supported on their hands, facing each other across the debris of a supermarket-bought picnic.

Rose pulled a face. 'I didn't like the last one – it looked so fake, especially Aslan.'

'I don't think even the cleverest, bravest lion-tamer in the world could have got a *real* one to do that stuff, though, could they?'

'Is it because there's lots of sex and you have to take your clothes off?'

Benedict laughed. 'I assume we're back on the fifteen rating to my latest movie rather than Aslan?'

'Well, is it?' Rose dug her nail into a patch of earth right under a scuttling ant. *An earthquake for him, she thought, and just a speck of mud for me.*

'In the latest one you do see my bum, yes,' Benedict confessed cheerfully.

Rose giggled. 'Yuk.'

'Precisely. I couldn't have put it better myself. Stay away as long as you can, that's my advice.' Benedict grinned, reaching out to stroke, briefly, the wild orange froth of her hair, resisting the urge to tell her, as he always wanted to, that she was a creature of violent, extraordinary beauty. He rolled over on to his back and squinted up at the sky, deciding that that was a thing of extraordinary beauty too, a flat blue sea pitted with scudding sails. He loved April, its freshness, its bright promise of summer. 'So that new school of yours is bearable now, is it?'

'Yep.' Rose dug deeper, searching for the ant, which had disappeared. 'It's good actually. There's a boy I like.'

'Lucky chap,' remarked her uncle, who, unlike most adults she knew, always said unexpected things, things that made it easier to talk. 'I hope he knows he's lucky.'

'Yes, I think so.' The ant had reappeared on top of the little pile of mud and was on its back legs, like an explorer peering off the top of a mountain. 'We write letters to each other, that's all.'

'Letters? What a wonderfully surprising girl you are. Don't change, will you, ever?'

'Silly, of course not.' Rose balanced the ant on her fingernail, then blew it off.

'You look cold, sweetheart, shall we go?'

'I'm not.'

'Yes, you are. Your knees are purple – look.'

Rose sat up and examined her legs. 'They're always that colour.'

'We should still go, or Dad will give me a bollocking for loafing in the park till you're frozen blue and feeding you junk food and not making sure you've washed behind your ears or whatever it is I'm supposed to do.'

'Silly,' Rose said again, shoving at his chest with both hands and prompting Benedict to perform two backwards somersaults before leaping to his feet.

'I adore your daughter,' he remarked later the same

evening, sitting opposite Dominic, who was expertly scissoring chopsticks through tinfoil boxes of beef, seaweed and noodles.

'And she adores you,' Dominic replied, continuing to eat ravenously, catching dribbles of sauce with the back of his hand. 'Thank you so much for helping out.'

'Resting actors have their uses,' remarked Benedict, drily, picking with more caution at the takeaway, wary as always of overdoing the calories. 'By the way, she seems to have acquired a sort of boyfriend.'

Dominic, mouth open, the chopsticks dangling with a fresh load, looked across the table in astonishment. 'Are you sure?'

Benedict nodded.

'Oh, God.'

'There's nothing "oh, God" about it. They write *letters*, for goodness' sake. How cute is that?'

Dominic shook his head in wonderment, recalling the handwritten envelope for which Rose had never, after all, volunteered an explanation.

'And while we're on the subject of relationships . . .' Benedict paused, leaning back in his armchair and steering a space among the cartons to rest his feet. 'Has Petra been in touch yet?'

Dominic, shovelling loose noodles into his mouth, raised his eyes to the ceiling. 'You're nothing but a meddler, do you know that?'

'I am indeed.' Benedict smiled, fixing his large, long-lashed brown eyes on Dominic's face as he added, 'I found you Maggie, didn't I?'

It took Dominic a moment to respond. His brother was probing, he knew, deliberately bringing Maggie into it as he always did – as most people did not dare to – wanting to check how he was, where he was on a scale that, for three years, had been longer, darker than Dominic could ever have imagined. 'Yes, yes, you did, you bastard, and that was quite enough match-making for one lifetime, thank you very much. But to answer your question, since you put it so nicely, with your usual *delicate* touch, your Polish starlet friend Petra and I have been playing phone tennis, leaving messages, missing each other. It was my turn last time and she hasn't got back to me . . . but I shall pursue the matter,' he promised, waggling his chopsticks and laughing at the concern on his sibling's face. 'I'm all right, Ben,' he added softly. 'I really am.'

Benedict, who had been holding his breath, released it slowly. 'Good, because I've got a proposition for you. A business proposition.'

'Good God, man, have a heart. My women, my house, for Christ's sake –'

'That wasn't me interfering, that was just plain common sense. Katie's parents were wanting a nice quick sale on a fantastic place and you needed to buy, urgently, to get out of this dump. Sorry, but it is dingy. You've said so yourself a hundred times.' Benedict rubbed his hands together and slipped them behind his head, wriggling deeper into the sofa. 'Rose seems really excited about the move, by the way. The packers tomorrow, I gather – congratulations.'

'Why does she talk to you and not to me?' Dominic burst out, giving up on the noodles and reaching for his bottle of beer.

'Because I'm outside,' replied Benedict, quietly, 'because she hasn't seen me howling like a dog, because there is nothing between us except my adoration.'

They sat in silence for a while, each absorbing the truth of these observations. Somewhere in the street a motorbike roared, then suddenly cut out.

'And gay men are always good with women,' joked Benedict, lifting his feet clear of the coffee-table and starting to stack the cartons. 'Surely you know that by now, brother.' He paused next to Dominic's chair and kissed the top of his head. 'Even those who haven't come out and never will, for fear of giving publicists, agents, fans and aged parents multiple heart-attacks. Any chance of another beer?'

'Of course. Grab one for me while you're at it . . .

'Okay, this business proposition, out with it,' Dominic urged, once they had successfully – competitively – lobbed the bottle caps into the waste-paper basket. 'I know you're busting to tell me.'

'Just hear me out, okay?' Benedict entreated, lining up the empty bottles along the middle of the coffee-table. 'The key things to remember are,' he pushed one bottle out of line, 'that you have never much enjoyed working in the City but need an occupation, second . . .' he slid the second bottle next to the first '. . . that you want, for a few years at least, to have more time for Rose, and finally,' he leant forward, abandoning his props and clasping his hands, 'that although you live and behave as if it were not so, you do in fact, thanks to several years of City bonuses, have enough money to consider a spot of risk and *investment*.'

'And let us not forget either,' quipped Dominic, 'that you are an exaggerating bastard with too much time on his hands.' He raked his fingers through his hair with a theatrical sigh. 'Okay, let's hear it, then, but make it snappy. Some of us have horrible jobs to wake up for.'

A thin band of mist was floating, as it had each morning, round the walls of the barn and the stout wooden fence that guarded the cottage against the surrounding fields. The trees, their tops frothing with blossom and fresh green leaves, were like statues submerged waist-high in a sea of milky water. It meant good weather not bad, Charlotte reminded herself, hugging her first mug of tea as she admired the scene from her bedroom window, summoning what she could recall of Henry's affectionate diatribe about Suffolk in early summer, how the chill of a clear night pressed down on the warm air of a clear day, producing this dawn magic carpet that would shimmer ever more thinly as the rising sun got down to the business of dispersing it. He spoke well about such things, with a tender interest that made it impossible not to be enthralled. He would have a good bedside manner, she decided, blowing the steam off her tea, offering that perfect combination of information and kindness that so few doctors managed. Yes, if she ever contracted lung cancer from her teenage years of puffing cigarettes out of windows and on icy school fire escapes with Bella, Henry would definitely be her man.

Having embarked on the brief holiday with little more than a vague desire to get away – for a change, for more sleep, for some perspective on the recent tangles of her life in London – Charlotte had been nothing short of astonished at how much both she and Sam had enjoyed themselves. There was only one full day left now and she wished there were ten, or twenty. And there was no denying that this was largely thanks to Henry – Henry, the prospect of whose presence she had rather dreaded but who had lit up each day with his kite-flying and crab-catching and knowledge of the best walks and pubs, and how to lay a fire that roared instead of fizzled. On one level Charlotte felt guilty, of course. The poor man had done barely any work, but every time she pointed this out he insisted that there would be plenty of time after she and Sam had gone and that he would apply himself all the better for having relaxed so well. A lot of the preparation went on in his subconscious anyway, he had explained, chewing the rather tasteless stew she had prepared the night before, so that even when he wasn't poring over his papers his brain was tussling with problems, thereby making them easier to solve when the push for proper application arrived.

Pulling on a jumper over her nightie, Charlotte spotted the object of these musings up to his knees in mist and striding towards the shack he rather grandly referred to as the garage. A few minutes later he reappeared, wheeling a large old-fashioned bicycle with a broken front basket and two flat tyres. Charlotte watched as he turned it upside-down on to the saddle and began energetically levering off the tyres and pulling out the inner tubes. She was on the point of turning away when he glanced up at her bedroom window and waved.

Charlotte undid the catch on the window and stuck her head out, momentarily catching her breath at the bite of the morning air. 'A bit early for that, isn't it? And with all this fog – I'm surprised you can see,' she exclaimed, laughing.

Henry grinned and put his hand to his brow as if protecting himself from a blinding light. 'It's like darkness – much easier to see through when you're in the thick of it. And tomorrow, when you and your car are gone, I may well be in need of it.'

'Oh dear, I suppose you will. Would tea help? I was just going to put the kettle on.'

'Indeed it would. Tea. Fabulous.'

'And toast?'

Henry groaned and clutched his stomach. 'Toast. Heaven.'

'Won't be a tick.' Charlotte tugged the window shut, pulled on some socks, got halfway downstairs and then – in the interests of decorum – went back up in search of her jeans. Ten minutes later they were seated opposite each other at the kitchen table, with a plate of buttered toast, an assortment of jams and the cottage teapot, which was in the gimmicky shape of a square cow and impossible to pour.

'Allow me – years of practice. It needs one sharp tip.'

Charlotte giggled as Henry's attempt resulted in a pool of spilt tea even larger than the one she had managed. 'I'll get a cloth.' She trotted over to the sink then let out a cry of annoyance as a mild irritation in her left eye sharpened into real pain.

'What is it?'

'Nothing. Something in my eye. Toast probably. Hang on.' Charlotte tugged at her upper lid, then blinked furiously. 'There, that's better. No, it isn't.' She blinked harder, her eye streaming. 'Bugger, I need a mirror.'

'No, wait, let me take a look.'

Charlotte, one hand over the afflicted eye, was already halfway to the door but Henry blocked her path. 'I'm good at this sort of thing. I even have a clean handkerchief – *voilà*.' He pulled a crisply folded blue hanky out of his back pocket and shook it with a flourish. 'Keep still now ... Look left ... Look right ... Up ... Ah, there we are ... there ... Don't move ... don't ...' Henry, steady-handed with the sharpest scalpel, willed the tremor from his fingers and knees as he pushed the lid upwards. He had located the tiny offending black speck, but could see only her eye – her beautiful eye – a Catherine wheel of greens and browns and blacks. And the first image of her that morning was still clouding his vision too, the tumble of hair as she pulled on her jumper, the glimpse of her ribcage through the flimsy material of her nightdress.

Charlotte, waiting patiently, face tipped up, like a most

dutiful patient, was at first merely uncomfortable. Then, like the tiniest breeze changing direction, she became aware of something different, something not right – not right at all. Henry was looking into her eye and she was trying to look at the ceiling, trying now not to blink, focusing on the antics of a fat fly trampolining near a cobweb. All was as it had been, and yet . . . not. For there was suspense suddenly, suspense and expectation and an *atmosphere* so thick she could have sliced it. Charlotte was still registering this change, hoping it would disappear back into the invisible, baffling place whence it came, when Henry, having deftly removed the speck with a corner of his handkerchief, cupped both hands round the back of her head and groaned, 'Charlotte . . . Oh, God, Charlotte.'

For a moment Charlotte couldn't speak. Henry's eyes, magnified a little through the lenses of his glasses, were closed, the lids trembling. The sight, so vulnerable, so obvious in its expectation of physical bliss, was curiously moving. He was going to kiss her and part of her wanted him to. Yes, it did. Dear sweet Henry, who had spent three selfless days fathering Sam and tending her, showing the pair of them what they had never really known. Family holidays with Martin had been such battlegrounds, with poor Sam caught in the middle, the reason, often, for the arguments and the solace when they spun out of control.

Henry had an appealing mouth too – Charlotte had thought so more than once – generous, playful, agile, perfect for kissing. More importantly he was nice, really *nice*. And if he liked her in this astonishing, unexpected way then did she – the independent, no-strings party – really have to take on the huge, painful responsibility of pushing him away? Life was such a mess. Surely one could justify grabbing happiness where one could, squeezing the joy out of each second, living for the moment? Wasn't that precisely what she had vowed to do?

Henry, sensing the possibility of reciprocation, murmured her name again and pulled her face towards his. Their lips were barely an inch apart when two things happened in quick succession: Charlotte, coming to her senses, jerked out of reach and Henry's phone rang in his trouser pocket.

'It's Theresa.' He stared bleakly at the handset, not answering.

'I'll speak to her, shall I?' Charlotte snapped.

'No ... I ...' Henry carried on looking at the phone although it had stopped ringing. His shoulder was still throbbing where Charlotte had pushed him away: firm, sharp as a gunshot. 'Charlotte, being with you has been ... I ...'

'You,' she hissed, 'are an idiot. As am I.'

'No, never you, never ...'

'Oh, Henry, grow up and stop playing games. I came down here in good faith, with no agenda except a break with Sam. It never *occurred* to me that – my God, all that dancing around us, all that *pandering* ... I don't even have the words to say how it makes me feel.'

'Charlotte.' Henry's knees had finally given way and he was supporting himself against the old pine dresser that had belonged to his mother and still displayed what had been her favourite cut-glass vase. 'Charlotte, my feelings for you – I thought you knew ... I thought that you ... these last few days ...'

'Feelings?' Charlotte snorted, too angry to care about being kind. 'And what about Theresa's *feelings*? She doesn't deserve this, Henry, and what's more, I know you love her, I *know* it, because I've seen it over years and years – seen it and been jealous of it, because although I loved Martin once, it went wrong through his total lack of ability to be *faithful*,' she spat the word, 'and though I'm glad to be *un*married because of how hopeless and mutually horrible that made us, I have lately realized the size and scale of the thing we managed to throw away. And if I could get it back I would – I bloody *would*.'

Charlotte stood clenching and unclenching her fists, breathing hard, her eyes burning. 'Now call Theresa back, for God's sake. It might have been urgent.'

'Urgent?' Henry gripped the edge of the dresser, struggling to accommodate this new horror alongside Charlotte's shattering hostility: all that vulnerability, all that intoxicating neediness, where had it gone? But she was absolutely right – for Theresa to call at eight on a holiday morning, it had to be pretty important. He turned away to make the call, dreading to hear his wife's voice and what she might detect in his.

Charlotte was on the doorstep, shivering with aftershock rather than cold, when Henry came rushing out of the kitchen waving the phone. 'It's not me Theresa wants, it's you. Your phone was off.'

'No, it's not, it's just the signal,' Charlotte muttered, too sickened still to look at him.

'It's your mother, Charlotte.'

'My mother?' He had her attention now. 'My mother?' she repeated, as Henry hovered, chewing his lips, his face flexing in an unreadable mesh of emotions.

'I'm sorry, but apparently she's had a fall. Here.'

Henry retreated to the bike while the two women talked. It was still parked on its saddle next to the barn, the inner tubes hanging limply out of the tyres. Slowly, carefully, miserably, he teased and stretched them, using his clever doctor fingers to search for holes. The collision of fantasy and reality – Charlotte's revulsion, Theresa's call – had been like the worst physical pain. It was with him still, in the pump of his heart and in the sensation of standing not on the cottage's gravelled drive but on two separating tectonic plates; his life had cracked down the middle and he was astride the widening chasm, certain to tumble into it, to lose everything he had ever wanted and held dear.

The mist had cleared, revealing the flat brown and green counterpane of the fields and the gauzy grey-blue strip of the sea beyond. Turning his back on the stricken bike, Henry stared till the colours blurred, wretched that not even such a well-loved sight could offer comfort.

Chapter Eleven

On Sam's second birthday I buy a set of Mickey Mouse-themed paper plates, cups, napkins and hooters from the supermarket. Five small playmates from Tumble Tots are coming to tea and I have made a cake that sagged so badly on cooling that I filled the hole with Smarties, smothered it in icing and called it a treasure chest. The camouflage is to satisfy the beady eyes of the other mothers: Sam is still too young to recognize a pirate, let alone his booty. Squirming for release from the supermarket trolley, he is enthralled into silence not by the papery images of the cartoon mouse but by the crackle of the cellophane encasing it.

The beauty of my child still takes my breath away. His hair is white blond, with a gully of frizzed ringlets running from his crown to the nape of his neck. Martin likes to joke that they make him look like a girl and should be cut off. But the ringlets, especially, make me weak with love. I would sooner hack at my own hand than cut them off. On the rare occasions that Sam is sleepy, he winds his fingers through them while his mouth chomps on his left thumb. Martin enjoys remarking on this too, saying he'll grow up with a bald patch and buck teeth and should have the habits trained out of him before it's too late.

I know Martin only means to tease, but these days I find it harder to laugh. We're not on the same, effortless wavelength we once were. Before Newcastle it was Birmingham and before that Leeds. The computer companies are changing, getting larger, but we need more money, more space. I lack sleep and friends. Bella stayed in Australia and Eve, seeking her fortune in America, is rarely in touch. Sometimes I feel as if I only really have Sam.

I pause at the checkout to consider this, wondering whether to worry, *whether such feelings are normal after eight years together and the vortex of mothering. Martin would like more sex, I know that, but often I am too physically crushed by fatigue to respond (colic, teething pain, ear infections, eczema, croup — Sam leaves nothing out in the gamut of possibilities to offer disturbance).*

'He's gorgeous!' exclaims the checkout girl, cocking her head at the trolley where Sam, having bitten through the wrapping is now sucking the napkins. 'Hello, gorgeous.' She waves and Sam, kicking, offers an obliging smile.

But we made love that morning, I remind myself, pressing the worry away as I unload the bags and Sam into the car. Wary, as ever, of disturbing our boy, still parked at my insistence (for convenience) at the bottom of our double bed, we touched and moved with some furtiveness, but a glimmer of the old, effortless closeness was there. Afterwards I said sorry for so seldom being in the mood and Martin said he understood and not to worry. I explained also, for the first time, how — with my history — being a good mother meant the world and he said he understood that too.

Later, downstairs, while Sam banged his spoon against the sides of his high-chair, spraying blobs of baby porridge across the wall, I straightened Martin's tie fondly and reminded him of the birthday tea. He kissed me on the lips, saying he wouldn't miss it for the world, then made Sam wave and gurgle one of his 'bye-byes' before offering a valedictory thumbs-up at the lumpy treasure chest, now sprouting two candles and a spangled sign saying, 'You Are 2!'.

Yet when the party starts he is not there. The women offer reassurance and sympathy between attending to full nappies and tantrums. I want to wait for Martin, but time is racing and noise levels rising. My friends pick at the finger food, exchange anecdotes about minor domestic dramas and say, 'No hurry', but they have to be away by five. It's no big deal, I tell myself, swallowing analgesics for a pounding head before giving up the wait and embarking on a search for matches. 'It's no big deal,' I say aloud, smiling defiantly at the faces round the table, as

I pluck Sam out of his high-chair and bolster his baby puffing at the two little flames.

I'm surveying the debris of the party when Martin rushes in, pushing the hair from his eyes, his tie flying over one shoulder. He is apologetic but cheerful, full of quick-fire talk about late trains and overrun meetings. He would help clear up, he says, but he has to work. There is a possibility of promotion, to London, if he doesn't make a hash of things with his new boss, Fiona, a first in Maths from Oxford, a PhD from Harvard and sharp as nails. Talk about being kept on one's toes. He takes his briefcase into the sitting room and then, when Sam's tears of exhaustion grow too loud, stomps impatiently along the hall to our bedroom and closes the door.

A promotion might mean a house instead of a cramped flat and I want that badly, even if it means another move. A play room, a garden, an extra loo. I think of these things as I scrape the soggy remains of the cake into the bin and cajole Sam into the bath.

Suspicion arrives later that night, quietly, like a thief, tiptoeing in search of valuables. It is the suspicion not of infidelity – not yet – but of emotional desertion. To miss a birthday tea is a small crime; it is the ease with which it was missed that hurts – no phone call, no real attempt to atone, just talk of work, promotions and his big-brained boss. With such priorities how can there be room for love, either for me or Sam? I move closer, nuzzling the little forest of curls on the patch of neck under his hairline, seeking reassurance. But there is no response, only Martin's own skin-smell and the faint scent of something else, something sweeter – the new body-wash, probably, that I bought for the shower.

I roll away and close my eyes, blinking them open in an instant when the first snuffles come from the cot. Everything is as it should be, I tell myself. My world, since Martin entered it, is safe. And yet I am aware of a new alertness that has no connection to the patchy sleeping patterns of our child. It is an alertness to danger – of patterns repeating, of losing love, losing Martin.

*

Sam ducked past the barn window, climbed over the gate he was supposed, always, to open and close, and picked up a hefty branch, which he thrashed as he walked. He felt bad about his granny, but probably not as bad as he guessed he was supposed to feel. A broken bone was serious, of course, but the fact that she had done it slipping as she got out of the bath conjured unwelcome images of her old-lady body, wobbling and slithery, sprawling on the tiled floor. He wasn't sure he could have brought himself to touch her as Prue, the poor cleaning lady, had presumably had to while they waited for the ambulance.

Spotting a sturdier, leafless stick, Sam flung aside the branch and picked it up. It had an end as sharp as a tent pole and growths hanging off it like pendulous fat grey warts. Sam shook it and charged a squirrel, which scampered up a tree, causing two large black birds to erupt out of the branches in a frenzy of flapping that made him jump. 'Fuck you,' he shouted, pointing his mouth at the sky as the birds shrank to pinpricks. 'Fucking fuck you.'

Sam knew he would have felt better about his granny (i.e. worse) if it hadn't been for the other stuff, the stuff just before the phone call. His mum and George's dad, *in each other's arms*. If he hadn't seen it through the open door of the kitchen with his own eyes he wouldn't have believed it. In fact, even though he *had* seen it, Sam still couldn't believe it. If such things could happen the world made no sense. If such things could happen, he wanted no part of them.

George's map turned out to be pretty useless, arrows and curves supposedly indicating a big dip in the dunes near a broken tree; but there were several broken trees and loads and loads of dips. Sam searched for a bit, studying the map from different angles, wondering if he had got the sea muddled with the sky, until a woman in wellingtons, using a ball-thrower for a muddy-legged Labrador, asked if he was lost and could she help. He shouted no and ran back the way he had come, then dived behind one of the steepest dunes when she wasn't looking. Peeping out, Sam watched the waves pushing and pulling along the shore, leaving rings of foam and straggles of seaweed. He could still make out the clear double path of his footprints embedded along the edge of the water where the sand was heavy and damp. In contrast, the sand in the dunes was dry and silky cool, spilling into the indentations his body made the moment he shifted his weight.

After the woman and the dog had gone Sam rolled on to his back and swished his arms to make angel wings. Overhead the sky was like a domed ceiling, impossibly blue, impossibly huge. It's just a planet, he told himself, with no god, no rules. It didn't matter that he had divorcing parents and a mother who kissed other people's fathers. It didn't matter that his granny had flopped like a fish on a bathmat and that, with his dad too busy, apparently, to take him in, he would almost certainly end up enduring the horror of accompanying his mum to visit her in hospital.

'If only Theresa was in London,' Charlotte had wailed between phone calls, her mood of general despair worsened by having to hold the handset at odd angles to get a signal and the fact of his father's work crisis. Sam, unable to imagine ever wanting to see George's mum or George's dad – especially not his dad – ever again, had chosen that moment to grab the hideout map and slip out of the back door.

He closed his eyes and pressed the back of his head into the sand. There was only one person he really felt like seeing, one impossible secret person who almost certainly hadn't got his latest letter and who would probably laugh if he told her what had happened. Sam opened his eyes and squinted as the sun slid out from behind a cloud and beamed into his face like a torch. He sat up, scratching the grit out of his hair. Rose wouldn't laugh. He knew she wouldn't because she wasn't like other kids. She knew when things were serious, what could be made fun of and what couldn't. Rose didn't have to be told that life was shitty because she knew already.

When Sam arrived back at the edge of the field they were both there, hands cupped round their mouths, hollering his name. Hearing the terror in his mother's voice, Sam broke into a run and waved his arms. A few minutes later she was clasping him and kissing him and calling him stupid and saying in a weird, strangled voice that they needed to pack up the car and get going.

George's dad stood well back, with folded arms, shaking his head. When the three of them turned back for the house, he muttered, 'Not your best move, mate. The tides round here are very dangerous.'

Sam shrugged and ran on ahead. When his mum caught up with him he said, speaking in a great rush for fear of losing courage, that he was really sorry about Granny's accident and running off and he would of course come to the hospital if she wanted, but he had thought of someone else with whom he might be able to stay, given that George wasn't around and his dad was too busy.

'Really?' She looked astonished and almost happy, as if the unexpectedness of such a thing had driven out the other worries of the day. 'Who's that, then?'

Sam mumbled Rose's name, then said it louder, looking her right in the eye, daring her to laugh or refuse, feeling suddenly that his new knowledge of her awful, gross secret gave him power – the power of *not* caring.

'*Rose Porter?* But you . . . surely you . . .'

'We're friends now,' Sam snapped. 'Her dad might say no, but I'd like you to ask. I know they're not going away because they were moving to that house, the one you liked.'

'Yes . . . they were . . . Okay, then . . . Well, we can try, I suppose, if I can get hold of the phone number . . . Sam, darling, are you absolutely *sure?*' Charlotte carried on staring at him, clearly amazed still, like she was seeing him for the first time and didn't have a clue what else to say.

Tim's morning had begun, unpromisingly, with a piece of tooth catapulting into the basin off the end of his toothbrush. Although the chip was small, the hole in his mouth felt, to the probing tip of his tongue, terrifyingly decrepit and huge. Tim had had fillings decompose on several occasions, but never a section of his own enamel, and could not help but regard the experience as a grim reminder that, no matter how hard he worked at the gym, no matter how solid a keyboard of abdominals emerged as a result, the next three decades would be about the creeping loss of physical resilience, teeth, hair, testosterone and all the other things that made life worth living.

With someone at his side to cosset him through such uncharacteristic troughs of pessimism and fan his ego with loads of rampant sex, he was sure he wouldn't have felt so bad. But since the horrible anti-climax of his date with Charlotte, his personal life had deflated to the point of non-existence. Sitting alone with a can of beer on the sofa the previous evening, watching an episode of an American soap he had seen at least three times, surrounded by the usual domestic detritus of unwashed mugs, old newspapers and abandoned clothes too crumpled to wear but not yet worthy of the washing-machine, he had felt sufficiently miserable to click on his laptop and tap 'dating agencies' into the Google search engine. Scores of possibilities had come up – *Perfect Partner*, *Lonely Hearts*, *Love4Life*, *Brief Encounters* – and although in the end male pride, coupled with a reluctance to part with several hundred pounds, had got the better of him, Tim had felt greatly reassured that such options were there, should he ever decide he *did* need them.

Everyone required safety-nets, he had comforted himself, snapping shut his laptop and embarking on a clear-up that included swishing a duster across the leopard print and then, with more tenderness, the mounted photo of Phoebe in the Caribbean. The picture had only retained its prominent position because its removal would have displayed an unsightly square of dirt; but it was, in fact, a bloody good shot, Tim had decided, leaning closer to admire the sharp focus of his ex-wife's face and the handsome backdrop of emerald sea and azure sky. How was she *really* doing now, he had wondered, in Dorset with – according to various grapevine reports – a lawyer boyfriend, platinum highlights in her hair and weekend riding lessons? Was Phoebe happy enough not to need a safety-net? Did she miss him as he, in unguarded moments, missed her?

Queuing at the dentist's reception desk, Tim's thoughts reverted, accusingly, to Charlotte. Talk about a knee in the balls. Lover to rapist in one second – when all he had done was follow her signals. She hadn't *said* as much, of course – mostly, from what he could recall, she had apologized – but Tim had seen it in her eyes, the accusing hurt, as if he'd stuck a knife into her instead of his dick. Angry at the memory – at being in thrall to it still – Tim flipped open one of the magazines lying on the waiting-room table: 'DENIAL ANGER ACCEPTANCE – GETTING HER OUT OF YOUR SYSTEM'.

'Mr Croft, ah, yes, we're squeezing you in. If you'd like to follow me, we need some forms filling in first.' The young receptionist peered over her clipboard. Green eyes, Irish, creamy blonde hair – but flat-chested *and* an engagement ring. Tim, a little weary of his own relentless assessment of females, swallowed the quip he'd had ready about following her anywhere and stepped meekly past the other waiting patients.

He was fish-mouthed, jaw aching, palms damp, having a temporary crown glued into place when the jaunty ring-tone of his mobile broke through the hum of soporific tunes, which Tim had decided offered a sinister rather than soothing counterpoint to the experiences he was enduring in the sloping leather chair.

'Just a minute or two and you'll be able to answer that, Mr Croft.'

Tim released an agreeing groan that bore little correlation to his true state of wretchedness. The protective glasses that the nurse had slotted across his face were cutting into the top of his left ear. Novocaine always made him feel queasy, yet work was still manic and required him to be on top form. Worse, he knew of no woman who wished to spend time with him or to touch his body. A terrible tear squeezed out of the corner of Tim's left eye, trickled down his cheekbone and into the corner of his mouth. He licked it away, steadying himself with the vicious reflection that a man with such cavernous nostrils might have thought twice before applying to dental school.

The phone, demoted to 'vibrate mode', buzzed again when he was struggling through numbed lips to rinse his mouth and then again when he was handing over his switch card and making an appointment to have the real crown installed. Not studying the list of missed calls until he got back to his car, Tim let out an involuntary cry of triumphant delight on seeing that they were from Charlotte. But steady, he warned himself, winding down the car window before replying, and taking a breath as deep as those required for a length underwater at his gym's Olympic pool.

'Tim?'

'I've been to the dentist,' he managed, all vestiges of steadiness or calm dispersing at the familiar, attractive sound of Charlotte's voice and the reminder that half his face and mouth were immobile.

'Poor you, and I'm so sorry to be a bother but, Tim, I need your help. My mother has had a fall and is in hospital and it's too complicated to explain why but I need Mrs Stowe's phone number – that is, I need the number of the person now living in her house, Dominic Porter. You probably remember him – the widower who hated my place. Unbelievable that *he* should end up with Chalkdown, but there we are. Small world and all that, and although I was upset at first I really don't care now. He might have changed the number, of course, but I'd like to try and you're my only hope as I'm stuck in Suffolk without my address book or list of class phone numbers, although that wouldn't have it anyway.' She breathed at last. 'So, Mrs Stowe's number, *please*, Tim, it's an emergency so *please* don't say anything about it being unethical.'

A woman in crisis, and he almost without the wherewithal to utter consonants . . . Tim could see no option but to swallow his misery and comply. Pressing his fingers to his cheek in a bid to encourage the functioning of the muscles, he managed a response to the effect that he would check his contacts list and text her the number if he had it. There was a rushed 'Thank you,' and that was it. All over. No hope, no recrimination, no regret, nothing. Tim stared out of his open window for several minutes, wondering if he might be sick.

The text took a little while to compose, not because Tim had any trouble finding or forwarding Mrs Stowe's number but because he set about it with the intention of communicating a couple of things in addition to Charlotte's request – like the untruth that he shared her evident indifference to their failed romance, and a calculatedly vengeful release of the recent rumour about the two puffs selling the bookshop. He might have no power over her heart, but he could put the wind up her at least. With the elder of the two reputed to have AIDS, the pair were said to be planning to cut their losses and retreat to their pad in Spain. Ravens Books would probably be replaced by a chic café, or one of those local branches of the major supermarkets. 'Here is tel. Hope ur mum get better. Sorry to hear ur bkshop up 4 sale. Life mad busy. T.'

Not much more coherent than anything he could have managed out loud. Nonetheless Tim pressed 'send' with a certain vicious glee, then phoned Savitri to explain he was in no fit state to work and taking his heavy heart and throbbing mouth home. He would go to the gym, he decided grimly, lift his mood with endorphins, make eyes at the chubby receptionist with big tits and a laugh like a strangled donkey.

But as he closed his front door Tim had to steady himself against the wall. His mouth tingled and the root of his tooth was pulsing. He couldn't exercise without some food and he couldn't eat, not for several hours, the dentist had said, and then only on the other side of his mouth. Nothing tasted good on one side of the mouth, nothing.

Tim sank to his knees and riffled glumly through the pile of post on the doormat. All the envelopes were brown, but the one uppermost, now bearing a faint imprint of the sole of his shoe, was particularly large and thick. Curious, Tim turned it over, only to find his spirits plummeting to a new low at recognition of the name of the company from which he had, with such buoyant hopes, purchased Charlotte's fortieth birthday gift a few weeks and an eternity before. All those good intentions, all that money – the bitch! But there was no anger left to come, no petty spite, only a dizzying wave of recognition that it was over. It was over and it had never really begun. Acceptance, just like the stupid article in the waiting room had said.

Which meant his suffering wasn't even original, Tim reflected grimly. It was just a feeling experienced by millions, a passing phase, suitable for packaging in glossy magazines. He prepared to tear the envelope in two, but hesitated, absently running his tongue along the familiar geography of his teeth, feeling for the gap. The temporary crown felt snug, solid. The throbbing was turning into a pleasant sort of prickle. The gift had cost a lot and the company might give him a refund. He slapped the envelope against his thigh as he got to his feet, scolding himself for so nearly losing focus, for almost allowing a woman to run rings round him when he had vowed never to do so again.

Keeping a wary eye open for police and cameras, Charlotte accelerated into the empty outer lane of the A20 until the speedometer needle was bouncing around ninety. The Volkswagen, thankfully, responded like a child to a treat, moving through its usual protesting coughs to a deep, steady purr.

The peculiar ordeal of posting Sam through the rose-fringed door of number forty-two Chalkdown Road was upon her still. Holstered and ready to fire with politeness and gratitude, she had been disarmed to find herself greeted not by Dominic but by the famous actor brother, with his dashing, tousled hair and piercing hazelnut eyes. He appeared to be dressed for high summer, in bright pink flip-flops, baggy knee-length shorts and a crumpled T-shirt. There were even sunglasses on his head, perched elegantly among the dark, perfectly messed-up waves.

'This is so kind.'

'Not at all. With me as her only playmate, Rose was dying of boredom, weren't you, Rosie?' He patted his niece, who was hanging on to the edge of his T-shirt, holding an awkward pigeon-footed pose and staring at the floor.

Charlotte wondered for by no means the first time whether the whole dubious arrangement should be abandoned. After some understandable surprise and a brief muffled consultation with his daughter, Dominic had agreed readily that Sam should come and stay. But now the girl looked decidedly reluctant, while Sam was lurking behind a flourish of roses somewhere to her left. They had had a horrible journey too, of bad traffic and punishing silence – hers on account of worry and Sam's, she presumed, because she had seen fit to reiterate her scolding for his jaunt to the beach.

'Dom was supposed to be home all day but something blew up at the office. He said to apologize. Do you have time for tea?'

'No, I –'

'Coffee? Gin?' Rose and Sam caught each other's eye and giggled.

'No, my mother . . . I . . .'

'Of course – *Christ*, of course. I'm so sorry – your mother's *accident*.' Benedict slapped a palm to his forehead. 'She's in hospital, I gather?'

'Yes, a broken wrist, bruising. It could have been a lot worse.' Charlotte reached for Sam's arm and tried to extract him from behind the briar, managing only to scatter a shower of dusky white petals across the doorstep. The giggle with Rose had been encouraging, though. 'It won't be for long, probably just a night, with it being Easter this weekend. I know it's a terrible imposition. If, for some reason, I'm not back tomorrow then Sam's father . . .' Charlotte let the sentence hang as a gust of fresh annoyance at Martin's lack of co-operation swept over her. Lack of flexibility, work first, no question of Cindy stepping in – some things never changed.

'As long as you want, Dom said. Easter, Christmas, no worries. Hey, Sam, good to meet you,' Benedict added easily, ducking round the flowers to make eye contact. 'I hope you're good with bonfires. Rosie and I have had a bit of a clear-out in the garden. Just a tiny fire, nothing to upset the neighbours . . . or your mum,' he added, offering Charlotte a broad grin, followed by an imperceptible wink as Sam, clutching his overnight bag, shuffled through the door.

On any other day it might have been rather thrilling to exchange complicit looks with a handsome celebrity, even one occupying the house of her dreams, Charlotte mused, moving across into the slow lane so as not to miss the turning off the motorway. The day, with its unexpected twists, seemed to have gone on for ever. It felt like years since the débâcle with Henry in the cottage kitchen, the dreadful hope in his blinking owl-eyes, her even more dreadful urge to respond to it. It felt like years and yet her stomach still churned with shame. How stupid she had been in not recognizing the signs – so obvious in retrospect – seeing only Theresa's husband, seeing *Henry*, for goodness' sake, solid, married Henry, safe to accept lifts from and even flirt with a little over a glass or two or on a country walk. Except not safe. Not safe at all. There were boundaries – she of all people knew that, she of all people should have been on the lookout for them.

Charlotte was well aware that the distressing news about her mother's accident had been a tremendous help, not just in breaking the horror of the moment but also in seeing her through its aftermath. Although she would gladly have forgone the distraction of Sam's walkabout, it had been a relief to have the phoning and packing to get on with, not to mention such a perfect pretext for early escape. What she was still agonizing over was the follow-up: what to *do* about what had happened. Henry, with what seemed to her to be sickening *male* predictability, had behaved like a shit, and part of her could not help thinking that this might be something Theresa had a right to know. She was so proud and strong, Theresa, the sort of woman who valued straight talking, who, having been presented with an unpalatable truth, would know exactly what to do with it.

It took some effort to shift the focus of her thoughts to her mother. In fact, Charlotte realized guiltily, shaking her purse for the right change for the machine in the hospital car park, thinking about her mother held very little appeal. She would be helpless, sorry for herself, with the bruising and the plaster. The situation was going to demand a show of daughterly bedside vigilance to which she would have felt unequal even without the horrors of the morning . . . horrors that had included – Charlotte froze, pound coin poised in the slot as her thoughts veered away from Jean yet again to the throwaway remark in Tim's text. What would she do without her job? It would simply be too cruel to lose it now, just as she was getting the hang of things.

She was having a difficult day, she scolded herself, ramming the coin home and striding back to place the ticket in the car. She would *not* let the hopelessness back in. Life was about difficult days. All she had to do was keep her head, deal with one problem at a time and the lovely new sense of direction would return. And right now the problem requiring her attention most urgently was her mother. A decent interval at her bedside, saying the right things, taking down a list of what she wanted from home, stocking up the fridge, checking the house was clean and tidy – yes, she could manage that. And she would speak to the nurses about follow-up care too, secure the relevant forms and information in case a home visit or two was called for when Jean was discharged.

By the hospital entrance there was a large, circular flowerbed, a floral soup of colours – sweet williams, pansies, busy lizzies, all pert and freshly bedded. Charlotte paused, breathing in the scents, trying to get herself in the right mood. Instead her mind swung back – with sudden, winding force – to the moment when Henry had charged at her with the phone on the doorstep of the cottage. *She's dead*, Charlotte had thought. *She's dead and this is how it feels and it's not too bad, not too bad at all.* Absorbing the rest of Henry's sentence, that Jean had suffered a fall rather than perished, Charlotte had been aware of a diabolical pulse of anti-climax.

Unnerved, she hurried to the gift shop to make amends. Twenty minutes later, she arrived at the entrance to the ward, armed with a bunch of carnations, a bag of seedless grapes and the most expensive box of chocolates she had been able to find.

'Ah, Mrs Boot's daughter,' exclaimed the nurse, after she had introduced herself. 'Lovely – I think they're nearly ready for you. I'll see if I can find Nurse Telson to give you a hand getting her to the car.'

'To the car? But I thought –'

'Fortunately the break isn't nearly as bad as the doctor first feared. It's her confidence that's taken a knock more than anything. Seeing as there's someone to look after her, we're very happy for her to go home. Recovery is always quicker there – especially with a loved one around. Lucky thing,' the nurse added, beaming. 'In these situations you wouldn't believe how many children just don't want to know.'

'Do you do an egg hunt, then?'

'Always. Dad hides them. I'm not supposed to look but of course I try to. Each year he makes it harder and harder. Last time he'd stuck one into this hosepipe thing and I had to use a knife to get it out. There were twelve, but I'm only allowed to eat three a day, so it took four days, obviously.'

'Obviously,' Sam murmured, sending up a small urgent prayer for his granny to be sick enough and his father busy enough to keep him at the Porters' through the weekend. Rose had a knack of making the simplest things good fun. Like building the den they were lying in now, nibbling biscuits, slumped among cushions like Roman emperors. He had said something about George's useless map and the next thing he knew she was leaping around the house ordering him to grab cushions and sheets and tugging mattresses off beds. Their first couple of efforts hadn't worked too well – collapsing walls, too many rooms – but they had simplified it into a brilliant space with two sections, so high in one bit that they could kneel upright without touching the sheet ceiling.

Sam had never met a girl who was into dens before. Pattie had only ever wanted to do drawings and watch TV. Secretly, he wondered if both of them shouldn't have outgrown such hobbies. They were thirteen, after all. But

Rose, as he had already seen a million times, in her strong, nose-in-the-air solitariness at school, wasn't the sort of girl who cared much about one was *supposed* to think or do. And Sam found it made him want to care less too. In the park that morning her dad had sat on a bench reading a news-paper while they played a game of spying on walkers, mostly from the branches of a large tree. She had produced a sugared ball of pink bubble gum, then a squashed cigarette, stolen, she claimed proudly, from a pack her uncle kept hidden in the inside pocket of his coat. 'He's trying to give up but just *can't*,' she had claimed, shaking her head as if it was something to be really sad about, then instructing Sam to cup his hands while she struck a match. The flame guttered madly, but Rose puffed till her lips squeaked and soon, amid much coughing and laughing, the cigarette tip was glowing and they were passing it between them. After-wards they had a bubble-blowing competition, which Rose won by producing a massive wobbling orb that made her cross-eyed and bounced on her nose before exploding across her lips and cheeks, mixing pink flecks among the brown galaxies of her freckles.

How on earth did you kiss a girl? Sam wondered now, watching Rose shovel a fourth biscuit into her mouth and recalling, with some distaste, the cold soggy feel of her saliva on the cork tip of their shared cigarette. Lips, he could imagine, but tongues ... *Eh-yew*, as Rose would say. No, Sam decided, definitely no. He tried to think about some-thing else, only for a vivid flashback to swoop in from nowhere: the half-open kitchen door, George's dad's arms across his mother's back, their faces close. He put his own biscuit back on the plate, feeling too hot, too horrible even to swallow.

'What's up?'

'Nothing.'

'Yes, there is. You look weird, like you're going to puke.'

Sam breathed hard. 'Can you keep a secret?'

Rose snorted, managing to communicate disdain as well as reassurance. 'Of course.'

Sam crawled to the sheet hanging over the entrance to check they were alone, then scrambled into a cross-legged position facing her. Mumbling most of the words into his hands, he attempted to describe the obscenity he had witnessed in Suffolk, the one that had ruined the holiday far more than his granny belly-flopping on to the bathmat.

Rose, as he had anticipated correctly, didn't laugh. She murmured, 'Gross,' several times, then refolded her skinny legs tidily and used both hands to push the springy corkscrew curls out of her eyes. 'Problems always have solutions — that's what Dad says.'

Sam nodded gloomily. The overhead sheet was starting to sag badly; bits of Rose's hair were sticking to it as she talked. 'I don't suppose,' she lowered her voice to a whisper and leant towards him, 'there's been anyone else your mum's liked, has there?'

Sam nodded slowly, scowling at the recollection of the hairy-faced estate agent and the bouquet of flowers.

'Tell me everything,' she commanded, burrowing to find a pad of paper, then making notes, as if she was a detective in a TV show taking evidence.

Sam obeyed without hesitation, not just because Rose's enthusiasm and confidence were catching but because, as far as their mattress and sheet edifice was concerned, they were clearly living on borrowed time.

It was odd being on the train during the afternoon, surrounded by returning shoppers and children instead of commuters huddled behind free-sheets, clutching briefcases. It was also unpleasantly warm – the railway network's heating system had not been adjusted to accommodate the strength of the afternoon sun, now firing directly along the train windows. Dominic loosened his tie, had another go at opening the window, then sat down again, offering a half-apologetic smile at the young woman opposite, who had several bulging shopping-bags and had watched his efforts to cool the carriage with what he had taken to be support. He tried broadening the smile but her face froze into a mask of wariness.

Dominic looked out of the window instead, at the may-hem of warehouses and scrapyards, terraced houses and high streets. He liked being back in London far more than he could ever have imagined; he loved its sheer busyness, so many colours, creeds and personalities living on top of each other, trying to make a living, and, presumably, like him, endeavouring to be happy. There was something noble in the effort, he decided, as the train trundled above market stalls in full flow and strings of pegged washing flapped on tower-block balconies.

Redundant. Dominic tested the word in his head, trying for the umpteenth time to get a grip on his true reactions, but not managing to progress beyond another knee-jerking sensation of personal rejection. The word itself had never been used, of course, not by his sympathetic colleagues or the sharply dressed female MD who had been mandated to deliver the decision. He was being 'released', 'let go'; the bank was rationalizing, economizing, streamlining. Several other heads had rolled as well, although only Dominic could boast the distinction of having been summoned in from a day off for the privilege.

Benedict, in pitching his kindly intended but absurd

business proposition the other evening (Dominic had rejected it out of hand), had been right in pointing out that his brother did not enjoy his job particularly, but that did not make the inconvenience of losing it any easier to bear. It was true that he would, in an ideal world, like to spend more time with Rose, and that he did have a lot of savings – although most of the latter had been swallowed up in the purchase of the new house. It was wonderful to have no mortgage but, Dominic reflected bitterly, the overheads of life still required a salary.

He felt somewhat bitter, too, about the timing of his ejection from the world of high finance: the ink on his house purchase was still virtually wet, his daughter had settled into school at last and was at that very moment enjoying the company of her first publicly acknowledged friend since losing her mother (the most unlikely unexpected friend, of course, forced into the open by sheer chance, but that was Rose for you). Such developments had taken so much effort and yet now, with his *redundancy*, Dominic couldn't help thinking that the necessity of all that effort had been some-what undermined. They needn't have moved back to London. He could have taken their grieving state and his talent for advising clients on investments to Scotland or Bath or Timbuktu.

Dominic hugged his briefcase, brooding over whether the time off round Maggie's death had done for him, all that compassionate leave; his employers had probably had the knives hovering ever since, paying lip service to accom-modating the work compromises required by his personal tragedy while secretly condemning him for it.

He was gripping the briefcase a little too hard, he realized. The girl with the bags was looking at him strangely. Although several minutes from his stop, he left his seat and went to stand by the doors. He would tell no one about his sacking, he decided, at least, not until the bank holiday was over; not Rose, not Benedict – especially not Benedict, who would start lining up beer bottles again and telling him what to do. An employment lawyer was what he needed, but not until Tuesday when Rose went back for the start of the summer term.

Dominic walked home via the supermarket, where he filled his trolley with a ridiculous quantity of oval-shaped confectionary of all sizes, several large foil-wrapped rabbits and, for good measure, a box of chicks that squawked, 'Happy Easter,' when you tapped their beaks. It was panic-buying of sorts – he was in shock, he knew – but there was also something pleasingly reckless about it. Maggie – zealot of things home-made, of keeping treats in moderation – would have been appalled.

'Your kids will love you,' chuckled the woman at the till.

'I certainly hope so.' Dominic blazed a smile at her, a little nervous at this inadvertent reminder of their house-guest. Rose had been so thrilled and pleading when he had taken Charlotte's surprising call for help that morning that there had been no question of saying no, but now he found himself wondering about more practical matters, like whether Sam would eat the shepherd's pie he planned for supper and whether he should expend any concern over sleeping arrangements. Rose clearly assumed that Sam would occupy the lower bunk in her bedroom, but they were a girl and a boy, teenagers now, and Sam was almost certainly the correspondent Benedict had been told about. Who knew what they had been saying in their letters, or what their hopes were? For a moment Dominic was even tempted to consult the woman at the checkout, who looked the jolly, maternal sort, easily old enough to have been through a few similar quandaries herself.

Instead he was interrupted by the trill of his mobile. 'Hello?' Dominic slipped the phone between his shoulder and his ear so that he could continue packing his shopping.

'Ah, I have you at last.'

'Petra, indeed you do, so to speak . . . except that I'm in the supermarket, about to pay for a ton of Easter eggs. If you could give me two minutes,' Dominic pleaded, struggling now with his wallet, the bags and the phone, and turning his back on the checkout woman, who was clearly enjoying the show. 'Don't go away. Keep the phone in your hand. Two minutes – and I'll call you back.'

'I want to meet with you, Dominic,' she said. 'If you do not want me, please, I prefer that you say it.'

'Of course I want you,' he whispered. 'That is, I would like to meet you very much. And in two minutes I will call you back to arrange it.'

The checkout lady's face had closed like a fist. From hands-on dad to sneaky husband – that was what she thought, Dominic realized helplessly, as she snatched his receipt out of the till and slapped it into his palm. He offered a firm thank-you but she was already beaming at the next customer, giving a fresh face the chance he had unwittingly thrown away.

He called Petra back the moment he had slung his bags into the car, only to be told, 'This is Petra, please leave your message.'

Dominic slammed both hands on the roof of the car so hard that his wedding ring clanged against the metal. He remembered in the same instant, with some astonishment, that he had forgotten to buy a goose. Goose, potatoes, carrots, peas for Easter Sunday lunch ... Benedict was coming, he had it all planned. He must be in an even greater state of shock than he had thought. A little wearily, Dominic pulled his phone back out of his pocket but found himself studying his wedding ring instead: white gold, engraved with the date of their marriage. Maggie had had it made specially. Tucking the phone under his arm, taking a deep breath, he removed the ring and dropped it into his back pocket. It came easily, even over the knuckle, as if it was ready.

'I would like to see you,' he insisted, in response to the recording of Petra's voice when he dialled again, 'very much *indeed*. I will have a lot more free time from now on and will make lunch with you a number-one priority. I'm not one for giving up,' he added, before stabbing his electronic key lock in the direction of his car and plunging back into the supermarket.

Chapter Twelve

After the flat there is so much space in the Wandsworth house that I dance from room to room with outstretched arms, proving to myself, and Sam, skipping behind, that we can now live and move and have our being without bouncing off walls. Martin, more usefully employed with speaker wire and screwdrivers, pauses to watch, laughing with an abandon that makes my heart sing. A change of geography may not cure, but already it is helping. She – whoever she was (Fiona, probably, but he never admitted anything) – is far away now, a thing of the past, like the too-small flat and the ill-lit street corners and Martin's ridiculous working hours. I stop dancing, catching my breath as some of the sourness, the suspicion, threatens to return. Fifteen-hour days . . . He might as well have invited her home.

We heave at furniture together and hang pictures, taking it in turns to balance on the arms of chairs and call out guidance as to where to bang the nail. For supper we order pizza because the oven doesn't work; a fuse, Martin thinks, but he has no spares and the shops are closed. We keep Sam up late to tire him out, letting him chew the pizza crusts and play among the boxes while we slave at the unpacking. We are a team again, I feel, at last. And when Martin wins the battle with the speaker wire and puts on one of our old favourites, I slip into his arms with something like the reverence of our very first time. We dance, cheek to cheek, eyes closed; a new rare perfect moment. I vow to hold on to it. Nothing with Fiona could ever have felt so good, so close.

A vital screw has gone missing in the move so we can't put up the bed. We sleep sprawling on the mattress, too exhausted to care. Across the landing, Sam, in his own room for the first time, wakes in the middle of the night and howls, rattling the bars of his new safety rail

*like a despairing prisoner. Martin growls, 'Leave him,' but I can't.
Of course I can't.*

*'Hey, sweetheart.' His little arms clamp round my neck. I try to
lay him back down but he won't let go. I try a drink of water from
his beaker but he blows and spits and giggles. 'You bad, bad boy,'
I scold softly.*

'Bad, bad,' Sam echoes, rubbing his knuckles in his eyes, yawning.

*'Come on, then.' I carry him back to our mattress, trying to keep
him on my side so as not to disturb Martin, but within seconds Sam
is clambering across me to the middle, fearless — heedless, as every
four-year-old must be, of any desires but his own.*

Martin, disturbed, groans. 'He has his own room. Take him back.'

'You do it.'

'You know that won't work.'

'You never try.'

*Moments later my husband and my son are fast asleep, lying on
their backs, arms by their sides, as if sunbathing in the moonlight
spilling in through the still curtainless windows. Tears prick my eyes,
partly because I am tired but mostly because my faith is returning —
in us, in the fruit of our love, lying between, the point that separates,
but also the one that keeps us whole.*

In the end it took a couple of hours to leave the hospital.
Jean was having a final test somewhere and Nurse Telson
couldn't be found, which Charlotte took as an opportunity
to move the car nearer and make enquiries about nurses
visiting patients at home. Feeling a little more on top of
things, she did a double-take when the arrival of the patient
back on the ward was announced and she turned to find
herself staring at a hunched figure in a wheelchair. 'Mum.'
The word caught in her throat.

'The chair is just to save energy for getting to the car,'
explained the nurse in charge brightly. 'We're doing very

well, aren't we, Mrs Boot? We've had a scare more than anything, haven't we? Right as rain in no time, eh? What a lucky girl to have such a lovely daughter to come and look after you.'

Jean allowed a flicker of a smile to cross her face. Her right arm rested on her lap, like some disconnected, precious object, plastered from the fingers to the elbow. She was wearing her old blue Paisley dress, one sleeve hitched up to accommodate the plaster, and a faded grey cardigan, draped over her shoulders like a shawl. Her legs were swathed in their usual too-loose stockings, her feet in ancient sheepskin slippers instead of shoes. Through the stockings Charlotte could make out a couple of inky bruises on her shins and one that looked almost black, spreading from her right knee above her hemline. Her hair, meanwhile, without the attention usually paid to it, had lost its sprightliness and shrunk to flimsy, lifeless strands that made no secret of the chalky liver-spotted scalp from which they grew.

Charlotte waited in some suspense, certain that her real lack of loveliness must be showing through. But all Jean did was glance meekly from her to the nurse and murmur, 'Yes, indeed,' in a voice so whispered and flat that it was impossible to know if it was ironic or truly meant.

As they embarked on an obstacle course of stiff-hinged fire doors, over-populated corridors and tardy lifts, Charlotte found herself slipping into the same false heartiness as the nurse. *Soon have you home. A cup of tea and lots of rest work wonders.* It was a survival technique, a stopper for difficult thoughts. Inside, meanwhile, she could feel the dread she had experienced in the car park congealing into something far worse, something closer to revulsion.

She drove with exaggerated care, asking about the accident and the prognosis, trying not to be irritated by the feeble monosyllables that continued to come in response. As they pulled up outside the house Prue appeared round the corner with Jasper tugging unhappily on his lead. The cleaner, unsurprisingly, given her new duties, seemed delighted to see them, as did her charge, who had to be physically deterred from abseiling up the baggy stockings to have its head patted. It was the antics of her pet, however, that brought the first real smile to Jean's face, and she talked to it, too, Charlotte noted wryly, cooing nonsense throughout their laborious, hobbling progress to the front door.

Escaping in the car to the supermarket the following morning, Charlotte let out a small scream, then a much louder one that made her eardrums vibrate. Sam had pleaded to stay with the Porters and Martin had sounded relieved. A rota of carers would make home visits but not until after the bank-holiday weekend. Which meant she had four more days to endure, FOUR MORE DAYS. A hushed conversation with Prue had offered the back-up of thrice-weekly visits, 'If I'm paid,' the cleaner had added, which was perfectly allowable, understandable and what Charlotte would have expected anyway, but which had nonetheless made her flinch. Where were the bridge friends, she had wondered, and the names on the church flower rota? When had that hectic phase been replaced by daily communion with no one other than a dog?

The screaming helped. And the supermarket, in a vast clean complex, fringed with coffee shops and aisles as wide as small roads, was somehow soothing too. Charlotte took her time, doing her best to resist the urge to shop for her own tastes, selecting products either with long sell-by dates or which could be stored in her mother's tiny fridge-freezer.

Having paid, but wanting to defer the ordeal of returning,

Charlotte steered her laden trolley into the most salubrious coffee shop and settled herself into a deep leather chair with a latte and a chocolate brownie. She was midway through them, flipping the pages of an abandoned newspaper, when she experienced the shivering sixth-sense certainty that she was being stared at. It took a minute to locate the source – not by the buns and the coffee machines, but behind her, at another table, with an equally laden shopping trolley parked alongside. Cindy. Charlotte, having swivelled, managed a grimace of a smile. Ex-wife bumps into ex-husband's girlfriend – there was no etiquette manual for such encounters. She stretched the grimace for a moment longer, cursing the instinct that had prompted her to turn round.

Cindy's smile was equally starchy. She had no paper to read, Charlotte noticed, and maybe because of that seemed even more at a loss than her. She was somewhat dishevelled too, with her hair scooped into a messy ponytail and, for the first time that Charlotte could ever recall, parading a face that bore not a single trace of makeup. And what on earth was she doing in Tunbridge Wells on Good Friday, with a shopping trolley, looking so out of sorts? Slowly, with mounting curiosity that was not entirely benign, Charlotte turned for a second look. Cindy smiled again, with more assurance, then stood up, reaching for her coffee cup. 'I could join you?'

Charlotte hesitated, spellbound, not by the suggestion, although that felt bizarre enough, but by the clear view of Cindy, now that she was standing upright. A stranger, unacquainted with the carefully groomed, svelte creature who had stolen her husband's interest, might not have noticed, but to Charlotte it was instantly clear that her ex's new love was pregnant, not heavily so – there was just the beginnings of a swelling under her T-shirt – but enough to have filled out the once enviable indentation of her waist. It made sense, too, of the lacklustre look to her face, the dark circles under her eyes, the puffiness along her jaw – telltale signs that, Charlotte realized, had been in evidence for many weeks.

How quickly the world could turn . . . how unexpectedly. Somewhere, amid the surprise, Charlotte was aware of a pinprick of envy. It had taken several years to make Sam. 'Okay, if you like,' she replied tersely, gesturing at the spare seat opposite, too curious to refuse. Cindy, looking miserable, alone, pregnant, and wanting to talk to *her*. It was mystifying. She recalled the plangent voice that had answered Martin's mobile back during the Sam crisis, sounding as sleepless as her, as lost. The memory produced a jolt of power. She, Charlotte, wasn't lost any more. And she certainly wasn't in the bewildering thick of pregnancy, with lank hair and a blotchy complexion, agonizing over some new, desperate rift with Martin. All that was for Cindy to deal with now and good luck to her. You reap what you sow, Charlotte reflected viciously, as Cindy sat down. 'Quite unexpected, seeing you here.'

'I'm staying with my sister.'

'Ah. And I'm at my mother's – she's fractured her wrist.'

'Oh dear, I'm sorry.'

So Martin hadn't even mentioned it. Or they weren't talking. Charlotte fiddled with her paper cup, torn still between the desire to put a speedy end to the encounter and a burgeoning need to know more. To be spending a bank holiday with her sister – no wonder Martin had sounded stressed on the phone. No wonder he had said he wasn't up to helping out with Sam. All her suspicions about trouble brewing had obviously been correct. They were spending time apart and Cindy was *pregnant*. The condition was even more obvious now, from the way she had sunk into the chair with her legs slightly parted, as if in anticipation of the latter months when sheer weight would demand such inelegance.

'I'm expecting,' Cindy blurted. 'That's what I wanted to tell you.'

'Gosh . . . actually, I did sort of think so.' Her companion was such a picture of distraction – her eyes darting round the café, her thighs jigging together to some urgent, private rhythm – that in other circumstances Charlotte decided she might even have felt sorry for her.

'I hope you don't mind or anything.'

'Of course not.'

'It's been terrible, actually, the most hateful sixteen weeks of my life.'

'Really?' Charlotte hoped she didn't sound smug. There were so many memories popping inside her head, like bubbles, that it was hard to concentrate. *Wanting* to become parents had been part of the early, happy time with Martin – the shared longing, the common goal. It was with the actual pregnancy that the first hint of distance had come, she saw now, the creeping sense of separating wavelengths. Seeing Cindy so grey-faced and wretched was bringing it back to her. 'It's a difficult time. Poor you,' she added, breathing hard, enthralled. Leopards like Martin didn't change their spots. 'I mean . . .' Charlotte hesitated. It was Cindy after all. But a different, needy Cindy, she reminded herself, in the thick of something she herself was uniquely positioned to understand. 'I know *exactly* what you're going through,' she gushed, giving up all resistance. 'It was when I was pregnant with Sam that Martin first began to pull away from me. But, unlike you, I didn't have a sister to take me in.'

Charlotte wondered whether her confidence stretched to patting her erstwhile rival's hand. She felt *fantastic* suddenly, more than up to the magnanimity that this and any other situation might demand. Bring on mothers with broken wrists, the lecherous husbands of best friends, and employers with sneaky plans – she would despatch the lot of them.

Cindy had clapped a hand to her mouth and was rolling her eyes. 'Oh, no, Charlotte, you don't understand. I'm only staying with my sister because I've spent the last few weeks being crabby and ill and weepy and horrible and I wanted to give poor Martin a break. He's been wonderful, just wonderful, in spite of being frantic at work – hard at it even today. Oh, God, here they come, bloody tears.' She fanned her face with her fingers, as if hoping to blow the emotion back up her tear ducts. 'I never meant for a moment to suggest . . . All I wanted was to tell you – felt it would be *right* to tell you in person – about the baby. We've only just started letting people know and Martin's been worried you'd take it badly.'

Charlotte made a strangled sound, intended as a laugh.

Cindy was still talking, softly, steadily, as if the misunderstanding and the bout of crying had relaxed her. 'I'm really sorry you got the wrong end of the stick. Of course I knew that things between the two of you weren't right for a long time. In fact, Martin always used to say –' She stopped abruptly, as if the context of the conversation, the identity of her would-be confidante, had suddenly come back into focus.

'What?' Charlotte had tightened every muscle in her body and was sitting on the edge of her chair, the grimace-smile back in place. 'What did Martin say?'

'Charlotte, really, I shouldn't have –'

'Please tell me. I want to know.'

Cindy dabbed at her nose. 'That he lost you to Sam.' She muttered the words round the side of the tissue, as if half hoping they might miss their mark.

'But . . .' Charlotte could hear the tremble in her voice, pushing through the tight muscles. 'That's pathetic – outrageous.' She hung on to the edge of the chair, gripping it with the backs of her knees. 'Lost me to Sam?'

'Look, here comes my sister – I've got to go.' Cindy grabbed the handle of her trolley and began, with manifest desperation, to try to manoeuvre it out between the café furniture.

Charlotte could see the sister coming towards them, tight jeans, white T-shirt, slim, blonde, a little younger, a Cindy clone. 'Martin is a liar. He always was.'

Cindy spun, tears spilling again, her face twitching. 'He isn't. He's honourable and wonderful and –'

'*Honourable?*' It was a relief to laugh properly. The sister had arrived and was looking concerned.

'Cindy, what's up? What's going on?'

'Yes, honourable.' Cindy spat the word back at her.

'Let's go, babe,' the sister murmured, tugging at the trolley.

'Yes, honourable,' Cindy repeated, turning back to Charlotte. 'I could give you an example if you like.'

Charlotte stood up, folding her arms. She could feel her kneecaps vibrating. She dug her nails into her elbows. 'Please, do.'

'Years, it was, years . . . *and he wouldn't sleep with me because of you.*'

All heads were swivelling in their direction now. Near the till a group of waiting customers had turned their backs on the cabinets of sandwiches and pastries and were watching

230

with the expectancy of a ringside audience. The young man in charge of the coffee machines was leaning on the counter on his elbows, one finger stuck absently in his mouth, another fiddling with his earring, as if the entertainment so far had not been dynamic enough to engage his attention fully. The sister now had hold of both the trolley and Cindy's arm, which she was pulling hard.

'And you expect me to believe that?' Charlotte hissed, her mouth dry. 'Martin must have *infected* you with his lying. How sad. How *pitiful*.' Her knees had vibrated to a state of peculiar numbness, forcing her to sit down. She was aware of Cindy shaking her head at her sister and the pair starting to move away. She had held her own, managed the riposte, but her thoughts were zigzagging violently, to the past and back again, reassessing, processing, trying to come up with a picture that made sense. Through it all, like the twang of a tuning fork, was the still indigestible possibility that Cindy had spoken the truth. Martin's denials of infidelity, her disbelieving accusations – it had been the theme tune of their marriage, the pattern that gave it shape. Charlotte's mind lurched. Of course, there were levels of infidelity – it didn't need to involve actual sex . . . She tried to keep a grip on this thought but it slithered away, leaving instead, unbidden, a sharp image of the snide little note. *A well-wisher*. Like hell.

Charlotte seized her trolley and charged out of the café, apologizing as she dodged small children and glowering adults. They had reached the automatic doors. The sister was pushing the shopping and Cindy was walking alongside, holding on to the trolley with one hand and pressing the other protectively over the little bulge in her stomach.

'It was you all along, wasn't it? That *anonymous* note, it was you.' Charlotte had intended rage, or indignation at the very least, but her tone, as she released the challenge, sounded merely pleading.

'For God's sake,' began the sister.

'It's okay, Lu. What note?'

Charlotte, the energy, the certainty withering, had to explain again. 'Obviously it doesn't change anything, but I need to know,' she ended hoarsely, 'if you wrote it.'

Cindy hesitated, her expression a mask of calm, while privately she recalled her joy upon hearing of the sly message and – best of all – Charlotte's reaction to it, kicking her beloved out, at last, into her arms. An answer to the longest prayer of her life, she even felt momentarily ashamed to have forgotten it. But when she spoke her voice was haughty and offended. 'I would never have done that, Charlotte. If you knew me at all you wouldn't even have asked.'

Charlotte watched the sisters disappear among the sea of parked cars. She was glad she had asked. For a moment she felt serene to the point of giddiness. She had had every *right* to ask. And it didn't matter, she reminded herself. None of it mattered, not any more.

But it was hard to steer a straight course, with the trolley wheels twirling and snatches of the conversation coming back at her. *He wouldn't sleep with me because of you.* Even taking levels of infidelity into account, it seemed an extraordinary possibility. Charlotte grappled with the wayward trolley, feeling all the while as if she was trying to keep a fix on her own memories. She had been the *honourable* one, hanging in there, forgiving the Cambridge genius and all the others . . . the ones before Cindy.

Charlotte unloaded the bags into the boot one by one, then drove slowly back to her mother's house. After turning off the engine, she sat still for a few seconds, ignoring the twitch of the front curtains and the faint yelping of the dachshund. Of course Cindy would collude in defending Martin, of course she would. The gibe about Martin having lost her to Sam was part of it – a spiteful dig, designed to make her feel bad. Charlotte re-approached the accusation as she might a cliff-edge. She had loved Sam as any mother had a right to love her child. And no wonder, she reflected wryly, as the curtain was yanked rather than twitched and Jean's face appeared at the window, anxious and frowning.

Charlotte offered a jaunty thumbs-up sign and got out of the car. Three more days of playing the dutiful daughter: it wasn't much in a lifetime. It was actually a relief to have something else to attend to, something solidly practical, away from pointless speculating and the bitchy stirring of the hateful – *pregnant* – Cindy. She would give herself over to the situation, the need to be a nursemaid, instead of fighting it. Thus buoyed, Charlotte managed to wave again as she walked up the path, the plastic handles of the shopping-bags knifing into her forearms, then kept the lid on her impatience during the long minutes it took her mother to locate her stick and shuffle to the front door.

Chapter Thirteen

Sometimes Theresa hated that a decade of living in the same community made it impossible to set foot outside her front door without bumping into an acquaintance, but back in London that Easter Saturday, hurrying from the butcher's to the florist's, with Matty in tow, wobbling fearlessly between her stabilizers, she found herself positively scanning the street for familiar faces. Typically, there were few to be found, just a glimpse of Naomi in a passing car (Graham, at the wheel, had been the one to turn his head) and a nod with Charlotte's neighbour, Mr Beasley, who was on his usual bench by the traffic-lights, watching the world go by.

It was all down to mood, Theresa thought. She wanted to engage with people because she was feeling good – about life, about herself, about Henry. The break in Cornwall had been just what she needed. Space, rest in the springy old double bed that swallowed her like no other, big unfussy meals, nothing to worry about except the children tramping sand into the house and whether they had had one ice-cream or three. It helped her recognize how much she managed in her London life, with four (five, if you counted Henry) sets of routines and demands crammed into every single day, not to mention her own meagre needs, squeezed among everybody else's. No wonder things got her down.

Her mother, waiting, as predicted, with the soup and biscuits, had spotted it at once. Having shooed the children into their beds and splashed sherry into the mugs of soup, she had immediately asked what was wrong. Theresa had said, 'Nothing,' then burst into tears, babbling out her miserable suspicions about Charlotte and Suffolk between sobs. Her mother had listened, topped up the soup, announced, as if she had first-hand experience of the matter, that divorcées were a dangerous breed, then asked what Theresa's deepest instincts told her about her husband's feelings.

'That he loves me,' she had wailed, raising her face from her hands. 'And Charlotte ... I *like* Charlotte, a lot, but she's so terribly pretty and doesn't seem to know it.'

'Good. Then you've done the right thing and it will be all right ... somehow. Don't call him,' she had advised next, fixing her daughter with steely eyes. 'Don't crowd him. There's no phone down there anyway, is there?'

All of which had gone to pot with Theresa finding herself caught up in the chain of communication (the cleaner had got hold of Martin who, defeated by unresponsive mobiles, had called her) about Charlotte's mother's accident. Henry had sounded a little weird, but then so had she, probably, as indeed had poor Charlotte. Being summoned to a hospital bedside was a terrible ordeal, but worse, Theresa supposed, if the subject of the disaster was famously prickly and unlovable. Her heart – as well as rejoicing in the break-up of the Suffolk party – had gone out to her friend. And it had made her feel incomparably fortunate, too, to have a mother who was not only healthy, but warm and insightful, who, after the flurry of phone calls to East Anglia, had tapped her nose and smiled knowingly over the heads of her grandchildren.

Since then Henry had called several times, reporting frustration, mental blockage, the collapse of a section of fencing and the arrival time of his train that afternoon. She was right, he had added gruffly, reluctantly, about trying to work with Sam and Charlotte around: the whole project had been an unmitigated disaster.

A disaster! Unmitigated! Theresa skipped, even though she was now, temporarily, carrying the four-wheeled bicycle, her daughter, her purse and a weighty bag containing a large plucked turkey and two dozen sausages.

Sam, emerging first from the estate agent's and seeing Theresa, ducked back into the doorway, bumping into Rose, who screeched and slapped his back.

'It's her,' Sam hissed, pointing a few yards down the high street, where Theresa was now crouching between Matty and the bike, patting the little pink leather saddle in an obvious attempt to encourage her daughter to sit on it.

'So?' Rose tossed her mop of curls and stepped out into the sun.

'I don't want to see any of them ever again.'

'But that's never going to happen, is it?' She folded her arms, frowning at him. 'And, anyway, you like George.'

Defeated by logic, as he so often seemed to be in any debate with Rose, Sam hunched his shoulders and emerged from the doorway. He was keen to be gone anyway, before Mr Croft got back and found the envelope they had left on his desk. It had been Rose's logic that had led to that, too, and Sam was fast losing faith in it.

My mum would like you to ask her out again. She is shy and alone and really enjoys your company. Please do not give up on her or mention that I have written this. Yours sincerely, Sam Turner

Rose had dictated the words, pacing her bedroom and chewing a pencil like an angst-ridden novelist. Glancing at her as he dutifully took it down, his heart thudding with doubt and daring, it had occurred to Sam to worry about his new friend's unusual predilection for written correspondence. But then, without it, they wouldn't have become friends, and it seemed impossible to unwish that. On top of which, Rose was brilliant at writing – he knew that from her letters, not to mention the essays that had been read out in class, History, English, anything that required a string of sentences. As if that wasn't enough, late the previous night, after her dad had turned out their light, she had slithered down the bunk-bed ladder carrying a torch between her teeth and a battered shoebox of papers that turned out to be poems, reams and reams of them, all set down in her tiny neat caterpillar handwriting.

Certain he was unequal to the task of offering any response that wouldn't sound inadequate or stupid, Sam had picked up the nearest and scanned it in frantic silence. Whereupon Rose had plucked out several others and begun to read the verses out loud, all of which rhymed and were about people they knew, and so wickedly funny that they had ended up stuffing the duvet into their mouths to muffle their laughter.

'And then there's this one,' she had said, pulling another piece of paper from the bottom of the box, 'which is different.' Her voice had changed – gone high and tight – so Sam guessed that whatever was coming wasn't supposed to cause more clutching of the bedclothes. Clicking off the torch, she had reached for his hand, squeezing the fingers really hard, like she was dangling in a precipice and needed him to haul her out. Then she recited the poem, holding up the paper like she was reading, although it was too dark to see and she clearly knew it off by heart. It was about a girl whose mum had got thinner and thinner and then died, full of short, broken sentences that didn't even try to rhyme.

Feeling even less up to a response when she had finished, Sam gripped her hand in return, far harder than he had ever squeezed anything in his life, even her elbow during their stupid fight. A few seconds later she had pulled away and scampered back up the ladder. Sam had lain on his back for what felt like hours, feeling awkward and wishing she would speak, until it dawned on him that the snuffling noises coming from overhead meant she had fallen asleep.

It was a while before he had been able to follow suit. He felt sorry for Rose, obviously, but he also felt sorry for himself, for having a mother whom he was glad was still alive, but whom – since Thursday morning – he also rather hated. The hatred was new and quite exciting in its way. It was like not needing her, like being set free. But then an image of her with George's dad would shoot into his head and he would feel as hot and sick and powerless as he had tearing across the field towards the beach, pumping his arms to fight the wind as it tried to press him back.

Rose's madcap plan had been something to cling to, something in the end that had helped him to sleep.

'What about your dad anyway?' he snapped, as they turned towards the high street. 'Have you ever seen *him* snog someone?'

Rose stopped walking, put her hands on her hips and stared hard at the chewing-gum blobs on the pavement. Sam held his breath, certain he had overstepped some sort of invisible boundary. But when she lifted her head she was grinning and dismissive. 'Of course not. After my mum he doesn't want anybody else.'

'Okay. Right.' Humbled into silence, Sam trailed his fingers along the top of a low stone wall and scuffed the heels of his trainers among the soggy patches of fallen blossom skirting the street trees. Up ahead there was now no sign of Theresa. Sam lifted his head higher, glad of this and that he was walking with Rose. He checked the clock on his phone. They had another twenty minutes until they were due to meet her dad – for lunch in the café that had towering plates of pastries in its windows. The uncle was coming back that afternoon to build a barbecue, he said, right on the still blackened spot where they had burnt the boxes. Sam could not remember when he had ever had such a great time. He wasn't missing his parents at all; his mum for obvious reasons and his dad because a phone call to say happy Easter had turned into a long spiel about a concert that his and Cindy's choir were doing and how much it would mean to them both if he was there, even though it wasn't his kind of music, and they'd go out for a special meal afterwards blah-blah.

Sam slowed his pace so that Rose would catch up. She was dawdling annoyingly, whistling a complicated tune that seemed to be taking up all her energy and attention. *Tweet, tweety-tweet*. It was an awful sound. And she looked like a chipmunk, Sam decided, shuffling nearer when she came alongside and observing, rather to his amazement, that she wasn't as tall as she used to be and that if he bounced on his trainers he could almost bring his eye-level up to hers.

'Hold my hand, then,' she said, between whistles, not turning her head.

Sam did as he was commanded, not like the night before but with the loosest of interlocking fingers, so it would be easy to pull away should the need arise.

I am lying on the floor, staring up at the dusty curves of the central stem supporting our dining-table. Although he closed the front door quietly, I can feel the physical reverberations of Martin's departure. Shifting on to my right side, I pick at a scab of dried food on a table leg. It leaves an unsightly white scar when it comes away, making me wish I had left it alone.

It is the eve of our fifteenth wedding anniversary. Out of sight overhead lies the detritus of the dinner party I organized in celebration: half-eaten bread crusts, smears of chocolate mousse, grains of rice, crumbs of Stilton, grape pips; for a bad cook I did a good job. Four courses, four couples, lively conversation about schools and interest rates and where to holiday in France – a show of such normality that at certain moments I almost caught myself believing in it.

Exchanging farewells on the doorstep, with Theresa and Henry and the rest of them, masks of graciousness in place as we received their compliments – on the food, the enjoyment, the achievement of the anniversary – it occurred to me that maybe pretending was the key, that if Martin and I could only feign happiness for long enough, it would eventually become real. But then, having closed the door on the last of them, the reality was back with us in an instant, concussing in its violence, like walking into a wall.

'So you still want me to go?'

He was standing at the foot of the stairs, squinting under the glare of the hall light, looking – with his blond hair flopping across his forehead – so like the creature who had pointed his index finger at my heart in the college rehearsal room two decades before that for a moment I almost lost my nerve. For strength I reached out and tugged open the hall drawer, groping for the hand-delivered envelope, which I had spotted on the doormat half an hour before the arrival of our guests. An extraordinary calm had descended then, powering my insistence both that we continue with the grisly charade of the dinner party and that he leave the house – and our marriage – immediately afterwards. It was hard to muster the same calm a second time, with the exhaustion of the evening's performance washing through me and the sight of him, so beautiful and wronged, at the bottom of the stairs. 'It's over, Martin.'

'So you believe some stupid malicious note over the word of your husband?'

'Yes.'

He spun on his heel, placed one foot on the bottom stair, then stopped. 'Look,' he snarled, only half turning his face towards me, 'there has been someone, but only as a friend — okay? Just a friend, Charlotte, someone to talk to, for Christ's sake, but nothing has happened, okay? Nothing.'

Pressure producing a confession — after so many years of denial — I experienced a moment of pure elation. What a lot of wasted time, I thought next, all those years of questing for the truth, probing through each bad patch like some delicate-fingered archaeologist, when all along a simple sledgehammer of an ultimatum would have done the trick. 'This "friend" of yours, what is she called?'

'That's irrelevant.'

'Not to me.' I shuffled my feet further apart, steadying myself. 'And not to you either, I assume, since some helpful soul has felt duty-bound to alert me to her existence.'

Martin sighed, clenching his teeth. 'Do you have any idea what it's been like, all these years, your suspicions, never trusting, on and on and —'

'The name of your friend, Martin. What's this one called?'

'She is indeed a friend, a true friend, and she's called Cindy.'

'Cindy! How perfect. And will you be going to Cindy's now, or is she, too, inconveniently shackled to a spouse?'

'Charlotte —'

'Is she married?'

'No, she's not. And I wouldn't dream of calling her now, I'll go to a hotel.'

Wavering again, I gripped the insides of my shoes with all ten toes while Martin continued up the stairs and along the landing. I remained in my rigid pose, blinking up the empty stairs, listening to the sounds of drawers and cupboards being opened and shut and, finally, the closing clicks of the suitcase. It was at the soft tread of his feet on the upper stairs that I had retreated to the dining room. I didn't want to think about his farewell to Sam, or the kindness in the quietness of the footsteps, a father with enough love not to want to wake the child from whom he is being separated.

The candles, mere wicks slumped in lakes of wax, go out. Chilled, I curl up, hugging my arms and knees to my chest. It is easier to think in the dark. I slip my thumb into my mouth and suck gently. I mustn't be too hard on myself. I have had to be brave and need time now to recover. What I most dreaded has happened. I have lost Martin. Somewhere inside I always knew I would.

But how much better to be alone than lonely! Not for me the fate of my mother – a lifetime of self-protective ignorance, the blind eye turned. It has taken time but the boil has been lanced at last. The recovery can begin. The well-wisher indeed wished me well. I fall asleep on the carpet to the tune of such comforts. I can't feel glad yet, but I will. I know I will.

Chapter Fourteen

Cutting through the narrow alley in the middle of the cul-de-sac, turning left, then second right past the garage, Charlotte soon found herself at the children's playground her mother had described, with the forested slope as its backdrop and a lush field to one side. With Jasper tugging at the lead the entire way, she could probably have managed without the instructions. The little dog was pulling even harder now, its eyes popping from near-strangulation and eagerness to continue on a route it clearly knew and loved. In the field there were several horses and a foal, twig-legged and tufty-coated. When Jasper barked it hopped in alarm, then hurriedly nuzzled under its mother's belly for a feed.

As instructed, Charlotte waited until the forest path before unclipping the lead. Jasper scuttled happily up the slope for a few yards, then slowed as the gradient took its toll. Charlotte, who had been worried the treasured creature might disappear among the trees, felt almost sorry for it, so old and silly, so ultimately helpless. The trees were tall and mostly branchless till their upper reaches. Spread beneath them, rippling over roots and round the base of brambles, shimmering in the dappled evening light, were oceans of bluebells. The air was cool and still, traced with scents of wild garlic and pine. Here and there clusters of midges hung in sunbeams, as clearly savouring the day's premature burst of summer heat as the mums she had passed in shorts and T-shirts wheeling charges in sunhats out of the playground.

When a bench appeared on the side of the path Jasper

flopped in front of it, looking at Charlotte and panting hard.

'So you stop here, do you? Fine,' she muttered, stepping over him to sit down. The path was still an empty corridor in both directions, steep-sided, speckled with light and so undeniably beautiful that Charlotte felt a surge of guilt for never having set foot in the place before. The playground had once been a petrol station, she remembered. On the rare occasions she had driven past or made use of it, the possibility of appreciating – let alone exploring – the surrounding land had never occurred to her. How many other things in the world had passed her by? Charlotte wondered idly. She pulled out her mobile phone to have another go at getting hold of Jason, but then decided it wouldn't feel right to break the hush of the forest. She had left a message already and it was Easter Sunday, she reminded herself, hardly an appropriate time to pester anybody, even about something important.

Instead Charlotte let her thoughts wend their way back, with an effort at ghoulish humour now, to her dire confrontation with the sisters in the supermarket: Cindy's blotchy-faced sincerity, her charging after them through the automatic doors – it had been like something out of a farce: one had to laugh or go mad. For Cindy's claims were insane, surely. Pregnant with Martin's child, hormones rampaging, the sad woman was probably just seeing what she needed to see, caught in the blinding glare of love as Charlotte herself had been, twenty years before; a rabbit in headlights, poised for crushing.

Since then a frenzy of housework had done marvels for her state of mind – the exercise, the display of daughterly virtue. If she could have awarded herself a medal, she would have. Keeping busy meant she didn't have to talk to her mother too much either, which was another plus.

Charlotte rested one foot gently on the dog and closed her eyes. The forest wasn't quiet: dense with rustles and creaks and whispers, it breathed noise. It was a question of listening hard enough, she mused, and in the right way, letting one's senses get in tune with a dimension beneath the obvious. These happy meditations were interrupted by the bleep of her phone, which proved to be a text, not from Jason – to her regret – but Martin: 'Concert date May 28th venue not quite sorted but really want Sam to be there hope J recovering ok'.

Charlotte chuckled darkly. Clearly Cindy hadn't mentioned their little run-in yet, which was good, possibly even generous, but here was the true Martin, the one *she* knew: self-centred, *dis*honourable, making demands, paying only the merest lip-service to any needs other than his own. He had added severely to her stress levels on Thursday by being too busy to help out with Sam and now all he really cared about was the date for his and Cindy's insufferable *concert*. And why should she be responsible for getting Sam there anyway? It was *his* gig so *he* could organize transport for Sam. Charlotte dangled the lead in front of the dog's nose to get him moving and set off up the path. Cindy, as she had reminded herself many times, was *welcome*.

She found such a long route through the forest that by the time they got back to the playground the sun was sinking and the dog dawdling so badly that Charlotte picked him up and tucked him, protesting, under her arm. She kept him there, ignoring looks of doggy bemusement and attempts to lick her neck, until they were almost back at the house, rejoicing all the while that, thanks to the collapse of her house plans, the bluff about getting a canine companion for Sam had never been called.

'Only me,' she exclaimed, having let herself in with the

keys Jean insisted she take with her, even for a two-minute stroll to the postbox. 'Only me,' she repeated, more softly, checking the kitchen and then the sitting room where the TV had been left on and the mug of tea she had made sat, grey and untouched, on the footstool. Gingerly, she pushed open the door to the downstairs loo, but that, too, was empty, and still looking dingy in spite of the hours she had spent scrubbing at the ridges of lime-scale round the taps and the dreary avocado wall tiles. A bag containing fresh bread and milk was where she had left it in the hall, thanks to a flurry of other requirements upon her return from the corner shop – tea, finding the TV console and a particular cushion, and taking the dog for his usual lengthy weekend walk.

It wasn't until Charlotte was halfway up the stairs that it occurred to her to feel worried. The house was deathly quiet. Her mother couldn't have gone out, surely. Unless the sun had drawn her . . . Charlotte pressed her face to the porthole window on the landing, surveying what she could of the back garden – the potting shed, the rustic chair, lichen-covered, these days, and too fragile to sit on, three large molehills, an empty plastic bag, blown in from somewhere. What was left of the sun had collapsed to a fiery smudge of red, illuminating silhouettes rather than shedding light. Charlotte hurried on up the stairs, checking the bathroom before finally reaching the bedroom. The door was ajar and squeaked as she pushed it open. Jean was lying on her bedcovers with her eyes closed and her head tipped back awkwardly over the crest of her pillow. The Paisley dress, worn solidly since the hospital, was hitched halfway up her thighs, showing the lavish extent of the purple-black bruise on her left leg and an expanse of petticoat.

Charlotte was transfixed, momentarily, by the petticoat: an obsolete, pointless garment to most people, these days, and yet she could remember, with sudden shocking lucidity, a tiny version of herself watching a stocking being pulled up under a similar hem of pretty lace, watching in awe and happy acceptance of the impossible, longed-for ambition of ever becoming such a creature herself, so elegant, so perfectly beautiful, so grown-up.

'Mum?' Charlotte took another step towards the bed. She was lying so still, so awkwardly. Absorbing the implications of this, Charlotte was aware not so much of horror as a deepening shame that she could ever, no matter how briefly, have imagined taking the death of this woman – loved, hated, never understood – in her stride.

'Did Jasper enjoy his walk?'

Charlotte gave a gasp of relief. 'Yes . . . at least . . .' She hesitated, recovering still. 'Good, you're okay, then . . . That's good. Jasper, yes, I think so. He was tired, actually,' she confessed, guiltily recalling the dog's ride home in the crook of her arm.

Jean tilted her chin to a more natural position and eyed her daughter steadily. 'Another pillow would be nice.'

'Another pillow . . . of course.'

'In the top cupboard. You'll need to stand on the chair.'

'Got it. Fine. Here we are. Can you sit up? That's it . . . Better? I was going to make supper. Pasta and some lovely sauce – I'll add extra mushrooms and things, make it really tasty.'

'Thank you, dear, but I'm not very hungry. Just a piece of toast will do and maybe some Bovril.'

'Bovril? On the toast?'

'Butter on the toast, Bovril in a mug, with hot water. But first, I wonder, would you mind . . .'

'Yes?' Charlotte was fumbling with the window catch. The room was so stuffy she could barely breathe.

'Please don't, there'll be a draught.'

'A draught . . . right.' Charlotte replaced the latch and folded her arms tightly across her chest, tucking her fingers into her armpits as if to prevent them doing any more harm. Two more days. Just two more days and she would be free again – to be impatient and undaughterly and get on with her life. A team of four would cover the visits for a week, the health-care people had said – work in a rota and without any of the irritation, probably, that Charlotte felt, with her dark thoughts about the self-pity behind the helplessness, the fact that (as the nurse had said) it was her mother's confidence rather than her body that had taken the real bruising. 'You were saying?'

'My hair . . . I wondered if you could help me wash it?'

Charlotte's first instinct was to find a pretext to refuse. She had done so much, shopping, fetching, cleaning, carrying, walking, shutting herself off from the outside world, with the hateful Cindy débâcle gnawing at her and no comfort except the occasional call to Sam, who seemed to have nothing to communicate but a hurtful eagerness to get off the phone and race back to his baffling new friendship with the Porters. Their conversation the previous evening had lasted for precisely fifty seconds.

'A hairwash – of course. You should have said before.' She spoke brusquely in a bid to mask her reluctance. 'Would you like to do it now or after your –'

'Now.'

It wasn't easy. The bathroom was small, the basin at precisely the wrong height. They tried it with Jean sitting in a chair – sideways, front ways, backwards. She got very wet, then distressed. 'It's not my arm, it's my neck. I can't bend it the right way – it's hopeless.'

'Perhaps I could tape up the plaster with clingfilm and

help you stand under the shower,' Charlotte suggested, eyeing her mother and the old fixed showerhead uncertainly. She, too, was rather wet now, splashed down her front and with sodden shirt cuffs, in spite of efforts to keep them out of the way.

'No. Let's leave it. Never mind. It's all too *hopeless*.'

She was crying, Charlotte realized, astonished, glad of the steamy mirror that had allowed her to make the observation without any obvious scrutiny.

'I want my Bovril,' Jean barked next, standing up. 'And my toast. Could you do *that* at least?'

'I've a better idea,' Charlotte replied, pressing her gently back into the chair. 'Don't move.' She returned a few minutes later with an old plastic shower attachment, a cherished accoutrement during her teenage years, dug out of a bottom drawer in her bedroom, and several more towels. 'Kneel on these,' she ordered, placing two of the towels on the floor and one across Jean's shoulders, then pushed and cajoled the crusty old suctioned ends of the hose over the snouts of the taps. 'There. Now, lean forward as far as you can on your good elbow. That's it. Close your eyes. The towel will help, but you're so wet anyway a bit more dousing won't do any harm. We'll find dry things afterwards.'

Jean did as she was told without another word, and after a moment or two Charlotte fell silent too. She worked quickly, moving her fingertips deftly through the froth of the shampoo, feeling the soft contours of the scalp, not with revulsion, or self-righteousness, or reluctance, or any other of the unedifying emotions that had dominated the last few days – the last thirty years – but with a simple, respectful tenderness. At the reapplication of water for rinsing (nicely warm, not too hot, Charlotte found herself taking as much care as she had during the early, joyful, gurgling years of bathing Sam), and Jean released several audible sighs of pleasure. There was no soap left to rinse but Charlotte kept the water running, stroking the thin wet streaks of hair till they squeaked under her fingertips.

It was such a simple task, not just the cleansing, the soothing warmth of the water, but the act of human physical contact, performed with caring hands. Turning the taps off at last, it dawned on Charlotte that she had experienced a few moments of the same nurturing attention herself, a couple of months before, kneeling on almost the same patch of lino, drooling and wretched, when Jean had held her hair for her and pressed the soft hot flannel to her aching head.

Invisible, infinitesimal as they were, the sense of these two connecting moments flooded Charlotte's heart; almost, she decided later, trying to describe it to herself as she lay in bed, how she might have imagined a state of grace, were she sufficiently religious to believe in such things. Whatever it was, she knew that Jean had felt it too: it had been like a conversation between them, unspoken and yet the most powerful they had ever had. Afterwards, giddy with the surprise of it – the *joy* of it – Charlotte had helped Jean into dry clothes, then happily accepted expulsion to the kitchen to do battle with gluey spoonfuls of Bovril and the toaster that only popped when its contents were blackened beyond salvaging.

By the evening of bank-holiday Monday the two-day spell of tropical blue skies had thickened and darkened to a ceiling of lowering grey. The muggy breeze that had been teasing under the rugs and skirt hems of afternoon picnickers began to whip its targets in greater earnest, driving them home to seek the comfort of thicker clothes and hot meals.

'They'll be fine.'

'I know they will. I'm not worried about them in the least.'

'Then stop looking out of the window.'

'They missed an egg – in the hinge of the gatepost. I can see it from here.'

'You could do some more unpacking.'

'And you could return to your own home.'

'I'm cooking, remember? Goose fricassée.'

Dominic turned from the window, frowning. 'Yes, what *is* that exactly?'

Benedict was lying the length of the sofa, sucking a pencil and studying a script for an audition the following day. 'Same as my chicken fricassée except with goose, to the accompaniment of French beans, new potatoes – a veritable feast. Christ, you're lucky to have me as a brother.'

Dominic returned his attention to the front window. In fact he had been on the lookout for a black Volkswagen more than the children, both of whom had phones, not to mention the protection of the father who had been hardy enough to suggest a pre-school get-together for their class in the park – rounders and bring-your-own picnic. Five o'clock, Charlotte had said, and it was almost six. He had tried to call to tell her about the rounders, to warn her not to hurry on account of it, but her phone had been off, for the journey, he had assumed, but that had been two hours ago. 'How long do you reckon the drive is from Tunbridge Wells?'

'An hour?' hazarded Benedict, returning his concentration to his character (a lawyer with a fondness for Persian cats and a vengeful ex-wife) and fighting a mushrooming urge to trade the flaking end of his pencil for a cigarette. 'Maybe two if the traffic's bad.'

'Which it would be today, of course – especially the South

Circular – Catford, Lewisham . . .' Dominic shuddered on Charlotte's behalf.

'Keen to get rid of Sam, then?'

Dominic wrenched himself away from the window and began to plump up cushions and stack the weekend newspapers in tidy piles. 'On the contrary. In spite of their decidedly unpromising start, he seems a good kid. On the quiet side, secretive – just Rose's cup of tea. I thought you liked him too – all that bonfire and barbecue business, you had him in raptures.'

'The boy's okay.' Benedict put down his script and levered himself upright. 'What's up?'

'Nothing.'

'Are you worried about him and Rose *liking* each other?'

'Don't be absurd.'

'Well, you're worried about *something*.'

'No, I am not.' Dominic punched the last of the cushions and dropped it into place, puzzling over the business of loving someone who could be so wilfully irksome. He wondered, too, whether the moment had arrived to reveal the latest unfortunate twist in his City career, a twist about which he, bizarrely perhaps, could still muster no real concern beyond hurt pride. If Benedict was picking up anxiety on that score it was entirely subconscious.

'Hah. I've got it.' Benedict slapped the script against his knees. 'The lovely Petra. You haven't mentioned her, from which omission I can only deduce . . .'

'Bugger-all. Shouldn't you be doing something useful like tearing goosemeat off a carcass?'

Benedict swung himself off the sofa, grinning smugly as he hitched up his shorts. One cigarette in the back garden before the rain had started, a treat for eating only half the mountain of chocolate he had accrued during the course of the weekend's festivities and for managing to pass on seconds of Dominic's apple pie at lunch the previous day. 'You are seeing her, aren't you, you sly fox? I put her your way and then you don't even have the decency to –'

'We're having lunch on Friday,' Dominic cut in, suddenly weary, not just of his sibling's curiosity, which, as they both knew, arose as much from brotherly fondness as a serious deficiency in his own life, but also of the human knee-jerk assumption (his own included) that every adult needed to find a *partner*. He had been feeling good lately, much more secure, and increasingly able to recall Maggie's maddening habits with the genuine irritation he had experienced at the time rather than through the cunning prism of nostalgia. There was an emotional freedom to being alone that he was also starting to enjoy and would not, again, surrender readily.

Petra's contribution to this more secure state of mind had been as a walk-on part in the occasional sexual fantasy, playing the role with such unwitting efficiency that Dominic had even wondered whether it wouldn't be better to keep her in such confinement, untested, unable to disappoint, the blank sheet he so craved, rather than throwing her into the dragon's den of real life, so messy in comparison, so full of scars and skeletons, maddening habits and dashed hopes. He wasn't worried about Sam and Rose *per se*, but he feared for the rawness of their young hearts, for their innocent ignorance of the fact that acquiring the capacity to love went hand in hand with the power to disappoint and inflict pain.

'That is excellent news.'

'Glad, as ever, to have your approval,' remarked Dominic, drily, moving back to the front window and noting that the foil-wrapped egg had disappeared from its perch on the gatepost – blown off, probably, by the wind. Behind him, he was aware of his brother retreating into the kitchen, banging a few drawers and then, softly (like the dope he was, thinking he could fool anyone), opening the back door to sneak out into the garden for a smoke. Such a great, warm, open, talented man, yet hamstrung by secret vices, Dominic mused with familiar, cheery despair as he held back the curtain for a better view of the street. He stood there for a few moments, using his free hand to fire off a text to Rose saying that if rain didn't end the get-together he wanted the pair of them home by seven p.m.

It was only as he was letting the curtain drop that Dominic spotted the car – patches of black behind a fuzz of pink blossom – parked a good fifty yards away, opposite the derelict church, which was soon, according to laminated council plans pinned to lampposts, to be converted into a primary school. It might not be the Volkswagen, of course – it was impossible to be absolutely sure from the angle he had and at such a distance – but Dominic, for no good reason other than a curious stirring in his gut, felt certain that it was.

'I'm going out,' he called, pushing open the back door and surprising Benedict, who spun round like a guilty school-boy, face pink, keeping the offending item cupped behind his back. 'Bury the stub, won't you?' Dominic added, chuckling to himself as he grabbed his jacket and hurried out into the street.

It was definitely a Volkswagen. Dominic slowed his pace, recalling the last occasion he had approached her car in that same street, when he had been finalizing things with the Stowes. There had been a gale blowing and she had treated his offer of help like a bad smell. Dominic began to smile, then stopped abruptly. The car was empty and dusted with blossom. It could have been there for hours. Not hers, then. Idiot. Christ, as if it mattered when the bloody woman arrived. She used him as it suited her, treated kindness as a commodity rather than a gift.

Dominic continued down the street, nursing the vague intention of joining in with the tail end of the class picnic, maybe offering his services as a deep fielder. He had been good with a ball once upon a time – cricket and footie – before marriage and work had eaten up the time necessary to pursue such hobbies. That was another thing he could consider now – a spot of weekend cricket. It would be perfect with the summer approaching; he might make some new friends into the bargain, like-minded souls to raise a pint with on a Sunday evening – yes, that would be nice.

Dominic proceeded slowly and with diminishing conviction. His appearance at the rounders fest, he realized, might not be greeted with unbridled glee, either by his daughter or her new friend. They might think, for instance, with their still so recently acquired, still fragile thirteen-year-old independence, that he had decided they needed an escort home. Which wouldn't do . . . wouldn't do at all.

Dominic stopped again. He had crossed the road by now and was by the church, right next to the no-trespassers sign that hung at an angle on the fence, as if someone had tried to prise it off. The sorry state of the fence itself made the warning seem pointless – slats broken and missing like a set of rotten teeth. The primary school would seem like a palace in comparison. The church, with its pock-marked red bricks and boarded-up windows, looked embattled to the point of defeat. Strewn around its base was a rich assortment of litter – cans, bottles, Styrofoam containers, the odd gnarled item of clothing; almost, Dominic decided, as if some of the in-habitants of the graveyard had tunnelled out of their resting-places for a spot of nocturnal partying and not cleared up afterwards. Through the trees crowding the side of the church he could just make out the tops of a couple of headstones pitched at angles in the long grass. And a woman. Dominic blinked. A woman with a blue top and red hair was visible . . . ducking behind a gravestone and then . . . Where had she gone? A ghost? Dominic squinted, uncertain of his emotions and his eyesight in the failing grey light. Maggie? He opened his mouth to call, then eased himself sideways through a gap in the fence instead, the widest one, right next to the wonky sign forbidding entry.

'I'm sorry.'

'Don't be silly. There's nothing to be *sorry* for. It happens.' Theresa eyed her socks as she pulled her pants up, wondering dimly if they could have been to blame: ankle-length, grey, serviceable, comfortable, with a small ladder over the left anklebone, they were hardly what one might have described as erotic. Henry had been so eager, prising her away from loading the dishwasher, chivvying her upstairs, tugging at zips and buttons, that it hadn't occurred to her to worry about the need to appear especially alluring. It was the first real physical interest her husband had shown in more than two months so it also hadn't occurred to her to refuse, even though there were a thousand other things she had planned to do before George and his brothers were dropped back from their various play-dates in and around the park. She had especially enjoyed their ungainly progress up the stairs, giggling and shushing each other on account of Matilda, who had ultimately to take credit for their opportunity: she had performed the unprecedented act of falling instantly asleep after her bath.

Once in the bedroom, they had taken the precaution of locking the door nonetheless, then fallen on to the bed, separating only briefly to attend to the business of removing garments. Except socks ... had Henry left his on as well? Theresa had been too embroiled in rediscovering the ancient pleasure of desiring and being desired to notice. He had them on now, certainly, along with the chinos that needed washing and a checked shirt he had been so eager to button up again that the entire set was misaligned.

'Hang on a minute . . .'

Henry pulled away, misreading the approach as a fresh effort to stir his passions.

'Your buttons,' said Theresa, anger pushing through the wifely compassion. What had she done wrong, after all, except respond to his advances and then, when he had gone irretrievably, inexplicably, off the boil, try to be understanding? She knew plenty of women who found sex tedious, who joked that the pretext of a week off provided by their monthly cycle was a blessed relief. Not her ... at least, not recently. Deprived, she had rediscovered real physical hunger. No one, when assaulted next to a dishwasher, could have been more eager, more willing to please, more delighted. 'Your buttons,' she pointed out tersely. 'They're wrong.'

After Henry had gone Theresa lay back on the bed to do up her trousers, which were tight – far too tight – and closed her eyes. She wished suddenly that she could leapfrog over what she knew would be a hectic few hours, and cut straight to the business of falling asleep. The boys would be tired, but hungry too, no doubt, in spite of their respective teas and picnics. George was supposed to have done a project on the Taj Mahal and the two younger ones had had spelling lists and Alfie had said first that his trainers were too small and then that they weren't and now she wished she had bought some anyway.

Theresa opened her eyes and raised one leg, wiggling the

toes. Socks were a better reason for going off the boil than the other thing, the thing she had ruled out. Suffolk had been an *unmitigated disaster*, she reminded herself. Henry had stumbled off the train and into her arms on Saturday afternoon in such a curious, unHenry-like state of exhausted relief that she had been momentarily concerned he might be ill. Just happy to be home, he had assured her, turning his attention to their three youngest and throwing each of them in the air, even Jack who was densely built and decidedly unwieldy. Normally one to let Easter pass him by, leaving it to her to assuage the children's expectations with regard to rabbits and confectionary, Henry had then spent the rest of the weekend making enormous efforts to participate in every ritual. On Sunday morning he had even presented her with a vast, expensive dark chocolate egg, rattling with truffles, and a card – a proper Easter one, exploding with spring flowers, lambs and baby chicks. A *card*! Henry usually only stretched to such extravagance on her birthday and even then he had been known to forget or to hand over something tacky or inappropriate, clearly bought at the last minute from the corner shop near the station. *Darling Theresa, Happy Easter, all my love, H.*

Theresa wagged her foot harder, not liking her train of thought, but unable to resist it. The egg, the card . . . It was all wrong. It smacked of penitence. What had Henry to be sorry for? Being a pig for three months, or for something worse, something more recent, more threatening . . . ?

The front door thumped and Henry called up the stairs, 'Tessy, the boys are back and I'm making scrambled eggs. Shall I do some for us, too, or do you want to wait?'

Theresa rolled off the bed. 'Yup – great. Let's all eat now.' She could hear the boys pounding round the ground floor, running as they always seemed to, as if nowhere could be got to fast enough. What bliss, she reflected wistfully, to want to speed on to the next thing, to have no fear of what might be waiting. One was calling her – Alfie, with his funny low growl of a voice, always the neediest of the four.

'Coming.' She straightened her hair and swiped away the makeup smears under her eyes. Henry, for whatever reason, was *trying*, and so would she. Nothing he had said about his few days with Charlotte and Sam had offered grounds for the reignition of suspicion; on the contrary. The pair had been a distraction, a nuisance, he had claimed many times. Charlotte, meanwhile, would have had a gruelling weekend tending her injured mother and would be in need of support. She would suggest they had a girls' lunch, Theresa decided, hurrying down the stairs, somewhere thoroughly nice for a change instead of the café, maybe even the new place she had posited as a possible venue for Charlotte's fortieth. They could order three courses and wine – go the whole hog – call it research. And she could probe about Suffolk, throw out questions and leave the instincts to which her mother had referred to do the rest. Innocent until proven guilty, as the old adage said.

After admiring the wobbling tooth that had prompted Alfie's summons, Theresa joined Henry in the kitchen, where she mopped up egg spills, fetched cutlery and generally played the role of dutiful sous-chef even though she was longing to seize the wooden spoon from his hands and take over. Henry never put enough butter in, or milk, or salt. The eggs would be dry instead of sloppy as she and the boys preferred. Once she wouldn't have thought twice before barging him out of the way. She would have called him a useless nincompoop and he would have said she was a bossy harridan and settled happily behind the newspaper.

But that night, after laying the table, Theresa was the one

who shook out the newspaper. War-zones, murder, injustice – the stories were torrid and varied. Yet she was too swamped in the story of her own life to care; a life that, in spite of her efforts, seemed somehow to be unravelling, behind the scenes, in a place that she couldn't pin down. Out of kilter, out of control, draining. How, Theresa marvelled, had she ever found managing something as mercurial as a marriage easy? How, too, had she dared privately, smugly, to criticize separating couples for lacking stamina? Henry, for whatever reason, had grown unreachable. It wasn't about staying power, it was about fissures too deep to see, a subterranean landscape that shifted every time she thought she had got close to understanding it.

Tim was surprised to see a woman crouched in the front garden, a woman in such a multi-layered frilled skirt and with so many beads and braids hanging off her arms and round her neck that he even wondered, momentarily, if Charlotte was being doorstepped by one of the travellers who had lately been loitering with smeary-faced offspring beside the local cash machine. Disconcerted, the speech he had been rehearsing scattering into nonsense, Tim stopped halfway through the gate, which had been fixed, he noticed suddenly, glancing at the gleaming new brass hinge. But when the woman stood up, he saw that she was sitting on a large leather holdall and that the layered skirt was well cut, stopping a few inches short of round, shapely calves and eye-catching toffee-suede high heels. 'Are you after Charlotte?' she asked, folding her arms and cocking her head at him.

Tim almost turned and ran back to his car, which he had taken the precaution of parking well out of sight, both for fear of alerting the object of his visit to his impending arrival and because he had wanted to give himself the walk as a chance to change his mind. The woman's question, so innocuous in its intent, bulged with significance. Was he after Charlotte? For reassurance, Tim groped for a line or two of his speech – the funny bit about children playing go-between, the light-hearted tone of *enquiry* that had felt so easy in his head. After all, Charlotte herself might appear at any moment and coherence would be required. But his earlier lucidity remained irretrievable and the woman's cocked head and decidedly entertained expression demanded a response. 'Yes, but only on the off-chance.'

'Like me,' she squealed, with evident satisfaction, bracelets jingling as she clapped her hands together. 'I'm not supposed to arrive until the end of next week – I live in America, you see – but my plans changed, as plans do, so I was ringing the bell on the off-chance. Except that Charlotte isn't here and now it's going to rain and I've got a brother to visit too.'

A silence followed while they both studied the sky.

'We could wait together?'

Tim groped behind him for the gate latch, shaking his head. He had promised himself he would trust things to Fate and here it was – an empty house, a locked door. Stupid to have paid any attention to the message from the kid anyway, letting his feelings get stirred up again when he had been so close to burying them for good. It had been an endearing thing to do – he had never got the impression the boy liked him that much – but what did a thirteen-year-old know about anything?

'I'm surprised she isn't here, frankly, as I'm sure she said Sam's summer term starts straight after Easter. Her son is my godson,' the woman added, with evident pride. 'I'm called Eve, by the way. Charlotte and I go back a long way, a *very* long way. We lost touch for a bit, but then I decided to track her down – the wonders of cyberspace, eh?' She rolled her eyes and then, in a bashful, tottering rush, came down the path to offer him her hand.

It was a very small hand, cold to the touch, and jammed with rings. She was fuller figured than Tim had realized, with a deep, openly displayed cleavage and a distinct swell to her backside, curving up towards a strikingly narrow waist that had been accentuated by a wide leather belt. 'I'm Tim – Tim Croft.'

'And what do you do, Tim Croft?'

'I manage an estate agency,' he began automatically.

'I thought she'd taken the house off the market.'

'She has ... Look ...' he stammered '... could you, perhaps, just tell Charlotte that I came by?'

'If I see her,' murmured Eve, with a quizzical look. 'I'm not going to hang on here much longer.'

Tim stuck his hands into his pockets as he sauntered back down the street, turning to offer a smile of surprise when the Eve woman called out an extra goodbye, waving so vigorously that he could see the bangles spinning down to her elbow.

Charlotte crossed her bare legs for warmth as she huddled against the gritty stone wall of the church and tried, for the umpteenth time, to block out sufficient quantities of gusting air to allow the lighting of a cigarette. Jasper, bored by so confined a location, tugged with fresh, surprising strength on his lead. Charlotte jerked it back, assailed as she did so by a wave of the old hatred for her mother – insisting she bring the bloody animal to London. How selfish, how inconsiderate, how ... But her thoughts dried up at the recollection of Jean's tremulous pleading for her to look after him. It had, Charlotte knew, been an act of sacrifice, not selfishness. With her leg so bruised and her arm in plaster, Jean had explained, she was afraid that he would be deprived of too many of his daily pleasures. Prue, who tolerated him (tolerated *her*, if the truth were told, Jean had muttered darkly), would do the bare minimum, even if paid. He was small and old but he was energetic. He wouldn't understand. He would spend all day whimpering. It would break her heart. If Charlotte could bear to have him just for a few weeks, until she had got her strength back . . .

They had been sitting across the kitchen table, Jean in her washed-out yellow candlewick dressing-gown, Charlotte in her nightshirt with a blanket across her shoulders, an old, stiff one that smelt of mothballs. They had met on the landing in the small hours, a pair of insomniacs who had never once talked to each other about not being able to sleep. Charlotte had suggested a hot drink and led the way downstairs to put the kettle on, marvelling still at the new quiet closeness between them, at the secular state of grace that had wrapped itself round her heart. The request about looking after the dog had followed soon after – unwelcome, inconvenient, but impossible to refuse. Charlotte had said, 'Of course,' and started rinsing out the milk saucepan, consoling herself with how pleased Sam would be and experiencing a stab of longing to see her son's sunny smile.

When she turned from the sink, ready to suggest they return to their respective beds, she was surprised to find her mother shuffling back into the kitchen from the sitting room, her eyes unnaturally bright, her breath coming in small gasps.

'What's happened? Are you all right?'

'Yes – quite. Give me a minute.' Jean closed her eyes and

made a visible effort to breathe more slowly. 'Oh dear,' she said opening them and making her way to a chair. 'I'm not going to be very good at this.'

'Good at what?' Charlotte had pressed gently, venturing a hand on her mother's shoulder and then a stroke of the soft silvery hair . . . the hair she had washed. The new lovely feeling surged again, like a door opening, letting warmth into a cold room.

'This.' Jean put her hand into her dressing-gown pocket and pulled out a folded piece of paper. 'Don't blame me, Charlotte.'

'Blame you? Of course not. Whatever for?'

'I was trying to protect you.'

'From what? Mum, what *is* this?'

'Sit down, dear, would you?' Jean patted the seat next to hers and sighed heavily. 'That day Dad and I took you to Durham, do you remember?'

'Of course.' Charlotte, sitting now, started a smile, then didn't dare to finish it.

Jean had put the folded paper between them and was darting glances at her – afraid, ashamed, timid – impossible to read, but leading nowhere good, Charlotte was sure of that. She knew, too, that what was coming was because of the new invisible bond between them – the open door – and it made her long to kick it back shut for good.

'That day, he was so ill, wasn't he?'

Charlotte waited. Her own version of the day, locked tightly inside, needed no expression. 'That money he gave you . . . there was also this.' The fingers of Jean's good hand, the knuckles swollen with arthritis, the nails ridged and yellowing, had crept back to the folded piece of paper. 'I took it out . . .'

Charlotte stared stupidly at the table. 'You took it *out*?'

'Kept it safe . . . I didn't think you were ready . . . You were still so unsure of yourself, about to begin a whole new life. Don't read it now, Charlotte . . . please not right now . . . Let me explain first. I kept it back because I *loved* you and knew how much you loved *him* . . .' But Charlotte had already pulled the paper out from the unsteady grip of her mother's fingers and was shaking it open. She was terrified but also full of a wild, happy curiosity. There were answers in life, after all. They just never came quite when one expected them.

Charlotte tucked herself closer to the church wall and sucked hard, tasting an unpleasant burst of sulphur from the flaring match. The cigarette tip glowed, then died. She took the packet of ten – bought from a roadside newsagent – out of her pocket and tried to put the cigarette back among its nine companions, but it broke, scattering shreds of tobacco, which were whipped away by the wind. Grinding what was left under her shoe, Charlotte remembered suddenly the bare, Blu-Tack stained walls of her college room and another cigarette balanced on the ugly Formica desk – such drama and then such anti-climax as the four fifty-pound notes fell on to her lap.

For a while, sitting at the kitchen table, with her mother talking quickly, breathily, explaining the background to her father's words, Charlotte had felt okay. She had folded and reopened the paper several times, sliding her fingers along the creases. The blur of the first quarter of her life had come into focus. Everything made sense. And he *had* tried to tell her – the shock of that alone was almost euphoric. She had helped Jean to bed and hugged her tenderly, said it was all right and thanked her. She had even slept well and been busy and helpful all day. It was only *en route* to London, passing the run-down shop fronts and tenement blocks as the suburbs thickened, that the feeling of being turned upside-down had taken hold, making it so hard to concentrate that she had wound down the windows and put a music station on at full blast to keep herself connected to the reality of the road and the purpose of her journey.

'I wouldn't have had you down as a smoker.'

Charlotte screamed and dropped the packet of cigarettes, then trod on it and on several of Dominic's fingers as he scrabbled at her feet to pick it up. 'Sorry!' she gasped. 'You gave me such a fright – your hand, is it all right?'

Dominic, upright again, the squashed packet handed over, made as small a to-do as he could of shaking his fingers, which were throbbing badly. 'You scared me, too . . . and you appear to have a dog,' he muttered, distracted by Jasper, who was springing between them. 'I didn't know. Sam never said you had a dog. I suppose you were walking it?' he ventured, ramming his sore hand into his pocket and glancing up as two crows screeched their arrival on a crumbling window-ledge above their heads.

'No, I . . . yes . . .' Charlotte faltered at the impossibility of describing to anyone the state of mind that had driven her to stop short of the house and plunge into the churchyard, clutching the sorry little packet of Silk Cut. Sam, the Porters, the *normality* of the present had felt part of another world, a world with which she simply could not yet engage, not until she had had a little more time to . . . to do what exactly? To think, to absorb, to reconfigure. Yes, that was it, she had been *reconfiguring* her life, using information that, it was clear now, had been pressing at her consciousness for thirty-nine years, tugging and distorting her efforts to feel balanced and whole. 'It's not my dog, it's my mother's and, yes, it has made me late,' she managed, with a Herculean effort to deliver a response appropriate to the circumstances. 'For which I can only apologize most sincerely when you've been so very kind already. I never meant it to get so late . . .'

'It doesn't matter. I tried to call you. Rose and Sam are still at the park. They won't be back until seven. More importantly, how is your mother?' Dominic added, satisfied that the dog had been the reason behind the eccentricity of a visit to a derelict churchyard, and turning to retrace his steps along the corridor he had made through the long grass. He could see where she had walked now, a chopped-up route round clumps of brambles and half-buried monuments.

'Does the past matter?' Charlotte blurted. 'That's what I want to know.'

Dominic, who had expected to be followed back to the road, with some cosy small-talk about ageing parents and fractured limbs, stopped and turned in astonishment. She was still standing against the wall, the back of her head and her palms pressed against the stone. She was in a state. She had been in a state the last time he had met her and the time before that and probably on the phone the previous week when she had called to ask if Sam could come and stay. She had scrambled through the broken fence not to walk the dog but to hide and be unhappy. She was miserable and messed up and should, at all costs, be given a wide berth. 'The past always matters.'

'Why?' she countered angrily, as if they were having a heated argument.

Dominic shrugged helplessly. 'I suppose because it makes sense of the present.'

'But it's all over and done with, gone – for ever – and different people remember it differently so it *doesn't* make sense.' Charlotte turned her head and pressed her cheek hard against the roughness of the wall. Her lips were trembling violently, embarrassingly. The situation was intolerable and yet she could gain no mastery over it. The door on to the past had been flung off its hinges and she was now at the mercy of everything flooding through it. Meanwhile, this poor man standing in front of her, with his slightly too large nose and big brown eyes, had every reason to look puzzled. All he had wanted was for her to pick up her son after a visit that had stretched from twenty-four hours to *four days*. At the very least he would have been expecting a timely arrival and a thank-you box of chocolates. Instead, here she was skulking and ranting in a graveyard, no doubt confirming his earliest, worst fears about her fitness as a mother. In fact, he had every reason to go straight home and report her to Miss Brigstock or Social Services.

Dominic was indeed at a loss. The rain had held off, but it was getting increasingly cold. He could see the goosebumps on Charlotte's bare legs and the fine hairs on her arms standing up with cold. The mother's injury was obviously much worse than she had let on. It was clear that she needed tea or brandy, but as he pushed his way back out of the long grass Charlotte only tucked herself more tightly into her stony corner, folding her arms as if to ward off approach. The little dog shuffled closer to her feet, then slumped down, as if having settled, reluctantly, on a decision to keep guard.

'Is it your mother?' Dominic asked, tentatively now, pulling the sleeves of his jumper, which was old and loose, right down over the tips of his fingers. 'Is she very unwell?'

'I suppose you know where you came from, don't you?' Charlotte snapped in response. 'A solid background, solid family, solid education – you're just the sort.'

'I beg your pardon?'

'And your wife, I suppose you miss her.' She was looking

268

at him over her shoulder, her green eyes like flints. 'I envy you, feeling things *clearly*.'

Dominic puffed out his cheeks, struggling and failing to find the wherewithal to take offence at this garbled interrogation. She was clearly messed up, he reminded himself, suffering, and he knew too well what suffering could do, how it could warp what had once been a perfectly balanced view of the world. 'Grief is very unclear, actually. Up and down, angry and relieved . . . that sort of thing. And Maggie was a vegetarian, I don't miss that.' He paused, hoping she would smile. 'In fact, if you want proof of how *unclearly* I see things, when I glimpsed you just now, from the road, I thought you might be her ghost. That's why I followed. She had red hair, too, you see, but much more orange than yours – a real carrot-top, like Rose.'

Charlotte blinked and looked away again, saying after a few moments, 'I'm so glad our children have become such good friends.'

'So am I. Shall we go now? Have some tea – or something stronger, if you like?' Dominic rubbed his palms together, fighting real impatience now, and thoroughly chilled.

'I'm sorry,' Charlotte murmured, 'behaving like this . . . what you must think of me . . .'

'Nonsense. Tea, that's the thing.'

'I've had some difficult news.'

'Yes, of course, your mother –'

'No. Not her. My father . . . It turns out he wasn't my father. My mother was pregnant by someone else – a *married* someone who had no interest in leaving his wife and died soon afterwards anyway. She told me last night. Dad took her in, saved her reputation with marriage. He must have thought he loved her, but it didn't last. Then she had nowhere else to go, no money. They stayed together because of that – and because of me,' Charlotte added in a small voice. 'He tried to explain it all to me just before he died but she stepped in without his knowing. To protect me, she says.'

'Well, I guess that's understandable.'

'The thing is, I loved him so much more than her. He was a lousy, unfaithful husband. He *fucked* around.' Charlotte spat the word, expecting a flinch, but Dominic, who had moved closer and was staring at her intently, didn't move. 'I knew that. I even *saw* him with one of his women once, when I was little – it fucked *me* up for years – and yet . . . and yet I would have chosen him over my mother any day.'

'Love is a funny thing.'

'He wrote me this, you see, just before he died, explaining . . .' Charlotte thrust her hand into the pocket of her skirt and pulled out the now crumpled piece of paper with its faint, scrawled biro writing, read so many times she could have recited it. 'He wrote me this and she took it away. Till last night.'

'To protect you,' Dominic reminded her, a little desperately, 'because *she* loved *you*. Like I said, love is a funny business – no rules, absolutely none.'

'Yes, maybe, but . . . there we were, my mum and I, being nice to each other, being *natural* for the first time *ever*, and she goes and –' Charlotte pressed her upper teeth into her lower lip, but the convulsions came anyway, dry, strange sounds from deep inside. She gripped her ribcage, as if fighting a caged malevolence. 'Everything – keeps – *changing* – every time – I try – and get – a grip – it *changes* . . . I don't know anything any more – what's real, who I am.'

'That's nonsense.' Spellbound but feeling increasingly out of his depth, Dominic was almost pleased when the weeping started, and the dreadful body-shakes, since an obvious need for physical consolation presented itself. Setting the wide-berth policy temporarily to one side (the hardest of hearts would have done no less), he said, 'Hey, now,' and put his arms round her. Charlotte remained curled into herself, tucking her head and arms into her chest, as if she would have pulled herself into a shell had she possessed one. 'Nobody really knows who they are,' he ventured, finding quiet comfort in the platitude himself, as if seeing the truth behind it for the first time. 'Most lives are spent trying to work it out.'

'All this,' she gasped, 'I'm so sorry.'

'Please stop apologizing. I broke down in the post office once – an old lady took me home for tea. And in a cinema – that was almost worse, being hissed at for ruining the film. Oh, yes, and in the school playground *twice* – poor Rosie –' He broke off, as Charlotte, merely sniffing now, having gained control of herself at last, pulled free of his support.

'You're very kind, Dominic.' She blinked at him, red-eyed and intensely calm, as if a tempest had literally blown through her and left a new stillness. 'In the last few months things – demons – have been catching up with me . . . ancient things, creeping out of the past.'

'I think Maggie might have been unfaithful. A school-teacher. I found emails after she had died.'

'Oh dear . . . I – I'm so sorry.'

'Please, don't be. It took me a while but eventually I realized that it didn't change anything. We were mostly very happy. And I've come to see that we can only hope ever to know parts of other people, let alone ourselves.'

'That's so true,' Charlotte agreed softly, then added, on a burst of harsh cheeriness, 'Does unhappiness make you wise, do you think?'

Dominic laughed. 'That would be nice, wouldn't it? Some compensation but, sadly, no, I don't think it necessarily follows.'

'I've been mostly unhappy for so long I think it might have become a *habit*,' she confessed. 'Do you think that's possible? And through it all,' she rushed on, not waiting for an answer, 'I'm beginning to understand that I've always looked for other things – other people – to blame. In fact,' she paused, releasing a sharp wild laugh, 'it's a wonder I've got any friends left. No wonder . . .'

'Yes?'

'Never mind.' Charlotte shook her head. The poor man had done enough. He was blue with cold and she felt the same. Whether she had driven Martin into the arms (no matter how outstretched) of Cindy was hardly something anyone else could be expected to comment on, let alone a hapless semi-stranger whose capacity for tolerance must already have been tested to its limit. 'That tea you mentioned, is it still on offer?'

'Absolutely. And if my dear brother has got his act together there might be some supper too, if you like.'

'Gosh! Supper, on top of a free counselling session in a graveyard. Thank you so much, but I really couldn't.'

'Who said it was free?' Dominic murmured.

'Pardon?'

'Feel free to change your mind – about supper.'

'Okay, thanks.'

He led the way back into the overgrown grass and this time she followed, with Jasper trotting happily behind. As they were about to go through the hole in the fence, Dominic stopped and put a hand on her arm. 'That thing about Maggie, I've never told anyone else – ever.'

'Thank you,' Charlotte said, since the confidence had felt

like a gift. 'The thing about my dad, about seeing him with someone, I never told anyone that either.'

'What a pair,' said Dominic, grinning as he held back one of the loose slats, widening the gap for her to pass safely through the fence on to the pavement.

Chapter Fifteen

Benedict had his own system when preparing for auditions: no alcohol the night before, an early alarm call, an hour of yoga, then a morning run while his stomach was still roaring for food. Hunger could be energizing, he had discovered, especially if one was performing the ever-draining, arduous task of inhabiting another psyche. That morning he had thought himself sufficiently deeply into the character of the divorced lawyer to decide that the man had a soft spot not only for Persian cats but also for romantic poetry (Keats's 'Ode on a Grecian Urn' being an especial favourite), and that behind vicious cynicism there lurked a damaged heart longing to be healed. By the time Benedict had completed three circuits of the park and was jogging down the high street he not only knew every detail down to the lawyer's preferred brand of aftershave, but had conjured a back-story of such heartbreak and intensity that it would have served in its own right as the synopsis for a feature-length film.

Pleased with himself, starving, Benedict paused for a moment of on-the-spot jogging outside the Italian café only to find himself peering through the glass window over a pagoda of fresh pastries at his brother. Occupied by the day's paper and a large plate of cooked breakfast, Dominic didn't look up until Benedict, ignoring the stares of other diners at his half-familiar face and sweating, dishevelled state, tapped him on the shoulder.

'Hey, mate, taking a little extension on the bank holiday, are we?'

'Ben – hey! Christ, you look revolting.'

'Thanks.' Benedict untied his fleece from his waist, placed it on the chair and sat down. He summoned the waiter, then ordered a pint of orange juice and a cooked breakfast with extra bacon. 'This is great, isn't it, running into each other? I'm always telling people London's a village, but no one believes me.'

'Ben, you're talking as if we haven't met for twelve years when it's been a mere twelve hours. Your house is now *half a mile* from mine, so it's hardly any wonder our paths should, occasionally, coincide.'

'Why aren't you at work?'

Dominic slowly carved his last sausage into quarters. With Charlotte holding back to drive and Benedict on a dry run for his audition, he had washed down the tasty but slightly odd goose concoction the previous evening with sufficient quantities of wine to feel very much in need of a fried breakfast once he had waved Rose off to school. Jobless, faintly hung-over, he should have been feeling blue but instead, strolling towards the café with the sun in full bloom – again – and a newspaper under one arm, he had been aware of a tingling of contentment and hope, as if he were about to embark on some long, well-deserved holiday. Unwilling to risk shattering this happy illusion now, he skewered a piece of sausage and countered Benedict's challenge by asking why he wasn't at – or on his way to – his audition.

'Because it isn't until this afternoon . . . I say, she didn't stay, did she?'

'I beg your pardon?'

'You've got that look about you – tail up, daft grin, dopy eyes. And you were all over her last night – so keen on the bookshop all of a sudden because it turned out she works there and had only just heard about it being up for sale, and yet when I suggested you buy the lease off Dean and Jason the other day you dismissed it out of hand. Whereas last night it was Mr Bountiful, wasn't it? "Yes, it *might* be an interesting challenge to run a *book*shop,"' Benedict mimicked, hitting the lower, slower timbre of Dominic's voice exactly, then breaking into guffaws that were silenced only by the arrival of the waiter with his food.

'Yes, well . . .' Dominic began stiffly, his buoyant spirits deflating just as he had feared, albeit for a reason he couldn't possibly have anticipated. 'That was *before* I lost my job. And no, for Christ's sake, of course Charlotte Turner didn't stay the night. Really, Ben, sometimes your taste for gossip is pretty hard to take.'

'Lost your job?' Benedict spluttered, his mouth bulging with bacon and fried egg.

'Yes, I am now, officially, *redundant.* I'd have thought you, of all people, would be pleased,' remarked Dominic, drily.

'Yes, well . . . so long as you're cool about it,' Benedict conceded, pressing his napkin to his mouth to stifle a burp. 'Redundancy isn't quite the same as resignation, is it? Blimey . . . the bastards.' He tossed the napkin on to his side-plate. 'No *wonder* you were all over that woman about books last night.'

'I was *not* all over her,' Dominic wailed. 'In fact,' he added, tightening his voice into a tone of genuine anger and waving at the waiter to bring the bill, 'fuck off about the whole subject, okay? Just fuck – right – off.'

Benedict sprawled, unoffended, in his chair. The sweat had dried now, leaving his hair in clumps and his shirt feeling stiff and rough against his skin. 'Seriously, bro, steady on there, okay?'

'By "there" you mean?'

'She's very pretty, I grant you. Amazing skin, cheekbones, and that vulnerable look, which I'm told reduces a large percentage of the male population to jelly, and as for the colouring . . .' Catching his brother's deathly glare, Benedict skipped on hurriedly: 'A nice kid too, in spite of his dodgy beginnings, as we've agreed, and I'm sure that if you choose to take up the reins of the book trade his mother will prove a wonderfully effective employee but . . .'

Dominic pretended not to listen. He offered the waiter a brief, broad smile and paid the bill for them both. Benedict, he thought grimly, did not know when to stop. He would endure a few more minutes, then go home and pack his things for a trip to the aerodrome. Space, air, a view of the world, that was what he needed; perspective, peace. Yes, he had enjoyed the previous evening enormously. So what? So had Benedict, and the children for that matter, both begging Charlotte to have another coffee so it wouldn't end. It had been a good, happy occasion, merriment round a kitchen table, innocent and heart-warming. Of course, her working in the bookshop had been a pleasant surprise, as had her knowledge of the issues facing independents. But Sam's imitation of Miss Brigstock had been just as enjoyable, while Rose pretending to be a tree had made them all beg for mercy, they were laughing so much. Watching how Charlotte clutched her stomach, the tears streaming down her face, Dominic had half wondered if he hadn't dreamt their encounter by the crumbling church. It had caused him to marvel, too, at the extremities of human emotion – grief and joy – poles apart, and yet with such similar blunt tools of expression.

'You're thinking about her now,' Benedict accused, wagging his finger. 'You bloody are, aren't you?'

'No, dear Benedict, I'm thinking that if I don't leave this

place in the next few minutes too much of the morning will have been eaten up for me to get down to Redhill aerodrome, take to the skies and be back again before Rosie gets home from school.'

'Good. Excellent. Because . . .' Benedict hesitated. They were out in the street now, squinting into the sunshine and Dominic was walking fast. 'Because if you *had* been thinking of Mrs Charlotte Turner I would advise you not to.'

'Benedict, for *Christ's sake!*' Dominic turned to face his brother, real despair in his voice.

'No, Dom, hear me out,' Benedict pleaded. 'She might look single but she isn't. She's seeing someone – a *married* someone.'

'And you would know,' Dominic sneered, rolling his eyes.

'Yes . . .' Benedict hesitated again. He didn't like breaking confidences, but he liked even less the thought of his still fragile sibling getting hurt by some divorced siren who looked mellow enough on the outside but within whom there clearly lurked a ruthless capacity to snatch happiness without thought for the feelings of others. He sighed. 'Rosie, as you know, tells me things.'

'Yup. I'm aware of that.' Dominic put his hands into his pockets and glanced up and down the street in a manner designed to communicate extreme impatience.

'Well, apparently Charlotte's having a thing with George's father – you know George in their class, thick, tar-brush hair, very sporty. The mother looks nice – roundish figure, big hair. She and Charlotte are supposed to be best friends. The father is some kind of consultant, hearts or lungs, I can't remember which. He was in Suffolk last week,' Benedict pressed on, speaking urgently now in a bid to trigger some sign that Dominic was actually listening. 'That, presumably, is why she and Sam went there. And there's an estate agent in the frame too, the one she fired for failing to sell her house. So stick with Petra,' he advised, when still Dominic offered no response, 'for everyone's sake.'

'And you,' Dominic replied at last, poking Benedict in the chest with his index finger, 'stick with getting yourself another big part before you get so sucked into playground tittle-tattle that you start believing it.'

'I think it's true, brother.'

Dominic flung open his arms. 'It probably is but, as I have been *trying* to tell you, Charlotte Turner could shag every man in south London, married or otherwise, and I would not consider it any business of mine. Okay? As you know, I'm meeting your Polish *protégée* soon and intend to take full advantage of her. Okay? And one final thing. I love you dearly, as you know, and you have helped me all my life in ways too generous and numerous to count, but could you now, please, back off a little bit?'

'Sure.' Benedict, hurt at last, shuffled towards the kerb, shaking his head. 'Whatever. Have a good fly,' he muttered, then bolted across the road between cars, his fleece flapping round his waist.

'And good luck this afternoon,' Dominic called feebly, already cursing his loss of temper. Breaking into a jog for the rest of the journey home, he found himself cursing several other things as well, like the selfish imprudence of an otherwise intelligent, attractive woman, and his dear brother for knowing him so well.

'Don't be gloomy – the summer term's always the most fun. Look, Jasper's trying to cheer you up,' Charlotte joked, as the dog, granted the treat of riding to school, performed a series of leaping attempts to lick Sam's ears and chin. In her own heart something akin to the state of grace had returned, thanks probably to the most extraordinary night's sleep – deep, dreamless, energizing – almost as if her body had learnt some incredible new trick as physical and fabulous as flying or breathing under water. 'Nobody likes going back to school, not even teachers. And Rose will be there, won't she?'

Sam's only response was a scowl of accusatory incomprehension. 'I'm fine. School will be fine.' He pushed the dog back on to his lap, making what she could see was a deliberate effort to look bored.

Wrong tack, Charlotte chided herself, returning her attention to the road and resolving not to let this new phase of filial hostility sour her own unexpected and wonderful peace of mind. The traffic was solid as usual, which meant there would be nowhere to park. The same problems, yet life was moving on in exactly the direction it should. Sam was entitled to mood-swings. He was a teenager, after all. She glanced across at the passenger seat noting, as if for the first time, the thickening features, the nose wider, longer, the jaw and cheekbones more prominent. He was going to be a good-looking man, she realized suddenly, like his father. When had that happened? Large blue eyes, floppy blond hair, slim hips and, most remarkable of all, *long* legs. That morning, between shooing Jasper in and out of the garden, helping find pencils, rubbers, ink cartridges, and getting herself ready for work, she had unpicked the hem of his school trousers and pressed an iron over them in an unsuccessful bid to extend their length to meet the edges of his shoes, which turned out to be too small as well, his big toes pushing visibly against the worn leather. 'I'll phone the school shop, get new trousers. And shoes, we'll do those at the weekend.'

'Yeah, you said.'

When Charlotte pulled over – double-parked, the hazard lights flashing – Sam got out of the car and strolled towards a cluster of children at the school gates without a backward glance, his bag dangling carelessly over one shoulder, his hand darting to adjust the complicated mess of his hair. Charlotte delayed moving on, straining to make out faces in the crowd, wondering – hoping – if one might be Rose's. Rose, who had metamorphosed from venomous accuser to closest ally, who had burst out of shy silence at the dinner table the night before to deliver a hilarious rendition of an oak tree in a high wind; who, in spite of her stick-like physique, had consumed two heaped platefuls of the main course and pudding; who, without a trace of affectation, had hugged Charlotte's dear, difficult, prickly son farewell in the manner of such honest and trusting friendship that Charlotte had wanted to hug her too, feeling for those few seconds that she could tolerate any amount of adolescent see-sawing in Sam's affections if she knew he was so treasured in another quarter.

And then there was the other, now significant, aspect of Rose – the fact that she was the daughter of Dominic Porter, a man whose very name had once been sufficient to make Charlotte sick at heart, but who now, thanks to the unforeseeable and rather striking events of the previous evening, seemed to be occupying a rather more positive place in her thoughts. Indeed, waking up that morning from her delicious sleep, Dominic had been the first subject that sprang to mind. Several hours later he was still there, rather like a large object blocking a view, Charlotte decided now, something that had to be thought round, or taken into account, or heaved out of the way to get a clear picture of the other things requiring her attention.

He had been kind, that was why, she reasoned, scouring

a new group of children, joshing and ricocheting off each other as they moved along the pavement towards the entrance. He had been kind, and if she could only spot Rose among all the bobbing heads she might spot Dominic too and be able to thank him properly; with the counselling, kindness, food, wine, the exciting possibility of him buying the lease on the bookshop now that he no longer had a job in the City . . . there really was an awful lot to say. Recklessly having changed her mind about the invitation to dinner, giddy still with the shock – the relief – of disburdenment about her father, trying to see signs of affection in the blank looks she was receiving across the table from Sam, the previous evening hadn't exactly seen her at her most articulate. But now she could tell him again – properly – how grateful she was, how utterly delighted at the prospect of the bookshop lease passing into safe hands. She might even confide how Dean and Jason had always run the place like two whispering old women, no canvassing of opinions, leaping on bad ideas. And then, if the moment felt right, she might venture to say that she had slept in a way that was entirely new and restorative, without the usual fitfulness and dreams of unanswered questions; and that while this was obviously connected to the momentous explanatory new light cast upon her past, she was certain that it was largely thanks to his patience and gentle wisdom that she had been able, so quickly, to process this new information to the point of peace rather than torment . . .

Charlotte jumped at the toot of a horn. It dawned on her in the same instant that Rose, newly resident in nearby Chalkdown Road, would require no parental accompaniment for the walk to school. Which meant there would be no Dominic to look out for that morning or any other. The same car horn sounded a second time, more briefly and sharply. Turning towards its source, Charlotte found herself looking at Theresa, popping her head in and out of the window of the Volvo as it moved in the stream of traffic going in the opposite direction.

Theresa – *Henry* – the blood rushed to Charlotte's face. Theresa was gesticulating, mouthing, her hair plastered across her face like netting. Charlotte's lips felt too dry to smile. Her heart thumped. Henry had said something and Theresa was shrieking at her, obscenities, hatred. As the car drew parallel, she gingerly wound down the window.

'Are you okay?' Theresa hollered cheerfully, rolling her eyes in sympathetic horror when Jasper's pointy little face and front paws appeared at the open window.

'Yes – oh, yes, thanks.' Charlotte patted the dog's head. 'I've just got him till Mum's better.'

'Yikes – bad luck. I want us to have lunch this Friday – the one after is our mah-jong, isn't it? Is that prodigal friend of yours still coming? Your bookshop's up for sale – did you know?' she shouted, as the traffic moved and she began to pull away.

Charlotte just had time to screech, a 'Yes,' before the flashing lights of a lorry forced her to rejoin the flow on her own side of the road. She turned off as soon as she could, cutting down the grid of residential streets that offered a circuitous but relatively peaceful route to the bookshop.

Of course Henry hadn't said anything. He had been the guilty party, Charlotte reminded herself, reaching with some difficulty across the dramas of the intervening five days to a recollection of the embarrassing near-collision in the Suffolk kitchen. Her only crime had been to behave like a blind idiot. The once urgent compulsion to tell Theresa had grown distant too. Some truths were massive, and some were small, Charlotte reflected, slowing with impatience for the bumps, then coming to a complete halt while a dustbin lorry spilt a team of whistling men into her path. In fact, she thought drumming her fingers on the steering-wheel, it was often how – when – truth was released that determined its significance. *A time to keep silence, and a time to speak*. Where had that come from?

Her mother had withheld information in a bid to protect her. It was entirely understandable, forgivable, not at all the same as lying, not remotely base. And she now wished to keep something from Theresa because she liked her too much to want to cause her unnecessary pain. Life, if looked at in the right way, could be so beautifully simple. The truth of Henry's affections – or lack of them – would be apparent to Theresa in other ways that Charlotte had neither to know nor to worry about. In the meantime she would agree to lunch and be supportive in any manner Theresa required, happy in the knowledge that she would receive the same in return about her mother's belated revelations, Dominic's kindness, Sam's sulkiness, mounting qualms about seeing Eve again and any other subject she chose to confide. They had been friends through thick and thin and never, Charlotte vowed, was she going to risk or take that for granted again.

Released by the rubbish truck at last, Charlotte arrived at the bookshop just as the man who had hammered a for-sale board into place was getting back into his van. Inside, Jason was waiting for her with crossed arms and a grave face, not about selling his livelihood, as it turned out, but on account of Dean, who was dying.

'Lung cancer – six months, a year at most. We're going to Spain,' he said, before falling upon Charlotte with so much of his body weight that she had to stagger with him to a chair, as if he was the invalid rather than his friend.

*

'I think I hate her,' Sam muttered, staring after the Volkswagen as it roared away.

'Nothing's happened, then?'

Sam shrugged. He liked the way Rose had come up to him from nowhere and was standing really close, not caring now about it being obvious they were friends. 'I wouldn't know, I suppose, would I? I mean, not yet anyway, not until he turns up in his fancy car again to take her out to dinner or something. But there she was just now, waving at George's mum – like nothing was going on. It makes me sick . . .' Sam broke off quickly as George ambled across the playground towards them.

'Hey.'

'Hey.'

'Did you find the den?'

'Yeah, I think so.'

'Cool. Hey, Rose.'

'Hello, George. What are you looking like that for?'

'Like what?'

'That stupid grin, that's what.'

George sniggered. 'You two, that's what.'

'Yeah, and what about it, Fat Face? You like Melanie Cooper and don't deny it. You just can't get her to like you.'

George had gone so very red that Sam, rather to his surprise, felt sorry for him. Rose, perhaps similarly moved, added much more kindly, 'She does like you, actually, if you want to know.'

George's colour deepened. 'Does she?' He looked incredulous and horrified in equal measure.

'Does she really?' Sam asked, as they walked away, inwardly vowing to warn George if this wasn't the case. Seeing him again, remembering the fun of skating and the map for the den, which, in spite of failing, had been a truly decent effort, it had come back to him in a rush just how well he and George had once got on. Nursery, primary, St Leonard's – they had known each other *for ever*. If their parents behaved like idiots it was hardly their fault.

'She totally does,' Rose replied, with her usual airy confidence. 'Totally,' she repeated, breaking into a trot as the school bell sounded, then turning to face him while she jogged backwards. 'You know you're my best friend ever, don't you? For now anyway.' She giggled. 'Beat you to assembly, though.' She spun round and took off in the direction of the main school building, like some ungainly spider with her long, thin legs, her school bag bouncing, and so slow – so beatable – that Sam allowed himself a few moments of compassionate hesitation before tearing past her with a Red Indian whoop of victory.

Jean made herself a cup of tea with the intention of taking it into the sitting room, then decided that a stick and a full mug couldn't be managed. She hobbled back and drank it standing next to the kettle instead, slopping some on her dress because of the shakiness – the feeling of not-caring – that had taken hold. It shouldn't have been too much to ask, to drink the tea at the desk, with Reggie's ribbed gold fountain pen in her good hand, the writing-pad open and waiting, as inviting to human imprint as a fall of fresh snow.

And a broken wrist was probably just the beginning. The old-lady osteoporosis responsible for it would no doubt make other claims on her health and dignity as time went by. And now there was nothing really for company either, except the TV, and the brusque carer who had chivvied her through her ablutions that morning – eight more calls to make, she said – and bossy, bristling Prue who, even in charge of a Hoover, had always reminded Jean of a strutting turkey with its neck feathers ruffled, too pumped up with indignation at her own troubles (the husband with the bad hips, the daughter with no husband and a sickly child) to extend any genuine tenderness towards the sufferings of others.

Prue had left a cottage pie, which was kind in theory but had not *felt* kind to Jean in the manner of its delivery – heavy sighs, an expression of martyrdom fit for a saint at the stake, and a concluding rat-a-tat of instructions about how it would stretch to two suppers if not tackled too greedily, if cooked and stored with sufficient care . . . as if she was talking to someone with dementia instead of a fractured limb, enjoying lauding her own relative robustness, as if it really was only pure financial necessity that had driven her to ring the doorbell every week for fifteen years. Jean had groaned with relief when the front door slammed, then looked round for the comfort of Jasper and remembered he wasn't there.

Standing alone with her tea in the kitchen, Jean forgot again and turned sharply as something moved out of the corner of her eye. Yet there was nothing to see, except the pattern on her kitchen curtains, large silvery shapes on mossy green, flat and still. She put down the empty mug, conjuring an image of the bridge companion who had tried to put her off dachshunds – Camilla something. They were like rodents, the woman had claimed, snapping the cards neatly between shuffles, all sharp points and ratty tails. Jean had gone ahead anyway and found Jasper, tactile and loving from the moment of his arrival, hopping into her shopping basket if he saw she was going out, curling up under the hem of her counterpane like a little stowaway the moment he sensed it might be nearing the time for his overnight incarceration in the kitchen.

Jean breathed slowly as the ache of longing intensified, then receded. She thought she had prepared herself but, really, it was as if she had lost her own shadow.

But there were things to be done, she reminded herself, reaching for her stick and setting off towards the desk in the sitting room where the pen and pad awaited her. There were things to be done and life changed, not gradually but in sudden unforeseeable moments: Charlotte's conception, for instance – terror, timidity, acute discomfort, over in seconds, but with a lifetime in which to live out the consequences; or the stupid stumble in the bathroom the week before – so slight, a misjudgement of a mere half an inch as she lifted her leg over the side of the bath, yet here she was, tottering round like a cripple. Once, not so very long ago, she could have put an arm out to steady herself, even against the steamed slippery tiles of the bathroom wall. Once, rather longer ago, the suppleness in her bones would have meant a bruise or perhaps a sprain at worst, even after the sliding and tumbling – arm first, knee second – on to the bathroom floor.

Jean, halfway down the passageway connecting the kitchen to the sitting room, paused to rest her forehead against the wall, recalling how once, even longer ago, before the brief promiscuity that had produced her daughter, there had still been the loveliness of hoping to live life well instead of making do. She squeezed her eyes shut, blocking out the songbirds on the wallpaper and seeing Reggie, carefree, handsome, the proverbial rolling stone, then the wizened undignified thing he had become at the end, labouring between each rattling wheeze until she'd wanted to grab the pillow, press it over his face and scream that it was time to let go, for her release as much as his. Ending well, there could be real virtue – real dignity – in that. Jean opened her eyes and tightened her grip on her stick. She had done nothing to help Reggie manage it – but *she* still might.

And already she had achieved a lot, she consoled herself, dropping into the desk chair with a sigh and letting the stick fall to the carpet: she had made her peace with Charlotte – told her the awkward dark thing that had had to be told and seen the brave, mature way her daughter was already accommodating it; and darling Jasper had been taken care of; and both the carer and the turkey-faced Prue had swallowed the story about Charlotte returning to undertake nursing duties for the rest of the week. Most cunning of all, she had cut across Charlotte's excited and endearing babble about leases and bookshops on the phone that morning to say that the line was crackly and definitely on the blink and she was thinking of calling BT. Yes, the stage was set and she was in charge at last, determined to exercise more control over the end of her life than she had ever managed in the living of it.

Jean reached for the pad, wrote the date and paused. Reggie had been the one for letters, when he put his mind to it. *So you weren't mine, but I have always been your devoted father.* What a lovely line. No wonder Charlotte had flinched with emotion when she reached it. Seeing it for the first time herself, after steaming open the envelope on the eve of the grand trip up north twenty years before, Jean had flinched too – fear, jealousy, protectiveness. It was as if every weakness, every failure of her life had been compressed into a single instant.

It was extraordinary, she decided, starting at last to write, how one could *remember* emotions but no longer *feel* them; how, with time, the most ardent passions could be relegated to the cooler, safer storage of humdrum memory. All her fervour for Reggie, for instance, that had faded now, as had the early secret hopes of what might evolve from his gallant, noble, mostly brotherly offer of marriage, not to mention the ensuing disappointment and dreaded jealousy, as first Charlotte, then the other women (wives, servant girls, he wasn't fussy) stole his attention. It was exhausting even to think about. It had exhausted her at the time too, wrung her out, made her unlovable and powerless and quite unfit, probably, to be a mother. And yet she had clung out of old habit, old hope; clung on until suddenly there were the faltering lungs to worry about and a turning of the tables and Reggie needing her and the realization that the love that had compelled her to behave in the best interests of her daughter had other manifestations, too, no matter how reluctant she was to acknowledge them.

My darling Charlotte,
Another letter – please forgive that and everything else I have put you through.

Please understand also that, from the moment of your conception, I have always tried to act in your best interests. As I attempted to explain during our talk, marrying Reggie, staying with him, keeping back so much of the truth, was simply an effort to protect you. And though much of that process has not been easy, I have no regrets. For instance, one of the reasons (other than darling Sam, of course) that I so badly wanted you to patch things up with Martin was so you could find out, as I did – unexpectedly – that there is always good to be found in bad, that no relationship is without its warts and warps and compromise, and that there is the most astonishing satisfaction to be had in seeing something through to the end.

Jean stopped writing and frowned, wondering whether to tear the page off and start again. So soon, and the words –

the meaning – was going off the rails, finding paths she had never intended. She had meant to apologize, to explain, and say her farewells. And, of course, she had regrets, hadn't she? Not telling Charlotte of her true beginnings, for one thing: that was truly regrettable. Poor Charlotte. But then . . . Jean ran the end of the pen along her lips as she recalled her daughter's fragility, not just as a lonely, shy, self-conscious child (so painfully in need of playmates that she and Reggie had broken their hearts in deciding to send her away to school) but in the extremes of emotion that had characterized Charlotte's adulthood – in pieces at Reggie's death, ecstatic at meeting Martin, so caught up with Sam, and then increasingly miserable once more as marital distrust had taken hold. The years, flying by, had never been without their justification for silence. And how, Jean wondered suddenly, could one regret things that – given the same situation, the same information – one would do again?

She wasn't thinking straight. She would be better off sitting up in bed, she decided, with the pad on her knees, the pillows propping her back and a full glass of water – heavens, she mustn't forget that, or the stockpile of tablets that would need rummaging for at the back of her bedside-table drawer.

At London Bridge station that morning Henry paused in front of a flower stall. He remembered a thing on the telly once in which a philandering husband had been found out through a lavish, guilt-ridden bunch of flowers – such a sudden gesture of romance from a lifelong sceptic that the canny wife in the drama had been on to him at once. He wasn't even a philanderer and his wife was still on to him, Henry reflected miserably, glancing at his crotch, then sideways in alarm at the unlikely possibility of an onlooker following his train of thought. Everything was in perfect working order (he had taken the precaution of testing it several times since the shameful bedroom fiasco over the long weekend) and yet it seemed – Henry released a soft groan – no longer to be relied on when he was most in need.

Famous for his professional nerves of steel, for the steadiness of his long, delicate fingers under the pressure of bright lights and the highest human hopes, Henry could hardly believe the private demolishment he had felt at having tried and failed to make love to his wife. Terrified it might happen again, he had spent every subsequent night feigning exhaustion, then lying sleepless in the dark. To get to the brink like that, to be so full of genuine ardour and virtuous determination to re-embrace his wife, his marriage, for good . . . It was almost as if his system had, literally, been poisoned by guilt; that while his brain might be ready to erase the memories of an ill-founded, inappropriate desire to sweep Charlotte Turner off her feet (pathetically triggered, as he kept reminding himself, by late-night pity and a glimpse of faded bra), some separate, stronger part of him remained determined that the path to recovery could not be so easy.

Theresa, meanwhile, was unbearably quiet, unbearably kind, tiptoeing round his emotions and his body as if he had some terminal disease. They couldn't speak, they couldn't touch, and now there was the new fear of the girls' lunch they were having that Friday when Charlotte might decide to blow everything sky-high anyway. Theresa had broken the news of this unhappy arrangement when Henry had been half out of the door that morning, her mouth still full of toast, her voice resounding with the new brittle cheerfulness that communicated distrust, hurt and the word '*Why?*' as clearly as if it had been emblazoned on her forehead. They were going to treat themselves to Santini's, she chirruped, have a trial run for Charlotte's birthday dinner. Wasn't that a lark?

Henry had nodded heavily, thinking of tongues, loosened by wine and the terrifying, peculiarly female capacity for mutual emotional exposure. Charlotte, after all, had spent years pouring out her marital miseries to Theresa. So what was to prevent a handy switch of roles? All Theresa had to confess to was a certain unease, and who knew what might spill out? It was like waiting for a bomb to go off.

There were some roses in a bucket near his feet, dusky pink, interlaced with sprigs of white. Would Theresa raise her eyebrows like the actress on the telly? Or would she get that distant dreamy look in her eye that Henry had lately been remembering so fondly, the one he had once been able to conjure with a single word or caress; the one that had always assured him she was his for the loving, and would be until worms chomped them both into soil.

'Anniversary?'

Henry spun round to find Martin standing at his shoulder. He looked impressively smooth-shaven and immaculate in a navy suit, offset by a crisp pink shirt and a tie of such shockingly electric fuchsia that Henry immediately suspected the handiwork of Cindy rather than Martin himself. 'No.' He managed a smile, colouring slightly.

'Not the right time of day anyway, is it?' Martin quipped, grinning, clearly on top form. He held up his wrist and shook out his watch from under the starched cuff, making a face as he registered the time. 'Unless you've reverted to night shifts and are on your way home.'

'Happily not. I was just looking . . . Some of these places sell out of the good stuff pretty early on.'

'Yes,' Martin murmured, eyeing his friend and the flower stall doubtfully.

'Thanks so much for the party, by the way,' Henry went on. 'I don't know if Theresa wrote but –'

'Yes, she did – thanks.'

'Excellent, yes, she's good like that, Theresa ... but, seriously, it was a great do. And *you* look great. Clearly, things are going well.'

Martin's grin broadened, crumpling his handsome face to a more accurate representation of his forty-three years. 'They are, mate, they really are.' He lowered his voice, 'Cindy's expecting – we've only just started telling people.'

'Hey, congratulations! That's tremendous.' Henry patted Martin's arm, genuine delight pushing through his preoccupations. 'We must get the pair of you over. I'll talk to Tess about it – see if we can get the women to come up with a date.'

'Yeah, absolutely.' There was a pause while both confronted, privately, the unlikelihood of such an event coming to pass. 'Or you two could come and support a good cause,' Martin suggested. 'Our choir's doing a charity concert in a couple of weeks. It's taken a while but we've got a lovely venue lined up – St Gregory's, not far from the Albert Hall.'

'The Albert Hall – goodness.'

'No, the church is *near* the Albert Hall. It's a breast-cancer charity. Cindy's mother died from it – she and her sister Lu both have to have regular checks. But, hey, I'll get Cindy to send you some bumph and you can decide for yourself.' He glanced again at his watch, this time with a frown. 'Look, mate, I've got to dash – I'm in need of a taxi and there's bound to be a queue. See you at the concert hopefully,' he added, delivering a farewell punch to Henry's arm.

Henry, who had only to walk the remaining few hundred yards to the hospital where he saw patients privately two mornings a week, stayed where he was, watching Martin and his exquisitely cut suit weave deftly through the crowds towards the station's main entrance. The noise of announcements and hurrying people shrank to a blur as he remembered the envy he had felt for Martin at the party, still youthful, embarking on a second chance, with the curvy, radiant, goddess-like Cindy at his side. He could muster no trace of an equivalent emotion now, not for his friend's new life, new wife, designer home and designer aftershave, probably, lingering still in the space he had occupied during their faltering conversation, and certainly not for the prospect of a new baby. Who would want to be at the beginning again, facing the hard slog of negotiating roles and trying to find out who each of you really was? Not to mention the invariably doomed efforts to reshuffle old acquaintances that the acquisition of a new partner demanded, as if friendships were as flat and flexible as an old pack of cards.

As the noisy reality of his surroundings came back into focus, Henry propelled himself away from the flower stall towards the nearest exit. He wanted a second chance, all right, but with Theresa. He wanted what they'd once had back again – the easy intimacy, tempting to dismiss it precisely because it was so familiar but which had taken so many hours and days and weeks and years to construct that he had utterly overlooked its value and fragility.

By the time he reached the street Henry's heart was beating so hard he had to stop and make himself breathe. Such treasure and he had thrown it away. Unless . . . unless he talked to Charlotte and somehow secured her silence. Yes, that was it. A simple thing – why hadn't he thought of it before? He would grasp the proverbial nettle, put his case, eke out some kind of peace of mind. Henry stepped into the road, then leapt back as a white van trundled past, so close that he could smell the driver's cigarette. Across the street he caught sight of Martin, his upper body framed in the rear window of a taxi, grinning still, waving madly. Henry raised a hand in return, then shuffled up the street to attempt a second crossing under the safer guidance of the traffic-lights, where he waited patiently for the green man to flash, even though the road was clear.

Chapter Sixteen

For the rest of the week April resumed the more rapidly changing weather patterns for which it is famous, but in such an extreme manner – patches of eye-achingly brilliant sunshine interleaved with torrential downpours – that by Friday Charlotte was quite used to seeing vast, vibrant rainbows arching across gun-metal skies beyond the fence in the back garden. Caught out several times, she had taken to carrying a brolly for even the shortest walk with Jasper and tried in vain to persuade Sam to pack a waterproof when setting off each morning on his bicycle – a new craze that Charlotte was sure she would have been able to celebrate more freely but for the sneaking suspicion that her son had adopted it out of spite to curtail the amount of time he had to endure with her.

'A teenager, with pimples on his chin, a new sense of his own seriousness, a girlfriend, and you expected to be *liked*?' Eve teased, when she phoned to confirm her arrival at the end of the following week, in good time, she promised, to help with preparations for the mah-jong party.

'I'm not sure Rose is a girlfriend and, actually, he hasn't got pimples – at least not yet.' Charlotte let her gaze drift to the kitchen window where there were no rainbows, only Jasper sniffing at something in the grass. Her mother's dog was proving a surprisingly complicated house-guest, only venturing into the garden if accompanied and then only staying there on his own if the back door was left open. The moment she prepared to go out he somehow knew it, no matter how tightly curled up in his little basket he was, or how softly she tiptoed towards the front door. If she persisted with the abandonment, he would start to howl, so blood-curdlingly, so relentlessly, that on Wednesday Mr Beasley had been round to complain, muttering about noise-pollution assessments and cruelty to animals. Fearful on both counts, Charlotte had taken the dog with her for her next work shift, first keeping him in the car and then, when she discovered Jason tapping and cooing at the passenger window, into the shop, where Jasper had bedded down among the folds of her old green cardigan on a shelf in the stock room, as if his God-given doggy rights had at last been satisfied.

Eve laughed at Charlotte's defence of Sam's complexion. 'Well, that won't last, you doting mother, you. But I can't wait to see him, I truly can't. Not having any of my own . . .' She let the sentence hang, adding quickly, 'I called round on the off-chance on Monday night, by the way, but no one was home. You were stuck dealing with your mother's accident, I assume. How *is* the old dear?'

Charlotte hesitated, partly at the uncharitable edge in Eve's tone, for which she knew she was responsible (the distance between her and Jean had been the subject of many energetic conversations during their student years), and partly because, thanks to either the sloth or inefficiency of the Kent-area telephone-repair workforce, it was now almost three days since she and Jean had had any contact. 'She seems to be managing, thanks. Carers, help from her cleaning lady, that sort of thing.'

'Oh, good. I can't wait to have a proper lovely catch-up about absolutely everything. And it will be hilarious to play mah-jong again – an aunt of mine had a set but it's been years.'

Charlotte put the phone down with a fresh surge of doubt about reigniting an acquaintance that had lain dormant and not been much missed for a decade. She had been pleased at the bolt-from-the-blue email before Christmas and enjoyed the exchanges that had followed. But hearing Eve's voice again was peculiar. She had sounded odd, different. Very much a part of her early happy memories of Martin. It would also be unsettling, Charlotte realized, to see her old friend now that she was separated and single – closer, in many ways, to the shy student whom Eve had befriended with shortbread and hot drinks twenty years before. Except no, Charlotte corrected herself, retrieving the phone and starting, with some defiance, to dial her mother's number, she couldn't be further from the girl she had been then: sad, lost, confused, angry, waiting for a parent to die and life to start making sense. It had been a truly desperate time, bearable only because there had been nothing else to know.

Halfway through dialling she stopped, pondering with the sudden clarity only ever granted by hindsight the obvious fact that when she had met Martin she had been on the rebound – not in a conventional sense but from the death of the man she had known and loved deeply as her father. And there had been that nagging sense of business unfinished to deal with too, of things unsaid and unexplained. No wonder she had constructed a tall pedestal and plonked Martin on top of it. No wonder he had fallen off.

It took Charlotte several seconds to register the engaged tone, beeping into her left ear as it had on every one of her attempts to contact Jean since Tuesday. Impatient, experiencing a spurt of real concern, she slammed the phone down and flipped through her address book on the slim off-chance that she had the cleaner's number stored under 'P'. She hadn't, and had to console herself instead with the acknowledgement that Prue had *her* number and was the sort who, in the event of any problem, would be only too keen to get in touch and disgorge the details.

Glancing at the page in the address book again, Charlotte's eye stopped at the last entry, made a couple of days before in her own careful handwriting: 'PORTER' and then, in smaller letters, 'Dominic and Rose'. She chuckled. As if she – or Sam for that matter – was likely to forget those two names in a hurry. And the man's nose wasn't really large at all, she decided, just a tad *aquiline*, an imperfection that was more than made up for by the deep, dark, dreamy brown eyes – like chocolate, but flecked with black, like – Whoa there, whoa there.

Charlotte closed the book and forced the room back into focus. Jasper had trotted in through the open door and was slumped against her left ankle, using it as he might a sturdy leg of furniture to lean against while performing the gymnastic feat of using a back paw to scratch behind an ear.

She had work to get ready for, not to mention the grand lunch with Theresa. Some proper makeup was in order for once and more than a passing effort at pinning up her hair. And Dominic might come into the shop, she told herself, hurrying up the stairs. He had apparently dropped in on Wednesday, when she was out on errands, and stayed for ages. Jason had given her a blow-by-blow on the questions he had asked, so intricate, some of them, that Dean, the true expert when it came to detail, had had to be consulted several times on the phone. Even Shona had mentioned the visit, saying, 'What a nice man,' in such a gushing way that Charlotte had begun to wonder (while recognizing her own insanity) whether the girl was playing some dark, competitive game over their prospective new employer's affections. She had had to remind herself that, thanks to various lines of conversation during the Monday dinner, Dominic already knew enough of the shortcomings of her co-worker to have sworn Shona would be one of the various things he would choose not to inherit should his purchase of the lease go ahead. The order for the expensive new carpet would be jettisoned too, he had promised, along with Jason's pet long-term project to surrender the little cast-iron Victorian fireplace for a measly few extra feet of shelves.

Charlotte hummed as she dusted her eyelids and cheeks with the assortment of worn makeup brushes that lived in an old toothmug next to the bathroom mirror, falling silent for the closer concentration required to apply lipstick. She was staring disconsolately at the dry sticky mess of her mascara, doubtful of any residual power it might have to enhance her looks, when her mobile rang. Thinking at once of her mother, she dropped the stick into the bin and hastily scooped the phone out of her pocket.

But instead of Prue or Jean, a man's voice was on the line, so croaky and uncertain that it took an instant or two for Charlotte to recognize it as Henry's. 'I assume this is about your car mechanic.'

'No, I – I'm sorry, Charlotte, I'd forgotten about that . . . Christ – sorry. It's Mr Jarvis, at the bottom of Moreton Road under the railway arches. Unfortunately I don't have his number to hand right now.'

Henry clenched his mobile. Standing in his own kitchen, he could easily have found Jarvis's number, but he was in too much of a lather to think about such things. Theresa had set off so early on the school run that he had found himself with this unexpected breathing space – a bubble of quiet in which to address, at last, his plan of calling Charlotte. It had been hovering over him all week, surging and fading, depending on how busy he was and the level of his own inner calm. 'You're meeting Theresa today.'

'Yes. We're having lunch at Santini's. If the food's good and not too expensive I might decide to have my fortieth birthday dinner there. Why? Were you thinking of joining us?'

'Charlotte . . . please.'

It occurred to Charlotte to hang up. Just in case he was on the verge of saying something truly awful – about liking her or wanting to see her again. But then it also occurred to her that he might simply be trying to apologize.

'All I want,' Henry blurted, 'is for you not to tell her anything about what happened – please, Charlotte. Things haven't been great, you see, so she might just . . . Look, don't tell Tess *anything*, okay?'

No apology, then. No renewal of affections either, which was good. Charlotte hesitated, needing to think rather than because there was any pleasure to be had in prolonging Henry's evident discomfort. 'What if she asks me something outright?' she offered at last.

'Oh, my God, she wouldn't, would she?'

'Henry, she's your wife. You've just told me you've not been getting on too well. Maybe she suspects something. Maybe she thinks something happened in Suffolk. How do I know? All I can tell you is that, for reasons I'm not prepared to go into right now, I'm not a huge fan of the bare-faced lie.'

There was a long pause. 'But if she doesn't ask, you won't say anything?'

'No. I'd already decided that.'

'Right.'

She could hear him breathing out.

'Thanks.'

'Don't mention it.'

Charlotte stuck out her tongue at her reflection as she tackled her hair. She stabbed roughly with the clips and grips, not minding as she nicked her scalp, wishing she could turn the clock back to the time when Henry had been safely boxed as Theresa's clever, slightly bumbling husband and she the disaster-prone friend.

By the time she was ready to leave, however, her good spirits had resurfaced. Guilt was robbing Henry of common sense. Theresa was as she always was. Since the shouting through the car windows they had enjoyed several thoroughly 'normal' phone conversations, covering a range of matters that included the maddening inefficiency of telephone companies and whether to make a fuss about Martin's request *vis-à-vis* his and Cindy's concert. On Theresa's advice she hadn't, with the happy result that Martin had offered to collect Sam straight from school the following Friday to give her a clear run to prepare for Eve and mah-jong. Charlotte was looking forward to the lunch enormously, not just because it seemed wise to fix on some plan for her hateful milestone birthday but because she was keen to move off such mundane matters and confide some of the other, much more seismic, things that had been going on in her life. Like the business of her father, and the miraculous new peace with Jean – subjects that required the intimacy of face-to-face contact as opposed to the impersonality of the telephone. And there was the Dominic Porter thing, too, of course, if she could muster enough courage.

Jasper was waiting for her on the landing, lying across the bottom of her bedroom door like a draught-excluder. As Charlotte set off down the stairs he followed, in the tumbling near-somersault fashion necessitated by his short legs and the deep Victorian stairs. 'I suppose you're coming too,' she muttered, shaking her head in amused despair as he scuttled ahead to take up his do-or-die pose by the front door. Charlotte paused to smile, understanding suddenly how deep attachments could form with such creatures – to be waited for, to have one's company sought, it was sheer flattery, no matter how dumb the animal. As she bent down to scoop up the morning's post, it occurred to her to wonder suddenly how on earth Jean could bear to be deprived of such attachment, and in the distressing aftermath of her accident too, when one might have assumed she needed it most . . . Charlotte froze, post in hand. It didn't make sense. And the phone not working. That didn't make sense either. Something was wrong.

Dropping the letters on the hall table, she embarked on a proper whirlwind search for the cleaner's number, flinging papers off shelves and out of drawers, riffling through notebooks and old diaries. Not finding it would mean driving to Kent. She searched harder, propelling herself with thoughts of Jason's dismay if she were to cry off her morning shift, and Theresa's, if she cancelled lunch. Leaving a paper-trail of mess, Charlotte eventually found herself back at the hall table, all set for a final desperate rummage in its two small brass-handled drawers. Instead, her gaze was drawn to a crooked second-class stamp on an envelope sticking out from the bottom of the pile of post. Near it – misaligned so as to be *too* near it – and clearly visible, was the last half of her surname, written in her mother's unmistakable hand, with real ink and letters so shaky that, as Charlotte stared at them, her heart for some reason gathered speed.

Gently, she tugged the envelope out of the pile, fighting the faint but growing conviction that her world, so recently righted, was about to be overturned again. The flap was tightly gummed. As Charlotte teased it free, the feeling of dread grew, but alongside it there was also a burgeoning, almost sweet sensation of surrender. Why fight anything any more? Maybe a part of her was that lost little girl still and always would be. Some lives zigzagged off course and others didn't. She had as much hope of righting such mysterious imbalances as abseiling up one of the rainbows sprouting out of her garden fence.

When the door slammed Henry hastily abandoned his phone, reached for a glass from the draining-board and turned on the cold tap. A moment later Theresa, marching into the kitchen, experienced a moment of equal surprise. She had come back for Matty's ballet shoes, she explained, stretching across him to turn down the tap, which was splashing up his suit front, and wasn't he going to miss his train?

'Headache,' Henry explained, tapping his temple and swigging the water. 'Came back to take something . . . Might still catch it if I run.' And run he did, out of the front door and up the street, only remembering as he hurled himself, along with a couple of other late arrivals, between the sliding doors of the eight thirty-two, that he had forgotten his phone.

Theresa, in a fluster about the shoes, acutely aware of her daughter still strapped into the unlocked car, late for school, but also – with her winning grin and plaits – a prime target for child-snatchers and paedophiles, bounced around the ground floor of the house ransacking plastic bags and back-packs. She had *seen* the ballet shoes somewhere that morning – seen them, thought they must be remembered and forgotten about them. It was only because the 'somewhere' turned out to be between the fruit bowl and the biscuit jar that she spotted Henry's mobile. Less easy to understand was why, with the pumps found and her haste so urgent, Theresa paused not only to pick up the little phone but to press the buttons taking her to the information entitled 'last number dialled'.

She emerged on the doorstep several minutes later, moving in a manner so obviously drained of haste that Matilda stuck her pig-tailed head out of the car window to scold, 'Come *on*, Mummy, come *on*.'

'Good shower?' Eve asked lazily, rolling over to study her new lover through the tumble of her hair, enjoying the sight of the miniskirt of a towel that stopped several inches short of the bulging muscles above his knees. His torso was glistening still with water, flattering the dark triangle of his chest hair and the smooth muscled panels of his stomach. Watching him move around the bedroom, opening drawers and riffling through a rail of shirts, it was clear to Eve that he was deliberately showing these assets off. So he's vain, she thought, rather enjoying the observation, since there was little she didn't know about vanity, and in her experience a man who cared about his appearance could be trusted to conduct himself in other ways that she judged important – hygiene, manners, the right outfit for the right occasion. Yes, this one would do very nicely. 'So, no time for a quickie, then?' she teased, keeping her voice low and full of playful disappointment as the torso disappeared inside a lemon shirt.

'Sorry, babe.' Tim grinned at her in the wardrobe mirror, sticking to the task of doing up the shirt buttons even though he would far have preferred to be tearing them apart. A good lay was so exactly what he had needed. And she was just his type, saucy, confident, full of surprises. 'I'd love to, but I'm late as it is.'

'Too bad.' Eve levered herself upright, tucking the duvet

under her arms as she dropped her phone back into her handbag and plucked out her lighter and cigarettes.

'Ah,' Tim wagged a finger, 'not in here, if you don't mind.'

'Open the window, there's a darling. Then you won't notice.' Eve placed a cigarette between her lips, snapped open her lighter and inhaled with a groan of satisfaction. 'Like I said last night, my sins and I come as a package – all-or-nothing, non-negotiable.' She watched through half-closed lids as Tim, with a show of amused reluctance, obediently opened the window. As a reward for this compliance she leant out of bed to blow a jet stream of smoke in its direction, making sure in the process that the duvet slipped down to her waist.

'You're terrible,' said Tim softly, pausing to admire the sight.

'I know.' Eve lay back, stretching both arms above her head invitingly. 'Show me again how terrible I am . . .'

'Baby, I can't. Later.'

'Who says I'll still be here?'

'You did,' Tim reminded her, laughing. 'Until Friday, you said.'

'Ah, yes, *Friday*, when I see Charlotte. I'll have to wear dark glasses and a big hat in the meantime.'

'Not on my account.' Tim flung a tie round his neck. 'Like I told you, as far as I was concerned, things on that front never really got going.' He worked at the tie until it was a fat, loose knot, sitting just below the top button of his shirt.

'You look good.'

'Thanks . . . So do you, come to that.'

Eve got out of bed to tap her ash out of the open window, trailing the duvet like an extravagant ballgown. Unable to resist the sight, Tim crossed the room to kiss her, unravelling what he could of the bedding in the process. He didn't even mind the smokiness. He was too thrilled with how everything was going, that he hadn't lost his touch after all. He still couldn't believe his luck – such a woman dropping into his life on Charlotte's doorstep of all places. Although Eve had to take the credit for charging after him to exchange phone numbers, promising to be in touch after the visit to her brother. A woman with balls for a change, a woman who knew what she wanted. Tim had waited for her phone call like a palpitating teenager.

Eve put out her cigarette on the window-ledge and leant out, enjoying the morning sun on her face. She tossed the stub at a bush, but it rolled short on to the jutting rectangle of Tim's neat, empty patio. 'But if I bump into her, I'll have to come clean, obviously.' She threw the sentence over her shoulder, studying Tim carefully. He was back in front of the mirror with a comb now, smoothing the sides and stabbing for a messier look on top, presumably to disguise the small patch where the hair was thinning.

She had been thoroughly entertained by his account of the brief fling with Charlotte, how her old friend had got too clingy, obliging him to call a halt. And Sam's dear little note asking him to change his mind (prompting the non-starter of a mercy mission, which she had so unwittingly interrupted), that, too, had been delightful. The idea of being adored and looked out for like that by a *child* – even a sulky one – intrigued Eve. It had even made her wonder, momentarily, whether she should consider getting her tubes untied to produce a similarly loyal and devoted little darling of her own. But then, right from the beginning, Charlotte had been so sickeningly *smitten* by motherhood and Eve knew she never would be: the squawks, the smells, the puke, the *neediness* – she had watched first Charlotte and then various other friends go through it in repulsed bafflement.

Tim had paused in his grooming. 'Whatever you think best, babe, though she was pretty cut up.' He pulled a face.

'I'll be careful, then,' Eve promised. 'And I *will* be here when you get back,' she called, snuggling back under the bedclothes as he bounded down the stairs.

With the weather mostly clement and business brisk, Santini's had recently opened its rear doors to a large, paved courtyard, attractively hemmed in by mossy stone walls and ripening thickets of honeysuckle and clematis. There were eight tables in all, each with an attendant heater, weighted tablecloths and large, solid canvas umbrellas, sporting the same green and gold stripes that blazed from the canopy outside the restaurant's front entrance. That Friday it was too warm for the heaters and the brollies were splayed by way of protection against the sun, offering such an effective carapace that the long, low bulge of charcoal clouds on the skyline amassed unseen, stretching and gathering energy as stealthily as a cat preparing to stalk its prey.

Theresa, observing them from her bedroom window, had changed into a thicker long-sleeved top. She had seen the Volkswagen, too, parked in one of the few spaces right outside the restaurant, one window left slightly open on account of the little dog, which had had its paws up against the glass as she walked past. But at the sight of Charlotte seated under the furthest of the canvas umbrellas, her chin resting on the tops of both hands as she studied the menu, Theresa murmured an apology to the waiter guiding her to the table and ducked downstairs to seek refuge in the ladies'.

Avoiding her reflection in the rows of mirrors, she perched on a small velvet chair next to a vase of lilies and dabbed her hot forehead with a tissue. Her mother, on the phone, had advised restraint, maintaining cool, keeping her counsel, waiting and seeing, but to Theresa it was clear that a turning point had been reached and needed to be acted upon – albeit in her own time when the moment was exactly right. She could enjoy that luxury at least, of deciding *when* to bring the edifice of her life tumbling down. In fact, after so many weeks of exhausting uncertainty and fuggy suspicions, getting the whole business finally out in the open would be a relief. She took it steadily as she proceeded back up the stairs, then strode with as much purpose as she could manage across the restaurant's polished stone floor.

Charlotte grinned and stood up long before Theresa reached the table. She was waving the piece of paper she had been studying – not the menu at all, but what looked like a letter. From her mother, Charlotte explained, her face still creased with smiles as they exchanged kisses, breaking her chatter only to agree, exuberantly, to the waiter's suggestion of champagne.

Champagne? Theresa managed a nod and a frozen smile as she sat down. Her head felt heavy – full – because of the question coiled inside, a hair's breadth from release. *Are you and Henry having an affair?* Yes, that would do it. The difficulty was the follow-up. *Take him. Give him back. Finish it. Carry on. Fuck off.* The possibilities were really too endless.

'So the letter explains that she has gone away somewhere,' Charlotte was saying, 'on her *own*, which is, of course, remarkable, given her enfeebled condition, but she says she's managing fine, give or take the occasional dousing of her plaster, and that she's realized it's all an attitude of mind. I can't tell you the relief – you wouldn't believe the state I got myself into this morning. I was so sure something *awful* had happened ... I mean, it is odd, of course, but she has every right to go where she pleases and I honestly cannot remember the last time she went *anywhere*, except to walk the bloody dog. Although Jasper isn't actually bloody at all but really rather sweet, and when she takes him back I have a feeling I'm going to miss him terribly – far more than Sam, whom I thought would be so thrilled to have the loan of a pet, but who has taken barely any notice. On top of all that –' Charlotte paused to sip her champagne '– she appears to be trying to give me some money.' She flapped the letter again, pointing at a sentence and reading out loud, '"The enclosed is for you to do with as you choose." A cheque in other words.'

'Wow,' offered Theresa, taking a long, steadying swig from her glass.

'Except,' continued Charlotte, laughing, 'the silly old thing forgot to enclose the *enclosed*, so I've no idea how grateful to be. And since she's gone away somewhere *secret* I can't even ask, for the time being, and maybe I shouldn't anyway – I mean, it would be a bit awkward, wouldn't it? Although we're getting on *so* much better ... I can't really explain it, but last week, after the hospital, I was dreading it so much but, looking after her, something *happened* – a sort of connection. I've been dying to tell you because it led – at least I think it did – to her telling me this most incredible, unbelievable thing about ...' Charlotte, having slowed, came to a halt at last. She had been talking with imbecilic speed and selfishness, she realized. Poor Theresa looked like some bewildered creature weathering a storm. 'Forgive me, I'm gabbling. There's just so much stuff I've been bursting to tell you. Sorry.'

'No, go on,' Theresa urged, impressed with her own sureness of tone. 'You and your mum getting along at last

– that's great. Wow,' she repeated, with less conviction, pressing her champagne glass back to her lips.

'You are my closest friend,' said Charlotte, quietly, sufficiently reassured to reach for Theresa's hand and keep a tight hold of it while she confided the discovery that the man she thought of as her father had married her mother when she was already pregnant out of deep friendship and a gallant desire to offer social respectability rather than passion; that from what she could gather her own existence was the result of a one-night stand with a married man who had died without ever having been made aware of the consequences of his infidelity.

A laugh of disbelief escaped Theresa, not in sympathetic wonderment, as Charlotte understandably supposed, but at the wild, unforeseeable injustice of being presented with such poignant, intimate information at such a moment. On occasions she had been genuinely curious about Charlotte's past – the pre-Martin Charlotte – but it seemed laughably cruel to have that curiosity satisfied *now* and so dramatically, just as she was poised with her cudgel, ready to beat out other, fresher and, to her, much more devastating truths.

'Theresa? Are you okay? I didn't mean . . .'

'*No*, I am not *okay*,' she hissed, letting the miserable anger fill her voice and her expression at last.

'Oh dear . . . I . . .'

'Your father . . . what you said . . . Of course I sympathize . . . but . . .'

'No, I'm fine with it, actually,' Charlotte stammered, a possible reason for her companion's miserable bewilderment beginning to dawn. She sat back in her chair, which felt hard and uncomfortable suddenly, all the wrong angles. Up under the curve of their umbrella she glimpsed a dark cloud, advancing upon the clear sky like a breaking wave. 'Every-

thing sort of makes sense,' she mumbled, 'it's like understanding it means I don't have to think about it any more.'

'Oh, *good.*'

Charlotte, hearing the sneer, braced herself. A waiter, who
had approached to take their order and sensed the intensity
of the conversation, tactfully withdrew to show some more
arrivals to their seats.

Dominic hovered under the green and gold canopy, staring
in disbelief at the mud-spattered black Volkswagen and its
small canine occupant, curled up on a tartan rug on the back
seat. There was a chance, of course, that she wasn't dining
at the same venue, that the Fates, though mischievous, were
not cruel. Dominic peered hopefully through the glass front
of the restaurant, but it was difficult to make out anything
beyond the dim outlines of a few scattered diners. He
checked his watch. Ten minutes late already – maybe she
wouldn't show. He felt a fresh surge of hope and then a
kick of dismay. What was he thinking? Of *course* he wanted
Petra to show. Only an idiot or a creature on the verge of
taking holy orders wouldn't. And being stood up would be
pretty shattering too, Dominic reflected, after the phone-
tennis and with his ego still shaky from Maggie and lack of
practice and being given the boot at work, not to mention
being passed over for a fat married doctor with old-man
bushy eyebrows . . .

'Domineec!'

'Hey, Petra. I was giving up hope.'

'Oh, no, I am so sorry. It was the traffic and nowhere to
park in this bloody city.' She kissed him on both cheeks,
then ran her fingers through her hair, which had grown
considerably since their first encounter and been cut into
long, feathery layers that accentuated the strong rounded

triangle of her face. 'It is so good to see you – at last!' She looped one arm companionably through his, then sprang away, clapping her hand to her mouth. 'The bloody meter machine – I have forgotten to put in my money. I have to run and come back soon. You go – I am coming.'

Dominic laughed as she took off back down the street. What a great girl. He pushed open the door of the restaurant, pausing to enjoy a final glimpse of the floppy mane of fair hair and the memorable legs moving inside the confines of her tight skirt.

There was no fluency to misery, Charlotte reflected wretchedly; it was only in films and books that suffering people were ever articulate or beautiful. In real life they were like poor dear Theresa now, puffy-faced, tugging at her lips with her teeth, too at the mercy of her emotions to mount her challenge with any coherence. And for her too, waiting with her hands clenched in her lap, knowing now full well what the challenge would be, steeling herself to answer honestly, there was nothing but an overwhelming – guilty – awareness of the ugliness of human weakness and its power to wound those held dear.

'I *know*,' Theresa burst out, after a huge gulp of air, 'about you and Henry – he phoned you this morning – I *know* – and you two in Suffolk – how *could* you?'

'What?'

'You and Henry –'

'*What?*' Charlotte repeated the word with more force. The incredulity in her voice was not only easy but *truthful*, she realized. There was no her-and-Henry. Honesty had levels. Wanting life to be black and white didn't make it so. 'Theresa, what are you *saying*? Stop, this instant.' Out of the corner of her eye she was aware of Dominic – *Dominic!* –

being shown to an outside table on the other side of the patio. It caused her a fresh bolt of energy – of confidence in the path she was taking. And Theresa's face, that was heartening too, as the puffiness and trembling momentarily gave way to an illuminated expression of pure hope.

'He phoned you just this morning,' Theresa pressed on, uncertainty clouding her face again, working visibly to push out each word.

At this Charlotte managed a laugh, of sufficient volume and high enough pitch to prompt Dominic to turn round. Charlotte's heart leapt in response. 'Your car man, you dope.' She grinned, almost enjoying herself. 'Henry phoned me this morning about your *car* man – Mr Jarvis, under the railway arches. He'd promised to give me the number for the bloody Volkswagen – though, typically, my wilful little machine is now behaving like a lamb.'

'But Suffolk.' The tone was dogged now. 'It was like the two of you *arranged* it.'

'Nonsense – what *nonsense*.' Again, there was sufficient truth in the denial to make outrage easy. 'You offered that week to me and I felt *awful* about Henry wanting to work there – *awful*.' The waiter, hovering in some desperation, topped up their glasses of champagne.

'But that business of the keys,' Theresa persisted, although with audibly less conviction now, 'all that last-minute phoning when you offered Henry a ride down in your car.'

Charlotte went very still. The keys muddle had been a genuine oversight on her part, but it was Henry who had taken advantage of it, throwing the suggestion of a lift at her, putting her on the spot at the very last minute when he pitched up in the taxi. Which meant he must have lied about the arrangement to Theresa, presented it as *her* suggestion rather than his and one that had been made before the morning rather than during the course of it. Charlotte could feel her brain tugging at the knot of this tiny conundrum, this fresh need to be false. Meanwhile, a tall, blonde woman was arriving at Dominic's table, turning heads in a short fitted skirt and a tailored jacket, which she proceeded to peel off – with Dominic's help – to reveal a skimpy grey linen top and broad bare shoulders. Hanging round her neck was a large, flat, stone pendant on a delicate silver hoop, neatly centred in the strikingly deep cleft of her collarbone.

What a beautiful girl. Christ. So there was no hope, then. Fool ever to have thought otherwise. Thank God she hadn't said anything to Theresa. Thank God *for* Theresa, Charlotte reflected, as her companion's still hopeful expression came back into focus, reminding her that this friendship, in its delicate and trembling state, was still within the palm of her hand to crush or nurture as she chose. And there were other things to rejoice in too, like Sam – always Sam – even in his recent dark mood, and her mad, muddled, spirited mother, with her forgotten cheques and new gentleness and . . . The girl was patting Dominic's arm, emphasizing something that was making him shake his head and laugh.

'Oh, Theresa.' Charlotte took both her hands this time, cradling the fingers. 'I just forgot the stupid keys – I really did – and when Henry so kindly volunteered to drop them round it seemed to make sense to offer him a lift. I was being utterly selfish, as it happens – you know me, worried about the directions and the stupid car, of course, which *did* almost break down and, to be honest, he was wonderful, your husband, then and countless other times during Sam's and my lovely stay in your cottage, but only to the point where I thought, lucky, lucky you, and lucky Henry, and quite right, too, because you two are so good and deserving and . . .'

Theresa, visibly embarrassed, unthreaded her fingers from Charlotte's and clutched her head. 'Oh, god, sorry, oh, *God*. You should be angry – why aren't you angry?' she wailed.

'Because it's all too stupid and none of it matters,' Charlotte replied hastily, 'and I know you've been having a bit of a hard time lately . . .'

Theresa released her head, staring across the table in astonishment. 'How do you know that?'

Charlotte swallowed. Not home and dry, then, but soon, if she could hang on, stay focused, not think about Dominic and the girl. 'On the phone this morning, Henry mentioned you'd seemed a bit down – said he hoped our lunch would cheer you up.'

'Did he?' she replied softly, the note of challenge gone. 'That was nice. Charlotte, I'm *so* sorry . . .'

'Please don't be. It's fine. Honestly. Wires get crossed. It happens all the time. I admire you for coming out and asking me straight. Typical you.' She grinned encouragingly.

Theresa responded with a steady gaze, some bravery returning now that she had been reassured. 'He does have a soft spot for you, you know.'

'Yes,' Charlotte replied, as lightly as she could, glad the surge in her pulse-rate could be felt by none but her. She had chosen a path of half-truth and would stick to it, not for her own sake but for Theresa's. Relationships could hang by such threads; one had to protect them. 'And I for him, come to that. Like I said, you're very lucky.'

'I'm *so* sorry,' Theresa whispered again, aghast. 'It's just that . . . well, to be honest, I have been a bit down recently but that's because Henry's been mysteriously distant – just not *Henry* – and I guess, seeing how well the two of you were getting on, I put two and two together and made –'

'Five,' interjected Charlotte, 'and if we don't order soon either I'll fall off my chair from all this champagne or that stormy-faced waiter will kick us out for dawdling.'

It was testimony to their friendship, Charlotte reflected afterwards, walking down to the river with Jasper, the rain bouncing off her brolly, that from the rubble of these exchanges they had managed to construct a genuinely enjoyable time. A bottle of Pinot Grigio had helped, although the food was fussy and sufficiently overpriced for them to agree that it probably wasn't an ideal birthday party venue after all. Theresa had said she would put her thinking cap on but Charlotte had said not to bother and she might just spend her birthday visiting her mother.

'*Very* nice,' Theresa had muttered, spotting Dominic and his dining companion as they were leaving. 'A dark horse, that one – give me the brother any day. Great that Rose and Sam have settled their differences, though,' she had added, giving Charlotte a final hug before pulling her jacket over her head for the run to her car.

Charlotte peered over the wall at the river. Its surface was murky grey and violently pock-marked, as if under siege from a hail of bullets rather than mere rain. Her brolly was small and no match for the damp gusts driving in horizontal assaults off the water, spraying her face and chest. The backs of her legs were wet already from the walk, while her hair, subsiding throughout the lunch, had sunk into a moist heap at the nape of her neck. In fact, the brolly was no use at all, she decided suddenly, shaking it closed and tipping her face up to the sky. How silly to try to stay dry. How silly! She performed a little skip of a dance with her eyes closed, wondering if she was still a little drunk but not minding much. She had done what she could to make things okay for Theresa, that was the main thing. And all her daft fantasies over Dominic had caused no harm. No one knew. No one need ever know. Charlotte twirled, shedding hair-clips as her sodden bun performed a final collapse.

Waiting at the traffic-lights a few minutes later, her eyes streaming mascara, both arms clasping the squirming muddy parcel of the dog, it was perhaps fortunate that Charlotte did not recognize the occupants of the small black sports car that shot past, spurting an arc of dirty water at her already sodden ankles.

Dominic, who did recognize the bedraggled figure standing on the pavement, shrank a little in his seat, grateful for his Polish companion's wild driving. As they sped away he kept the image in the wing mirror for as long as he could, wondering, as he had countless times during lunch, at the brazen insouciance of one who could share a meal so enthusiastically with the wife of a lover. It wasn't his place to judge, of course – as he had said to Benedict – but it was hard nonetheless to discover that there could be such a different, such a harsh side to someone he had thought he might like to get to know. On top of which it had triggered painful memories of stumbling across Maggie's 'other' side and the desolate period that had followed, when faith in love had felt lost along with everything else.

It rained hard in Kent that afternoon, too, bestowing a glossy sheen on the lichen hugging the oldest of the grave-stones and the new slate tiles of the church roof. Jean, dressed more sensibly than her daughter, in a mac and wellies, walked slowly down the gravelled path, while Bill, the driver who had been looking after her so beautifully for four days now, kept them both dry under the vast multicoloured umbrella that lived in the boot of his smart silver Audi. He used it for his golf, Bill had explained, during one of their many pleasant exchanges, and for special customers, he had added, offering one of the winks Jean had learnt to look forward to, for the perfect balance they achieved between respect and familiarity.

Bill held the umbrella steady and fixed his gaze over the stone wall of the churchyard while Jean set down her bunch of flowers – her favourites, irises and purple campanula. Using her good hand, she traced her index finger slowly round the letter 'R' engraved in the headstone. It felt wonderfully simple, as seemingly complicated things often were in the end. Forgiveness, embracing all the imperfection of the love that had kept her by Reggie's side for four decades – there was really nothing to it.

'He was always so kind,' she told Bill, as they made their way back to the car. 'So kind,' she repeated, in a murmur, keeping back the private observation that this was precisely what had always been so hard: how the gentlest handling could feel like an insult to one seeking the reciprocation of something more akin to passion.

Bill held out his arm for her to grip as she levered herself into the car. 'Back to the hotel, then?'

'I'd like to sit here for a bit, if that's all right,' Jean replied, winding down the window.

'I'll have a walkabout, then,' he said cheerfully, pulling out his cigarettes and tapping the earpiece that connected him to his mobile phone. 'Back in five. Hit the horn if you need me.' He marched off, balancing the arm of the umbrella on his shoulder while he lit up.

'Well, well,' said Jean out loud, shifting her sore wrist so she could get closer to the open window and sniff the wet air. Earth, tree bark, the scent of recently cut grass and the sweet, subtle smell of the rain itself . . . The layers were endless if one took the time to seek them out. It was noisy, too, an orchestra of drips and drumming threaded with birdsong and the hum of distant traffic from the motorway. It had been raining at Reggie's funeral, although of course she hadn't seen any beauty in it then.

'Sorry, Reggie, not coming before . . . Sorry, love.' Jean dusted away a tear, then put on her glasses, wanting a clear, final sight of the top of the gravestone through the slanting rain and the swaying branches. The air was cold on her face but her feet and hands were pleasantly warm. 'Who would have thought it?' she exclaimed next, both as a general remark at her circumstances and in a fresh attempt to understand exactly how she had arrived at them. A light, that was it. A light had appeared in her bedroom just as the weary hopelessness was tightening its stranglehold. The pad with the farewell letter to Charlotte – the third attempt – had been propped awkwardly against her knees. There had been ink on the bedclothes, she remembered; terrible black stains, and the galling realization that she had forgotten, after all, to gather up the wretched little stockpile of sleeping pills, that she was going to have to endure the painful ordeal of clambering back out of bed and rummaging for them. And then, quite without warning, there had been the light . . . or, at least, a warmth, a heat, a glow – *something*.

Jean waved to Bill as he reappeared among the trees, then wound the window back up. She didn't believe in ghosts; during the years abroad she had dismissed out of hand any servant tittle-tattle about spirits. But she was in no doubt that something had entered her room that night – some essence, or energy, filling her and leaving her filled, even after it had seeped away. The notion of this private pilgrimage had sprung to mind immediately afterwards, so like a need that the requirement of remaining alive to see it through did not need examining. She had phoned the taxi company that evening, gathering confidence when her tentative suggestion of a driver on a daily rate was so well received, as if people did it all the time instead of just lonely widows with broken wrists following mad ideas about revisiting old haunts.

She had taken the phone off the hook – not told anyone – for fear of losing her nerve. Packing, sorting out her route and accommodation, closing up the house, pushing her arm beyond limits at every turn, Jean had nearly baled out more than once. At times it was the sheer effort it would have taken to unscramble the arrangements that had kept her going, along with self-mocking mutterings about the harmlessness of lank hair and sodden arm plaster. And then Bill had arrived, whistling, smartly dressed, cleanshaven, opening doors, swinging her bags, cracking a joke about the barmy balmy weather and she had felt as irrevocably committed as a shy bride about to be swept off in the back of a limo.

'Back to the hotel now, please, Bill.'

'How lucky it was still going strong, eh, Mrs B, after all those years – and a lot smarter, you say?'

'So lucky . . . and, yes, a lot smarter.' Jean leant back against the headrest and closed her eyes, seeing again the grey walls of the poky room where she and Reggie had argued about England and houses and Charlotte . . . about every subject, in other words, but the one that, for those few weeks at least, had mattered so much: the one called Charity, the girl with the satin skin to whom her husband had, for the first time and unwittingly, almost lost his heart.

The arguments ebbed and surged until, like a gunshot in the dark, Charlotte had cried, 'Stop,' and banged the wall. Inches apart, all three had held their breath. Then, in the thick, dreadful, quiet darkness Jean had felt Reggie's hand touch hers. A minute later the hand was moving down her arm, her belly, her leg, with more explicit purpose, but with such urgent tenderness, too, as if, beneath the mechanics of that tireless appetite, there lay some passion after all.

Chapter Seventeen

By the time Martin and Sam pulled into the Rotherhithe cul-de-sac the following Friday evening, grass and concrete alike were glistening under the full force of the beaming sun following another afternoon of downpours. Informed during the course of the journey that he was to have a half-sibling and that, with Cindy still fragile and tired, he was to spend the next thirty-six hours being quiet and undemanding, it was not with the best of spirits that Sam lugged his rucksack upstairs. There were dubious smells coming from the kitchen, which turned out to be fish – three grey ones lying side by side in a pan, their dead, cloudy eyes fixed on the swirls of steam floating round the ceiling.

For a change and because it's healthy, Cindy said, when he went in to say hello, like she knew it was a rubbish meal even before she had served it.

'Can I go out on my bike?'

'After supper, I should think, if the rain stays away, if Dad agrees.'

'Agrees to what? Hmm, something smells good.' Martin bounced into the kitchen and slipped his arms round Cindy's waist, fondly cupping the new thicker waistline camouflaged by her apron.

Sam looked away quickly. Without his briefing in the car he wouldn't have noticed Cindy was any fatter, let alone pregnant. He had wanted a brother or sister once, but presented with the reality of it – and in this split version of a family too – he wasn't at all sure. He would still be number one, his dad had said, which had only got him thinking of George's siblings and how not one of them was ever number one, not really. 'I want to go out on my bike after supper.'

'I want never gets,' Martin murmured, 'and it'll be dark soon.'

'I said he could,' Cindy put in, making a special face at Sam. 'It won't be dark for a while yet. We're eating early because I am, as usual these days –' she made another, different, special face, this time for his father '– starving.'

'And I've got lights,' Sam added, brightening at the sight of mashed potato.

'Assaulted on all sides,' pronounced Martin, in a tone of happy defeat. He let go of Cindy and advanced on Sam instead, holding his fists up like a boxer spoiling for a fight. Sam ducked and made a run for the door, only to be swung off his feet and over his father's shoulder.

'Not so big yet, are you?' Martin growled, while Cindy tutted happily, rolled her eyes and drained the peas, and Sam, making a show of wriggling resistance, wondered when, if ever, a boy could announce that the time of genuinely enjoying such games had passed.

The fish weren't quite as horrible as Sam had anticipated, especially after he had been allowed to fetch the ketchup. He ate fast, keeping an eye on the slits of blue sky through the kitchen blinds, while his dad and Cindy talked about things to do with work, then ticket sales for their concert, occasionally putting questions his way, but really obviously, like they felt they had to try to make him feel included.

When he was ready to go, his dad, merrier still with a glass of wine in hand, rapped his helmet, told him to stay in the compound, not to run over any old ladies and be home the moment it got dark.

Sam let his bike roll down the slope of the hard-standing,

then pedalled slowly round the mini roundabout a few times, wishing he had thought to bring his mobile. He and Rose had recently exchanged telephone numbers – at last! – and he wanted badly to tell her about Cindy having a baby. She would, as usual, know how he felt without him having to explain. She was amazing like that – just *getting* things – like knowing, since the evident failure of their desperate little scheme, to leave the repellent subject of his mother's love life entirely alone. And wanting to stay just as friends – he was sure she knew that, felt it too – in spite of the stupid playground taunts.

The wheels of the bike made a lovely swishing sound on the wet Tarmac. Sam speeded up towards two fat pigeons scrapping over a crust, getting a lovely rush of power when they took off in fright. One day he would have a motorbike, he decided, pedalling as fast as he could now, away from the little roundabout and across the junction that led towards the compound entrance.

'Mah-jong. I'm afraid it's off.' Theresa's voice was crisp, unreadable. 'There's been something of a domestic crisis.'

Charlotte slowly put down her knife and reached for a tissue to wipe the onion tears out of her eyes. Her hair, wet still from a bath – a lovely long indulgent soak with the radio parked on the stool next to her – suddenly felt unpleasantly cold. 'Oh, no, Theresa . . . I'm so sorry.'

'It's Naomi,' Theresa said hurriedly, sufficiently aware of her friend's train of thought for a touch of embarrassment to creep into her tone.

'Naomi?' Charlotte sank into a chair, hoping she didn't sound too relieved. 'Why, what's happened?'

'She's just pitched up on Jo's doorstep in floods of tears with all three children in tow. Apparently she and Graham had some sort of row and he *hit* her – or tried to. She ducked and his fist landed on the wall . . . Can you *imagine*?'

Through the tone of appalled sympathy Theresa sounded almost excited. And no wonder, Charlotte mused. Not getting on with Henry must seem mild in comparison to such horrors.

Theresa, expounding on the grave revelations about their friend's life, was growing earnest and faintly hysterical. 'Admittedly she seemed a bit dazed when she came to tea – that time before Easter when the twins ran riot. She was definitely not quite on-the-ball . . . But I'd never have guessed anything was *that* wrong. And neither did Jo, who – let's face it – is the one to whom she has always been closest. And now it's come to this terrible head, and with Naomi's parents in France and that one sister who travels all the time she couldn't think where else to go. Jo says she's been trying to phone you about it this evening but there was no answer.'

'I probably had the taps running – I got drenched again on a walk with the dog. Christ, poor Naomi . . . I can't believe it, although I suppose it shows –'

'What? What does it show?'

'That . . . well, that there's always the other life.'

'Other life?'

'The one we try not to reveal to each other,' Charlotte murmured, thinking – inconveniently, selfishly – of Dominic in the restaurant the previous week; how her stomach had knotted every time he tipped his head towards his dining companion, how she had wanted to look every time he laughed. 'The one we keep in our heads.'

'Ah, yes . . .' Theresa muttered, her own thoughts also skipping from Naomi to her own situation. The only 'other life' she felt capable of caring about was her world with

Henry; a lost world that she wanted back so badly she had gone straight to the fridge after Jo's call to see if she could rustle up something surprising for supper, freshly determined to restore full domestic harmony in her household by whatever means at her disposal, no matter how pitiful or old-fashioned. Hopes thus raised, she had been standing, packet of frozen prawns in hand, when Henry called to remind her that he was delivering a lecture, didn't need feeding and wouldn't be back till after nine. 'Well, my head doesn't contain a *life* so much as a big ridiculous mess – as I'm afraid you now know only too well.'

'How can we help?' Charlotte was determined to stick to the matter in hand.

Theresa sighed. 'I don't think we can do anything, at least not for the time being. Jo seems to have everything under control. She's putting Naomi and the twins in the loft conversion and Pattie with one of the girls. Paul's going to talk to Graham. She's calling me tomorrow. You hadn't started cooking, I hope?'

Charlotte eyed her chopped onions, sitting in a pool of oil in the frying-pan. 'Not really, though I need to anyway, of course, for Eve.'

'Ah, Eve, I'd completely forgotten. Well, have a great time.'

'Theresa?'

'Yes.'

'Eve . . . she – she'll never be a friend like you.'

'Thank you, Charlotte. What a lovely thing to say . . . Thank you.'

'I mean it.'

'Me too . . . and our lunch,' Theresa blurted. 'I'm sorry we haven't really talked since. I've been putting it off, to be honest – I felt such a dope. But the fact is, you were great

– couldn't have been greater – about everything. And what you told me,' she rushed on, 'about your father not being your father . . . I didn't really know what to say. As you gathered, I had other things on my mind. But what I really think is that getting the whole truth is always good in the end. I mean, the *worst* thing in a life is feeling something's wrong and not knowing what it is, don't you agree?'

'Absolutely. The whole truth – we need it.' Honesty had levels, Charlotte reminded herself firmly, putting down the phone. Life was full of grey splodges. One had to clutch at what few certainties one could. Theresa and Henry were meant to be together and she had been right to do everything within her power to ensure that. Naomi's woes sounded terrible but would get sorted with time, just as her own had done. And as for the Dominic thing, it would no doubt wear off, gutter without the hope of reciprocity, like any flame deprived of oxygen. Her hand shook a little as she returned her attention to the onions. Shock on Naomi's account, of course, she told herself, stirring hard as the oil warmed and gleamed.

Eve wasn't sure what she had been expecting. Grey hairs, a middle-age spread, eyes pouched with suffering? Out of respect for Charlotte she had avoided not only the high street but also quizzing Tim on the subject. The poor woman had been through a lot, after all, if their recent burst of transatlantic email correspondence had been anything to go by: a divorce, money worries, Sam's bout of unhappiness in school – it had been quite a catalogue of woes. Long before the Tim thing, responding with news of her booming mail-order business, her satisfying personal life, her love of all things American, Eve had at times experienced the occasional unfamiliar stirring of compassion for her old friend.

'Charlotte!'

'Eve!'

There was an instant – as quick as a camera click – of mutual sizing up before they fell into each other's arms. 'Trust you to be in the thick of it and still look like Nicole bloody Kidman,' Eve accused, smiling hard while inside there stirred the old wariness of being outclassed, over-shadowed. 'And where is darling Sammy?' she exclaimed, pushing the feeling to one side and casting an anxious glance at Jasper, who was making small leaping efforts to join in the celebrations. 'I've bought him something horribly complicated to build – advanced Lego. You even need batteries.'

'How lovely,' Charlotte murmured, easily forgiving the inappropriate gift (how could Eve possibly know that Sam's dusty box of Lego had been the only thing with which he had gladly parted company during her recent clear-out?), and (slightly less easily) suppressing the urge to insist that 'Sammy' was not an acceptable option in the repertoire of possible abbreviations of her son's name.

The sheer oddity of having Eve on her doorstep was even more overwhelming than Charlotte had anticipated. She looked so exactly as she remembered her, yet not so. The dusty brown hair was still shoulder-length, still with a straight, girlish fringe, but had been streaked with blonde and gold and, instead of hanging in its old limp way, seemed to bounce off her head and neck as if it had an energy supply all of its own. More striking still was how the full, matronly figure, once shyly camouflaged under smock dresses and baggy dungarees, was now being shown off in a close-fitting skirt and a low-cut top, flaunting the large, shapely assets that the young Eve – usually amid groans and much tugging in front of mirrors – had laboured to conceal.

'You look *amazing*,' Charlotte cried, grabbing the dog, whose attentions, she could see, were not appreciated, and noticing as she bent down the extravagant soft suede of Eve's high-heeled shoes. 'Fantastic – you look fantastic.' Pushing the door further open, she stepped back to make room for her guest and a large wheeled suitcase to enter the hall. 'Sorry about the dog – it's my mother's. And Sam is at Martin's but only till tomorrow – and I'm afraid there's been a change of plan on the mah-jong front,' she gabbled, not knowing which subject to address first. 'There's been a bit of a drama, but come in, come in . . . I'll explain everything later. Oh, Evie, it is rather *incredible* to see you after all this time.'

'You too, and isn't this heavenly?' Eve gushed, parking her case at the bottom of the stairs and darting in and out of rooms in a show of enthusiasm designed to mask a reflex of distaste at the homely, faded furnishings and visibly scarred cream walls. It made her long to show Charlotte her sitting room in Boston, with its peachy silk scatter cushions that matched the ties on her curtains, and the milky carpet of such deep pile that, three years after its purchase, she still asked each and every visitor to take their shoes off at the door; a house-rule that often caused irritation, but which always ended up breaking the ice, even with dour-faced customers, like the grumpy Mexican who had come to spray the drains for cockroaches and ended up staying for a mug of iced tea, flashing two highways of cobbled gold every time he smiled.

'It's not remotely heavenly,' Charlotte corrected her cheerfully. 'It all needs a face-lift. I've got a decorator lined up but he's running late on another job – usual story. Oh, how kind,' she exclaimed, as Eve whisked a bottle of wine out of her shoulder bag.

While her host went in search of a corkscrew, Eve quietly rejoiced that the hideous mah-jong had been called off. And Sam not being there was a blessing too. Polite chit-chat with housewives, playing the adoring godmother were challenges at which she knew she could excel, but not nearly as appealing as rolling up her sleeves for a proper chinwag. She had another bottle in her suitcase, but would keep that for later, when the juices were really flowing and they'd reached that lovely stage of not counting glasses, by which time – she sincerely hoped – Charlotte might have dropped some of the stiff, wide-eyed, rabbit-in-headlights look and begun to let her hair down in a manner that bore some relation to the glorious auburn stuff still cascading off her head.

'I'll need to smoke, I'm afraid,' she confessed, when Charlotte returned with a corkscrew and two glasses. 'I know everyone's giving up, these days, but I've never been one to swim with the tide. I'll go outside, of course,' she added, with a brisk glance at the evening sky, darkening to purple ink through the sitting-room window. 'You've been off the weed for years, I presume?'

'A while, yes,' Charlotte admitted, dismissing a mild temptation to mention the recent near-relapse behind the church in Chalkdown Road. She wondered suddenly how Dominic had viewed the episode and her heart lurched. While she had imagined closeness – some sort of meaningful connection – with him there had clearly been nothing of the sort. Kindness, politeness, leading to an offer of dinner, that was all. And amid the jollity of the meal the brother had been noticeably cool, she remembered now, nothing like the warm, joking creature who had welcomed her on the doorstep when she dropped Sam off before Easter.

'Er . . . going outside *would* be best,' she ventured, brought back to the present by the sight of Eve blithely settling into a chair and lighting up. Where was the Eve who *did* swim with the tide? she marvelled. The Eve who used to fuss at *her* about lung cancer, who preferred comfortable clothes instead of five-inch heels and tops a size too small. The Eve, more pertinently, who would have offered to help with preparations for supper instead of standing next to the kitchen door, ineffectually puffing smoke in the direction of the garden while offering a running commentary about the joys of life on the East Coast.

'I'd like to freshen up,' she said, as Charlotte was draining a saucepan of easy-cook rice. 'I'll find my way. Won't be a tick.' The thump of the suitcase on the stairs followed, then everything went very quiet. After a few minutes, Charlotte placed lids on the dishes of hot food and went into the hall. Peering up the stairs, she could see the door of the spare room had been left ajar. She was on the point of calling, when Eve's muffled voice drifted out on to the landing, interlaced with bubbles of laughter. So she was on the phone, talking to a man by the sound of it. Charlotte smiled to herself as she retreated. Good for Eve. Without the consolation of motherhood, having someone would be all the more important. Without Sam, for instance . . . Charlotte looked back up the stairs as the door to the spare room swung open and Eve emerged on to the landing, her hair even more buoyant from a recent brushing and her lips softened with a fresh layer of pink.

'Hey!' Eve pulled an arm from behind her back to reveal another bottle of wine. 'Shiraz – always good after a merlot, – don't you think? New World, of course. I *love* the New World. And look what else I found!' She waved her other hand. 'Talk about a grisly memento, Charlotte darling . . . From a *well-wisher*. How sick is that?'

Charlotte folded her arms, trying to keep her smile in

place, fighting an absurd, dim sense of violation. She had expected to get on to the subject of divorcing – of Martin – of course, but not so early, or in a manner that made her feel so uncomfortable, so . . . hijacked. 'I'd forgotten it was in there. I –'

'And who was this *well-wisher*, that's what I'd like to know?'

'Me too. I mean, I – I never found out.'

Eve fell against the banisters with a theatrical gasp.

'I kept it because it was what ended us,' said Charlotte, simply. 'Martin and I, that thing you're holding is what brought it – finally – to an end.'

Eve was advancing down the stairs now, shaking her head. 'Are you serious? This?' She dangled the note between two fingers. 'This was why you let him go? Didn't it make you want to *fight* to keep him? Martin. *Martin.* You let him go for *this*?'

Charlotte took a step backwards. It dawned on her that her guest was more than a little drunk. During the chain-smoking session standing at the kitchen door, she had got through most of the first bottle on her own. 'Supper's ready.' Charlotte swiped the note out of Eve's fingers and stuffed it into her handbag as she led the way to the kitchen. 'It's getting cold.'

Eve clung to the banister post for a few moments while her body swayed in search of equilibrium. She had meant to bring things to such a head, but not quite so quickly. Having got back in touch with Charlotte on a spurt of something like nostalgia, a desire to reconnect with her English roots, the news of the separation from Martin had sharpened her focus to the point where a face-to-face encounter had felt imperative. Orchestrating it had been the easy part, she saw now. How to play things with Charlotte actually within her grasp was going to be far harder. Already the note, peeking out at her from the book in the bedside drawer, had almost fast-forwarded everything off course. Not to mention the wine, which – if she was honest with herself – had probably followed a little too closely upon the shots in her cup of tea and the vodka tonic that Tim had poured on his return from work, before pulling her skirt up and spinning her round to take her against his hall wall, knocking pictures and knick-knacks in his haste for release.

In the kitchen Charlotte was doling out spoonfuls of rice and runny mincemeat bobbing with kidney beans. 'I didn't know how much you wanted,' she said briskly. 'I hope that's okay.' She placed the steaming plate of food on one of the table mats, right next to a full glass of water. 'Please, Eve . . .' She gestured at the food – at the water. 'Sit.'

'I'll fetch the corkscrew first, shall I?' Eve tapped the shiraz bottle so that the rings on her fingers chimed against the glass. She didn't look directly at Charlotte or at the place setting. The glass of water was like an order, and she didn't take orders these days, not from anyone. 'I think it got left in the sitting room.' She could feel Charlotte's eyes – still remarkable after all these years, still men-winning – boring between her shoulder-blades as she left the room. 'In for a penny . . .' she muttered, steadying herself with thoughts of Tim (talk about a piece of luck) as she gripped the bottle between her knees. The cork resisted, then popped free with a squeak and such force that an arc of red drops sprayed on to the carpet. The bubbles of liquid subsided into the mottled blue, leaving a line as visible as row of hammered nails. Eve wondered idly whether to drop to her knees and dab at them with a tissue. She hated mess, especially her own. But it was such a horrid old carpet, she reasoned, stepping back over the stains, lifting her pointy shoes very high and with great care, as if the barrier being crossed for her return journey was far more impeding, far more treacherous than a few dribbles of wine.

Sam had no plan. One minute he was on the smooth new black-treacle surface of the compound's network of roads, the next he was bumping along the dirty, heaving pavement that ran along the main road, keeping a wary eye out for old ladies, as his father had jokingly instructed. There were several as it happened, one with a stick, one in a motorized wheelchair and one funny tottering one who walked side-ways and had long hairs sprouting out of her chin and who scared the life out of him by asking for help crossing the road. It wasn't easy with the bike and the old biddy squeezing his arm while he pressed the pedestrian button. But once he had got her over and watched her scurrying crab-walk into the courtyard of a high-rise Sam felt pretty good, as if his small adventure had been fully justified.

He turned back for the lights, but the road was once again log-jammed, the vehicles bumper to bumper, hissing and roaring like a herd of jostling beasts. So Sam walked on a bit further, pushing the bike, keeping an eye open for a shop in which to blow the fifty-pence piece he could feel jumping around in his pocket. There were none on the main road, but spotting a Walls ice-cream sign down a side-street, he hopped back into his saddle and rode towards that instead. Hopes high, he arrived to find that the sign was a leftover prop of a disused garage. Two boys, one white, one black, who looked a few years older than him, were skateboarding round the forecourt, taking it in turns to try jumps on and off the elevations that had once housed the pumps. They wore tracksuit bottoms and vests that showed off the muscles in their arms. Their wheels rumbled like thunder on the ruptured concrete.

'Hey, we got ourselves an audience, brother,' shouted the tallest one, after a couple of minutes. He nodded in Sam's direction. 'Shall we charge him or what?'

Sam looked away but didn't move. He could be quick on his bike, really quick. He felt angry, powerful. He had a mum who screwed other people's dads and a dad making babies with a woman hot enough to be a model. These two might be older, taller, but they couldn't touch him. And it felt cool too, to be perched in this strange place with the evening sun warm on the back of his neck, one foot on the pavement edge, ready at any instant he chose to push off. Both the boarders were good, but the smaller dark-skinned one was definitely the best, crouching low as he took off, then flinging out his arms like a ballet dancer as he nailed his landings.

'Are you watching, or what?'

Sam shrugged.

'Hey, brother, he thinks he can *watch*, man.'

Sam hesitated at this, not because the words themselves were more threatening but because they were directed over his right shoulder where he had registered no objects of interest beyond a couple of overflowing recycling containers. Turning slowly, like an animal taking stock of danger, he saw now that there were three other boys, emerging from between the two bins, scuffing heedlessly through the bottles and stray sheets of newspaper as if the debris was of no more consequence than water lapping at their ankles. Their arms hung a little away from their sides, like they fancied themselves as cowboys, ready for a race to a draw. Except there were no holsters, of course, or guns. And this wasn't the Wild West, but Rotherhithe on a sunny May evening, with people streaming home from work just yards away and his dad and Cindy not much further off, snuggling on the sofa, no doubt, making the most of not having him around.

Sam went for his push-off. He could see his escape in his head, as smooth as a new map: a U-turn, a sprint of acceleration, he would be back at the busy road – visible now like some slice of promised land, at the end of the street – before the five of them had even blinked. But as he started to turn the three boys quickened their pace and stepped into the gap through which he needed to pass. The other two, meanwhile, had abandoned their boards and were walking fast, rolling on the balls of their feet, towards the pavement. In the hand of the taller one Sam saw something flash as it caught the sun. The boy, seeing him look, grinned, revealing a line of messed-up teeth.

Sam abandoned the U-turn and began instead to cycle on past the garage. Out of the corner of his eye he was aware of the first two, running now to reach him, slicing the air with their hands for added speed. The taller one was faster, the knife like an extra gleaming finger shooting out of his palm. Sam stood up on his pedals, keeping his gaze fixed on the narrowing road. Much further ahead the street petered out into the shadows of a long low block of tiered flats. But before that there was a turning right; a turning he might be able to reach, if the faster one would only trip or slow down, or if the muscles in his legs could just stop shaking long enough for him to get the necessary purchase for a proper sprint – like the one he had managed so easily the afternoon before, racing against the second hand of his watch as he did the final belt down his street, improving his personal best by almost two full minutes.

Dominic lay on his back with his hands under his head, the points of his elbows just touching the edges of the pillow. The bed was a small double, wedged into a corner of the room to make space for a chest of drawers, a wardrobe and a tall rack overflowing with shoes. Even so, the wardrobe doors couldn't open fully without hitting the side of the bed; efforts to ignore this constraint had left two chiselled, symmetrical grooves in its wooden frame. Dominic had noticed them while he was kneeling with his head between Petra's long legs, trying to think about the task in hand rather than the discomfort of the hard floor against his kneecaps.

It had got better, though, much better. Petra, certainly, had seemed satisfied, scattering his face with kisses afterwards and saying, 'Lovely,' before springing out of bed to shower. Lying alone, Dominic had counted shoes, then thought about Rose who was on a birthday sleepover with a pretty Nigerian girl called Gabby, a new friend apparently – not displacing Sam, his daughter had explained, with her endearing seriousness, but in addition to him. This second date had been at Petra's instigation, as had the decision to cut straight to the business of taking off their clothes.

Dominic crossed his legs and looked at his feet, which Maggie had often told him were unusually elegant for a man, elegant and *long*, she had liked to tease, tweaking his toes. It had been rather lovely having his body known so well, he reflected now, to have it regarded as a terrain that held no secrets, possessed jointly for use and commentary and pleasure.

'Dominic, you are handsome,' remarked Petra, perhaps catching the dreamy look in his eye as she reappeared decked in two towels, one arranged as a turban, the other a mini-dress. 'I like you a lot.' She wagged a finger at him as she rummaged in a drawer spilling with underwear. 'But now I have to go out. It is a party. But only cocktails. I will be back so we can have dinner and sex again. In two hours. If you like?' She crossed to the bed and kissed him, sensuously this time, wetting his lips with her tongue before pushing her mouth hard against his.

'Actually, I'd better be getting home,' Dominic murmured. 'For Rose,' he added, surprising himself with the lie.

'That is very sad. Now I am sad.' She pouted as she pulled away, then busied herself with fastening her bra, not looking sad at all.

Outside, the sun was a smudge of bloody orange, like a dying ember in a dark hearth.

'It will rain again,' announced Petra as they emerged on to the pavement. She tugged up the collar of the black denim jacket that had been pulled on over a glittering silver T-shirt and crisp white jeans, and tucked her long hair inside.

'I have a brolly – an umbrella – in the car if you want.'

'No, I am late. I must go now.' She turned smartly on her heel, then spun back again. 'I could come to your house after my party, maybe? But no,' she added, correcting herself in the fraction of a second it took Dominic to hesitate. 'Your Rose, she wouldn't like it. Girls who love their daddies – I understand that.' She was shaking her head in amusement as she walked away.

Dominic drove home slowly, mulling over this parting remark and his needless sequestering of his daughter as an alibi. It bothered him, too, that during the course of their two recent, very intimate encounters, Petra had still told him practically nothing about herself, peppering him instead with questions about the city and Benedict and films, a subject on which she was both well informed and passionate. Whenever he, almost out of a sense of duty, steered the conversation towards Maggie, she had deftly steered it away again, pressing to hear more about his plans for the bookshop and warning him, in her somewhat monotone, textbook English, that he would probably miss the adrenalin of impossible deadlines and mesmerizing bonuses.

Maybe Benedict had given her a thorough briefing on the Maggie front, Dominic mused, fighting a downturn in spirits as he let himself into his empty house and checked for messages. Since their slightly terse exchange outside the café his brother had pointedly made no contact and Dominic was beginning to feel the silence. 'Okay, okay, I'm *sorry*,' he barked into the phone, after hearing the familiar recording of Benedict's voice, delivered irritatingly and affectedly over what sounded like a soundtrack of a Bach fugue. 'You were *right*. There is something about Charlotte Turner . . . but, yes, a woman like that would gobble me up for breakfast and spit me out by lunch and I happen to know that she's quite messed up, so I shall steer well clear. And,' he continued slyly, certain that the right hook would trigger a response, 'I have just spent a second delightful afternoon with the delectable Petra . . . and, let me see, what else? Ah, yes, it's Rose's sports day soon – and she'd like you to be there. Your performance in the three-legged in the Home Counties last year remains a vivid and dear memory. Look, just call me, you bugger, can't you?'

Tucking the house phone and his mobile into his trouser pockets, Dominic prepared himself a tray of cold meat, cheese, olives and bread and settled down on the sitting-room sofa with some paperwork. There was a lot to attend to – a long list of friends and institutions still requiring change-of-address slips, forms from utility companies and a letter from the employment lawyer, expressing an optimistic plan to negotiate a better settlement – six months' severance pay instead of three – if he could supply the following information . . .

Dominic had soon abandoned it in favour of the sales

figures from Ravens Books. The for-sale sign had triggered a couple of other interested parties, but on the phone that morning Jason, sounding tense and weary, had almost guaranteed the lease was his if he could meet their asking price of sixty thousand pounds. That was for the 'goodwill' element of the custom they were passing on. On top of that there would be an annual rent of twenty-five thousand, plus rates, of course, which totalled five thousand . . . Dominic paused, sucking the end of his pencil and pondering some of the ideas Charlotte had mentioned for rearranging the shop, improving stock and forging stronger links with local schools. No matter. He whacked his pencil against the notepad. He would get Charlotte to leave, he decided, along with the hapless Shona. He would explain that he needed one experienced full-time employee. With Sam in the mix she was bound to refuse. Dominic fetched a second beer to celebrate the decision and settled back on the sofa, giving up on his papers and channel-hopping vainly in search of something to match his mood.

By eight thirty Eve had picked at two courses and assailed the second bottle of wine with a speed and determination that seemed to Charlotte almost worthy of admiration. Rather less easy to commend, however, was the sight of her guest sprawling in the upright kitchen chair, tapping the ash of her endless cigarettes into the ruin of her uneaten food and resting her feet on the edge of the recycling box that lived next to Jasper's bed. The dachshund, after sniffing Eve's empty suede shoes, had retreated to his third favourite sleeping place, between the coat stand and the doormat in the hall.

A little on edge, thanks to Eve's outburst on the stairs, Charlotte had found that she, too, had little appetite, either for her chilli con carne or the second bottle of wine. Having to feign an interest in the anecdotes (some on their second outing already) about the glorious life of a self-made mail-order guru, the evening – not to mention the next few days – was starting to look decidedly uninviting. But it was also quite funny, Charlotte conceded privately, to be confronted by this new, extrovert version of her once staid friend. What Sam would make of her she could hardly imagine. And telling Theresa would be enjoyable, too. She swallowed a yawn as she started – with what she hoped was a tactful lack of fuss – to stack their dirty plates.

Eve sprang to life in the same instant, sliding her feet off the box and clutching the edge of the table. Charlotte, imagining she was to be offered assistance, fearing, mildly, for the safety of her crockery, gestured at her to relax back into her seat.

'Sam fucking Mendes.'

'Pardon?' Charlotte paused with her clutch of dishes.

'Martin . . . all that university directing . . . he could have been as good as Sam Mendes.'

Charlotte laughed as she continued clearing up. 'I'm not sure you're right about that, Eve, but Martin would certainly be flattered to hear it. That thing in the bedside table, by the way,' she added, unable to resist the urge to set the record straight, even with someone whom she knew would never again be a close friend, someone manifestly in danger of losing the power to make much sense of anything, 'it was the end of a long road, of course. Martin had been seeing other women – I'd suspected it for years – but that was the first hard evidence. It was a relief, to be honest. The woman to whom it refers is the one he's living with now. They're expecting their first child. It took a while, but I'm fine about it now – really fine.' She straightened from stacking the dishwasher and pulled a face. 'Marriage, children – nothing but trouble. How wise of you to avoid them.'

Eve frowned, trying to bring Charlotte more sharply into focus. For her the evening had now reached the final, always riveting stage when her mind had broken sufficiently free of her body and the tedious constraints of conscience and social nicety to cartwheel down any track it chose. She needed to grip the edge of the table because, like the other items of furniture in the room, it had started to rise and fall on an invisible sea and she feared that without physical security it might float out of the room. 'Wise?' Liking the word, and its effect upon Charlotte, who put down her bundle of knives and at last paid attention, Eve repeated it, more forcefully, flexing her lips like an opera singer. 'There was only ever one man for me.'

Charlotte picked up her cutlery again. 'And who was that?'

'Who do you think?' she snapped. 'Martin, of course. But you *knew* that. You *knew*.'

Charlotte's mouth opened, then closed. 'No, I . . . at least . . .'

'We'd slept together, did you know that? Before those stupid auditions. Just the once, and it might have been the start of something – but then you came along and he ended it. He was always a one-woman man, Martin . . . The girl before me – he cut her off too, ruthlessly, the same *day* he met me. Love, loyalty, till-death-do-us-part – he believed in that stuff.'

'And so did I,' Charlotte whispered, appalled but fascinated, as the past she kept trying to understand heaved, reconfiguring itself yet again. 'I knew that you . . . I mean, I thought it was a crush. I had no idea. I'm so sorry.'

'And he could have loved me.' Eve beat the table with her fist, losing another round in the fight against total inebriation. 'I know, because after Sam was born, with you on

Planet Zog – never there, always upstairs, or out, or sleeping or feeding or cooing over that bloody child of yours, always ignoring *him* – we got quite close again, the pair of us. But he wouldn't – he *wouldn't* admit it or do anything *about* it or even speak so much as a word against you.' She banged the table again, so hard that Charlotte jumped.

'Look, Eve, I had no idea, I –' Charlotte faltered, the idea dawning that this embitterment was what had prompted Eve to return, the reason, ultimately, for getting in touch. No wonder the rekindling of the friendship had felt so odd, so doomed.

Eve had dropped her head into her hands and was plucking at her hair. 'Part of going to the States was to get away from it – from you.' She lifted one hand and pointed a finger at Charlotte. 'Bloody, bloody you.'

'I think,' Charlotte ventured softly, 'that maybe it's time to put all this behind us, time, perhaps, to call it a day and go to bed.'

'And I think maybe you should shut the fuck up.'

Charlotte stood very still, trying to dredge some pity from within the outrage, trying, still, to make sense of everything. That Eve and Martin had briefly been close did not surprise her somehow. Neither did the pitiful disclosure that Eve had held a torch for him for years afterwards. No, what was truly shocking was this further evidence of Martin's resistance, of his *faithfulness*. A *one-woman man*, not speaking a word against her, fighting for their marriage, while she . . . What had she been doing? Loving Sam, wallowing in wifely self-pity, certain of betrayal before it had happened . . . maybe, even, *making* it happen. Charlotte caught her breath, recalling again the claims Cindy had made, how Martin had held out. 'I am sorry you're unhappy, Eve,' she murmured. 'I've made so many mistakes – I'm only just beginning to

345

realize quite how many – but your feelings . . . they're not among them. They, at least, are not my fault.'

Eve jerked her head up, her eyes flashing with fresh energy. 'Who said anything about being unhappy? I'm *marvellous*, thank you very much. I've met someone, you see, someone really special. He was the one I was on the phone to earlier. He was literally *begging* me to come round. So if you would be good enough to call a taxi . . .' She attempted to stand but fell back into her chair.

'Look, Eve,' Charlotte pleaded, unable to give up on the possibility that something might yet be retrieved from this calamity of a reunion, 'it's great that you've met someone, but maybe it would be better to stay here for tonight. After that, if you decide you want to cut short the visit –'

'But I'm more welcome *there*,' Eve muttered, examining her cigarette packet and looking faintly baffled when a shake produced nothing but a few tobacco shreds.

'But you're welcome here,' offered Charlotte, weakly, guilty that she couldn't really mean it.

Eve studied the cigarette packet again, then crushed it in her palm. 'The Someone is called Tim, by the way, Tim Croft. We met on your doorstep when I dropped by on the off-chance, which is sort of fitting if you think about it.'

'Tim Croft?'

'Believe me, Charlotte,' she cooed, her voice mockingly sympathetic, 'I *know* how you must feel. But it was instant – one of those love-at-first-sight things –' Eve broke off. Her lips were beginning to feel rubbery, like they were chasing the words. And the walls of the room were sloping towards her and there was none of the triumph she had imagined either about Tim or the longed-for talk about Martin, only the sound of Charlotte laughing and clapping her hands and saying love had no rules and she would be

346

only too delighted to order a minicab if Tim was expecting her and why hadn't she said so earlier, but only if she was absolutely certain she didn't want to postpone the visit until the following day.

The world did not come back into focus until Eve found herself being bounced over road humps on the back seat of a vehicle that smelt strongly – nauseatingly – of vanilla air-freshener. Memories of the evening were already jagged fragments, hard to place in the right order. It had gone wrong, she knew that. Then there had been coffee and Charlotte hugging her and calling Tim and the taxi . . .

Struggling upright, Eve leant forward and tapped the driver on the shoulder. 'Change of plan – the Heathrow Hilton, and a fag if you've got one.'

'Blimey, that'll cost you, love,' the cabbie growled, 'and there's a no-smoking sign, in case you hadn't noticed.'

But Eve had already let her head fall back and succumbed to the bliss of closing her eyes. She'd been away from England too long. What little there had been to return to was long gone. And the past could never be changed anyway, only left behind.

It was nine thirty when Henry reached his doorstep. There were no lights on in the house and the bulb in the porch had gone. Fumbling for his keys, he found himself recalling the night he had given Charlotte a lift home, the night it had all started. Her house had been so dark then, so empty, so utterly quiet apart from the squeak of the broken gate. The pity of it had choked him, duped him, destroyed him. Theresa knew of his miserable lapse – Henry was certain of it now. It was in the studied cheerfulness of her voice, the minimal reporting on the dreaded lunch, the vicious way in which she had explained the distressing reason for the last-minute cancellation of her beloved mah-jong that night. A small crime, perhaps, in the general scheme of human failing, to make a pass at a best friend, but not for them: for them it was proving huge, irreparable, devastating.

Finding the correct key at last, Henry jabbed it into the lock, muttering unhappily to himself ... A pitch-black house, the deliberate snub of an early night (*nine thirty!*) – they had never in their entire marriage gone to bed at such an early hour. Thus unhappily preoccupied, he almost missed the small piece of lined paper that had been Sellotaped to the knocker on the front door. Henry reeled backwards, leaving the keys dangling. Not just a dark but an *empty* house, then ... She'd gone. Oh, God, she'd gone. Henry ripped the note free and stumbled out of the porch, seeking the buttery light of the moon by which to read what already felt like a death sentence. His arms were leaden as he held the paper out – at full stretch because he was wearing the wrong glasses.

If you have given up on me, please don't come inside.

Henry turned and ran back so fast he tripped on the porch step. Then he couldn't make the keys work, or find the handle of his briefcase. Inside, pinned with Blu-tack next to the burglar-alarm panel, there was another.

I will never give up on you.

And on the top stair: *I am waiting for you. I can hear your steps. I am holding my breath. (NB DON'T wake children!)*

And on the bedroom-door handle, sealed this one, presumably against the possibility of prying minors stumbling to the landing loo: *I love you, always. Sex = icing on cake. Did I mention that I love you?*

Cindy couldn't believe they were rowing. Sam hadn't come back from his bike ride, and instead of pulling together they were rowing. Martin had been out to look for him, first on foot and then in the car. It was only at her insistence that he had phoned the police, and now he was pacing the perimeter of the sitting room, contradicting everything she said with a raised voice, as if it was *her* fault that his moody son had decided to play truant or been run over and not had the decency or common sense to take his mobile. But worse in her view – far worse – than all of this was Martin's refusal to call Charlotte.

'It's nearly ten o'clock. You have *got* to tell her. It's only right.' Cindy pressed both arms protectively round the tight swell of her stomach. 'If it was our . . .' She left the sentence hanging, hoping she had said enough for the fight to end, for Martin to stop glaring and soften his tone.

But Martin's expression had hardened. 'I told you what the police said. Hundreds of teenagers are reported missing every day and ninety-nine per cent of them turn up within twenty-four hours. Sam is at just that age – experimenting with boundaries, defying authority. He's been a handful all year. I was the same – drove my parents mad.'

'You should tell her,' repeated Cindy, doggedly. 'It's only fair.'

'What? Fair to make Charlotte worry, as I am? Fair to make her *suffer* when the little wretch will probably come skidding into the drive any minute now?'

Cindy flinched, but said steadily, 'Martin, it's nearly ten o'clock. Sam has been gone for *three hours*. Charlotte has the right to –' She stopped, aghast, as Martin made a sort of run at her, then dropped to his knees in front of the sofa, covering his face with his hands and shaking his head.

'I can't,' he whimpered through his fingers. 'She never thought I loved him enough. Ever. Right from the start, I always fell short. And now, with this, she'll –'

'Of course you love him,' Cindy whispered, shocked at this new vulnerability in a man she'd thought she knew better than any other, and the fresh spin it gave on the demise of his marriage. That he had lost Charlotte to Sam had been a favourite quip of Martin's during their early heart-to-hearts, and she had sympathized readily – an over-cosseting mother of an only child would be enough to drive any man away. But this was the first time Cindy had seen any hint of darker repercussions. 'Hey, baby.' She shuffled to the edge of the sofa and pulled his head into her lap, turning it so that his cheek rested on the bulge of their unborn child. 'Sweetheart. Of course you love him. Charlotte knows that. But you've got to tell her he's missing, just in case . . .' Cindy chewed her lip, drawing blood in her effort to find the courage to continue '. . . just in case it turns out that Sam is in that one per cent. I'll do it if you like.' She licked her lips, trying to sound matter-of-fact rather than brave.

'No.' Martin struggled upright, clenching his fists, not looking angry now but as if he was fighting off some invisible physical agony. 'I know you mean well, my love, but no. I'm going out to have one last look, okay? I'll take my bike – it'll be better – I should have done that before. If I don't find him, or he doesn't turn up while I'm gone, I'll call Charlotte, I promise. Okay?'

Cindy nodded, sucking the cut on her lip and swallowing at the lump in her throat. Tears wouldn't help. Martin wasn't coping too well, so it was up to her to be strong. That was how good couples functioned, after all, offering ballast, plugging each other's shortcomings. With the cancer, her mother had been cheerful and positive to the end, holding her dad together even though she was the one dying.

Cindy lurched round and pressed her face against the

window behind the sofa, steaming it with her breath, willing the silver frame of Sam's bike to glimmer out of the dark.

Tim gave it thirty minutes, then an hour, then another twenty minutes, then checked the street to see if the cabbie wasn't hovering outside the wrong house. Eve had sounded a bit worse for wear on the phone, so it was just possible she'd got the wrong number. He squinted into the lamp-lit dark, clutching his mobile, but fighting the urge to use it. She wasn't the sort who would like a man to appear too keen, too needy.

A skinny fox sprang out of the garden opposite and trotted across the road, disappearing between his neighbour's bins. Somewhere a cat mewed. The moon was almost full and very yellow. A summer moon, Tim decided idly, enjoying the feel of the cool night air against his bare skin and the prospect of Eve's soft body back in his arms. He checked his watch again, then turned back to the house. On the doorstep he paused, grinning in anticipation as a car appeared at the end of the street at last. It was going slowly, too, as if the occupants were on the lookout for the correct spot. But then, with a whine of the engine, it suddenly accelerated and shot past, its front wheel just missing the fox as it trotted back out to the kerb.

The phone was a bell in another world. Charlotte, absorbed in the recently discovered bliss of deep sleep, surfaced to consciousness slowly. Eve hadn't stayed, she remembered happily; she had been drunk and outspoken and gone to Tim Croft's instead. Tim and Eve – hurray! What a turn-up for the books! What perfect proof that life was random and therefore capable of offering resolution in the most unlikely ways.

As the ringing continued, she woke properly at last, noting with sleepy puzzlement rather than alarm that it was well past midnight. And at the sound of Martin's voice, it was to the conversation with Eve that her thoughts flew first, bringing with them the new humbling knowledge of having got things wrong. It took several seconds for her to register what Martin was saying, to connect with the need to feel fear.

'His bike? How long? The police?' Charlotte made him repeat everything, barking questions while numbness crept through her limbs and her mind exploded with unhelpful, uncontrollable images of Sam – pedalling to school that morning, not looking back, even though he knew she was hoping for it; wobbling as he turned the corner and adjusted his rucksack; lying on a road next to the twisted metal of his bike . . . but no, she couldn't picture that. She remembered instead a recent incredible news story of a toddler on a cliff ledge. How many days had that been? Found on a ledge, safe and sound. 'I'm coming to look.'

'I don't think that –'

'I need to look for him.'

'Charlotte, I'm so sorry – I – If something's happened –' Martin was gabbling suddenly, close to tears. 'I – Christ, I . . .'

'Hey, steady on, it's too soon for this, Martin, way too soon,' Charlotte interjected, aware of her own terror translating into an icy calm. 'He's out there somewhere. He probably had a puncture, or got lost, or – look, Martin,' her tone was logical, faintly reproving, 'if there had been an accident, the police would have heard by now, wouldn't they? They would have *heard*, I tell you. And besides which, he's thirteen, strong and sensible . . .' Charlotte thought again of the rescued toddler, lying on the cliff ledge for three days, with no experience or common sense. 'What about his phone? Did he have it?'

'No,' said Martin, in a small voice. 'Bring a torch,' he added, much more harshly, 'that big one on the hook in the broom cupboard.'

Charlotte arrived half an hour later, with the torch and a look of blazing intensity on her face, like someone staring into a bright light and refusing to blink. Cindy opened the door. 'Oh, Charlotte, he promised to be back by dark, to stay in the compound – to –' Her eyes bulged from crying. 'And then, just this minute, I had this other thought, that maybe we upset him about the baby. Do you think he could have been upset about the baby?' she pleaded, wringing her hands.

'If he is, that's fine by me,' Charlotte replied briskly. 'Sam sulking . . . yes, I'll settle for that.'

'Me too,' said Martin, appearing from the kitchen. He was pale and drained, as if the ordeal had already lasted several months instead of a few hours. 'Hey, Charlotte.' He glanced at her, then quickly away. 'You stay by the phone, babe,' he instructed Cindy, gently. 'The police are looking too. We could hear something at any moment.' There was hope in his voice, but his eyes, as he scanned the darkness through the open doorway behind Charlotte, were hollow with desperation.

They worked their way through the compound together, calling in the dark, ringing the doorbells of those houses still with lights on. Charlotte, in a moment of frantic inspiration had swiped Sam's latest school photo off the sitting-room mantelpiece, noting as she did so that it was already wrong – too baby-faced, the hair too short, the nose small and undefined. On seeing it, Martin ran back to the house to fetch a picture for himself – a more recent one, which Cindy must have taken, of him and Sam leaning on the railings skirting the walkway that ran along the river.

The river, oh, God, the river. 'Martin, have you been round the back, down the path, to the . . . river?' She had to fight to get the word out.

'No . . . I just assumed . . . It's hard to get a bike there – at least the first bit. You have to get off and walk. Sam never liked doing that. But maybe we –'

'I'll go.'

'Charlotte?'

She turned, remembering dimly – as if it were part of a previous existence – all that Eve had disclosed, shifting the mercurial landscape of the past. The story of her and Martin; they had loved, not loved. All that mattered now was that it had brought them to this moment, a moment of an anguish so shared that looking into the familiar face – kissed, distrusted, missed, not missed – was like staring into a mirror.

'If anything . . . to Sam . . .' he blurted '. . . I won't . . .'

'Stop, there's no need,' she whispered, mustering again the strength to be stern. 'I'll call you in ten minutes.' She sprinted down the path that led round the edge of the compound towards the river. Narrow and pitted with sets of iron bars to force cyclists off their saddles, Charlotte grew increasingly certain that Martin's first assumption had been right. Sam would consider it too much like hard work, too much bother, particularly given his recent detached, fiercely nonchalant frame of mind. But when she reached the stretch of Tarmac running along the Thames itself, Charlotte's certainty gave way to a bolt of pure terror. Left or right? And the river was so black, so menacing, so able to swallow a giant, let alone a child. Left or right? Time was so precious. She mustn't waste a second.

She turned left, along the backs of the houses, then changed her mind. Indecisive, hopeless . . . No, not hopeless, she scolded herself. The ledge, the toddler and that other one, several years ago – the boy in the drain – or had that been a drama on the telly? She phoned Martin after twenty minutes instead of ten, saying there was nothing to report, that she was going to take the next turning back towards the main road.

'The police – they've just found a silver bike,' said Martin, in a thick voice. 'They want me to look . . .'

'Where?' The word came out as a screech, breaking through the self-control. 'Where did they find the bike?' she repeated more steadily, reining the terror back in. 'And are they looking for him? The police, are they looking, Martin?'

'They say so.'

'Where have they found it?' Charlotte asked again, inwardly cursing the wasted time on the riverside path and trying to block out a vivid rush of new, more sinister scenarios. Sam loved his bicycle. Only under extreme circumstances would he have abandoned it.

'Outside a newsagent in Warren Road. I'm on my way there now. It's just off that street before the roundabout, the one we use for the short-cut through to the Old Kent Road.'

She could hear Martin running as he talked, the slap of his soles on Tarmac, the gasps of his breath. Charlotte began to run as well, not jogging this time, but as fast as she had ever run in her life. For Sam, she was running for Sam, and so was Martin and that, surely, was a force of good, a force to be reckoned with – two people who had failed each other but loved their child.

Ten minutes later, sweating but cold, she tore into the street that marked the beginning of the short-cut, only to see Martin coming towards her, shaking his head. 'Not his. Too big. Different make.'

Charlotte bent over her knees, catching her breath. The running had helped the panic. They would keep looking for ever, if necessary. For ever. It was that simple. As she straightened, her phone rang.

'That's probably Cindy – I've been talking to the police station.'

But it wasn't Cindy, it was Dominic Porter, ringing to say he had Sam in quite a state on his doorstep and he thought she'd better come round.

It was only then that Charlotte started to cry, falling against Martin, who – having gathered that it was good news rather than bad – also began to sob. Still weeping, clinging to each other like two drunks, they staggered back to tell the policeman hovering next to the newsagent.

'I'll kill him,' croaked Martin, grinning, wiping his eyes, as they turned for home. 'I'll bloody kill him.'

'Me too,' Charlotte gasped, squeezing Martin's fingers when they sought hers, aware of a bond of joy more intense than any they had ever shared as lovers or parents, not even during the wonderment in the delivery room thirteen years before. 'And I want you to know I'm sorry.'

'Sorry?' He was still half laughing, wiping the tears off his face.

'For us. How wrong we went. I know it was as much me as you.'

'Okay. Thanks. Me too.' He let go of her fingers, seeming uncertain.

'I just needed to say that,' Charlotte explained quickly, before switching the conversation back to Sam and keeping it there while they hurried back to the house.

Cindy, on the phone to her sister when they returned,

356

screamed and dived at them, simultaneously shrieking the news into the mouthpiece. Seconds later they were in their cars, heading for Wandsworth. Martin drove behind Charlotte, struggling to keep up as she broke speed limits, shot lights and soared over road humps like the woman she was – on a mission, learning to fly.

Chapter Eighteen

In spite of its early appearance in the school calendar, the Wednesday of the St Leonard's sports day dawned with Caribbean blue skies and a flaming sun suggestive of high summer. Jean, winding down the window of Bill's air-conditioned Audi as they cruised for a parking space, was momentarily transported back to her first step off the plane in Ceylon sixty years before, when the hot air had filled her mouth and whirled under the hem of her dress, fanning the dampness behind her knees.

'It must be here.' Bill craned his neck, trying to see over the hedge, which then conveniently became a fence, revealing a set of playing-fields swarming with children, small, brightly coloured cones and onlookers. 'Can you see if it's them?'

Jean squinted, putting up a hand to shield her eyes. 'I can't actually see *them*, but it looks right, doesn't it? Sam said it was by a church and there's a church.' She rummaged in her bag with her good hand for her glasses, finding only lipsticks, her purse and the mobile Bill had encouraged her to buy, then helped her to use, but of which she was still mostly very afraid, and the envelope with the cheque in it. Heavens, yes, she mustn't forget that . . . not again. Rediscovering a positive attitude to life had proved a lot easier than sharpening her memory.

'Perhaps I should take a look at that text, should I, Mrs B?'

'Oh, here's a man,' Jean cried, not ready yet for more

palaver with the mobile. 'Let's pull over and ask him. Excuse me . . . I say, excuse me,' she trilled, sticking her head as far out of the window as she could. 'You wouldn't happen to know if that's St Leonard's School sports day going on in there, would you?'

Tim Croft, too hot in his pinstripes, dabbing at his forehead with his handkerchief, smiled warmly. Grandparents, he decided, the old biddy riding in the back because she felt safer, the pair of them bewildered, no doubt, by London traffic, one-way systems and the heat. 'Yes, I believe it is. There's no parking here, though, I'm afraid. You'll have to try your luck in the next street over for that.'

Duty done, he turned back to the fence, tracking Charlotte as she moved through the crowd. Between viewings in neighbouring streets, it was pure coincidence that he had caught sight of her, arriving a few minutes earlier on a very old bicycle, with a basket on the front handlebars and a rusted rack fixed over the back wheel. Seeing the breeze press her lilac cotton skirt round her fabulous legs as she pedalled, the little dog trotting alongside, Tim had felt a sufficiently violent flare of the old desire to watch closely as she parked and tied the lead to the handlebars, asking himself what would have happened if she had been on her doorstep that evening instead of Eve, whether they could have made a go of things after all. Peering at her now, among the jolly throng of children and adults, he let the reverie continue, trying to imagine what it would be like at her side with the kid in tow, going to school events, playing a part in such a different world.

Eve's bolting had been a horrible shock. The so-and-so had made him wait until the next morning before getting in touch, calling from the concourse of Heathrow airport, surrounded by the hubbub of announcements, conversation and rumbling trolley-wheels. England pissed her off, she had said, as if that explained everything. It had been good to see Charlotte, and to meet him, of course, but she liked to act on impulse. And he could visit Boston whenever he wanted – an open invitation. An email had arrived two days later, reiterating the invitation with such flirtatious invention that Tim, forgiving her, had responded in kind. The correspondence, continuing heatedly ever since, was fun, as was the prospect of visiting America. In the meantime he had bumped into an old flame in the supermarket (far prettier than he remembered) and there was a new woman at the gym too, giving him signals – ash blonde, early forties, but fit as a cat . . . Like buses, Tim reflected happily. Nothing for ages, then several at the same time.

Far better to be a rolling stone, he decided, moving away from the fence and crossing the road: America in August, the old flame next week, the gym that night. Charlotte had been a mistake, a post-marital glitch, holding him back.

Hearing a rustle in his pocket, he pulled out the brown envelope that had arrived that morning. It contained the now dog-eared tickets for what he had misguidedly intended as Charlotte's birthday treat, with a curt note of referral to the small print describing the company policy not to offer refunds. Tim tapped the envelope against his palm, weighing the temptation to use the tickets to woo one of his new prospects against a dim notion that they might in some way be jinxed.

In the end the superstitious feeling got the better of him. And he had, after all, made the booking in Charlotte's name, he reasoned, pulling out a pen to overwrite his address with hers and scribble a hasty explanation on the flap of the envelope. And maybe – just maybe – a gesture of such obvious generosity would help dispel any lingering memories she might have of the horribly unsatisfactory encounter on his sofa. It didn't matter, of course, not now, but a man had his pride, he told himself, experiencing a small buzz of satisfaction as he dropped the packet into a postbox.

Charlotte had to force herself not to stand too close, not to touch, not to ask, every minute, if he was all right, if the headache had really gone, if he was sure that running four hundred metres might not cause the gash in his leg to split open and spill some more of his precious, precious blood. Dear God, she would have wrapped him in steel if she could, every delicate little inch of him, not just as protection against evil youths with knives but against future suffering of every kind.

But then again she wouldn't, Charlotte thought, moving further away, losing herself instead to the enjoyable sight of Sam among his peers, holding his own; the yellowing bruise, the plaster on his leg were the last things on his mind. It might have taken thirteen years but she was beginning to understand that a mother's desire to protect her offspring had at times to be controlled so as not to throw everything else off balance. The world, like the school playground, could be bullying and brutal, but no amount of mother-love or armoured plating would ever help anyone get through unscathed – not her, not Martin, not Eve, not Sam, no matter how much she wished it so. The best one could hope for was what, in fact, had happened: that presented with a crisis involving thugs and violence, her son had been instilled with enough sense, confidence, instinct, to try to pedal away from it – even after the fastest of his attackers had sliced through his calf with a flick-knife, even after he had fallen off taking the road-bend too quickly and been forced to complete his escape at a hobbling run, leaning on his bike for support. Charlotte was glad she hadn't seen any of what he had been through, that she had only Sam's spare, reluctant descriptions of the tall white boy with the blade who had run at such speed, and the railings where he had hit his head falling off, and the long spell of being so totally lost, before the main road and the big sign saying 'Clapham', which he knew was near Wandsworth.

For Charlotte, the vivid images started with her and Martin's arrival in Dominic's sitting room and the sight of Sam on the sofa, sheet-white apart from a bulbous blue bruise above his right eye, one leg of his jeans rolled up to reveal a long, ridged lump of caked blood. Dominic, in grey tracksuit bottoms and a T-shirt, pale and rumpled from sleep, had stood out of their way, murmuring that he had thought it better to wait for them before doing anything, that at the mention of an ambulance Sam had got upset. Glassy-eyed, breathless, they had knelt next to the sofa to listen to the first garbled version of the ordeal, before broaching the subject of getting him to a doctor themselves. 'And the police, mate,' Martin had added gently. 'You're going to have to tell them everything you can remember.'

'But I don't want stitches,' Sam had sobbed, clinging to creases in the sofa cover.

'It won't hurt any more than it does already, darling,' Charlotte assured him, trying to stroke his head and pulling back in dismay as he flinched. 'We'll take you there right now – get it over with. And they must look at that bump on your poor head too.'

'We could call George's dad, if you like,' Martin had suggested brightly, as Sam continued to cry, 'I know it's late, but Henry would be only too glad – I know he would – to give you a once-over, explain what's likely to happen at the hospital.'

But Sam, from having been upset, became hysterical. 'No – not him, Dad, no, please! I want – the hospital.'

'Okay, mate, okay. Steady on.'

'We'll go to St George's,' said Charlotte swiftly, seeing the cruelty of further delay, both for Sam, who was too shocked to be coherent, and Dominic, whose pained expression suggested that he was beginning to feel more than a little inconvenienced.

'Thank you *so* much.'

'He just turned up. I did nothing.' Dominic looked at the carpet, shuffling his feet, which were in beaten-up suede slippers, and then over her shoulder where Martin was gathering Sam into his arms for carrying to the car. 'Look, forgive this,' he lowered his voice, speaking in a rush, 'but I feel you should know – that business just then about George's father. Sam's reaction – it's because . . . I'm sorry, Charlotte, this is difficult – but it's because he *knows*. About you and the doctor father – after Suffolk he told Rose. Sam *knows*.'

Even remembering the moment now, with whistles blowing, children shrieking and Sam getting in line for a throw-the-furthest competition with a tennis ball, Charlotte could feel her lip curling in a smile of shocked disbelief. 'But –' was all she had managed. *But.* And then they had been out of the door and driving in convoy again, this time with Martin in the lead and Sam stretched out on his back seat, going via her house so she could abandon the Volkswagen to join them for the ride to A and E.

She had clambered in and clasped Sam to her, sensing the reticence in the limp response but understanding its origin at last. And when Martin said, 'Shit,' and pulled into a petrol station, granting them a few quiet minutes alone in the car, she had announced fluently, firmly, ignoring the crimson flush in Sam's pale face, that there was nothing going on between her and George's father and that if anything in Suffolk had led him to believe otherwise then he was wrong and she was sorry. They were friends and that was all, and he could trust her, because she had never lied to him and had no intention of starting now. 'And I like Cindy,' she had blurted, rather less fluently, 'and I am so pleased she and Dad are happy and having a baby, and you should be too.' And Sam had gripped her neck and pressed his face into her chest, with no reluctance now but just like in the very old days, when his love had had no agenda but pure need and she had been naïvely happy to close every other avenue of her life in responding to it.

Dominic, in contrast, had received a *but*, Charlotte reflected glumly. The man clearly wasn't a gossip but it still irked her. And, she recalled, indignation rising, if Jason (who *was* a gossip) was to be believed, Dominic's imminent tenure of Ravens Books was to begin with the search for a full-time assistant instead of an amateur enthusiast with limited hours. Since she hadn't had the chance to speak to him herself it was impossible to know. He had ventured into the shop once when she wasn't there, and two attempts to reiterate thanks over Sam had found only his answering-machine.

That he had his back to her now was almost certainly no coincidence either, Charlotte observed grimly. He was talking with some animation to Naomi, who was wearing a daringly short yellow sundress and looking greatly refreshed since her twenty-four-hour sojourn in Josephine's loft. She and Graham were having counselling (Josephine had informed Theresa, who had told her) but didn't want anyone to know. Naomi reckoned she had been fighting a touch of post-natal depression since the twins, while Graham had owned up to anger-management issues. They were making a clean breast of things, listening to each other's needs.

Like Theresa and Henry . . . Charlotte shifted her gaze to her friend and her husband, the latter celebrating the rare treat of an afternoon out of his consulting rooms by wearing a Panama hat and a Hawaiian shirt of livid orange and green. They had set up camp with Thermoses and sandwiches on a blanket near the marker for the long jump, casting fond glances at George who was limbering up nearby. Catching Charlotte's eye, Theresa waved a plastic mug and pointed at a Thermos, offering an exaggerated frown of disappointment when Charlotte shook her head.

But she was a little thirsty, Charlotte decided, wondering if she had time to fetch the bottle of water she had left in the basket of Mr Beasley's bicycle. She squinted back across the playing-field, noting with pleasure that an old lady was patting Jasper before gasping at the realization that it was her mother. Her mother who, since her mysterious road trip, had taken to making regular, sprightly telephone calls, probing for Charlotte's news, singing the praises of a taxi driver called Bill and, more recently, Bill's daughter, Jill, who had apparently displaced Prue and the visiting nurses and had a passion for playing cards.

'Sam, look, it's Granny,' she exclaimed, hurrying over to point out the surprise. 'I must go and give her a hand. Look, don't throw the ball yet, okay? Tell Mr Tyler, I've asked specially for you to go last.'

'Mu-um . . .' Sam groaned. 'I *can't* do that – the order's already been decided. And I knew Granny was coming because she texted me about it.'

'*Texted* you?'

'Yeah, she's got a phone,' replied Sam, in the manner of one having to explain something very simple to someone of limited intelligence. 'She wanted to surprise *you*. And Jasper. She's going to take him home.'

'Oh. Golly . . . Oh, look, here she comes – she's bringing him and dogs aren't allowed. Oh dear.'

Sam raised his eyes to the sky for the benefit of his friends as his mother hurried off, then checked for Rose, who was miserable at having been assigned the ignominy of the fancy-dress race – the event for losers, although none of the teachers admitted it. Secretly, Sam thought it was quite cool of his granny, who never usually went anywhere, to attend his sports day, even if it was mainly because she wanted to collect her pet. It helped to make up for the last-minute absence of his dad, who was in the hospital with Cindy, thanks to some drama with blood loss, which was too gross to contemplate but which had got Sam thinking that acquiring a baby sibling was probably preferable to having something going wrong with one *en route* to being born. They had both been brilliant since the attack, not once saying (even though they must have thought it a million times) that it had been his fault for leaving the compound. What his mum had said at the garage had been an incredible weight off his mind too. In fact everything had been going so much better since getting into trouble at school and now the knife fight (as he had taken to calling it in front of his friends) that Sam had even caught himself speculating whether bad stuff had to happen for life to feel really good.

He arched back for the throw, arm straight, picturing a cricketer on a boundary, trying to use all of his shoulder as he swung forwards for the release. He knew it was good from the smooth way the ball flew out of his hand, and because Miss Johnson, who was helping Mr Tyler, began trotting backwards from the marker flags of previous turns, stumbling in her effort to keep her eyes on the sky.

'Oh, hooray,' exclaimed Jean, delighted to be looking in the right direction as the ball bounced, momentarily forgetting poor dear Jasper, whom Charlotte had forced her to leave tethered to the bicycle. 'Hooray indeed. I just wish I could clap. Oh, and I've got something for you – that cheque. Were you ever going to tell me I'd forgotten to put it in the envelope, you dear silly girl? Could you fish it out of my bag? These things are so much easier when you've got two hands. It's in an envelope – there, that's it. In fact, it's just as well I *did* forget it as, thanks to the maturing of one of Reggie's little schemes, I was able to make it out for a bit more than I'd originally planned. I say, is that nice lady over there offering us tea? I think she is, Charlotte dear. Look, she's waving and pointing and I can't think who else she means.'

But Charlotte couldn't speak. With recent events she hadn't given her mother's oversight with the cheque a moment's thought. Even as she eased her finger under the flap of the envelope, her focus had been more on the joy of Sam's astonishing throw. 'Mum, I can't take this,' she murmured at last, staring in disbelief at the figures in the box, which, like the words – and in spite of being made out in Jean's uncertain, old-lady scrawl – made absolutely clear her intention to pay the bearer on demand the sum of sixty-three thousand pounds.

'Of course you can. It's only sensible. It turns out Reggie had a terror of dying in penury. All sorts of investments he made have been coming good gradually for years – most of them a surprise to my accountant, let alone me. And I can assure you I'm acting on his advice, because of the tax side of things, living seven more years and so on. Call it an early birthday present, Charlotte dear, if it makes you feel better. Oh, look, now she's coming over. The lady inviting us to tea – she's coming over, and a man in a horrible shirt. Is that her husband?'

'Mum, I – Thank you.' Charlotte slipped the cheque into her pocket as Theresa and Henry approached. 'Wow – we need sunglasses to look at you,' she quipped, trembling still on account of the cheque, and glad of the shirt, as a talking point and because it was so glaring and endearing, so typically the *old* Henry, that the silliness in Suffolk felt buried for good.

'I can't believe we haven't met,' exclaimed Theresa, sweetly, grasping Jean's good hand during the introductions, 'and I've been waving you over because we've made too big a picnic as usual, haven't we, Hen? Charlotte, you should have told us your mother was coming,' she scolded, her eyes blazing with warmth. 'She didn't tell us!'

Jean smiled, delighted at the fuss. 'She didn't know. It was a surprise. I wanted to see how Sam was doing for myself – after that *horrible* business the other weekend – and to collect Jasper at long last,' she added quickly, not wanting to darken her mood or anyone else's by instigating a post-mortem on her grandson's recent trauma. 'I feel up to walking him again now, you see. The dear little chap does *love* his walks. I should think he's quite worn you out, hasn't he, Charlotte?'

'As I've tried to tell you many times, Mum, I've loved every minute.'

'She has, honestly.' Theresa looped her arm through Charlotte's, fearing from her friend's somewhat dazed expression that some of the old mother-daughter prickliness might have been reasserting itself. 'But tell me, Charlotte, are you quite sure now was the best time to acquire a *bicycle*?'

'It's not mine,' Charlotte corrected her, laughing. 'It's Mr Beasley's – the bloody car finally chose this afternoon to conk out in earnest. I was getting cross because he was watching me through the curtains and then he goes and wheels that out of his front door. It belonged to his wife, apparently, so I'm very honoured.'

'You'll be needing Mr Jarvis the mechanic, then,' said Henry, latching on to what he imagined to be the safest of subjects. 'I never gave you the number.'

A long moment followed. At least, it felt long to Charlotte, still dizzy because of the money and trying not to grip Theresa's arm as she laboured for a response that would keep everything from blowing apart. A lie never went away, she realized, never blunted, never lost its power to be dis-covered and inflict pain. 'Oh, but you did, Henry,' she managed, keeping her voice dull and steady. 'You kindly phoned, remember? The day Theresa and I met for lunch? Although, needless to say, with all that's been going on, I couldn't find where I'd written it down so I'll probably have to ask for it again anyway.'

'No worries.' Henry coughed into his hand.

'Tea anyone?' Theresa sensed awkwardness but was pre-pared, in her new state of happiness, to overlook it. She and Henry were closer than they had been for years, agreeing about the children, laughing at the same things, making love like newly-weds at mad times and in new positions. It wouldn't last, she knew. It was a manic patch, before humdrum nor-mality reasserted itself, the product of a mutual, tacit cele-bration of Henry's return from an invisible leave of absence that had swept through their happy home like a cold wind. Something had almost happened, then not. Theresa wasn't sure what or with whom and no longer cared. They were in the same groove again, going forwards together, not looking back as surely as vertigo sufferers know never to look down.

*

Gathering for the grand finale of the sprint races, Charlotte noticed, but managed not to point out, that Sam's plaster was showing a smudge of leaked blood. Her mother was leaning on her now, visibly tired having been introduced to her friends, including Naomi and Jo, who had charmingly insisted that she organize a return visit to coincide with one of their mah-jong sessions. 'Such lovely friends, dear,' Jean had murmured. 'A girl needs good friends.'

Spotting Dominic again, this time with the young woman from the restaurant, Charlotte was glad she had colluded in their private game of mutual avoidance. The brother was there, too, attracting undercover stares because of his famous face, but doing a good job of appearing not to notice. The girl stood between them, her loose blonde hair streaming. She wore high-heeled gold sandals and a denim miniskirt cut high enough to reveal the splash of a large *café-au-lait* birth-mark across the back of her left thigh. She held a tiny crocodile-skin bag in one hand and a mobile in the other, pink and slim as two fingers and flecked with glitter.

Charlotte offered Sam the thumbs-up and checked on Jean, who had left her side to perch on a shooting-stick Theresa had kindly fetched from the boot of the Volvo. There was a false start and a second. Then the line of runners blurred as Charlotte's thoughts ricocheted back to the birth-mark and the suddenly crucial question of whether or not Dominic had placed his lips upon it. That soft, broad mouth travelling over one's skin . . . what would it feel like? She gripped her bare elbows, aware of her body goose-bumping in spite of the now belting afternoon heat.

The race was over and she hadn't watched. Sam had come third – or was it fourth? He looked happy, she saw with some relief, panting, wiping the sweat off his forehead, patting the shoulders of his competitors as if they had survived a battle on the same side. Catching his eye, Charlotte pulled a face of exaggerated sympathy. Sam shrugged, then dived into his kit-bag for a wad of papers he started hurriedly to press into the hands of the now dispersing crowd.

'Advertising Dad's concert,' he confessed, grinning guiltily, as he skipped past. 'I've had them for ages. George has asked me to tea, is that okay?'

'Of course.' Charlotte laughed at the tatty flyers. Having agreed to drop Sam off, she had lately been pondering whether to attend the event herself. Martin singing Mozart . . . she had to see it with her own eyes. And she was rich! The thought popped into her head like an exploding light.

'Excuse me. Do you have a moment?' Dominic had appeared from nowhere. She was pleased to notice that, close to, he was messy, unshaven, with dark circles under his eyes – a far cry from the alluring figure invading her thoughts a few minutes before.

'Oh. No. I mean . . . This is my mother.' Charlotte tripped over the words as she remembered Jean who, clearly restless to be gone, was now back at her side. 'Mum, this is Dominic Porter, the father of Sam's friend.'

'Ah, Charlotte has told me all about you, the man who saved our Sam.' Jean gripped Dominic's arm with her good hand. 'You bought that house she liked. And now you're buying the bookshop.'

'Mum . . .'

'I'm not sure that's an entirely fair summary,' Dominic muttered, flinching.

'But there's Bill,' Jean cried next. 'He'll be double-parked and he's been waiting so long, Charlotte, I've really got to go. I shall gather Jasper on the way.'

'But what about his bed and things?'

'They can wait till my next visit,' she replied gaily. 'I must

371

see if Jill can teach me mah-jong. Bye-bye, dear. And happy birthday, if I don't see you before, though we'll talk soon, of course.'

'Wow.'

'She's not normally like that.'

'When is your birthday?'

'What?'

'She said "happy birthday". When's your birthday?'

'Oh, in a few weeks . . .' In the distance Charlotte could see the brother, Benedict, scooping Rose, who had won the fancy-dress race, on to his shoulders. Along with most of the crowd now, they were walking back to the street. The blonde girl was walking alongside, gesticulating with her free hand as she talked into a pink phone.

'My mother . . . Something's happened – she's gone all cheerful. It's odd.'

'Nice, I should think . . . and maybe connected to – to what you told me that time by the church.'

'Oh, God, that time, yes . . . Something of a low spot.' Charlotte blushed. 'Sorry you got caught up in it. Look . . .' Sam had disappeared with the Curtis clan, but she was acutely aware of Dominic's faithful little trio waiting in the street. In fact, they were the only people in the entire playing-field now except for a disgruntled-looking young assistant picking up abandoned water-bottles and items of clothing. 'Look,' she repeated, fed up suddenly with the pussy-footing, her own silly fantasies and the rush of embarrassment at having him stand so close. 'For the record, not that it matters, there's nothing going on between me and Henry Curtis – or anyone else for that matter – only a bit of a misunderstanding because he felt sorry for me, I think, which is perhaps not surprising since I seem, until very recently, to have been in a pretty pitiable state – and – and

– Oh, yes.' Her voice hardened. 'If your real intention was to fire me the moment you sign that lease then you could at least have had the decency to offer a little warning.'

Dominic, colouring, folded his arms and began to drum the fingers of one hand on the wrist of the other. 'Well, obviously, I –'

'You might like to know that I haven't ruled out putting in a late bid for the bookshop myself. I've come into some money.' Charlotte gripped her hands into fists, enjoying the sight of his astonishment, the feeling of having him on the back foot for once. 'I might make Jason a better offer.'

'But you've got Sam to think of – you couldn't manage it.'

'We'll see, shall we?' she replied, managing an archness quite at odds with her pounding heart as she turned and strode back towards her bicycle.

It was only as she swung her leg over the saddle that Charlotte remembered Dominic had approached with the appearance of having something specific to say. She peered over the fence but the street was empty, apart from the young assistant, traipsing away with his bundle of lost property. She set off, pedalling slowly, sheepishly. She wouldn't do it, of course, the bookshop thing, she'd be sensible and put the money into a saver account instead, something with a high interest rate that couldn't be touched for years. But the rush of power had been fun, she reflected, laughing when she recalled the look on Dominic's face, as if she'd thrown a glass of cold water at him instead of a wild idea.

Chapter Nineteen

'What is a requiem anyway?'

'It's a piece of music for when someone has died –'

'Oh, *very* nice.' Sam folded his arms and stared gloomily at the set of temporary traffic-lights impeding their progress over Wandsworth Bridge.

'Mozart is *very* nice, yes. He wrote it when he was dying –'

'Blimey.' Sam slithered deeper into his seat, burying his face in his hands.

Charlotte laughed. 'I think you'll be surprised by how much you like it. I'm not, as you might know, a classical-music buff myself, but Mozart, I assure you, can be relied upon for a decent tune. And it's for a good cause.'

'Cancer, yeah, I know,' Sam put in quickly, keen to avoid the horror of hearing the word 'breast' out loud.

'Hey, the Beetle's going well, isn't it?'

'I thought we were going to get a new car.'

'We are. Soon. But I'm glad Mr Jarvis was able to do whatever it was he did. I like this car – it's a friend. We've been through some times together.'

'Yeah, like all the *bad* times of *not* starting,' Sam sneered, not getting it.

'That shirt looks nice,' Charlotte offered next, wondering if the light was ever going to change. 'Especially with those jeans,' she added slyly, observing from the corner of her eye that Sam was trying hard not to look pleased.

'Yep.' Sam gave in and grinned, holding out his arms to admire the shirt, which was long-sleeved, collared and striped blue and white. His mother had plucked it off a shop rail the previous weekend, and he had been astonished to find that it actually suited him. The same shopping expedition had seen the acquisition of the jeans, weathered, low-slung, baggy, which – with even more astonishment – he had found himself encouraged to wear that evening. Sam had gawped at himself in the mirror, unable to believe how good a set of clothes could look, how good it could make him feel. And because of his granny's cheque he was going to have an allowance, his mother had announced that evening, not poxy pocket money but an *allowance – thirty pounds a month* – for anything not to do with school, except his phone, which his dad was paying for so long as he kept each bill under twenty-five pounds.

Charlotte, sensing the contentment radiating from her no longer small companion, not caring that it was (and would be for a while yet, probably) often withheld from her, returned her attention happily to the road. In the creamy evening sunlight the river water looked blue for once, instead of brown. A small flock of birds was zigzagging across it, swooping and climbing, their shape shifting yet always miraculously – mathematically – precise. She gripped the steering-wheel as a surge of faith in the ordered beauty of the world swept through her. Just a few months ago life had appeared so fiendishly random, so beyond comprehension and control. The same water had shimmered like a malevolent blackness, capable of swallowing her son – her own happiness – whole.

But it wasn't the physical world that had changed, Charlotte realized, accelerating over the bridge as the lights changed at last, so much as human perceptions of it. Similarly, the energy – the optimism – with which she now got out of bed each morning was not because of any metamorphosis in the unedifying facts of her existence but simply because of her improved understanding of how they had come about.

There was a parking space almost outside the church, not easy, but just big enough. Charlotte manoeuvred into it, feeling again the benign order of the world. And she had been a bad wife. Yes, there was that, too. She yanked on the handbrake with a gasp as this new, still discomforting truth surfaced for attention – no more palatable for her having attempted to apologize for it. Obsessively loving, then neglectful, self-pitying, complaining, dining out on her misery as if it was the only thing capable of defining her. There had been reasons, of course, there were always reasons, but no wonder Martin had formed close relationships with other women, sex or no sex.

In spite of such broad-minded self-analysis, the sight of Cindy stepping on to the conductor's podium to deliver a speech of welcome – a stunning S shape in hugging black silk – caught Charlotte off guard. She looked extraordinary, not just for being undeniably beautiful – her blue eyes shining with emotion, her hair gold under the lights, her voice low and strong – but because pregnant, sincere, moved but articulate, with the orchestra and the choir, similarly attired in black, ranged behind her, she exuded a raw pulling power that had everyone shifting to the edge of their seats. Charlotte, equally spellbound, allowed herself a moment of quiet acknowledgement that Martin, in pursuit of a second soul-mate, had chosen well.

'It means so much to me and my sister, Lu . . .' necks craned and heads turned as Lu, slighter than Charlotte remembered and wearing a subdued outfit of mushroom brown, was pointed out in the front row '. . . that so many of you have come, so many friends and friends of friends . . .'

It was the church rather than the occasion itself that was getting to her, Charlotte decided, raising her eyes to the vaulted marble ceiling in a bid to clear the tears that had gathered by the time Cindy had retreated to her place among her fellow choristers, and the gentle, haunting opening bars of the Kyrie had begun. A vessel for the seminal events of human life – memorial fund-raisers, funerals, requiems, weddings, baptisms, confirmations – a church was bound to stir emotion. Especially one of such beauty, Charlotte reasoned, trying to focus on practical matters like stone-masons and architectural styles as her gaze moved from the clusters of angels and cherubs topping each pillar to the trumpeter's balcony housing the organ loft. Instead the music, washing through her, over her, each note floating upwards in whispered echoes, seemed determined to summon every recourse for joy and sadness that she had ever known: marrying Martin, burying her father (who was not her father), christening Sam – he had screamed, Charlotte remembered suddenly, then quietened at the touch of the priest's wet fingertip, out-staring the man with amazed blue-black eyes.

The same child was crossing and uncrossing his gangly legs beside her now, chewing with energy at a stick of gum that had been unwrapped as they were leaving the house. If she cried he would be appalled. Charlotte blinked, briefly clearing her vision, only to see a bird – of all things – a small brown one, perched on the crumbled stone nose of the angel at the top of the pillar nearest to her, cocking its head at the wall of music like a seasoned critic. The tears, instead of receding, gathered force. It was too much to contain – the little bird, the feelings, the memories, the threads of music thickening, soaring, merging, parting . . . Blinking furiously, her throat bursting, Charlotte plunged a hand into her bag in search of a tissue only to find herself pulling out the crumpled piece of paper she had hastily stuffed out of sight on the occasion of her unsatisfactory reunion with Eve. *Your husband . . . well-wisher . . .*

The jolt saw off the tears. The stupid thing had been hanging around for far too long, Charlotte thought, like a vile smell, a memory of bad luck, threatening always to drag her back, drag her down. She had the answers that mattered. She had done what she could to put things right in the lives of people for whom she cared. She had as much control over her own existence as anyone could hope for, especially now with a mass of money safely stowed in a building society and an updated version of her CV delivered to an employment agency that boasted imaginative placements for part-timers. She had even written to Dominic Porter, informing him of her decision to leave at the same time as her current employers, citing a desire for change and other platitudes designed to protect the inconvenient confusion of her true feelings.

Charlotte looked about her, dry-eyed now, wanting only to dispose of the sad, rumpled piece of paper. Even holding it felt horrible. Unwittingly, her gaze caught Henry's. He was seated in a side aisle next to Theresa. There was a second – of gratitude, regret, relief? It was hard to be sure. Henry looked away first, swivelling to face the front, slipping his arm protectively along the back of the pew behind Theresa, who sat erect, eyes closed, nodding in a manner suggestive of quiet ecstasy. Charlotte returned her attention to the top of the pillar, but the bird had gone and the angel looked like a stone carving with a broken nose.

Feeling a tug on her sleeve, she turned sideways to find Sam pointing, with a theatrically pained expression, at his mouthful of stale gum. Without a qualm Charlotte held out the note for him to spit it into, then settled back to enjoy the music, absently kneading gum and paper into a tight ball, ready for dropping into a bin during the interval.

'I thought there would be an interval.'

'It would have broken the spell, I suppose. Wonderful, wasn't it?'

'Exquisite. Aren't you staying for a drink? There's champagne and nibbles. Henry's promised to come back laden. I'm on this new diet – soup and vegetables – but one night off won't do any harm.' Theresa paused for breath. Part of her wanted badly to say that she – that they – were happy, but another, wiser, part knew that Charlotte could see this truth for herself and that such a delicate tendril as personal happiness was best left for private savouring rather than public declamation. She had taken it for granted once, felt impregnable, complacent, not recognized that the key to the treasuring of contentment was the knowledge that it could be snatched away. 'Go on – one glass. I'll signal to Henry.'

'No, Theresa, really. I've loved it but I'm not going to hang around. I've delivered Sam to Martin – they're taking him out for a meal and hanging on to him. I kind of feel I've done my bit, to be honest.'

'You have,' Theresa cried, kissing her, 'you so absolutely have. And it's bloody well done, as far as I'm concerned, the way you've brought it all round, made sure everyone's getting on. To think how it used to be . . .'

'I know.' Charlotte gave a pointed jangle of her car keys. Theresa meant well and she did indeed feel quite proud of how she had managed, but it was catching up with her now . . . blossoming Cindy, beaming Martin. To behave well on such an occasion was the least she could do for him but, still, she wasn't up to a moment more.

'But your birthday,' Theresa shrieked, grabbing Charlotte's elbow as she tried to set off through the crowd thronging round the tables of food and drink. 'We still haven't decided what you're going to do.'

'But I have, actually,' Charlotte admitted with a smile. 'An unexpected thing. Two tickets to go ballooning in West Sussex. I'm taking Sam. It's all I want, honestly,' she added, as concern broke through Theresa's look of surprise.

'Well, that's lovely, of course. Goodness, how did you come by those?'

Charlotte chuckled. 'Would you believe it – Tim Croft, of all people! Apparently he bought them when he still had hopes of winning my heart – before Eve won his. He scribbled me this note, saying they were destined to be mine and I should consider them a thank-you for Eve. Remember? I told you about the Eve business,' she prompted, as Theresa continued to shake her head in wonderment.

'Yes, yes, you did. Well, goodness, I suppose that is a treat of sorts. Ballooning!'

'Sam's thrilled at the idea.'

'I bet he is but, still, it doesn't seem –'

'Theresa, I'm fine,' Charlotte assured her, with some urgency, since Henry was visible now, twisting through the merry-makers with a plate of food balanced on two flutes of champagne. Worse, the sister, Lu, was right behind him, heading their way purposefully. Charlotte knew her flagging courage certainly didn't extend that far.

With a hasty kiss of farewell, she set off in the opposite direction, choosing a more circuitous route to the exit that involved crossing through the choir stalls behind the altar. Among them – empty, smelling strongly of polish and incense – Charlotte paused to enjoy the reverential hush of the church, the worn stone floor, the crests and names of their benefactors carved into the seats. But then the clack of approaching heels broke the spell and she hurried on, ducking through the archway that led to the less congested side of the church and turning left towards its large wooden doors. The clacking heels stopped in the same instant, as Cindy's sister blocked her way.

'Charlotte – I wanted to say thank you for coming.' The mushroom outfit had long floating sleeves, which she tweaked nervously as she spoke.

'Not at all.' Charlotte managed a smile and stepped past her. Snapshots of the débâcle in the supermarket were going off like fireworks, flushing her cheeks as she relived the humiliation. Thank God she'd moved on from all of that. The incident was just another tiny fragment of the past now, one of many stepping-stones on a difficult journey, not forgotten but despatched as certainly as the sticky gobbet of gum and paper she had dropped into a rubbish box next to the drinks table.

'I wanted you to know –'

'Thanks, Lu. Yes. I've really got to go.' Charlotte quickened her pace, her own heels clip-clopping on the hard, uneven tiles.

'– that it was me,' Lu blurted, running after her. 'The well-wisher. It was me. Cindy doesn't know. I did it because she was so unhappy – and from what I could gather you were too. All three of you, trapped by misery. I – I thought it needed . . . something.'

It was a few moments before Charlotte, frozen mid-escape, could bring herself to turn round. Lu was peering out through the long silky slats of her fringe, clearly terrified. 'Something,' she mumbled again, flapping the wispy material dangling from her arms, then clasping her elbows.

'You had no right,' Charlotte managed at last, her voice a whisper.

'I know.' Lu, fidgeting less, held her gaze now, glints of defiance in the big blue eyes. 'Mum had just died, Cindy was so unhappy – all of you so unhappy – but Martin wouldn't leave or commit properly or . . . So I did what I did. I honestly believe it would have happened anyway, that I just speeded everything up.'

'*Speeded everything up?*'

Lu dropped her eyes. 'I know that sounds terrible. What I did was terrible and it's been eating away at me, but then Cinds said you'd met someone and I was so glad because I thought you must be happier too, that it was working out. But in the supermarket café I saw that, happy or not, it was still eating away at you, too – the *not* knowing. I mean, thinking it was Cinds of all people. And ever since I've had this burning need to confess, to say sorry . . .' Lu fiddled with the strap of her bag, looking, though Charlotte was loath to acknowledge it, genuinely distraught.

'You can't be sorry for something with such a happy outcome, surely,' she pointed out bitterly.

Lu sighed, pushing at the floppy blonde fringe, which fell straight back into her eyes. 'But for whatever you've been through – I can't pretend to know – I'm sorry.'

'Well, *thank you.*'

'Charlotte, would you mind . . . not telling her – not telling Cindy, please?'

Charlotte gave a barely perceptible nod as she strode away. She kept her back stiff and walked tall, communicating all the things that it seemed to her Lu deserved to see – affront, pride, anger. But once outside the church she let her shoulders drop and breathed deeply. So there it was, the last answer, the one that didn't matter, the one that had never mattered. One day, soon, she would admit as much to Lu. The marriage had died anyway, by her hand and Martin's. They *were* happier now, all three of them – four if you counted Sam. And how could one not count Sam? Charlotte scolded herself, smiling as she strolled the last few yards to the car.

'There!' Dominic cried, unclasping his seatbelt and lunging forwards to point as the cabbie swung into the street at last. 'There!'

'I thought you said it was a church you were after, mate.'

'It is – it was – but we're too late and I need to speak to that woman.'

'Oh, do you now?' the cabbie chuckled, entirely unsurprised to find that this irritating and most unfortunate of customers should turn out to be on some do-or-die mission involving the opposite sex. 'Oy, and I need paying,' he called, with altogether less good humour as Dominic hurled himself out of the cab and sprinted with cartoon-like urgency – jacket and arms flapping – towards the black Volkswagen edging out of its parking space. When he returned to the window a few minutes later, he was breathless, sweating, his dark hair wild. 'She says she'll wait.'

'Well, that's a relief for both of us, mate, but I'm afraid the grand reckoning still comes to forty-five pounds – a lot, I know, but we had that trip to the garage for petrol, didn't we? And the wait while we realized your problems went beyond an empty tank and then the call when you found your AA membership had run out.'

Dominic plucked three twenty-pound notes out of his wallet, not listening. He didn't need the cabbie to tell him it had been a hell of an evening. Sitting in the tail-back on to Wandsworth Bridge, after Benedict had arrived so late for baby-sitting, then the fiasco with the car breaking down, he had begun to feel like some desperate salmon attempting to hurl itself up a waterfall when all he had wanted was to attend a charity concert, to get there on time, in a modestly presentable state, early enough to find a friendly face to sit next to . . . But no, that wasn't quite true, Dominic corrected himself, making a desultory attempt to impose some order on his hair as he approached the Volkswagen. There was one face he had had especially in mind, a not particularly friendly one.

He walked slowly, aware of the cabbie watching and that he seemed to make a habit of approaching Charlotte when she was in her own famously temperamental vehicle. 'Thanks so much for waiting. I just wanted a quick word.' He squatted on the pavement next to the open window.

She frowned. 'You do know the concert's over, don't you? It began at seven.'

'Sadly, yes, I am aware of that fact. I've had something of an epic journey.'

'But there are drinks going on inside.'

'That's splendid news, but I don't want a drink.'

'I assume you got my letter,' she cut in, folding her arms, every last trace of friendliness gone.

'Indeed I did.' Dominic flexed his legs into a half-standing position. His knees were cramping and it had been deluded, he realized, to have hoped for the conversation to play out with any of the smoothness he had imagined during the countless silent rehearsals in his head.

'Are you all right?' She stuck her head further out of the window and peered with something like concern at his legs.

'My knees hurt.'

384

'Oh dear, I –'

'My knees hurt and lately I've been arguing with my brother, which I never do. Ever.'

'Benedict?'

'The same. Look, there isn't a chance you could give me a lift home, is there?'

Charlotte let out an incredulous laugh. 'But you've only just got here.'

'I know. The entire evening has been a catastrophe. But I wanted to talk to you anyway.'

'Well, I suppose so.' She leant across the passenger seat and flicked up the lock, dismissively, angrily even, or so it seemed to Dominic, busy thinking of black-widow spiders and webs and others of his brother's graphic warnings as he levered his long legs into the car. Buckled in next to her, such doubts worsened to total speechlessness. Charlotte drove in equal silence, flexing her eyebrows, before enquiring at last, with some savagery, what had caused the brotherly disagreement.

'You,' Dominic muttered.

'Me?' She performed an unorthodox version of an emergency stop, slung him a look of horror, then ground her way noisily back up through the gears, delivering, as both her sentences and the Volkswagen gathered speed, a heated defence of her threat to buy the bookshop lease and the decision to resign that had supplanted it. 'I haven't got a head for figures and of course you were right – the last thing I want is a job that stops me being there for Sam. *But*,' she added viciously, 'I also have enough pride to want to *walk* before I'm *pushed*.'

'Yes, I was going to try to get rid of you,' Dominic admitted quietly.

She slapped the steering-wheel, seeming more triumphant

than insulted. 'Good. I'm glad we've got that out in the open. And was that the happy news you didn't quite deliver at the sports day?'

'Yup.'

'Fine. Excellent. So we're all clear. And has Benedict been trying to argue you out of it?' she continued, cautious curiosity breaking through the bravado.

'No, on the contrary. Benedict thinks I should avoid contact with you at all costs.'

Charlotte swerved into a bus stop, pulled up the hand-brake and folded her arms. 'I think maybe you should get out and find yourself another taxi. Which might seem harsh, but this conversation doesn't seem to be going anywhere good and I don't need it, I really don't.'

Dominic sat very still. He was aware that he was making a mess of things, but that was because he knew he was standing on the edge again – the invisible edge of wanting something so badly that any movement felt like a risk of disappointment, of pain. 'I think Benedict's wrong,' he said at last, turning in his seat so he could look at her properly, the palest pinpoint freckles dotting her nose, the neat, obstinate chin, the wispy flames of hair curling under her earlobes. 'Charlotte, I want you to reconsider your idea to purchase the lease,' he blurted, 'not as sole owner but with me. Fifty-fifty. I think we'd make a good team. I *am* good at figures, and you'd be the expert on stock, not to mention customers. We could share the workload, both have time for our children – and, er, there's a bus coming, one of those long bendy ones.' He pointed at the glare of headlights in the rear-view mirror. 'A bus?' he repeated, when she failed to move or even look at him. 'Okay, forget the bus. What about my proposition? What do you think?'

'I think, no,' said Charlotte, in a small voice. 'Impossible.

No.' She shook her head, slowly, marvelling at how heavy a head could be when forced to move against its natural inclination. 'Thanks, but no,' she repeated, louder, staring straight ahead, as if transfixed by the flecks of dead insects spattering the windscreen.

'Reasons?'

'Lots.'

'I see. Right. Well, it was worth a shot.' Dominic slapped his thighs and reached for the door handle. 'I'll find my own way home, then, as you so sweetly suggested.'

Half out of the door he hesitated, secretly astonished she wasn't leaping to rescind his banishment from the car, out of neighbourly decency if nothing else, what with it being late and the bus hissing inches from her bumper, like a beast bent upon revenge.

Many hours later, wide-eyed, sleepless, Charlotte was still taking herself through every moment, studying it with the forensic intensity of a detective searching for a clue in a sequence of mysterious events. Had Dominic seen the reluctance in the slow, sad swivel of her head? Was that why he had taken so long to cross the road, making sure she had time to notice the street into which he disappeared? And as for her, what exactly had prompted the deft, traffic-stopping, highly uncharacteristic three-point turn that took her past the no-entry sign and into the alley down which he was supposedly attempting to escape? It certainly hadn't felt like courage at that stage, merely foolhardiness, and perhaps, lurking deep beneath that, a small urgent pulse not to let this moment – of all moments in her life – go by without as good an articulation of the truth as she could manage. Perhaps Lu had inspired her, or the heartening truce between the Curtises, or the thwarted attempt at a confession from her dying father? For it was all there surely, each turning point in a life being the product of the trillion moments that had gone before.

When Charlotte caught up with him, Dominic kept walking, forcing her to kerb-crawl. 'You've just broken the law,' he shouted, when she wound down the window. 'This area is heaving with cameras too – you might go to jail. Licence suspension at the very least.' He kicked a stone. 'Or harassment. Perhaps I could get you for that.'

'Dominic.' It was hard to project her voice and drive at the same time. 'Your proposition, the answer is still no, but it's not what you think. The reasons . . . they're not what you think.'

He stopped at once, crestfallen. 'I was only pretending to be cross. Driving like that – I thought you must have changed your mind. Where did you learn to drive like that? Change your mind, *please*.' He had come right up to the window and dropped to his knees, pressing his palms together in a mockery of prayer.

'Dominic, stop! Get up, this is unbearable.' Charlotte hung her head. 'And awkward. And your *knees* – I thought they were hurting . . . Aren't they hurting?' she pleaded, when he stayed where he was.

'Not till I've heard these reasons. I'll suffer until then.'

'Oh, God.' Charlotte groaned, dropping her forehead on to the steering-wheel. 'The fact is . . .' she turned off the engine and flicked on the hazard lights, although the street was empty '. . . your proposal – the bookshop – it holds a lot of . . . appeal. I've even put my money in one of those accounts where you can make a withdrawal every three months without losing interest.'

'Well, that's splendid.' Dominic dropped his arms to his sides, looking puzzled. 'So what's the problem?'

Charlotte swallowed. 'The *problem* is that – as they say in America – I have *feelings* . . .' She blew out her cheeks and whistled, her face burning.

'We all have those, Charlotte.'

He had sat back on his heels and was staring at her, his dark brown eyes unreadable.

'For you,' she spluttered, slapping her forehead with a palm and keeping her face averted. 'There. That's probably the hardest thing I've ever had to say, so . . . er . . . tread carefully and all that. In fact, in the circumstances, it's probably best if we stick to the taxi plan.'

'No, I can't say I agree with you there. And the refusing of my proposal, I'm against that too. And what was the other thing? Oh, yes, *feelings*. I might have to take issue with you on that score as well.' Dominic shuffled closer to the window. 'Charlotte? Look at me, please. I need you to look at me when I say this next thing.' He took hold of her chin and turned her head until she was facing him. 'I was frozen. Rose and I were frozen. You and Sam –'

'Sam hit Rose.'

'There was that, yes, but she's a complicated minx and in those days a very sad one, too. Sam was the first to get through. I'll love him for that, always, whatever on earth happens between them . . . Relationships at thirteen –' He scowled. 'Can you even begin to remember what that was like?'

'Yes, actually,' Charlotte admitted, her thoughts flying back to Adrian's kind blunt features and milk-jug ears. 'Yes, I can. Though I believe Sam and Rose are just really good friends.' She wasn't euphoric yet, just calm – calmer than she could ever recall being in her life – as if she knew already that, after all the stumbling, her instincts were leading her in the right direction at last.

'Now, where were we? Ah, yes, you were saying you had feelings. Is that correct?' He took her hand like a doctor about to test for a pulse.

Charlotte nodded, trying to concentrate, trying, even at this relatively late stage when she could feel the warmth of his interest and energy, not to get her hopes up. 'I think it began in that bloody churchyard –'

'Ah, and thank God for that bloody churchyard and for Sam, and for house sales and ill-functioning cars and all the other things that have led me to you.'

'What?'

His mouth was so close she could smell a faint sweetness on his breath; chocolate or maybe coffee. 'But what about –'

'What about what?' He was slipping both hands through her hair now, combing her scalp, until his fingertips cupped the curve of her skull.

'Your – that woman . . .' Charlotte gasped. 'In the restaurant – at sports – oh, please stop,' she begged, 'or I won't be able to. I won't be responsible for my actions.'

'I don't want you to be,' he whispered, 'ever again, not with me.' He nuzzled his lips and the long nose she had tried so hard not to like, against her hair, her forehead and into the hollows of her eyes.

'That woman –' It was hard to speak. The freefall of wanting and being wanted, she had forgotten it. How had she forgotten?

'She's called Petra. She's Polish. I tried my best to like her because Benedict commanded it and obeying my brother has led me to much happiness in the past.' He brushed his lips along her chin. 'I have many theories about Petra, current favourite being that she's on the lookout for an English – preferably rich – husband. Benedict's thinking of obliging – for his own convenience.'

'Benedict?' Charlotte pulled back in astonishment.

Dominic took the opportunity to struggle – with exaggerated grimacing – to his feet. 'I don't suppose I'm allowed back in the car, am I? That is, if I'm still capable of walking.'

'Of course, of course – get in!' Charlotte cried, guilty for his discomfort, which she had quite forgotten, but unable to resist laughing as he made a show of hobbling round to the passenger seat. 'Poor old man – is that premature arthritis or what?'

'Insults. That's a *very* good sign,' Dominic muttered, closing the door and pulling her as far into his arms as the gear stick would allow. 'Now I've lost my thread again. Where were we?'

'Benedict.'

'Ah, yes.' He stroked her hair, looking serious for a moment. 'My brother is gay but in need of wife. Rock Hudson syndrome. It's a secret, but we've done that before, haven't we, Charlotte – told each other secrets and I thought it felt bloody marvellous, didn't you?'

'Bloody marvellous,' she murmured, wondering that waiting to be kissed could feel almost as good as the thing itself. 'I wish he did like me, all the same.' She sighed, then added with mock-petulance, 'He's so handsome and famous – I *want* him to like me.'

Dominic laughed, pulling her closer. 'Benedict likes you very much indeed. He's just protective. He thought you were far too beautiful to be interested in a donkey like me, and then, of course, there was the red hair, which worried him because of Maggie. But you're nothing like her, *nothing*.' He paused. 'And, of course, he believed that odious rumour your son started – the bloody doctor. Christ, at those sports the other week, when he kissed you, I was close to murder, I tell you.'

'Did Henry kiss me?' Charlotte exclaimed, delighted. 'I don't even remember.'

'Twice. Once on each cheek . . . like this. But not like this, or like this, or . . .'

Now Charlotte, tangled in her sheets, rolled her face into her pillows. A four-by-four, attempting to drive the correct way down the street, had disturbed them with several indignant hoots. She had had to reverse the Volkswagen, with her ears singing and the world spinning and Dominic, not entirely himself either, offering unreliable advice about whether to put her left or right hand up or down.

Rolling on to her back, Charlotte opened her eyes to watch the silvery light of dawn thicken through the gap in the curtains. Her body, pumped with hope and excitement, was more than ready for the day. She turned to her alarm clock, willing the hands to move faster.

'And there was me thinking I'd worn you out,' Dominic murmured, sliding across the bed and slipping his arms round her.

'You did, totally. I'm awake because I'm buzzing . . . happy.'

'Hmm, that doesn't bode well . . . Your happiness, sleep – can't I have both?'

Charlotte lay as still as she could, fighting a bursting urge to ask if it could really be okay – them, the recklessness of running a business together. Dominic would say yes, because he was kind and basking still in the after-glow of having made love. But he didn't know. He couldn't know. And neither could she. No one could. And he was exhausted, she reminded herself, because of her, he had said, all the weeks of weighing up what to do, afraid of rejection, of defying Benedict, of following his heart.

He had fallen quiet, his chin resting lightly on her shoulder.

Charlotte, too, let her eyes close, not to sleep but to savour his warmth and the lazy, lovely knowledge that she was back at the beginning again, ready not to need answers, ready to believe and be believed in.

Chapter Twenty

Having asserted her desire for a quiet birthday so volubly, Charlotte was aware that she had no right whatsoever to bemoan a mild sense of let-down when the day presented itself with no more fanfare than making herself an exceptionally early cup of tea. Nor was there much to celebrate in the task of having to rouse a sleepy teenager for a drive to a field in the middle of West Sussex.

'Will there be food?'

'Of course there won't be food. It's a balloon, not a cafeteria.'

'Happy birthday by the way,' Sam muttered, shuffling into the kitchen in his pyjamas a few minutes later. 'I made you something at school but it needs to be fired. Shall I tell you what it is?'

'No!' Charlotte pretended to be appalled. 'I'd much prefer a surprise.' In a bid to enliven things a little, she fetched the small parcel her mother had so prematurely handed over in March and opened it while they ate breakfast, making as big a to-do as she could of picking off the Sellotape. Sam watched sleepily, taking desultory bites of toast and jam until, from among a froth of tissue paper, Charlotte pulled out her once beloved set of babushka dolls. 'Well, my goodness.' Surprised, disappointed, having expected bath salts or something useful for the kitchen, she turned the ornament over, wondering if Jean in her new, more positive frame of mind would ever have chosen to make a gift of something so unlikely.

'Can I have a go?' Sam begged, wide awake suddenly, hastily licking the jam off his fingers.

'Of course. It was mine when I was little. I expect Granny thought I missed it.'

Still puzzling, Charlotte drifted to the sink with their dirty breakfast plates. She had been very fond of the dolls once upon a time. And Reggie had varnished some brightness back into the paintwork, she remembered suddenly, shortly before he died. Maybe that was it – Reggie's handiwork, a memento infused with his love . . .

Behind her, Sam let out an unguarded, girlish squeal.

'Wow, awesome! Mum, look what I found – right in the middle. Do you think Granny meant to put it there? Is it real gold? It's got a picture on it of a lion. Awesome,' he repeated, trying what Charlotte could see now was a ring – gleaming and huge – on each of his fingers, and frowning in disappointment when not one of the ten proved big enough.

'Well, my goodness, it's his signet ring,' she said quietly, taking it from Sam and cupping it in the palm of her hand, feeling its weight, remembering the groove it had worn in the little finger of Reggie's left hand. 'It was your – your grandfather's . . . my father's . . . That is, he *was* my father because he looked after me from when I was born but my real father died before I ever knew him.'

Sam had taken back the ring and was studying the crest. 'That's bad luck, but I guess if you never knew him, you couldn't really miss him, could you?'

'No,' Charlotte murmured, humbled by this guileless summary and the still innocent heart responsible for it. Her world had darkened when she was so young; a small piece of bad timing – stumbling into the shed – and she had been turned upside-down. Sam had his troubles aplenty, but nothing yet – give or take a close shave or two – on that scale. 'It's what they call seal-engraved,' she continued, sneaking the chance for a quick ruffle of his hair, 'which means you can dip it in sealing wax and close letters and envelopes with it – like in the olden days.'

'Wow,' Sam exclaimed, even more fervently. 'I want to do that now.' He began looking around, as if sealing wax might be found in one of the kitchen drawers.

'Not now. Now it's going somewhere safe and you are going upstairs to get dressed.'

'Will it be mine one day?' he persisted, hovering in the doorway.

'Yes, I suppose it might,' Charlotte conceded, laughing. 'But for now it's *mine*, and today is *my* birthday and if you don't get a move on that balloon will take off without us.'

Sam reappeared a few minutes later, not only dressed but clutching a card – clearly printed off the computer – with the number forty emblazoned in crimson across the front. 'The thing I made, it's jewellery, too, but not a ring,' he blurted, clearly fearing the inadequacy of his offering, both on account of its absence and the tremendous treasure that had been concealed in the gift from his grandmother.

'I shall love it,' Charlotte assured him, every trace of let-down gone as they sped off with no rush-hour traffic to worry about – it was only just seven o'clock on a Saturday – and the clear skies the forecasters had promised already in evidence overhead.

Sam was soon fast asleep, his fleece bunched up to cushion his head against the car window. He was tired because it was so early, of course, but Charlotte also suspected he might have guessed at her hopes of using the enforced intimacy of the car to quiz him on his feelings about the Dominic situation. 'But it doesn't matter,' he had cried, with some exasperation the last time she tried, 'because it's just what's happening, isn't it?'

It was indeed what was happening, Charlotte mused, and she was as powerless in the face of it as a pebble against a tidal wave. And, as Dominic had once so wisely pointed out, to know another's heart was a rare privilege and if Sam wanted leaving alone she would jolly well have to manage it.

With only a small truck parked in the corner of the field, Charlotte thought at first that she had the wrong time or place. But soon they and a few of the other fourteen would-be passengers had been invited to sign registration forms and assist with the unpacking of the equipment, which included a fat bale-shaped bag containing the balloon in its deflated form. Sam, taking orders from the burly man in charge, was in heaven, tugging and pulling at the contents of the bag until an astonishing sea of material had emerged, covering most of the field. They then stood side by side, equally entranced, as pumping blasts of cold air from a small, noisy machine on the back of the truck inflated the sea into a floating, brightly striped bubble the size of a multi-storey car park.

'And here's your other present,' Sam shouted, over the roar, as a silver Mercedes swept to the end of the line of other parked cars. 'I told them to do it, I hope you don't mind.'

'Who to do what?' Charlotte shouted back, knowing the answer even before Dominic and Rose scrambled into view, rubbing their pale faces and in an assortment of clothes – wellingtons, shorts, scarves – which suggested that they, too, had struggled somewhat with the dawn start.

Sam was already running across the field to greet the new arrivals. Charlotte approached more slowly, shy of eliciting one of Rose's icy stares, noting that Dominic was wearing

397

the unforgettable scarlet woollen pom-pom hat in a bid to ward off the morning chill. 'What a fantastic surprise.' She confined herself to a peck on the cheek by way of a greeting. 'And I've always loved that hat – do you know, Rose, your father wore it the very first time I met him, when he came to view our house and didn't like it?'

'I did like it – it just wasn't right for me,' Dominic protested. 'And I could never have made it as nice as you have now. If you ever put it on the market again, they'll be queuing down the street.'

They grinned at each other, happy in the knowledge that, thanks to the presence of their offspring, they were holding back. Similar sensitivity had led to the agreement not to share a bed yet either – at least, not openly, a deprivation they would have felt more keenly had private opportunities to express their mutual enthusiasm – at less traditional times of day – not been in ready supply.

But Rose was too transfixed to bother with receiving compliments or the already somewhat tedious challenge of having a rival for her father's affections. The balloon had become a giant planet, taut and beautiful, taking up most of the sky. 'Oh, but it's *huge*,' she gasped, trotting after Sam, who was keen to show off his friendship with the bulky man in charge.

'It is, isn't it?' Dominic remarked, gazing upwards, like everyone else now assembled in the field. 'Happy birthday, by the way.'

'Don't remind me.' Charlotte pulled a face.

'It's only a number.'

'That's what people who are younger always say.'

Dominic chuckled. 'I'm only a few months behind. We'll be forty together, eh?' He wrested his gaze from the sky and took her hand, holding on to it even when Rose raced back to announce that they'd better hurry as it was time to get on board and you had to go in twos and she wanted to be with Sam. 'And happy birthday,' she added breathlessly, turning to smile at Charlotte. 'The balloon, it's so cool, just the *coolest* . . .' and with that she ran back again, lolloping with evident difficulty in her wellingtons.

'I've got a present, but it's for when we're alone, okay?'

'You being here is a present.'

'It was easy – two slots left – like it was meant to be.' He squeezed the tips of her fingers.

During lift-off the balloon hovered so steadily and with such precision just a few inches above the ground that Charlotte wondered whether the burly man's instructions about taking up brace positions for landing had been necessary. It was so hot too, under the blast of the contraption responsible for keeping them afloat, that by the time the basket was rising in earnest she had peeled off her fleece and Dominic's woolly hat had been stuffed into a trouser pocket.

'Oh, Christ.'

'What?'

'I'm not sure I can manage this.'

'But you're the flyer,' Charlotte reminded him, laughing as she leant over the edge of the basket to enjoy the sight of the ground falling away, shrinking vehicles, houses, cows and sheep to the size of farmyard toys. In the neighbouring compartment Sam and Rose, shrieking, pointing and grabbing each other, were evidently just as thrilled.

Dominic, meanwhile, was pressing himself against the rear of the wicker compartment, his face ashen.

'It's okay.' Charlotte slipped an arm round him, realizing at last that the fear was serious.

'It's not. It's not okay at all.'

'But, darling, you fly aeroplanes,' she reminded him gently.

'I don't care. It's not the same.'

'Because you're not at the controls?'

He nodded, biting his lip. 'Maybe. I can't look down, I just can't.'

'Don't, then. Look at the sky. Look at all the greens in the trees and fields. Look at how trim and prim the country-side looks, like a place for garden gnomes, a Toytown, so unscary and manageable . . .'

'That means looking down . . . to see those things.'

'Oh, yes, sorry. Just the sky then – keep your eyes on that. And there's a cloud over there, small and fluffy – like a lost sheep.'

Dominic edged forwards, keeping a tight grip on her hand. 'Maggie was the one who got vertigo. Not me.'

'This better not mean you're going to give up flying.'

Dominic laughed, relaxing a little. 'No, never . . . I'd miss it.'

'A month of promising and you still haven't taken me up.'

'I will. There's been quite a lot going on, in case you hadn't noticed.' He shuffled closer to the edge of the basket and peered over gingerly. 'It's better now, being higher, more like the plane. God, I feel so . . . *exposed*, though, don't you? One sneeze and I could fall out.'

Charlotte giggled. 'Nonsense. And, besides, I'd hold you.'

'Then you'd fall with me.'

'Then I'd fall with you,' she echoed, smiling.

Up high, it was silent and still, as if they were suspended from some invisible hook in the sky rather than actually moving. Below, the world was a carpet, smooth and safe, unpeopled, untroubled. Thoroughly relaxed now, they rested their elbows side by side on the edge of the basket and feasted on the sight – the bands of colour in the sky, the lost sheep of a cloud, which shrank to a wisp, a speck and then was gone.

'We're going down,' Dominic shouted, relaxed and exuberant, when the balloon, some forty minutes later, began its descent. 'I hope you remember the drill.'

'Easy – look.' Charlotte turned her back to the edge, took hold of the safety handle and squatted as they had been shown.

'Very impressive, but,' he added slyly, 'there's the other thing to prepare for too, the thing I haven't mentioned yet.'

'What other thing? What are you talking about?' She punched his arm.

'If you look now, you might see.' Dominic pointed down to the road where the truck – in walkie-talkie contact with their captain – was racing to the field that had been identified as the best spot for landing. 'There's a bit of a welcome committee behind that thing down there. Sorry, but Theresa can be quite formidable when she latches on to something can't she? The whole birthday-party idea, she wouldn't give up on it.'

Charlotte stared, speechless, as the line of cars behind the truck came into focus, the windows of each open and spilling, she could see now, with familiar heads and waving arms. Theresa, Naomi, Josephine – husbands, children, they were all there; and the saintly Bill's sparkling Audi was bringing up the rear, with her mother riding up front for once, her face a small blur through the windscreen. Four, five cars, counting the truck . . . Charlotte scanned the lane, checking for Martin's black convertible. It wasn't there, but it was good to have wanted it to be, good to know that he was an integral, positive part of her world.

'I am whole.' She whispered the words to the air. The

ground was rushing up at them, bringing with it the hiss of trees, the roar of car engines, a barking dog. Reality returning: it was time to adopt the emergency positions they had been shown. And it felt necessary, too, now that the moment had come. They were going so fast, anything could happen. Charlotte squatted, reaching not for the safety handle but for Dominic's hand, watching his face as they braced themselves to land.

Acknowledgements

'Research assistance' occurs constantly, in ways too numerous and subtle to list or pin down. Those clearly warranting formal thanks are Paula Carter, who took me flying, Ed and Louisa Brookfield, for my helpful birthday gift, Sara Westcott, for matters medical, and Greene's College, Oxford, for setting me straight on my Latin.

AMANDA BROOKFIELD

THE SIMPLE RULES OF LOVE

One family. Four seasons. Everything must change...

The Harrisons are a large and extremely close-knit family. But with the grandchildren fast becoming adults and elderly Pamela struggling to adapt to widowhood and the emptiness of Ashley House, the four children of the middle generation find themselves equally lost in a changing world.

As preparations for forty-two-old Cassie's long-awaited wedding gather pace and an exotic family holiday is planned, sibling and marital bonds are stretched to breaking point: adultery, an unwanted pregnancy, shadows of past losses... suddenly a year of celebration threatens to become one of painful upheaval.

Beset by such emotional chaos, how can the adults hope to guide their children in matters of the heart? Or are the children the ones who should be guiding them?

'Few contemporary British novelists explore the messy tangles of close human relationships with quite such warmth perceptiveness as Brookfield' *Mirror*

'A strong sense of humour, a natural narrative gift' *Evening Standard*

'Brookfield skillfully illuminates the relationships, dilemmas and compromises that define so many lives' *Sunday Express*

He just wanted a decent book to read ...

Not too much to ask, is it? It was in 1935 when Allen Lane, Managing Director of Bodley Head Publishers, stood on a platform at Exeter railway station looking for something good to read on his journey back to London. His choice was limited to popular magazines and poor-quality paperbacks – the same choice faced every day by the vast majority of readers, few of whom could afford hardbacks. Lane's disappointment and subsequent anger at the range of books generally available led him to found a company – and change the world.

'We believed in the existence in this country of a vast reading public for intelligent books at a low price, and staked everything on it'
Sir Allen Lane, 1902–1970, founder of Penguin Books

The quality paperback had arrived – and not just in bookshops. Lane was adamant that his Penguins should appear in chain stores and tobacconists, and should cost no more than a packet of cigarettes.

Reading habits (and cigarette prices) have changed since 1935, but Penguin still believes in publishing the best books for everybody to enjoy. We still believe that good design costs no more than bad design, and we still believe that quality books published passionately and responsibly make the world a better place.

So wherever you see the little bird – whether it's on a piece of prize-winning literary fiction or a celebrity autobiography, political tour de force or historical masterpiece, a serial-killer thriller, reference book, world classic or a piece of pure escapism – you can bet that it represents the very best that the genre has to offer.

Whatever you like to read – trust Penguin.